Miracles from Ashes

By Elizabeth Bourgeret

DCT Publishing
St. Louis, MO
Printed in the United States of America

Author Photo by Haley McQueen
Other Artwork by Kylie Prestein

www,elizabethbourgeret.com
www.facebook.com/EBourgeret
@ebourgeret on Twitter and Instagram

ISBN: 978-0-9982866-2-4

. . . for my husband

Miracles From Ashes

DCT PUBLISHING
St. Louis, MO

"Perhaps this is the moment for which you were created"

Esther 4:14

Chapter One

Hannah Michaelson walked down the corridor of the OB/GYN ward, flipping through the chart briefing her resident on the patient they were about to see.

In the middle of her third year of medical school, Hannah has worked her way through surgery, orthopedics, emergency and is now on the OB/GYN rotation.

"She's complaining of stomach pains. They just sent her up from the ER. No pregnancy test. Why are they sending her here?"

"How old?"

"Uh…" she ran her finger down the chart looking for the answer. "Fourteen?"

Ingrid Seager nodded, taking in the information.

They paused outside the door preparing to enter when they heard a high pitched scream coming from inside.

Hannah and Ingrid looked at each other confused and opened the door.

"Oh! Oh no… don't!" Hannah called out trying to bridge the distance between herself and the patient.

The girl was straddling a pool of blood streaming down between her legs.

"Stop! Stop! Don't push!"

"I can't help it!" the girl cried, and screamed as a rush of pain swept her body.

Hannah and Ingrid ran to her as she screamed once more and a tiny life form slipped out. Hannah dove in and caught it by the umbilical cord so it wouldn't hit the hard linoleum floor. The cord tore, sending blood spraying in all directions.

Ingrid took over with the girl, removing her blood soaked clothes and wrapping her in a gown. She placed plastic sheeting across the bed quickly before another contraction would expel the placenta.

Hannah took the infant to the corner of the room and swaddled him in a blanket. He had no color and no pulse. Hannah inserted her finger in the mouth to check for blockage and rubbed against his tiny little sternum before she began CPR, attempting to bring breath back to his under-developed body. It was too late. The baby had died internally long before the girl's body dispelled what it believed was now an invader.

Hannah looked to her resident and shook her head defeated.

The young girl sat on the bed after the placenta had been delivered and removed and cried. "I'm sorry. I'm sorry."

"Honey, how far along were you? Do you know?"

The girl just cried and looked away.

"Sweetie?"

She shrugged her shoulder but would not make eye contact.

Hannah stepped up and rested her hand on the child's shoulder. "Crystal, honey, you're not in any trouble. We want to help you."

Crystal looked down at the sheet that covered her naked body from the waist down.

"How did you get here?" Ingrid tried.

"Bus," she barely spoke above a whisper.

"Okay. Okay. Good. Good. Thank you." Ingrid praised. "Where are your parents?"

"Can we call someone for you?" Hannah added.

Crystal shook her head no.

The nurses took out the blood soaked sheets and wiped the floor as much as they could around the patient. Crystal was now hooked up to an I.V. and was given something to help calm her.

"Would you..." Hannah took a deep breath, "Would you... like to hold your baby?"

Crystal furrowed her brow as waves of emotion crossed her face. She started to shake her head, but then looked up at Hannah.

"You can if you want," Hannah encouraged.

"It's a boy?" she asked, meekly.

Ingrid nodded.

Crystal's tears began again. Silent, painful tears of a mother, no matter what age.

"Are you sure? You can..." Ingrid's words were soft.

Crystal shook her head again. "Didn't get to hold the last one neither." She shrugged her shoulder, "...just easier."

"The last one? Crystal, do you have another baby?"

She shrugged her shoulders again, not responding.

"Did you know you were pregnant?" Hannah asked.

Crystal paused and closed her eyes. The tears slipped down her cheeks. "No."

Hannah shoved the last of her sandwich in her mouth as she pulled out her dishwater blonde messy bun, only to put it right back up higher and tighter. Her bangs slipped out almost instantly and she unconsciously pushed them from her face, which lasted only seconds, before they were right back in the same place.

She grabbed the charts from the nurse who held them out for her as she rounded the corner of the nurse's station in one fluid movement.

"Twins in 236. Six centimeters in 238 and you need a haircut."

Hannah smiled and blew her bangs away again. "Who's got time for that?" she laughed, flipping the first chart and reading the contents.

As Hannah continued down the hall, she almost collided with a wheelchair transporting a very pregnant woman.

"I'm sorry, I..."

"Ma'am, can you help us? I'm having a baby. I mean, my wife is having a... a... our baby." He pulled the wheelchair back from Hannah's feet.

"I don't feel so well," the woman complained.

"Okay, sir... You're so close. Just keep going straight and you'll see the nurse's station right there, " Hannah explained. "They'll get you all set up, okay?"

A contraction began and the woman looked up at Hannah in complete panic.

Hannah reached down and placed her hand on the now tight pregnant belly as the contraction increased.

"Ooo, that's a good one. Just breathe through it. Come on, breathe with me."

And just as Hannah was going to work through the contraction with her, the woman threw up all over the front of Hannah's scrubs, down to her shoes.

Hannah stood up and turned her head to keep from inhaling the putrid stench.

The nurse was right beside her and swapped out the charts for a white towel that Hannah wiped her neck, hands and top with.

"You probably ought to go change before you see your next patient," the nurse suggested.

Hannah could only nod in agreement as she left the scene in the capable hands of the nurse as she went back to the doctor's lounge.

Hannah went running down the corridor to the ambulance bay to meet with the taxi cab that was pulling up. It screeched to a halt in front of the double sliding doors of the hospital's emergency room.

The driver, a man who could barely speak English, got out of the cab and started yelling and waving his arms around.

"Help! You must help me!"

"Can I get a wheelchair out here?" Hannah called back to the orderlies following her out to the driveway.

"No! No! You need to help now!"

"We're coming sir. Try and stay calm."

"She's in my cab!"

Hannah went to the back door and opened it to reveal a young woman in her twenties in labor and not doing well with it.

Her eyes were wild with fear and her stretch pants were soaked where her water had broken.

"Drape! Give me a drape!" Hannah yelled.

"Ma'am, I'm going to move your legs, okay? Can you turn this way?"

She stared at Hannah, terrified.

"I just need you to help me a little, okay? Can you come this way?"

"The baby's coming!" she cried. "He's coming!"

"Let's get you inside, okay?"

"He's coming! I can feel it! I don't know what to do!"

Hannah put her knee on the edge of the seat to reach in toward the woman. She grabbed her right foot and tugged it toward her.

A contraction began and the woman began to scream.

"All the time!" the driver yelled, in his thick foreign accent. "She did that all the time to here."

"Shhh… shhh…." Hannah leaned closer. "Try not to scream. You're wasting all your energy and you're going to need it. Can you hear me?"

The woman nodded and gritted her teeth, screeching through the pain, bouncing her left foot.

"Good, that's good. Okay, let's bring that other foot around," Hannah coached once the contraction subsided.

The woman helped as much as she could.

"What's your name?"

"Alison."

"Okay, Alison, we're going to get you into the wheelchair so we can all get out of this cold weather, okay?"

Alison nodded and tried to scoot closer to the edge of the seat.

Another contraction halted their progress as Alison kept eye contact with Hannah and tried her best not to scream.

"He's here… I can feel him. He's right here."

Hannah reached her arm out of the cab and was handed a drape to put under Alison and one to put over her waist and legs. She reached her arm out again and was handed surgical scissors which she used to cut into Alison's stretch pants, and it was like she said; the head was already crowning.

"Alright, folks," Hannah warned. "Baby's coming right now, let's get this done smoothly. Are we ready back there?" She asked the staff behind her.

"Ready."

"No… no… no… this is my cab. I have to work," the driver complained.

"I'm sorry, sir. Baby doesn't want to wait."

The driver grabbed his head and paced back and forth on the opposite side of the vehicle. "No… I… I cannot have this!"

"Okay, Alison, the head is coming, breathe nice and easy through this next contraction and if you feel the urge to push, go ahead, but gently…" Hannah looked up at the woman and made eye contact. Alison nodded in understanding.

"Cory, could you please get around to the other side and give this poor woman some back support?" She looked back at Alison, seeing that the next contraction was coming. "Okay, stay with me… you've got this. Just a little push… doin' good… okay, now, yes… there's the head. Well done! Great job! Now rest and then we can meet this little fella." While Hannah talked and coached Alison, she suctioned the baby's nose and mouth. It wasn't long before the next contraction and Hannah was soon holding a healthy baby boy in her arms.

The nurses wrapped the baby and set him on his mother's stomach as they were transported to a gurney to be taken inside under much more pleasant and controllable surroundings.

Hannah sat at an empty table in the doctor's lounge working on charting the day's events. It had been the first time she'd been able to sit all day.

"I heard you had quite a day," her attending and friend Dr. Mosha Joshi came up to the table to sit beside her. She was woman in her fifties, slim and well kept and had taken a liking to Hannah her first year of med school. Dr. Joshi wore her coal black hair in a bob just above her collar and always had it tucked behind her ears or pinned back with a wide barrette. Originally from India, she came over to America for college and quickly climbed her way to the top of the medical field.

Hannah just looked up from her paperwork and nodded. Anything she would say to this woman would be a mere drop in the bucket compared to what her days have been in her years of hospital practice.

"You have the day off tomorrow, don't you?"

Hannah nodded again. "Finally."

"You will spend it with the children, I am sure?"

A smile spread across Hannah's face just thinking of it. "Yes. Jeremy has already promised that I get to sleep in and that we have nothing scheduled. No games, no grocery shopping, no ballet. Just a family day."

"Don't you think you should get to it then? You don't want it to start without you," Dr. Joshi grinned ,looking down at her watch.

"Oh my gosh! I didn't realize it was so late!" She rubbed her face with her hand. "Thank you, yes, I need to get home."

Hannah stood and began collecting all of her belongings. "Will I see you Monday?"

"Of course, where else would I be?"

Hannah chuffed, "Right… where else would you be. You know one of these days, you'll take a day off and the entire hospital will probably fall to the ground."

Mosha nodded, "You see the pressure I am under then, don't you?"

"Hey, more power to you, but I have family day to get home to."

"Then you had better get to it."

Hannah pulled into their driveway. The fresh snow had been shoveled and a clear path was marked from the driveway to the front door. The house was dark and quiet and Hannah barely had enough energy to get inside.

She slipped quietly through the door and began removing her outside attire. Hat, dropped. Gloves, dropped. Scarf, draped across the coat rack. Coat, unbuttoned, dropped to the floor. She slipped from her shoes and padded across the wood floor to a set of stairs. She peeked into the living room and could see the glowing embers of an earlier fire in the fireplace. She took in a deep breath to capture what was left of the wood burning smell.

She padded her way up the stairs, keeping one hand on the bannister not trusting her own balance at the moment.

She passed two closed doors, which she opened and saw the sleeping forms in each of the beds. Her own room was only a few steps more.

She pushed open the half closed door and it creaked slightly at the strain.

Hannah slipped out of her sweatpants and her turtleneck then tucked herself into her bed next to the warm body of her husband.

He breathed in as she pressed her cold body against his. "Hey babe," he slurred.

"Mmmmmm," she purred, as she pulled his arm around her waist.

He kissed the back of her head. "Busy day?"

She nodded her head.

"Want to talk about it?"

She shook her head and held his arm tighter.

They lay silently for a couple minutes before…

"There was this fourteen year old girl today…"

Jeremy smiled as she began to unwind from her day.

"… that gave birth to a stillborn baby. You know who the father was? Her father! Can you believe that? What has this world come to? Needless to say, we had to set her up with DFS, and call the police and… and… that poor child. This was her second one. They gave the other one up for adoption. I told Mosha about it, but nothing even phases her any more…"

Jeremy smiled again and held her tight as she talked out her stresses before she passed out from exhaustion.

The sunshine flooded through the tall, lead windows of the bedroom of their old home. You could mistakenly think it was a warm sunny summer day with the warmth the sun created in the small room.

Hannah blinked her eyes, allowing a new day to begin… begrudgingly. She tried to lift up but felt her body being pressed to the bed.

Oscar, their black cat had turned himself into a kitty stole and draped himself across Hannah's neck. Her right arm and shoulder were pinned down by the seven year old, Rosie, still sound asleep. And when she lifted her head to see what had restrained her legs, there sat her three year old, Olivia.

She had pushed Hannah's feet together creating a "nest" between her legs. And there she sat, surrounded by stacks of books. Not knowing how to read, she quietly narrated her stories how she felt they should go.

Hannah dropped her head back down on the pillow deciding not to argue with her predicament, but instead smiled at the beauty of it all.

Oscar was the first to complain about the sudden activity disturbing his sleep and then, as if on cue, her husband, Jeremy came in the bedroom door.

"Hi Daddy," Olivia called out. And then remembering her vow to keep quiet, tried again at a forced whisper. "Hi Daddy…" She scrunched her shoulders and looked up at her father who couldn't deny her for anything. His spitting image.

Jeremy returned the smile, "Are you being quiet?" he asked, whispering as well.

She nodded faithfully. "I'm reading. Rosie is sleeping." She put her tiny finger to her lips to remind her daddy that he must mind the silent-while-mommy-is-sleeping-rule too.

Jeremy walked over to the edge of the bed and sat down, smiling at his wife. "You hungry?"

She nodded, attempting a limited stretch.

"Mommy! You're awake!" Olivia squealed.

Rosie blinked her sleepy eyelids at the sudden excitement.

Hannah wrapped her arm down the length of Rosie's body and pulled her closer. Olivia crawled up Hannah's chest and lay her head down squeezing her momma. Oscar had had enough and vacated the bed altogether.

"Good morning, my girls. I love to wake up and see my beautiful babies!"

"We let you sleep," Olivia reminded her.

"I miss you, Momma," Rosie mumbled, still pretty sleepy.

"I miss you, too, sweetie," Hannah replied, honestly.

"How much longer?"

Hannah shrugged her shoulder, "Not much, only another year and a half."

"That's a long time!" Rosie whined. "I'm almost going to be nine."

"That's right, you are. My smart girl…" H a n n a h stretched to kiss her on the forehead. She looked over at her husband, " Thank you for letting me sleep. I feel bad missing out on time with you."

He laughed, "You're no fun to be around when you're tired. It's better when you've had your sleep."

"Yeah, sorry about that," she giggled. "You mentioned something about being hungry?"

He laughed. "I did. I thought you'd like some breakfast."

"You thought right." She wove her free hand around the covers and Olivia body parts to clasp Jeremy's hand. He stroked the back of it with his thumb. "I love you, Mr. Michaelson."

"I love you, Mrs. Michaelson. Phyllis would be so proud of you."

At the mention of her mother's name, Hannah paused and smiled. "I believe she would. This is what she wanted for me."

"You're gonna make it," Jeremy leaned in to kiss her. "You are going to be a great doctor."

"I don't know about all that... but I hope I can help people. That's what I really want. To help people who are hurting."

"You will. You already do."

She reveled in the glow of the moment for as long as it would last, afraid that she was going to wake up to discover she had fallen asleep in the lounge. But she was here, with her family on a coveted Sunday morning. Her first full day off in three weeks.

"Okay kiddos, let's get up and see what Daddy has planned for breakfast."

"Pancakes," Rosie snitched. "I saw him mixing stuff before."

"Mmmm, pancakes," Hannah purred.

"Do you want some pancakes, Momma?" Olivia asked.

"I do."

"Come on, I'll go with you." Olivia slid over Hannah's body not worrying about where and with what pressure she stepped and squished. Hannah's over-exaggerated groans and flinching were merely laughed at.

Olivia stood on the edge of the bed and reached back out for her mother's hand. "I'll help you, Momma... I can help."

"But Daddy's got my hand."

She looked at the situation and put some thought to it. She looked up at her daddy's face and knew instantly that he was not going to help. She tried to pry the two hands apart with her tiny fingers, to no avail. "Daddy! Let go."

"I want to hold your mom's hand too."

"Olivia, I have two hands. Can't I hold your hand *and* Daddy's hand?"

She looked at the possible solution and was satisfied that it was plausible. She walked to the other side of her father and reached for the empty hand.

"Okay, you," Hannah nudged the other child. "You are in the way of me and pancakes."

Rosie laughed and decided to challenge the implied threat. So as not to be disappointed, Hannah released the one-handed tickle monster on the ribs of the stubborn child. Not to miss out, Olivia climbed back on the bed to "save" her sister, only to be attacked by the Daddy Tickle Monster.

The best of days, the best of memories, a family tickle fight prior to pancakes.

The doors of the hospital slipped open as she approached, and she was hit with the bitter cold from the outside. They were bracing for a severe snow storm and requested that all staff stay at the hospital until further notice.

Hannah had been on edge all day and just wanted to be home with her family. She had tried to find someone to cover her shift, but no one in their right mind was about to get "stuck" at their job through the worst-predicted storm of the season.

She tried to keep her mind busy, with charting and patient follow-up, but she just wanted to be home. The snow had been falling steadily for hours. She knew her family would all be asleep, probably all in her bed, but in these types of storms, she wanted to be at home, safe in her own bed.

Finally, three of the night crew were able to make it in to work, so Hannah begged and pleaded to be allowed to clock out. She lived within the city limits of the hospital and used that as a bargaining chip should things get busy.

She pulled her hat down a little tighter over her ears and nuzzled her nose into her scarf. She made her way to the parking garage and was thankful to be shielded from the abrasive winds. The snow was coming down heavy and the winds made it difficult to see.

She reached her car, an older silver Ford Capri. It's best days were long past, and they had agreed to save money while she was finishing school, but a new car was the first thing on the list.

She turned the key and it rumbled to life, yelling at her the whole time. She sat in the parking space breathing warm air into her hands as Old Reliable mustered up some heat.

When she pulled from the garage she had to pause as an ambulance raced in front of her to get to the emergency room entrance. A brief flutter of guilt passed through her wondering if she should stay. "No, Connor and Scott are there, they can handle things."

She pulled out on to the mostly empty street and fought against the winds beating on her car. She took her time, stopping before the intersection and was slow to go through just in case someone from another direction couldn't handle driving in the snow.

She got on the highway with no trouble but still decided to go under the speed limit and not compete with the morons that thought that just because they had four-wheel-drive that they could magically handle snow on the roads. If only they knew of all the accidents caused by such careless driving…

As she was thinking about the last car accident case she had to deal with, she saw the flashing lights of an emergency vehicle coming up behind her. The sirens were screeching and it was going at a pretty good pace.

"I rest my case," Hannah muttered under her breath, assuming that she'd be driving up to an accident in a mile or two.

She pulled over, allowing the fire truck and ambulance to pass her by.

When they passed, she cautiously pulled back out onto the highway. She didn't get very far when another set of emergency vehicles raced up behind her.

She was now wondering if she should turn around and go back to the hospital. Something big was going down. She looked ahead and the next exit wasn't for a few miles as she left the downtown area.

"They will be fine," she scolded herself. "That hospital has been functioning long before you came on the scene, Hannah Michaelson." Deciding not to let it bother her, she didn't give it another thought and made her way home. She opted not to call her husband to let him know she was coming but to surprise him and be there for the girls when they woke up. She smiled thinking of them stealing away a few hours before a nice warm fire.

It wasn't until she took the exit that lead toward her house that she thought about the possible injuries that might have incurred from the accident, because she could hear the sirens close by. Instead of taking her usual route through the quiet streets of the suburb, she took the main roads in hopes of seeing what was happening and if she needed to help in any way.

As she got closer to her home, the hairs on the back of her neck stood up as she realized that the fire trucks were in front of her house.

Billows of smoke were battling with the snow. Huge flames lighting up the night looking for something else to devour. The paneling on their detached garage was beginning to melt, and all the windows were busted.

Hannah shook her head and stopped her car in the middle of the street. She got out and had to hold on to the car door to keep her balance. The heat was so intense that the snow flakes disappeared the moment they touched the surface of her skin. She tried to walk away from her car toward the fire, not believing what was in front of her. Her house… that was her house and it was on fire.

A firetruck blocked most of her view where she was standing, so she stumbled closer, tripping over multiple hoses, fighting the wind, the snow and the mist of water coming from the spray of the fire hoses.

Neighbors lined the street talking and filming the entire incident with their phones. She felt like she was moving in slow motion.

Her home. Her home was on fire.

Suddenly, Hannah reached the front of her home and was able to take in the full spectacle. Men were running up the front stairs of her porch through the open front door. Black smoke hung under the eves pouring from split slats of wood and broken windows. Her eyes traveled up to the second story where her children and husband would have been sleeping. The right side of the house was still dark, the fire not spreading there as yet, but the left side and back were almost completely engulfed in flames. Hannah started screaming and running toward the front door. "My babies! My babies are in there!"

"Lady, lady, stop. You'll get burned up." A neighbor grabbed for her hand to stop her.

"My husband is here… with the girls…. I have to get in there."

"Ma'am, you can't go in there, it's about to fall."

"Noooo! Where's my husband?" She fought against the arms that tried to restrain her, "Jeremy! Jeremy where are you!" She looked at the man holding her. "Did you send anyone to the hospital? I have two little girls…. My…. My husband was in there with my daughters…."

The fire fighter looked everywhere but at her, hoping someone was going to come and help him with all the answers.

"Tell me! I saw an ambulance! Where are my children? I…. I work for Saints Memorial Hospital. Where did they get taken?"

"I'm sorry ma'am…. There were no survivors."

Hannah looked at the man as if he were an idiot, an underling who obviously didn't know what he was talking about. "Where is your supervisor. You don't … you can't…" she shook her head refusing to hear his words. She saw an ambulance with her own eyes.

"Get back! Get back!" Someone shouted.

Moments after three men came running from the house, the roof and top story fell into the structure. Black smoke and a spray of embers went up into the grey sky lighting it up.

Suddenly it felt as if the wind was knocked out of her. She felt dizzy and faint.

She rolled her shoulders to break free of his hold, and he allowed it. She walked away from him, staggering in no particular direction. She fell to her knees in the snow, not moving. Her body was shivering, but not from the cold. A paramedic came to lift her back to her feet. "Ma'am? Ma'am? Can you come with me?"

Hannah looked up at his face and smiled at him. "Are you taking me to my children? They live here. My husband and I live here."

"I need you to come with me, please." The paramedic led her away from the heat of the fire and took her into the back of a nearby ambulance.

The paramedic took off her winter coat which was soaked and wrapped her in a blanket even though her skin glistened with sweat. Her face was covered with ash. Her knit hat had both crystals of ice and perfectly placed ashes that drifted down from the sky. He proceeded to adhere the Velcro of the blood pressure cuff on her arm and attached a temperature-taking device to her forehead.

"What… what are you doing?"

"Just making sure you're alright, ma'am."

The doors to the ambulance opened and an older gentleman came in and sat down across from Hannah.

"Do you know where you are?" he asked.

"I'm currently in the back of an ambulance, for some reason and this person is checking *my* pulse," she answered a little sarcastically. "I'm a third year medical student at Saints Memorial Hospital."

The man patiently took in a deep breath and released it before continuing. "My name is Isaac Douglas, and I'm with Incident Command. Do you know your name?"

She looked at him almost confused for a moment, but after a second, answered, "Hannah. Hannah Michaelson."

"Do you know what day it is, Mrs. Michaelson?"

She looked off to the left thinking. "It's Thursday." She furrowed her brow suddenly questioning her answer. "It's Thursday, isn't it?" She laughed, embarrassed. "I'm sorry, I'm awfully tired. Feeling a little dizzy at the moment."

He nodded. "It is Thursday." He fidgeted in his seat before continuing.

"Do you know where you are? The address, I mean."

"My address? You want to know my address?"

"Yes,"

Hannah furrowed her brow thinking. She rubbed her forehead and slid her hand down her face. She leaned forward trying to see out of the windows. *There was a fire. A fire truck. People. There were people everywhere. At her house. They were at her house.*

"My house?" she asked. "My house?"

"Mrs. Michaelson..." the man reached out his hand seeing that reality had returned. "I... I need you to stay calm..."

She nodded in compliance.

"There's been an accident..." he began.

Hannah shook her head. She changed her mind. She didn't want to hear it. She didn't want to have to stay calm.

"The blizzard closed the flue of your chimney, which caused smoke, carbon dioxide, to back up into your house…"

"No…. no… don't say it… don't…"

Mr. Douglas paused for a moment wishing he could respect her wishes. He breathed out a heavy sigh, "Why don't we get you to the hospital to get checked out?"

"No! I'm not leaving without my children!" She tried to stand, but the paramedic halted her.

"Mrs. Michaelson…" Mr. Douglas reached out his hand to steady her. "Your children… they were caught in… They both perished from smoke inhalation.'

Hannah drew her hands to her mouth and gasped. Her heart was pounding, trying to escape from her chest. "That's not right.   That can't be true… my husband… he would have…"

Isaac Douglas looked away hating his job more than usual right about now. "Your husband… "

"Don't…"

"… has also passed away this night."

"No… no… NO!" Hannah broke down in tears. She covered her face and bent in half. She laid her face against her knees and cried out. "This can't be true!"

She sat back up and wiped her face. Her eyes were wild with fear, "Did you… I mean… did you check all the rooms? Maybe they could have…. Is Jeremy's car here? He could have taken them away to safety…" the tears slipped down her cheeks and her cries garbled her speech. "He wouldn't let them die… He just wouldn't…"

"I'm sorry, ma'am," Isaac attempted. "The fire has destroyed… we couldn't get here in time to…"

"No… no… please no…" she whimpered.

"They were all sleeping in the same bed. They didn't suffer. They just… stayed asleep… I'm so sorry for your loss."

"No… no… no…" Hannah was shaking her head and crying. She didn't want to hear the words. Her heart was breaking right then and there. Her whole world. Her everything. Gone… it can't be. Her mind was racing a mile a minute and yet producing no thoughts.

A dream… it must be a dream… "This isn't happening." She mumbled, looking around the ambulance for proof. "I see this everyday… ambulance… bandages are in that drawer… disposable gloves are in that drawer… I'm dreaming… I… I…" she looked to Mr. Douglas to confirm her decision.

"Mrs. Michaelson… " he shook his head never knowing the words to use. "I am so sorry to have to tell you this and I know there is no easy way to hear it. I wish I didn't have to bring this news to you."

Hannah shrugged; her tears drying and her eyes glassy, "It's okay. I'll wake up soon. It'll all be okay… you'll see."

Isaac nodded to the paramedic.

The paramedic handed Hannah a small plastic cup containing two white pills. "Here, take these, it will help you feel better," he said, while unscrewing a cap on a bottle of water.

Hannah held out her hand and let him spill the pills onto her hand and she took the opened bottle. She looked into the eyes of the man that she knew deep down was sedating her. Inwardly, she thanked him for relieving her of her pain, even if only for a little while, but outwardly, she pleaded with him to tell her it would all be okay, that things will go back to the way they were when she wakes up.

Chapter Two

Hannah opened her eyes and stared up at the white tiled ceiling. Her eyes were dry and swollen, her mouth felt pasty and her head felt cloudy. *Side effects from sleep aids,* she told herself.

How many days... she asked herself. *How many days will it take not to hurt so bad every time I open my eyes.* Every day, the wound was reopened again. She could feel the burning of a new set of tears.

She could still see him... so clearly... in her mind's eye. Her husband. The love of her life. Her best friend. The father of her children. Her children...

"My babies..." she spoke, out loud. She blinked and tears slid from the creases. "My babies..." she said, again.

The door to her room opened and Dr. Mosha Joshi walked in carrying a food tray and a mustard colored square bucket.

"You are awake. I am happy to see that."

Hannah nodded, but looked away.

"I know that you are hurting. I cannot imagine the pain you must be feeling. But it is time to get some things taken care of."

Hannah looked up at her friend and supervisor but still couldn't find words to speak.

Dr. Joshi set the food tray down on her side table and pushed the button on Hannah's bed to sit her upright.

"You eat this food. And," she nodded to the bucket, "I brought you some toiletries. Use them." She flipped her wrist to check her watch. "Your insurance agent will be here at two, to discuss your policies and what is to be done." She locked eyes with Hannah making sure she understood, but then her face softened. She came close to the edge of the bed, and tentatively touched Hannah's hand for only a moment. "Hannah…" she lowered her voice, and took the sternness out of its tone. "You need to put your family to rest."

Hannah's face tightened, allowing the tears to spill out once again. She turned away from her friend trying to swallow the lump in her throat.

"I am sorry, but it must be done. You must have closure. You must set them on their way."

Hannah let out the most pitiful squeak as she tried to maintain composure in front of her boss.

"You are a Christian, are you not?"

Hannah nodded.

"Then you know their souls are already in a good and happy place and they will wait for you; make a place for you… Is that not your belief?"

Hannah couldn't contain her sadness any longer and sobbed heavy, coughing sobs.

Mosha looked around the room, uncomfortable with the open display of emotions. She noncommittally patted her leg and stepped back from the bed. "I… I will make arrangements for you to use the meeting room when your insurance agent arrives." Mosha looked down at her feet and decided that there were no other words that she could offer. "I will check back with you at a later time... and... and... I am here to... help you... if I can." She nodded, completing her thought and exited the room.

Hannah stared vacantly as the Insurance agent, Angie explained what her husband had done with their insurance policies.

"You had complete coverage which means that we will take care of the outstanding balance of your mortgage.

Hannah was present as the two sat at the large oval table in the meeting room, but she wasn't really hearing a word. Her hair was still wet and hung down past her shoulders. She didn't even bother to brush it. The notebook sitting in front of her was blank and she kept her hands folded in her lap.

Angie continued, "You have lost everything."

Hannah's eyes followed along the fold creases in her light blue scrubs.

Angie's pen followed each line of the long type-written, tri-folded pages, as she explained each line. This is what her life looked like. Itemized lines to be tallied, and totaled.

She talked on about what was covered and what was not... she tapped into the importance of life insurance and how Jeremy had a small policy from when he was an infant... and luckily her husband's job included burial insurance.... Hannah barely heard muffled noise in the suddenly uncomfortably small meeting room.

Angie pulled a check from her black folder and slid it across the table in front of Hannah. Hannah took in a deep breath and glanced up at the check. Her entire life to this point has been boiled down to a dollar sign. This piece of paper tells her how much the lives of her husband and children were worth to the world.

Her chest felt heavy and she could hardly breathe.

"Do you have any questions?" Angie asked politely, ready to wrap up this account.

Hannah looked down and shook her head, giving her permission to conclude the meeting.

Angie slid the pen across the table for Hannah to sign in six places. Hannah looked at the names of the people she loved most on earth. She lifted her eyes to Angie, her eyes filling with tears. She silently emplored her to take the papers away. She didn't want to sign them. She didn't want to finalize their ... Hannah swallowed hard. She couldn't even think the word.

Angie swallowed her emotions and tried to keep everything on a professional keel. "If… if you could," she took in a jagged breath, "… sign here, on this first line…"

Hannah blinked forcing a tear over the edge of her eye. She obediently picked up the pen. Her breath caught in her throat as she brought the pen to the blank line. The pen hovered for just a second more before she scribbled her first initial and married name."

Angie breathed a sigh of relief and turned the page. "And… here…uh, please."

It was done now. Hannah went through the motions on each page. Angie stood and folded the pages and tied the tiny bow keeping them neat and tidy. She held out her hand and saw that Hannah wasn't "present" "You can… uh… keep the pen."

Angie collected her other papers and tucked them into her briefcase, and smoothed down her straight black skirt. "I am deeply sorry for your loss." She slipped her card across the table and positioned it just above the check. "If you need any other insurance needs, please don't hesitate to contact my office."

Hannah dropped her head to her chest, still clutching the pen as the woman quietly left the room, closing the door behind her.

Hannah sat at the large empty table looking at the only thing she had left. This neatly folded light blue set of papers. It was misleading. It looked like a pretty package but it was filled with sadness and emptiness. It didn't say anything about

Rosie's smiles. Or Olivia's blonde curls. Or Jeremy's strong arms. It didn't say anything about the hours and hours it took her and Jeremy to sand and spackle and paint all of the rooms in that beautiful old house. It didn't mention the antique dinning room table passed down through her family for three generations... all the dinners and the breakfast meals they had shared as a couple... and then with three and then four... completing their family... Two vehicles. The memories those two vehicles held. The miles and miles Jeremy's Jeep put on that motor... How do you put a price tag on all of it? Who can do that? It didn't seem worth it.

A small funeral was held for her family, which no one attended but a few of the other residents, and Dr. Joshi.

She wore a plain black dress which she bought at a second hand store. She pulled her hair up in a simple bun and didn't bother with make-up.

It was a dark and cold Tuesday afternoon. She stood beside the gaping hole in the ground and wondered how she would be able to sleep at night knowing that her family was left behind in that cold, dark hole.

The large casket was lowered in first, and the two smaller caskets were nestled in on either side of the large one.

A single marble plaque rested above the grave marking the names of the family.

Hannah walked to the edge and dropped in a single red rose for her husband and two pure white roses for her children. She watched them fall,   staring momentarily as they found their resting place on each one of the light wood-colored caskets.

Here, she had to say good-bye. Here, she had to let them go.   Here, she had to decide what she was going to do with the rest of the days that God made her stay on this earth all alone.

Hannah had found a mobile home to live in until she sorted things out. It wasn't the best of accommodations, but it was clean enough and was the right price.   She had accumulated a few items in order to survive, but most of the things were already part of the home.

She had missed her classes and rotations for two weeks now, and her inner dialogue continued the same. It berated her for being weak. It told her that she needed to get back into her routine; that she needed to get back on the horse, save her career and begin again.

And, every morning began with the best of intentions. Yet by the end of every day, Hannah considered putting on clean clothes and brushing her teeth an accomplishment.

She used some of her insurance money to get her car from the towing lot, where it was taken the night of the fire. She would go back to the remains of the house and kick things about looking for anything she couldn't live without. But most times, she would just sit… and stare. She didn't care what the neighbor's thought. She had been there a hundred times and was still shocked at the site of her home in piles of rubble, charred wood and ash mixed with pieces from her life

The clean-up crew, hired by the insurance company, found some items right after the accident and gave them to Hannah. She was informed that she was no longer allowed on the premises, which belonged to the bank now.

All that she had left from her home were some papers from a filing cabinet, a few of Jeremy's tools, and the item she was most grateful for, a metal fire box filled with photos, negatives, important papers… her wedding vows, the girls' birth certificates… their first tooth that came out, a lock of their hair… Jeremy's wedding band…

Hannah would spend nights with the contents of the box spread out around her on the lumpy, full size bed. She let herself cry and remember. She would tell herself that this was the last night for this behavior so it was all right to give in to her grief, because tomorrow, she had to begin again. She completely believed herself and at the end of the night, she would neatly clean everything up and put it away in the firebox and promise that the morning would bring a new day.

But then, when the morning came... it was just too hard. Too hard to get out of bed. Too hard to find a reason to keep her eyes open. Just... too hard. The mornings just kept coming...

Dr. Joshi knocked on the door one afternoon and was taken aback with the appearance of her star pupil. Her hair was up in a messy bun that had fallen to the side. Her face was pale and it looked like she hadn't eaten or slept for days.

Hannah looked at the reminder of her former life and felt a flutter of guilt in her stomach. She stepped back, allowing passageway into her living room.

Dr. Joshi stepped inside the dark paneled room and straightened her posture, visibly uncomfortable in these surroundings.

Hannah feebly attempted to adjust her hair and straighten her clothes, feeling suddenly self-conscious in the presence of her mentor who was always put together and never out of sorts in front of anyone.

"You have not been to class or rotation," she began, skipping the formalities.

Hannah looked down, ashamed. She had never been one to shirk her duties and responsibilities.

"I know. I'm sorry, but I…"

"You have to keep going."

Hannah nodded at the reprimand. She knew everything that Mosha was getting ready to tell her. She'd been telling herself the same things for days, but she just couldn't make herself move… or get dressed… or even eat most of the time.

Mosha walked over to the refrigerator and opened it. It showed one can of Pepsi, an empty egg carton and a package of American cheese.

She looked over the door at Hannah who still stood in the middle of the living room holding her one arm.

"You are not eating?"

"I'm not hungry."

Mosha Joshi dropped her head hating to have say the hard things, but ready to get it over with. She hoped that her words were going to force Hannah to wake up and get her life back on track, and not the opposite; to continue spiraling out of control until she had nothing of her earlier, vibrant, amazing self.

She walked back into the other room and forced herself to sit on the edge of a tattered recliner. "Hannah… come and sit with me."

Hannah crossed the matted brown carpet in her socked feet and sat in the corner of the very used couch. She folded her arms across her chest, not to be defiant, but she just realized that she wasn't wearing a bra... again. She looked down at her knees not wanting to hear the "speech" that was coming. "Snap out of it. You aren't the first person to lose someone. This too shall pass..." She knew what was coming and knew that all of the condolence cards, and words that were whispered as they hugged her were meant to be encouraging, but... they just ... weren't.

Mosha raised her chin and looked Hannah over from head to toe. A doctor's assessment.

"This will not do."

Hannah raised her eyes to meet the scrutinizing gaze of her mentor. It was not unkind; in fact, Hannah was sure she saw compassion. Hannah didn't know her backstory, as Dr. Joshi did not divulge any personal details to her students. Everyone just knew that she was alone and devoted most of her waking hours to the teaching hospital.

She lived in an apartment; mere blocks from the hospital and those who saw it said it was very simple but elegant... clean... too clean, no signs of living. Hannah wondered where her people were, if she had any...

"You are on the correct path to become a doctor."

Hannah blinked back from her thoughts to focus on what Dr. Joshi was saying.

"It's who you are and it is breaking my heart to watch you throw all of your hard work away. You need to think about the people who need you. You were put on this earth to help others. I know this about you. I need you to see it too."

Hannah dropped her head, ashamed. She hated disappointing people.

Finally after a moment of silence, Hannah responded. "I can't.

"Now is not the time to be selfish, Hannah. Your gift does not belong to just you. It was given to you to share with others."

Hannah furrowed her brow as she mindlessly shifted her wedding band so that the diamond was centered on her ring finger. "But... I..."

"You must get out of your head. You are so close to your goals..."

"But it doesn't matter anymore!" Hannah shouted, a bit too loud. And then barely above a whisper she added, "Nothing matters anymore."

"I hear you saying that, but you must look at things from another perspective. You matter greatly to the patients that you help. They need you. They need your skill and your kindness," she paused, attempting a new avenue, "I know that you are hurting..."

"Everything!" Hannah stood up and refolded her arms across her chest hugging herself. "I've lost everything. I wish I was in that bed too. I just don't..."

"Don't speak it." Mosha stood up and looked down to her feet before raising her eyes to Hannah's. "Don't give in. Don't stop fighting. Your loss has been great... this... I understand..."

Hannah broke down in tears and sat heavily on the edge of the couch. She covered her face with her hands as the tears poured through her fingers.

"You were not there for a reason. Your time on this earth is not finished. You still have work to do."

Hannah did not respond, but Mosha knew she was listening. "You must complete the life you were meant to live. You are hurting now but it won't always be this way." She paused, "There will be a piece that will always... bring sadness," she raised her head and squared her shoulders, "... but you have to fulfill your purpose. It is in your heart. You may try to ignore it. You may try to pretend that it does not exist, but it is there. You must fulfill your purpose."

Hannah looked up at her and furrowed her brow hearing a glimpse of a story underneath the stern, yet understanding words of advice.

"I will suspend your classes and grant you an extended leave of absence. Grieve. But don't stay in it. You are a healer. One way or another, you will come back to your calling. I know this." Dr. Mosha Joshi walked over to Hannah and stroked her hair. "Don't take too long," she whispered. She turned, not waiting for a reply and not looking back, and she left the mobile home.

Miracles from Ashes

Chapter Three

"Hank I need these eggs over easy, not over hard and I am missing a side of hash browns."

"Comin' up, Doc," Hank shrugged, and went about remaking three soft eggs, over easy. Not his dime. He was in his late twenties with the beginnings of a beard, or what was more like two days of not wanting to shave before his shift. Hank wanted to be a country music star. He believed that his being named Hank was his mother's way of putting the legacy on him. And while he could sing, as he did often from his kitchen, he lacked the motivation to "risk it all" and go to Nashville. He just told everyone that he was going to one day. "One day" had not happened as yet, so that made him lead cook at the Route 66 Diner and Truck Stop.

"Please don't call me that." Hannah stepped away from the counter, filled a short plastic cup with orange juice and grabbed the fresh brewed coffee pot.

"Here's your small orange juice, those hash browns will be out in just a minute, Joe. More coffee?"

Joe held out his half empty coffee mug for her to top off.

Hannah made her rounds to each table filling coffee and removing used dishes. She smiled and chatted with the regulars and treated all the guests with respect.

And they liked her too. Not very many people knew that she was almost a doctor and that she lost everything, but they responded to her and she could make the grumpiest of guests smile. She was always on time, extremely proficient and her boss dreaded the day when she finally wakes up from her nightmare and realizes her true potential.

Her boss, Wayne was in his fifties, a former truck driver himself. He wore his sandy-colored hair longer and ended up tucking it behind his ears when it got in his eyes. He was a fan of flannel and thermal. He looked like he should be hunting something if it wasn't for the black apron that he constantly wore. A lot smarter than he looks, he recognized lost dreams. He lives among those who have chosen to work here because they have no place else to go. He feeds those who have chased their dreams and have failed or have lost all the things they used to believe in. This was his world and he knew Hannah didn't belong here. He was hesitant to even hire her, but he also knew sometimes people had to really hit that rock bottom before they can begin their climb out.

She was willing to work as many hours as he would give her; and he was short on help. He could see that she was tired, but she just kept showing up. She was punishing herself; he could see it.

In Wayne's observation it seemed she was working through some serious guilt, but she never brought drama to work with her and when she was here, she was on her game. *One of these days*, he shook his head watching her glide from table to table smiling at his guests, working on her twelfth hour, *she won't show up.*

Hannah counted her tips, rolled them up and shoved them in her pocket. She changed into her jeans and tennis shoes, a hoodie and a coat and added a hat, scarf and gloves.

"Night all," she waved to her co-workers, and made her way out into the cold, snowy evening. The sun was beginning to set as she made her way to her car parked at the edge of the busy corner lot.

The radio had long since died in her beat up old Ford, so she rode along in silence. Sometimes it was the loneliest part of her day. She drove for a bit and pulled her car over to the side of the road and got out. She pulled her coat tighter around her and walked to where a sidewalk began that lead the way onto a bridge. She reached the middle where the arch was at its highest point. There was no one else to be seen from her left or to her right. She was completely alone.

The sun was setting at the edge of the water and she stood staring at it. Her breath would create a soft filter for the magnificent display of yellows and oranges and pinks spreading across the sky. She didn't even feel the tear slip from her eye and make its way down her cheek.

She took her eyes away from the sunset and looked down at the rushing water beneath her. It was moving fast, frothing over boulders in its way.

It would only take a second…

It could all be over. The pain. The memories.

It would only take a second.

She leaned against the railing and rubbed her forehead and her face with her gloved hand. She was angry at her lack of courage. She was angry for being afraid. She was angry that she was left all alone. All the people she loved were gone.

She closed her eyes and let the memory come… The bubbling and gurgling water transitioned into the familiar squeak and rub of metal from chains of the porch swing from her childhood. A sound as familiar and steady as her own heartbeat.

Her mother… sitting on the front porch swing. She had a lap blanket covering her legs and she was watching Hannah sort her medications before administering them to her.

"You are such a good girl," she would say. "You should be out doing teenager things and here you are taking care of your mother." Her mother had a thick Detroit, Michigan accent with a bit of Italian thrown in when she got mad or sentimental.

"I don't mind, Ma, " Hannah would say.

"You should be a doctor. You should. You care about people."

"I care about you, Ma. I don't care about everybody else."

"Oh… you do," she wagged a finger in Hannah's direction. "You got a big heart. God's got big things in store for you. You just wait and see."

"I'm sure God has other, more important things on His mind. Here, drink this."

"Don't you mock…" She raised her eyebrows. "He knows every hair on your head."

"Yeah? Then why is he making you suffer? Tell me that." As soon as the words left her mouth, she regretted them.

Her mother looked at her and Hannah could see her eyes glisten with emotion. "Maybe… my only purpose on this earth was to have you." She nodded her head, the Italian coming out. She cupped Hannah's chin with her frail, trembling fingers. "Maybe *you* are meant for great things. Not me. Maybe you were meant to find the cure for this terrible disease…"

Hannah rolled her eyes. "My grades say otherwise," she attempted humor.

"… and maybe," her mother continued, not to be dissuaded, "I don't get to spend as much time on this earth as other mothers… and this is the only time I have to be with my only child."

"Ma…"

"Listen to me…" Phyllis went on, "I have had a good life. I had a good husband and we had an amazing child. You are the light of my life, Baby Girl. I don't regret a thing. I am sorry that I'm a burden to you…"

"Ma… you're not… I…"

"But I am thankful that I get to spend my last days with you." She pulled Hannah in for a weak embrace and Hannah sat beside her on the swing and allowed herself to be held until it was time for her mother to go into bed.

That was their last afternoon together. Phyllis died in her sleep and Hannah was alone at nineteen.

Hannah shook away the memory and blew hot air onto her hands. The sun was just a small sliver in the distance.

She breathed out and tapped her hand against the rail. Defeated, she walked back to her car and headed home.

It was an hour before Hannah's shift was scheduled to end and she was low on sleep. She felt like she was a little extra emotional because she was so drained. All her hours training at the hospital, the long shifts and then the long hours at the truck stop, should have made her immune to such things, but today, she felt like crying every time she turned around. Maybe she had finally had enough. Maybe she had reached her limit. Maybe tonight, she'd be able to let go and be done with it all.

She went about her duties and smiled for the patrons but inside she was too sad to care about anything.

A woman came in with her three kids and ordered from the children's menu. She could see that they were struggling, so she padded their order with some extra fries... "on the house."

Joe came in for every meal, so when she saw him enter the door, she set him up in his regular spot at the counter with a diet Pepsi, a cup of coffee that he puts three scoops of sugar in and will most likely order the pie of the day... *why he bothers to order a diet soda...,* she laughs to herself.

The place was quiet tonight and it looked like Hannah just might be able to leave on time. She flipped through her stack of tips and paid for the extra fries. She shrugged her shoulder at the small amount of cash collected from hours of work... *doesn't matter, I won't need it soon anyway...*

Just then a man came into the diner and smiled in her direction. She returned the greeting and said, "Just sit anywhere." But under her breath she mumbled, "but please not my section." And it was as if the fates were laughing at her, as he sat in the middle of her perfectly cleaned section. Hannah sighed heavily and grabbed a cup of water and a menu for him.

"Good evening, welcome." She set the water and menu in front of him. "Can I get you anything to drink?"

He looked up and smiled at his server. He paused before speaking. "Just a coffee, please. Black."

She nodded and returned the smile. She looked him over and assessed his health, like she unconsciously did with every guest. *He is low on iron, and there is a sadness behind his eyes,* she observed. *I'm sure he has quite the backstory.*

He was an older gentleman, easily in his eighties. His hair was thinning to the point that he only had a crown of white, which was kept cropped short and neat. He was fairly short, and a little overweight, but not so much so that it would cause any serious health problems. His face was kind, but seemed sad and deep in thought. He smiled at all the appropriate times but didn't say much.

As Hannah came back to deliver his coffee, she noticed that he wore a light tan colored Member's Only jacket and a button down blue plaid shirt underneath which he tucked into his slacks which were also a lightweight fabric, along with a pair of loafers.

"Aren't you cold?" she asked. "Do you have a coat?" Her heart went out to him.

"Not cold, thank you."

She smiled and nodded, "Okay, anything else I can get you? Cream and sugar? A bowl of soup? A blanket?" she giggled.

He chuffed and smiled at her, appreciating her genuine warmth and generosity. "I'm good."

She nodded again and went about the business of her other guests and finishing off her closing duties.

She was rolling silverware when she realized that she hadn't checked on her tables in a while. The mother and children were gone and left a mess all over the table, benches and floor. Joe was still there, but he'd be there for a few more hours and Tracy, her co-worker would pick up where she left off. And the single gentleman who only ordered coffee had left.

Hannah admonished herself. "I hope he didn't leave hungry. I forgot to go check on him again. She rolled her eyes and went to wipe down his table.

She picked up the untouched cup of coffee. No tip. She wasn't surprised, she wasn't being a good server... but on a corner of a napkin was a note... it said, "Hold on".

She looked around the diner to see if anyone was watching her or if the man had just gone to the restroom or something, but nothing seemed out of the ordinary. She finished her duties, heavy in thought, and went home.

At home, her mobile home was clean. Everything was in its place, no dishes in the sink, no food in the fridge. She went into her bedroom and looked at the firebox that set beside her bed every night. She put it on the corner of the bed and flipped open the lid. A picture of her family smiled up at her but she looked past it to the corner of the box. A prescription bottle lay in waiting. She took in a deep breath and let it back out. No tears, no drama... she was just done fighting.

She crammed her hands in her pockets and pulled out the crumpled money from her shift and the napkin slipped out onto the photo. "Hold On" it read in bold blue ink letters.

Hold On. What did that mean? Was it for her? Was it for him?

She hadn't prayed in months… she sat on the edge of the bed and looked back at the note… she didn't feel like praying now, because she already knew what He would tell her…

Hold On…

That's what He would tell her…

She closed the box's lid with the napkin included and scooched her way to her pillow and fell in to a deep solid sleep… uniform and all.

Hannah woke up and stared at her white paneled ceiling, always a little disappointed that she woke up at all. She sighed and looked at her watch to see what time it was. She had a little over an hour to get to work. If she *had* to admit, she felt better today than she had in a long while. She could only assume it was because her body finally shut down and allowed her to sleep. She'd been asleep for twelve hours. She hadn't slept that long accumulatively in more than a month.

Hold On.

The words flashed through her mind again.

She shook it off and looked down at her wardrobe. "Well, I don't have to change for work," she said out loud to no one and went in to brush her teeth.

That night, the same gentleman came in. He sat in the same spot and ordered the same cup of coffee.

"I'm sorry I wasn't very attentive last night, I got distracted and completely forgot to check on you. Can I get you a slice of pie on me as a peace offering?" she offered.

"You don't have to do that. I'm not much for the sweets any more." He patted his stomach.

He sounded tired, but there was a kindness in his voice.

"Very well, anything else I can get you?"

He looked into her eyes and paused for a moment longer than was comfortable, "No thank you."

She nodded and left to grab his coffee.

The diner was busy tonight and Hannah's tables stayed full. She would glance over at the man sitting alone with his coffee cup situated in the circle of his arms that were resting on the table. He watched the people come and go but said nothing and never picked up his coffee cup. And at some point, he left. Didn't touch his coffee. No tip... no note.

This dance went on for a few evenings and Hannah was always kind to him and tried to get him to talk a little bit more each time. Tonight, was his fifth night in a row and Hannah couldn't help but notice that he wore the same outfit every single night. Same jacket, no matter how cold it was, same shoes no matter how wet it was. He didn't look, or smell dirty, and his clothes always looked as if they had just come from the dryer; wrinkle free and fresh.

She brought his coffee to him without his prompting and he smiled up at her, appreciating that she recognized their routine.

This time, Hannah gave him some time to people watch and be on his own for a bit, but before he was able to sneak out she went back to his table as if she was going to top off the cup of coffee that she knew had never been touched.

"Can I ask you a question?" she came right to the point.

"You may," he nodded politely, as if he anticipated this.

"The other night… you left a note… on the table," she paused, sorting out her thoughts. "Was that meant for me?"

He smiled and looked down as if he'd been waiting for her to ask for decades. "It was."

She shook her head, "I don't understand…" she shrugged her one shoulder.

"Don't you?"

She swallowed the lump in her throat, as if he could read her thoughts and a flutter of guilt pricked at her skin.

He pointed to the seat across from himself indicating that he was inviting her to sit. She looked around the room to quickly assess her choices. She could sit for a moment to talk with this man and his cryptic message or she could chalk him up to being another crazy person who found his way into her section. What could it hurt? She looked around and saw that all of her tables were empty.

She tentatively sat on the edge of the booth across from the man, ready to get up at a moment's notice if her boss called for her.

She looked over the man sitting there, waiting for him to speak. He was dark complexioned and when he spoke, she detected an Italian accent. Direct descendant or just one generation from Italy. He had hair sprouting up under his collar and also wore a thick gold chain with a cross dangling from it.

He looked into her face after what felt like a lifetime of silence. His hands started speaking before his mouth did. *Yep, Italian*, she thought to herself.

"He has seen your troubles. He wants to bless you. But… sometimes His blessings may not feel like a gift." He nodded as he spoke. "You are good inside and you have suffered much. He sees your suffering. You have the gift of healing. You must share it humbly with the world."

"How did…."

He continued on as if he did not hear her. "Do not bring attention to yourself and you can do great things with His blessing. You will have all you need when you need it. This is His promise to you."

He slid from the booth and laid a hundred dollar bill on the table, and a dollar and thirty-two cents, the exact amount for his cup of coffee. He patted her hand as he left the diner.

She sat there for a moment more, completely dumbfounded by his words. How did he know she was studying to be a doctor? How did he know her troubles?

Maybe he doesn't know the specifics, she thought. Maybe he's just super empathetic and can sense my hurting? She toyed with different reasons why he would say those things to her. She was baffled.

"You just gonna sit it out tonight, Doc?" Hank called to her from the kitchen window.

She scowled at him and grabbed the full cup of coffee, the hundred dollar bill and the payment. She wiped down the table, but couldn't quiet her thoughts.

That night, she fell asleep quickly, she slept hard. The whirring of the refrigerator motor that hummed and then clunked didn't even keep her awake like it did most nights.

Her eyelids fluttered and her breathing slowed. Her heartbeat, however, sped up. It thumped against her chest and she could feel it echo throughout her entire body. It pounded in her head... "You have the gift of healing and you must share it humbly with the world..." she heard his voice in her mind as if he was calling to her from the other end of a tunnel. Thump. Thump. Thump. She twitched and turned. "Sometimes His blessings may not seem like a gift. They cost much, before and after you are chosen to bestow His gifts..." She saw the image of her mother, her father, her husband, her children... they were smiling and holding out their arms to embrace her. She wanted to run to them, but her legs wouldn't move. She tried to call out to them, but she had no voice.

Finally her heart pounded so heavily she thought it was about to stop. She woke up with a start and put her hand on her heart. Her pulse was quick, but not dangerously so. She looked about her room. It was still dark, but the sun was beginning to stir. Photos of her past lay scattered about her on the bed.

She shook her head, and took in a deep breath to calm herself. She flopped back down on her pillow and stared at the ceiling before muttering the words… "Why, God… why are you keeping me here? There is nothing left for me. I have lost everything. And I have nothing to show for all that I have lost. There is no gift in this grief…" the tears slipped from the corners of her eyes and into her hair and ears but she lay still waiting to hear an answer. "Yeah, that's what I thought," she grumbled low, "…nothing."

She rolled to her side deciding to sleep a bit more, and there on the other pillow in clear view was the napkin… Hold On.

Miracles from Ashes

Chapter Four

At the stoplight, Hannah looked at her eyes in the rearview mirror. "I must be getting sick," she said out loud to no one. She stuck out her tongue assessing herself for any signs of illness. Her fingers were sensitive to the touch. Her stomach felt like it had butterflies, but she didn't feel nauseous. Her head felt hot like it should be fevered, but she had no temperature.

She watched someone walking down the street and furrowed her brow. She shook her head and looked again, not believing what she saw. She squinted and rubbed her eyes hoping that her vision would go back to normal, but she saw the same thing. A car honking behind her, reminded her to move forward. "Weird."

She kept her head down as she continued on her way to the parking lot.

She parked in her usual spot, in the far corner of the truck stop and diner, out of the way of the routine traffic. When she got out her car and closed the door, she heard a man coughing right behind her. Startled, she turned around to see who was so close to her, but there was no one there. She heard the coughing again. A deep smoker's cough. She looked around her but there was no one. "Seriously?" She scanned the parking lot and all the way on the other side was a man pumping diesel into his semi, coughing up a lung.

She leaned in and squinted at the man. It was his cough, but he was so far away and yet she heard it as if he were standing right in front of her.

The man spit on the ground and wiped his mouth with the cuff of his coat. And while that disgusted her, it was quickly forgotten when he stood up straight.

Hannah gasped and stumbled back onto the side of her car in disbelief. She could see his lungs! Literally SEE his lungs! They were covered in cancer spots and she was amazed that he could even draw breath at all. She couldn't stop staring. He wore a heavy winter coat, but she could see beyond his layers, into his chest and if she looked ever so slightly to the right, she could see his heart trying its best to beat. She couldn't see bones, she couldn't see anything else, but his rotting lungs and weak heart. They were clear as if he had a hole cut out from the center of his body.

She shook her head in disbelief... "This is not happening."

She looked down to the pavement watching her feet cross the slushy blacktop toward her job. "I don't drink. I don't smoke. I don't take any medications. My blood work was fine last time I got tested. I don't even eat a lot of...." She stopped and looked at nothing, as if all the answers had just come to her. "Oooh. I haven't eaten." She bobbed her head, satisfied with her diagnosis. "That explains a lot. I need to take better care of myself," she said out loud, but then her thoughts immediately admonished her, *what for*?

She walked into the diner and what was usually a mixture of voices and comfortable sounds became a cacophony in her head. Everything was so much louder. The voices, the silverware rattling against the platters, pots and pans scraping and … and… breathing. She heard breathing… hearts beating… blood pumping…

She paused, almost losing her balance and leaned against the doorframe. Her eyes wide with fear as she attempted to find the location of all the sounds.

She scanned the room and saw glimpses of the inner workings of people's bodies. An ulcerated stomach… a clogged artery in the left ventricle… a fractured femur… Her mouth dropped open as she tried to maintain some sort of normalcy.

"Hey! Doc! You comin' in or goin out?" Hank yelled at her from behind the window that led to his kitchen domain.

The room quieted when she focused in on Hank thankful, for once to hear his voice. She walked toward him and looked only at him.

"Why you lookin' at me like that, creeper?"

"I'm… I'm sorry. I guess I'm still tired."

"Yeah, well, you'd better snap out of it cause a bus just pulled up, and I'm guessin' they're gonna be hungry."

She nodded, taking off her coat and reaching for an apron.

"And if I were you, I wouldn't block off table twenty-two tonight, the boss is gonna be in."

She shook her head, not understanding. "What are you talking about?"

"The last few nights,   you've blocked table twenty-two." He pointed his spatula at the table in question, as if she had forgotten the diner's set-up.

She sighed heavily, no longer happy to hear his voice, "I know where the table is, I don't understand what you mean by 'blocking'."

"You've been putting a cup of coffee there for the last few nights so no one else would sit there. If you don't like that station, why not trade with someone. I mean, what do I know, I'm just the cook, but I see things."

Hannah frowned at him. "I did no such thing. Why would I do that?"

"Excuse me, Doc...   who knows why you girls do things. I know that Lisa gives all her people caffeinated coffee even when they ask for decaf." He shrugged. "You chicks are crazy."

"Hank, I wouldn't put coffee there unless someone asked for it." Hannah was exasperated.

"Zat why you were sittin' there the other night, too? Cause someone asked you to?"

"As a matter of..."   Hannah stopped short and furrowed her brow. "Wait, what?"

"You…" he over exaggerated pointing at her, "… deciding to take a break out on the floor, for some weird reason. You need to get a grip."

"There was a man…" Hannah spoke more to herself than to Hank.

"Yeah, okay… whatever you say, darlin'."

"So… you're telling me you didn't see an older gentleman sitting in that booth for the last few nights?"

Hank stopped his cooking and looked straight at her. "You serious right now? Sometimes I can't tell with your college-level sense of humor."

Hannah chuffed and looked away. "Right… you… caught… me…" She couldn't help but stare at him for a moment longer and furrowed her brow.

"What?" he snapped at her.

She blinked at him and pursed her lips before speaking. "Did you know… you have a cavity in your back right molar?" She stared blankly at his shocked expression and turned away before he had an opportunity to answer her.

He placed his palm on his lower jaw and frowned at her as she walked away, not even knowing what to say.

Hannah tried to tune out the sounds in her head and concentrate on her patrons as she discovered that when she spoke to one person, the other sounds faded to the background, so she became very diligent at focusing on each guest.

She was now suddenly privy to everyone's health secrets. She tried to keep eye contact but sometimes that was made difficult when other parts of their bodies were trying to get her attention. Colon cancer... UTI... congested lungs from the common cold... Asthma caused from black mold spores...

She was trying hard to keep her composure but was on the edge of breaking down. She wanted to scream for all the noises to stop. Just STOP!

She came to a table with a family of four, they had their food but she was just following up. "Everything good here?"

The father nodded. The mother looked to everyone's plates and glasses taking inventory before she nodded. The little boy held up his index finger, wrapped in a band-aid. "I gotta boo-boo."

"Oh, no..." Hannah leaned over to see it. And she could, through the band-aid. She saw a scratch about a half an inch long, already getting its first scab forming on it. She gasped at what she saw, but the child took it as just the right amount of sympathy and awe. "Don't you worry, it will heal up fast and you'll be good as new."

She patted his back and turned away from the table.

Her fingertips tingled as she walked away and she chalked it up to another side effect of her meltdown. It wasn't until she heard the little boy squeal, "Look Momma! It's all better!", that she felt her heart beat in her throat and she momentarily thought she was going to faint.

But she had no opportunity because Joe, her regular, started coughing. "He's choking!" someone called out.

Hannah ran over to Joe who was coughing, then gasping for air, doubling over as he sat at the counter. Hannah could see that there was food lodged in his esophagus and leaned in to perform CPR. But the moment her hand touched his body, the food exploded into tiny particles and made its way down. Hannah stepped away from Joe with her mouth open. His esophagus faded from her view and all she could see was heartburn at the top of his abdomen. She gasped and fell back bumping into someone who had gathered around to watch the drama unfold. They patted her on the shoulder. "You saved his life."

She shook her head…. "I didn't… I didn't…" Her face showed panic and fear, but Joe didn't seem to notice as he turned to hug her. "Thanks, girl." He wrapped his arms around her and she returned the hug, but when Joe pulled away, the heartburn was gone.

Hannah gasped again and fell backward trying to escape the scene.

"You okay?" Joe asked, as she pushed away from the surrounding people.

She nodded quickly and turned away.

Joe called out over the counter, "Hey Hank, I'm feelin' better than ever, what are the pies you got on special for today?"

Hannah could barely breathe. She ran to the front door and heard Hank call out to her, "Hey Doc, where ya goin? Joe wants a piece of my famous…."

She was out the front door. She didn't stop running until she got to her car. "That… that did not just happen…" she said out loud, the cold air turning her words into clouds. "What… what is happening to me…" She tried to pull the handle of her car door but it was locked. Her keys were inside the cafe, in her coat pocket. She couldn't bear to go back in there.

She hugged herself and walked back and forth the length of her car trying to decide what she should do next.

"This is it… this is what has become of me. I've gone crazy. It makes sense," she launched into another self-analyzing session… "No sleep, really. Poor diet. Suffered a lot of pain… loss… Reality can sometimes slip away and we project a world where we can make-do… looking for a purpose…"

She was startled out of her mental evaluation when Wayne tapped her on the shoulder.

She screeched and turned to face him. She looked down and saw that his lungs were coated in black tar from years and years of smoking. She immediately brought her eyes back up to his, "Uh… hi."

He raised his eyebrows, "Um… hello. Would you like to tell me why you're outside talking to yourself and not inside talking to your customers?"

Her eyes welled up with tears. "I can't."

His face immediately softened, "Why can't you?" Hannah didn't respond but just stared wide-eyed. "I'm pretty sure I've heard it all before," he offered.

She looked around wildly, "No... I... don't think you have..."

"Hannah. What's wrong. Talk to me."

She looked into his eyes and then back down to his chest and then back up again. "You need to quit smoking."

He was a little taken aback by her response, not quite what he was expecting. He raised his eyebrows again and took in a deep breath. "Okay. I can do that, but could we maybe discuss it inside."

"I can't. I can't go back in there."

"Did someone..."

She vehemently shook her head, "No..."

"Honey, Joe's gonna be okay. He's crowing that he feels better than ever. You did a good thing in there."

"I'm sorry, Wayne... I can't... I can't go back in there... the noise."

"Okay, okay..." he put his hands out in front of him and gave her plenty of warning that he was about to touch her. "Let me grab your coat for you and you take the rest of the night off, okay? You probably just need a good night's sleep." He rested his hands on her shoulders. He would have pulled her into an embrace, if for no other reason than to warm her until he could get her coat but she put her hand out to stop him.

At the moment she made contact with him, she started backward as if he burned her and bumped into her car. He pulled back with his hands in the air, un-aggressively.

She stared wide eyed at his chest and then back up to his eyes. She tentatively placed her hand back on his chest and watched it turn from black to pink and then fade away under his thermal top and flannel shirts.

Her jaw dropped open and she snapped her hand back feeling a tingle in her fingertips.

He took in a deep breath, and the look on his face told her that he noticed a difference and that she could be the cause of it.

He stepped back another pace, still looking at her and her shocked expression and breathed in the cold air allowing it to fill his lungs.

"What did you do?"

She could only shake her head her eyes wide with fear. "I don't know…." She gasped. "I don't know…. I'm sorry… I have to go."

She pushed off her silver car and took off into a sprint across the parking lot. She wove her way through cars and trucks entering and leaving the gas station. She barely looked both ways before crossing the busy street and running along side the highway through the outlying wilderness.

Her lungs were burning and the muscles in her back and legs ached, but she couldn't stop, didn't stop running.

She finally came to the bridge she was searching for. She paused at the edge of it and hunched over trying to catch her breath. When she stood back up she marched straight out to the middle and looked over. "I don't want to be crazy. I know you don't like it when people choose their own demise, but I can't… I can't rot away in a mental institution! Please… don't make me die like that. Please just look away and let me end it now. My life is not worth living and now I am losing my mind. Please, God… I know you can hear me. Please let me come home to my family."

She broke down in tears and sobbed, leaning her head on her hands that rested on the top rail. She cried until her tears ran out. She stood up tall and wiped her face, suddenly calm in her decision. She took in a deep breath and blew it out and stepped onto the lowest rail.

"You're not crazy."

She snapped her head in the direction of the voice. There, standing only a few feet from her was the man from the diner.

She looked at him for a moment before speaking, "You're not real."

He bobbed his head as if he'd heard that more than once.

"I assure you, that I am real. But it is true that no one else can see me… anymore."

She shook her head, "That's… that's not possible."

"It is if you're an angel."

She stepped away from the railing to face him. She looked down at her bare arms and realized that she was no longer cold. She was no longer out of breath and her body felt no pain.

"Am I dead?"

He chuffed. "Why does everybody ask that? No, you're not dead."

"I don't… what is…"

"You can call me Pete."

"Pete, the Angel?" she looked at him skeptically.

He shrugged his shoulders, "What can I say, I like it. It's easier to say than Paschar." He tried it out a few times, "Paschar. Paschar. Paschar…" He shrugged again. "Pete just seems more… down to earth." He chuckled at his own joke.

She just stared wide-eyed as he spoke, not knowing how to have a conversation with an Angel… or more likely, how to have a conversation with an invisible counterpart knowing perfectly well that she was probably standing on this bridge alone. This illusion was her own brain trying to save her from committing the biggest sin in her mother's repertoire. She has conjured him up as an angel because of her religious Italian/Catholic upbringing.

"Do I need to sprout the whole wings and glow for you?"

She just continued staring but shook her head slowly.

He took her silence as permission, possibly resignation allowing him to continue. "This is the 'gift' I spoke of before."

She shifted her eyes to the left scanning her memories of their previous conversation, but still said nothing.

"You're not crazy, Hannah. Go heal them. To heal your own suffering, you must put your focus outward; off your own suffering and help others. You have the ability to help others."

She swallowed and cleared her voice not trusting it. "But I... failed at being a doctor."

He shook his head "no" and pointed a finger at her. "Fail, you did not... you walked away from that avenue."

The truth stung and she shifted her eyes away from him.

"You were created to heal."

"But... I..."

Pete held a finger to silence her argumentative thought. "Now," he widened his stance and clasped his hands together and let them hang just below his little round belly. "God does give you free will..." He nodded, choosing his words carefully. "But, He also gives you a purpose. You were put on this earth with a purpose, do you believe that?"

Hannah reluctantly nodded.

He raised his clasped hands pointing his index finger once again, before letting his hands drop, "You were on the path of your purpose, and then you took a hard right. And that was your choice. However, your purpose was not getting done. Follow me?"

Hannah shrugged her shoulders, "I guess?" the mist puffed from her mouth around the words.

"Consider this..." he paused and pinched his chin, "This... gift. This is ... His way of getting you back on your path. You are a healer. You were meant to be a healer. Go be a healer." He spoke with his hands, saying, *simple as that*...

"But this... this..." she waved her hands in front of her face, "This doesn't make any sense."

"Help them."

For a brief second, she felt a glimmer of hope... a purpose for her future.

"Your hands now have a healing power. Your purpose is to heal. But you are still human, so you *still have* free will. You may choose who to heal and when."

She frowned at him, not understanding the many hidden implications with this new "gift".

He laughed slightly. "You'll find your way around."

"Why? Why me?"

"He sees your heart. You have become the person he designed you to be, but for some reason, you don't believe in yourself. You were meant to be a healer. He is helping you to heal. He is teaching the people about faith. He is bringing His miracles back to the people."

Her Christian history tugged at her. "But He wasn't going to do that unless He was returning..." she let her voice slip away not wanting to finish the sentence.

Pete just looked at her and smiled. He opened his hands up and bobbed his shoulders letting her thoughts go where they will.

Her heart suddenly felt heavy and full at the same time. She looked down to her feet and kicked a rock off the edge sending it to the roiling waves below.

"So what now? Where do I start?" She looked up for the answers, but realized she was standing on the bridge all alone.

She looked down at her hands. They looked the same. "What now?"

Chapter Five

She walked into the dingy back office. The walls had a film on them from being exposed to years of cigarette smoke. Wayne sat at his desk with papers and ledgers stacked up around him. She could see him through a little cut out space where he was writing.

He looked up raising his eyebrows to allow his bifocals to slip down his nose. "Hey, there she is. How ya feelin'?"

She looked around uncomfortably and gave a half smile. "Okay, I guess."

He nodded, not pushing for more. "Are you clocking in?"

She raised her eyes to his, "You mean, I can?"

"Are you kidding? I'd be an idiot to turn away such a hard worker."

"So, I'm… Uh, you can, you know. I'd understand…"

He took off his glasses and used them to point with. "Your coat and keys are over there in the corner if you want, or your apron is where it always is. Your choice, kiddo."

She smiled and decided to take the olive leaf giving her some time to decide what she was supposed to do. "Thanks," she said, and turned to leave.

"Oh hey, by the way, I quit smoking."

She looked back over her shoulder not knowing what to say.

"Went to the doctor this morning and he said I had a clean bill of health. 'Damnedest thing he ever saw' is what he really said."

She looked away again, but he pulled her attention back to himself. "Hey," he placed his index finger to his lips. "Just no more freaking out, got it?"

"I'll try."

"Good. Now get to work, I'm sure there's something for you to do somewhere."

Over next few days, she experimented with her "gift". She was learning how to tune out the massive amount of various noises and focus in on any given task at hand. She also discovered that smaller injuries could be healed by a passing touch where the recipient didn't even realize what had happened, but larger wounds, or problems took a bit more time and concentration. She wasn't able to do many of those without the person thinking she was inappropriate for keeping her hand on their shoulder for a little too long before it slipped over into uncomfortable.

She kept her gift quiet and only healed people that wouldn't really find out until they went to their doctor. Some probably didn't even know they had an ailment.

After about three days, with only Wayne as her confidant, she decided to use a day off to visit her friend from the hospital.

She drove over to the other side of town and made her way comfortably through the hospital corridors until she reached Dr. Mosha Joshi's office.

She tapped on the door and smiled knowing that once she looked up from her charts she could see her face through the glass window.

She smiled in return and waved Hannah to come in.

She stood from her seat and offered Hannah a chair across from her. "It is good to see you, my friend. You have lost weight, I think."

"Maybe a little. It's been a rough few months."

"I can understand that. Please, please, sit. What brings you to my office today? It would please me if you were to say that you were returning to the program."

"No, I'm sorry. I'm not here for that." She looked down at her hands suddenly not sure of how to tell her friend about all that happened. "I... I have something to show you. Do you have some time?"

"For you? Of course. What is it that you wish to show me?"

"I… I think it might be better to let things speak for themselves."

"As you like. Lead the way then."

Hannah and Mosha got caught up on the little things. Hannah told her that she was working at the diner and actually enjoyed it.

Mosha tried not to condemn the work, but she would shake her head and say, "Such a waste of your skills."

They walked to the emergency room and paused as the sliding doors whooshed to let them enter.

"What is this about? Do you have a friend you would like for me to see? Are you hurt? Hannah, it is time to tell me…"

Hannah nodded as she scanned the wall for the listing of patients and their ailments.

She looked again at her friend and took in a deep breath only to release it while puffing out her cheeks. She opened the curtain in Bay 7. On the bed, a young man lay still. Hannah read from his chart: "Male. 37. Sedated. Laceration on the forehead above the right eye. Stitches needed." Mosha nodded. The man had a bandage wrapped around his head that was beginning to bleed through.

Hannah lifted the bandage to reveal the wound to her. Mosha nodded again and turned her hands over wondering what the point of this visit was.

Hannah raised her finger, begging for her patience for just a moment more. She breathed in and released it, standing by the man's bedside. She closed her eyes and placed her right hand on his shoulder, waiting for the tingling in her fingers to stop.

She opened her eyes and stepped away. She glanced at Dr. Joshi before lifting the bandage. The wound was gone. There was no scar. No sign that there ever was a laceration of any kind.

Dr. Mosha Joshi gasped and took a step back. "What trick is this?"

"It's not a trick."

"I… I do not understand what you have done."

"I have healed him."

"You cannot do that."

"I know… but I have."

Mosha crossed her arms in front of her, her face suddenly serious. "I know you have been though some very difficult times." She paused. "I feel for you. I do. But I also feel that we have done everything we can do for you. I don't know what your end game is, here, with… this." She pointed to the sleeping man.

Hannah looked at her patiently, a little hurt but understood that this was a difficult thing to accept. "I know you don't believe me. I've had a tough time with it myself. But what you saw was real. I have been given a gift. And I don't really know how best to use it."

Mosha didn't move, but looked away disappointed, shaking her head. She was internally wondering who she should call that could best help her friend… psychologically.

Hannah shrugged her shoulders. "I know… I know what this looks like. All I can say, is let me prove it to you. You choose a patient. Let me heal them. Maybe then you will see."

Mosha frowned not expecting her response. "I don't have time for…"

"Please. Take me to a patient. Any patient."

"This is Ciara. She was in a car accident." Mosha grabbed her chart from the end of her bed. "She has multiple lacerations, two broken ribs, a punctured lung, brain trauma…" Mosha shook her head. "This woman will never walk again. We will feel it a success if she were to wake up on her own." She cocked her eyebrow challenging Hannah to undo the damage and save the life of this woman or walk away never to bother her again.

Hannah said nothing but walked to the side of the bed. The patient lay still, being held together with hoists and pulleys and bandages from head to toe. She was attached to every kind of assistance machine the hospital had to offer. Hannah brushed the hair from her cheek momentarily feeling the pain this woman was suffering. And then, she lay her hands on the woman's heart. She closed her eyes and stood very still.

Mosha looked on still in disbelief but gave Hannah a few moments to bury herself. Mosha took in a deep breath ready to finish the escapade, when the monitors started to go haywire. Loud beeps filled the room and Mosha couldn't decide if she should stop what was happening or play it out.

Hannah stayed very still maintaining the same position.

Nurses bolted into the room responding to the monitors but Dr. Joshi held them back giving Hannah space. The monitors soon quieted down and her heartbeat was at a steady pace.

Ciara took in a deep breath as if she had been deprived of oxygen. She blinked her eyes and looked up at Hannah confused. She smiled down at the patient. "How do you feel?"

"Where am I? Why can't I move my arms?." A tear slipped from the corner of her eye.

Hannah unhooked the restraints and set her arms and legs on the bed. "Do you have any pain?" Hannah asked.

Ciara shook her head from side to side which caused all present in the room to draw a shocked breath.

"Good. That's good." Hannah wiped away the tear. "Can you give me your hand?

Ciara did. There was another collective gasp in the room followed by low whispers and murmuring.

"Can you squeeze my fingers?" She did. "That's good. Very good. Do you think you can sit up?" She nodded and Hannah took her hand and supported her as she swung her legs over the side of the bed. "Just sit tight, and the doctors are going to check you over, okay?"

She nodded her head in response, and the doctors and nurses in the room whispered and gazed having witnessed a miracle.

Hannah locked eyes with Mosha. "She is healed."

Mosha barked orders, "Run tests, I want an MRI and x-rays on my desk immediately." She pointed at Hannah, "You. Come with me."

The group nodded and jumped to work.

As Hannah left the bedside, she could hear Ciara call out to her. "Thank you. God bless you."

Mosha waited for Hannah to catch up to her in the hallway. "How do you do it."

"I don't know."

"You must know."

"I don't. I just lay my hands on them and they heal themselves."

Mosha furrowed her brow. "Anything? You can heal anything?"

"I'm not really sure. I've only had this gift for a few days. I have no idea what the gift can achieve."

"Come with me."

Hannah followed as she walked in silence down the hall. She could see that she was being lead to the radiology department.

"You will do some tests for me?" Mosha asked.

Hannah nodded. They walked into an empty room and Mosha found a hospital gown for Hannah to wear.

"I have so many questions that I want to ask," she paused. "But I must follow the science first." She stepped outside the room allowing Hannah some privacy to change into the gown.

Hannah and Mosha went into an MRI room that wasn't being used at the moment.

Mosha had Hannah lay on the bed and explained that she wanted images of her brain and brain activity. "And then we will take some images of the heart and blood vessels."

Hannah shrugged, accepting the testing. She had no explanation of this new gift and as a student of medicine, she was curious of the findings as well.

"Lay back, now, this won't take long."

The huge machine whirred and rumbled around Hannah's still body. She could feel her body respond on a molecular level. It was almost as if she could feel her blood pulsing through her veins and her organs gravitated toward the magnetic pull as it circled around her. She closed her eyes to concentrate on the sensations.

Before Hannah got changed back into her street clothes, Mosha drew six vials of blood, took an inner cheek swab, and got her updated vital signs.

"Your heart rate is very slow. Are you feeling at all light headed?"

"No. I am tired though."

Mosha nodded and scribbled some notes on the chart she created for H. M. Female.

"Okay, you can get dressed now."

As they walked through the hallway in silence; Mosha thinking that she didn't want Hannah to leave and possibly not return and Hannah not wanting to keep passing all the patient's rooms wondering if she could heal them all.

"There's something else…" Hannah began.

Mosha turned to look at her waiting.

"I can see things."

Mosha frowned, "See things? What do you mean by this?"

Hannah wished she wouldn't look at her like she was some kind of freak, but dismissed it, because Hannah herself sometimes felt the same way. "I mean, I can see the actual ailment. I could see the broken bones," she pointed to a patient in a wheelchair passing by, "and the swollen spleen," she nodded to a patient being wheeled past them. Then she pointed with the tilt of her head toward a man doubled over sitting in a chair in the hallway, "And a terrible case of gallstones." They continued to walk and she added, "That's gonna need surgery."

Mosha stopped in front of the door to the Emergency Room. Her face showed that she really had no idea what to do with all of this information, so her expression read of one that was irritated, but Hannah recognized it as her friend taking in and sorting though all that was being thrown at her.

They continued through to the room and Hannah stood near the door and looked over the wide open room with curtained off temporary exam rooms around the edges.

They walked from bay to bay and Hannah would tell Mosha what she saw:

Bay7: A dog bite, no rabies.

Bay 8: She *does* have a migraine, but the person waiting in the lobby complaining about a migraine does not have one, but instead has nausea and vomiting from withdrawals of Methadone.

Bay 10: The chart says she has a stomach ulcer but instead has: a gluten sensitivity

Bay 12: The child has strep throat.

Mosha didn't want Hannah to heal anyone in that room so her staff could work through the traumas as they normally would and confirm if Hannah was correct in her assessments.

"There is one more thing I'd like to see, if you could indulge me."

"Sure."

Mosha got on her cell phone. "How far along are you? Ask Dr. Markess to stop. Tell him that I am on my way and to do no more cutting. Thank you." She turned to Hannah. "We are going to surgery. I want you to scrub in and see if we can heal this patient."

Hannah nodded, pleased that she was actually going to do some good.

When they arrived at the surgery, both she and Hannah washed their hands up to their elbows and dried them. They were dressed and gloved and escorted into the room.

"What is so important that you had me put my entire surgery on hold."

"If this works out right, you'll be able to take a longer lunch," Mosha cocked her eyebrow at her co-worker. "Hannah…"

Hannah walked beside the patient and made eye contact with the doctor. "Good afternoon, Dr. Markess. I'm sorry to interrupt."

"Dr. Michaelson? What are you… Dr. Joshi what is this…"

The female patient was draped and unconscious with her abdomen exposed. A single incision was in the center of the undraped section. Mosha shewed away the doctor that was holding the suction hose keeping the blood loss contained. The blood bubbled up to the top of the incision and trickled out. The surgery team all looked at each other not knowing what to do or what was happening.

Hannah was the only one touching the body and she stood perfectly still with her eyes closed, her hands on the patient's chest.

A few more moments passed and the doctors and students standing around the patient began to get visibly uncomfortable. It was right about then that the incision on the patients abdomen started to seal itself. The attendants could see the wound tighten, deep inside the cut. The blood decreased. The wound tightened again causing the top layer to spread open. A student gasped and fainted. There was no other sound in the room. The top layer of the incision began to close and when the two sides of skin came together, there was no sign of any cut. Her abdomen was as smooth as when she came into the room.

"What just happened?"

Hannah gasped and stepped away. "She is healed."

"That's impossible! Dr. Joshi, what kind of games are you playing here?"

"And what was her ailment, Hannah?"

"She had a severe case of PID."

"Did you see any damage to the fallopian tubes and the ovaries?"

Hannah nodded, but then added. "It is healed as well."

"Would it have required surgery?"

Hannah suddenly uncomfortable, shook her head "Uh… uh… no, not usually."

"You're asking your former students for their assessments now, Dr. Joshi?"

"You were cutting into this patient for no reason, Dr. Markess. Dr. Michaelson just saved this woman's life. Your patient is not dying of cancer, but merely has too many sexual partners. By the time you would have gotten in there only to find out that you were wrong, she could have died on this table."

"You don't know that!" Dr. Markess yelled.

"True. And now we shall never know, because this woman's body has been healed." She stared at the speechless doctor a second more daring him to speak, then she turned to Hannah. "Come, Hannah."

All eyes were on them as they left the room and tossed their scrubs in the laundry hamper.

But they could hear the conversation explode once they stepped outside the door.

"Why would you have me do that?" Hannah asked, sincerely.

Mosha took the accusation in stride. "It was wrong of me to take advantage, and I am sorry. Ryan and I argued about that patient for weeks. I told him that he was mistaken in his diagnosis, but he was the lead surgeon, so I had to stand aside."

"That's not what this gift is for," Hannah stopped in the middle of the hall.

"I have told you that I am sorry. And you healed the woman. That's what you wanted, correct? It seems to be exactly what the gift is for."

Hannah was still upset but said nothing more. By now, as they walked through the halls back to Mosha's office, she could feel people begin to stare. They were trying not to be obvious, but everyone she made eye contact with, quickly turned away.

Finally a familiar face stepped in front of their path.

"Hannah!"

"Nicole!" Hannah smiled and embraced the young woman in front of them.

"I heard you were here today. What's happening? Are you coming back?"

"She is here for tests..."Dr. Joshi interrupted.

"Tests? Are you alright?"

Hannah giggled. "I am. Are you?"

Nicole looked at her a little sideways, "I have been fighting the flu bug. It's been awful, but you know what it's like getting a day off around here."

Hannah's genuine smile spread across her face. "You don't have the flu, Nicole. You're pregnant."

Nicole's face paled and her jaw dropped. She snapped her head to her left where she caught the eye of Dr. Clemmons, who shared her shocked expression.

Hannah's smile faded and she looked back down to Nicole's midsection. She started to walk past her but whispered, "You're about eight weeks along, but everything looks healthy." Her eyes darted around the hallway, wondering if anyone else heard the surprise news about a three year resident having a baby with quite possibly an attending... a married attending.

By the time they reached Dr. Joshi's office, she had to draw the blinds because what seemed like the entire hospital was staring her way and not even trying to hide it.

Hannah sat in the chair across from Mosha's desk and looked down at her hands.

"Do not trouble yourself. They will forget all about it before the day is over. They are like children. Easily distracted by something new."

Hannah looked up at her mentor wanting to believe that but the words of her Angel came back to her. *"You have the gift of healing and you must share it humbly with the world."*

Humbly, she thought to herself. *I was not very humble today. I was not very cautious today. I am so confused. How do I heal without bringing attention to myself?*

"Hannah," Mosha's stern voice brought her back to what she was saying. "Are you hearing me?"

"I'm sorry, no. Could you please repeat that last part?"

"Your test results won't be in for two days, can you come back in?"

Hannah nodded, "Yes, of course. I'm curious to see them."

"What is a good number where I can reach you?"

"I don't have a phone."

Mosha looked at her as if she had three heads.

"I work at a diner. I barely have enough money to keep a roof over my head." Hannah felt the need to justify her meager spending.

A look of pity quickly fluttered across Mosha's face but was quickly replaced by her practiced stoic expression.

"Do you need some money?"

Hannah shook her head, "No, I'll get by."

"Do you need a place to stay?"

Hannah shook her head. "I'm still in the same place. It works."

Mosha looked at her not knowing what to say.

"I'll be back in two days, that's the best I can do for now." Hannah offered.

"It will do. I trust you."

Hannah thought that an odd thing to say at the moment, but couldn't connect it to anything specific.

Hannah left the hospital amid whispers and watchers, but no one bothered her. She walked around the back parking lot to her car.

As she was pulling her keys from her purse a woman came up behind her and tapped her on the shoulder. "Ma'am?"

Hannah started and turned around. A woman in her late twenties and a young boy stood in front of her.

"Please… please help my little boy."

She looked down at the child and could see the damage eating away at the child's insides as the woman spoke. "The doctors have turned us away. They told us that there's nothing else they can do for him. He has leukemia. They basically sent him home to die."

She began to cry and the child just looked up at Hannah. The dark circles under his eyes and the thin wisps of hair that stuck out from underneath his ballcap, along with his thin, frail frame told even an outsider that this little boy was gravely ill.

"I… I saw you in the emergency room this morning." She began wiping her eyes with her fingertips, determined to get the words out whether she believed them or not. "You can do… things."

Hannah looked away and looked back at the boy.

"Please. Can you help my son? He's all that I have. Help my Barry. Please."

Hannah knelt down in front of Barry. She looked up at his ball cap, "You're a Cardinal's fan?" she asked.

He nodded and a smile crossed his face. He pulled his cap off and showed her the inside. Names were scribbled along the hat band and on the inside.

"Is this an autographed hat?"

He nodded again. "By the whole team!" His raspy voice was still that of a happy eight year old.

"Now, that… is pretty cool." She said. "Can you show me where it hurts?" she asked.

Barry shook his head no.

"Why? Why can't you tell me?"

He raised his head up to look at his mother. "It makes my mom cry when I talk about it."

"Oh, baby… he's always trying to protect me." She leaned down and kissed his head. "You can tell her, honey. I won't listen."

"You must be pretty brave." Hannah saw the residue of chemo on his organs.

"I am. I am so brave that I... I... swam all... all the way across to the other side of the pool, by... uh... by myself. Without even wearing floaties."

Hannah showed him how impressed she was by her expression. "Wow..." She smiled at him again, "That IS really brave, your mom must be so proud."

He bobbed his shoulder, pretending that he was indifferent.

"Do you mind if I give you a hug?"

He held open his arms and she came into them wrapping hers around his tiny body. "Oh! You give such great hugs!" She said trying to prolong the moment. "Your mommy is so lucky to get these great hugs from you every day!"

She pulled away from him and smiled. She held him on both of his arms and talked while looking at him in the eye. "Now, I want you to take really good care of your mommy, okay?" He nodded. "And I want you to do really well in school so that someday you can teach others how to be super brave like you. Okay?"

He nodded and his body shook as if he felt a cold chill.

She stood up and nodded to the mom. "That's a pretty special lil' man you've got there. You take good care of him. It's going to be okay." She locked eyes with the woman and her words spoke volumes.

"Really?"

Hannah nodded.

"Oh, thank you. Thank you. I can never thank you enough." She shook Hannah's hand and then chose to embrace her instead. And then, once more.

"Come on, honey, let's go home."

They turned away and Barry automatically reached for his mother's hand. "Who was that lady, momma?" he asked

"She was the nicest woman we will ever meet and you mother will never stop praying for her."

"Then I will pray for her too."

Hannah watched them walk away and listened to them talk. The woman turned back around and took one last look before they disappeared in the sea of cars.

"I sure could use those prayers," she said out loud to no one, as she unlocked the door to her car and climbed in.

Chapter Six

Hannah walked into the diner and was greeted by a teenage girl. Her curly hair was pulled back with a wide headband.

"Table for one?" she asked.

Hannah stopped short at her question. "I... I work here." She unzipped her coat to reveal her pale pink uniform. She held out her hand to the girl. "Hi, I'm Hannah. I guess you're new here?"

"You're Hannah? You're the reason my uncle pulled me in here. You some kind of superstar waitress or somethin'?"

Wayne came out from behind the two-way mirror of his office to interrupt. "Hey, there's my girl."

"What's going on? We suddenly need a hostess?"

"Everyone keeps asking to sit in your section," the new hostess volunteered.

"This is my niece, Kristy. She's just helping us out for a bit."

Kristy crossed her arms, as if she was not given an opinion on the situation.

"You're gonna be busy."

Wayne put his arm around Hannah's shoulders and led her toward the back room. When they were out of earshot, he asked, "So? What happened? What'd the doc say?"

Hannah shrugged. "At first, like you said, she didn't believe me. But after I showed her a couple times, she decided to run some tests." Hannah took her coat off and hung it up on a hook on the wall. She turned back to Wayne. "This gift is really powerful! I can't believe some of the stuff that I did today! There was this one…"

"Honey, I wanna hear all about it, I do but… do you trust this… this Dr. Joshi person?"

"I… I guess. I'm supposed to go back and see her on Monday to find out the results of the tests."

Wayne dropped his head and squeezed the back of his neck as if he could massage away the giant lump of stress that he had created there. "I … I just don't want her to take advantage of you."

"Oh. I don't think she'd do that. She loves the science of medicine…"

"This gift you have… people could…" he swallowed, "people will take advantage of it." He looked up and away feeling guilty. "It could make someone a *lot* of money."

Hannah smiled at him, resting her hand on his arm reassuringly. "This gift is a good thing." She took down her ponytail only to put it back up again. "How could healing people be bad?"

"Hannah," he took her by her shoulders. "*I* am making money off of you." He scrunched his face saying the words all wrong. "I'm … I'm not trying to, but… people… once they find out about your gift and… they… they are coming here to see you. This is not coming out right." He ran his hand down his face and tried again. "They know that you are doing something. And… lucky for me, they feel obligated to buy something. They just pretend that they want whatever Hank is cooking back there. They are here to see you. So you can heal them."

Hannah smiled, "I think that's nice. It's what the gift is for."

"You're not hearing me, girl!" Wayne put his hands on his hips and paced in a small circle.

"I finally have a purpose. I can help people." She shrugged her shoulders, "God knew where I worked when I got this gift. Maybe he was giving you a gift too."

"I know but… " he ran his fingers through his hair and squeezed the back of his neck again. He closed his eyes not wanting to betray emotion. "I just want you to be careful."

She saluted him and bobbed her head in compliance.

Wayne rolled his eyes like a parent would with a willful child. "Go on then. Get out there and do what you do. They're waiting."

"You might want to go give Hank a hand in the kitchen then, so I don't have to spend all night healing all the heartburn he causes." She smiled, and walked away tying her apron.

He threw his head back and laughed showing the history of the deep lines around his eyes.

People poured into the diner and at first, things moved along smoothly. Hannah took orders, delivered food and healed people as covertly as she could.

The night wore on and the wait time for seating reached over two hours, but they waited. Big, fat, wet snowflakes fell outside and made the floors slick and wet and the guests cold and uncomfortable. The lobby benches were full, and the crowd spilled into the gas station side and out the door, making it difficult to keep it closed. But they waited. And waited.

The other waitresses abandon their stations and acted as support for Hannah. They pooled all their tips, so they were happy to help or run the risk of not making any tips at all because everyone wanted Hannah's services.

And then…

"Hey!" a voice called out from the front door of the lobby. "Excuse me!" A man pushed through the crowd toward Kristy. He was tall, very slim and wore a chocolate turtleneck and tan slacks that hugged his ankles. His leather shoes did not belong in the snowy slush and showed the watermarks from the depth of the collecting snow in the parking lot. He supported another man who was about the same height, but whose illness had made him a shadow of his former self. This man had a low stubble across his cheeks and chin, but it was neatly trimmed. He wore a pair of loose fitting high-end jogging pants and a long sleeve, light weight turtleneck. His hair was stuck to his head, drenched with sweat.

Both men made their way to the front of the line with great effort.

"We have been waiting for over an hour."

"I'm sorry sir, we are seating people in the order they come in and as soon as we possibly can. What was your name please?"

"Corbin."

Her eyes scanned down the list of names. She smiled as she brought her eyes back up to his. "I see your name here, party of two. But I'm sorry, it looks like your wait could be at least another thirty minutes. Would you like to order an appetizer for while you wait? I'd be happy to…"

"Oh, this is ridiculous. Couldn't we just skip this part?"

"I'm sorry?"

"I mean, I'll pay for a meal or whatever if that's what I need to do, but I'm certainly not going to eat it."

"Sir… um… everyone is…"

"Look, little girl…" he reached up and scratched his eyebrow, annoyed and trying to keep his composure. "My husband is dying. This is our last hope. We don't have time to mess around here. Can she really perform miracles?"

Kristy fidgeted and didn't know how to answer such a question. "Sir… I… uh.. I'm not sure I understand…?"

The crowd began to get restless behind the man and his sickly mate, trying to hear the details of their conversation but also not wanting to be bumped in line.

"Look, I'll pay more money, if that's what it takes… I just…"

At that moment, Hannah pushed through the kitchen doors holding a plate in each hand smiling.

"That's her! There she is!" shouted someone from the lobby.

"Ma'am! Ma'am?" Corbin called out to her.

"Does he get to go ahead?" someone asked.

"We were here before them." someone else called out.

"I don't want to eat either, is there a different list for that?"

People began to rush the hostess station with their questions. Kristy tried to calm them down as best she could, but they had gotten themselves pretty worked up.

Corbin and his husband pushed past the crowd and entered the dining area trying to flag down Hannah from her duties.

"Hey! You… you there…" he called to her.

Hannah delivered her plates to their waiting customers and turned back to the man calling her.

"I need you to save my husband. Can you? Can you really? He is dying and no one will help us."

Humble. Stay humble.

Hannah looked around the room, caught off guard. She wasn't used to people asking her to use her gift on demand.   She was so much happier with the game that everyone pretended that they were just there to eat a greasy meal and if they were lucky, they would go home leaving whatever dreadful ailment they came there with behind.

She looked over at the man, barely holding his own weight. He leaned heavily on Corbin to keep himself upright. His skin was paper thin and was covered in bruises.

Hannah's heart went out to him. She walked over to him and put her hands on his cheeks and smiled. "I will help you," she whispered.

She reached out and took his hands in hers.   He strained to raise his eyes to hers but she still looked at his face.

A few moments passed and he took in a deep breath. He lifted his head and put his feet flat on the floor supporting his own weight.

He straightened his spine to rise up to his full stature and the crowd behind him gasped.   He closed his fingers around Hannah's and looked into her eyes.

Corbin was crying so hard but stepped away to see that his husband was standing on his own and returning to the man he once knew right before his eyes.

The crowd collectively gasped and murmured at the transformation.   His sallow skin returned to a rosy complexion. There was color in his cheeks. He shivered from a cold draft.

Whispers fluttered from one person to the next until the whole room was no longer silent, but a cacophony of voices.

Hannah only saw the man in front of her and the smile that he returned.

Corbin wiped away his tears. "Thank you. Thank you," he said to Hannah and broke their connection. "Oh baby… you're well… you look amazing," Corbin blubbered.

"I feel amazing. Like new." He turned back to Hannah, "I can't thank you enough. I wouldn't have… I didn't believe but…"

"She's for real!"

"She healed him!"

"Help me!"

"Look this way, Hannah!" Cell phones were pointed in her direction from every angle.

"Heal me!"

"Save me!"

The tender moment was shattered as the mass of people pushed past the meek hostess and swarmed Hannah trying to touch her. They grabbed at her hands, her hair, her clothes. Hannah was pushed into a wall as the crowd of people climbed over each other to try and reach her. She wrapped her hands around her waist trying to protect her abdomen. They pawed at her and tore her clothes. They pulled at her hair and stretched their hands out attempting to make some kind of connection with her.

"Help me!"

"Save me!"

"I'll give you anything…"

"Please…"

Hannah slid down the wall into a ball wishing she could disappear into the floor.

"Get back! Get back!" Wayne and Hank pushed their way through the crowd, shoving people left and right to get to Hannah.

She was crying and had her head tucked down as far as it could go with one hand covering the top of her head and the other tucked in around her waist.

"Come on, honey. I've got you." Wayne bent down and wrapped his coat around her shoulders while Hank kept the others at a safe distance. "I've got you. I've got you." He strained as he picked her up but was able to lift her still curled up body and carried her back toward his office.

"She needs to heal me!"

"Where is she going?"

"I'll pay you!"

"Get back, you freaks!" Hank yelled at the people, and had no qualms about pushing people back when they tried to get too close while Wayne made a way for Hannah to escape.

The police were called to get the crowd back under control, but with Hannah now off the serving floor, the people either left the building or went back to their seats in the lobby hoping Hannah would make another appearance.

Wayne sat beside Hannah on a bench with his arm around her shoulder. He could hear the commotion just beyond the door of the break room. Every once in a while, one of the other waitresses would come back and check on her.

"Are you alright?"

Wayne would answer for her, as Hannah still sat slouched on the bench crying.

"Those people aren't going to leave," Wayne said under his breath, more or less to himself. The police got them to stop banging on the door, but they can't make them go away. They may leave, but they won't go far.

"What did you do, honey?" Wayne finally asked, after Hannah had some time to compose herself.

'Nothing.... I... I just did what I have been doing. I healed this man and then all of a sudden, everyone went crazy."

"You did it in front of people?"

"Well, I mean... he was right there... he needed me."

"But before, you just..."

"Yeah... many of the others may not ever know they were healed. Some may not figure it out until..."

"... they go to their doctor."

"Yes. But this man... he... he..." she paused and rubbed her face, trying to shake off the events of the night. She focused on the healed man. "You could ... literally see life come back into his body. It was the most beautiful thing I'd ever seen. There was this light that... that started at the center of his body and made its way to every single part... his organs were pink again and his..."

"Alright. Alright... I get it, you don't have to tell me all the guts and the details."

"I didn't mean to..."

"I know… I know."

It wasn't until six o'clock the next morning when the crowd finally dispersed enough for Wayne to sneak Hannah back to her house.

Hannah was so exhausted that she slept in the office as well as the short car ride.

Wayne fretted as he watched her sleep. His heart broke for her as he tried to imagine the life that was in front of her from this point on. He felt for her like she was the daughter he never had. He didn't know how to help her at this point but knew she wouldn't be able to come back to the diner.

"Hannah… Hannah… wake up."

She fluttered her eyelids and gasped slightly not remembering where she was but recalling the invasive feeling of being smothered by stranger's hands.

"It's okay… You're okay. You're at home. I drove around for miles, one, to make sure you got some sleep and two, to make sure we weren't followed. You're safe."

She looked over at him on the brink of tears.

His heart tore just a little bit, but he pushed through it, hiding behind his gruff persona. His raspy voice was still soft around the edges though as he spoke. "Now listen, you get in there and don't so much as stick your nose out that door for the next few days."

"But the diner… my car… what about…"

His stern look silenced her. He took in a deep breath and spoke again, "Darlin' I hate to have to say this, but you can't go back to the diner."

"But, Wayne, I didn't mean..."

He looked out the window so she couldn't read his expression. "It's not that. I don't care about all that. The diner will be fine. People will eventually forget. New people will come in... People get distracted by other things..."

"Then, I could just wait..."

He sighed out heavily, "No... you... you gotta..." he rubbed his face and pinched his eyes, "You can't come back. You're gonna have to live... a little more... quieter. Do you understand?"

He looked over at her and her eyes were red-rimmed with tears waiting for the slightest incentive to spill over the edge.

"It's for your safety. People can't know... about..."

"Humbly..." she spoke, barely above a whisper remembering Pete's words.

"Yeah," he shook his head, "something like that."

She didn't move, but sulked in the front seat just staring at her snow boots on his wet stained floor mat. The tears silently slipped down her cheeks and off her chin.

"Do... you want me to go in with you? Are you worried that..."

"I don't know if this is a blessing or a curse... this... this thing that I can do."

He knew she wasn't looking for a response so he sat silently and listened.

"I'm *supposed* to be helping people…"

"You are. You've already helped so many people. Even if they didn't know it. You do."

"So was that it? Was that all I was supposed to do? Will my gift go away again?"

Wayne opened his mouth to speak and for a moment was speechless, and then, "I don't know, darlin'. I've never come across anything like this before in all my life."

She glanced at him and went back to staring at her feet. "Yesterday, after…" her eyes darted about, her mind flooded with images of the night before. "They made me feel so… dirty. And I don't even know what happened to that guy. The one who had AIDS. I saw color come back to his face and his eyes had life behind them… and just as he stood up to claim his life back, he disappeared in a sea of people." Frown lines appeared on her forehead as she tried to process the beautiful and then dreadful evening of events. "The sad thing… all those people… who rushed at me… I couldn't help them. Not a single one."

He looked at her confused.

"It doesn't work like that. I can't heal anyone if they touch me, and I can't just heal someone in passing." She glanced up at Wayne just to make sure he wasn't sizing her up for a fancy white jacket that fastens in the back. He was listening, concentrating on what she was saying. "Like…" she continued, "If I were to shake hands or brush up against someone, they could be magically be healed if it was something small.   But for bigger ailments, I have to concentrate. I have to focus on healing them. Just them. Just that one person."

She tipped her head to the side, self analyzing again, "And... and... it doesn't seem to work if people touch me. And those people... all those people... they just... grabbed at me... pulled my hair... my clothes..." she gulped as a sob squeezed at her throat.   "The healing comes through my hands."   A single tear slipped down her cheek.   "I would have healed them. All of them, if they could have just..."

She went quiet for a moment processing her next thought. "So, how am I supposed to heal people, but keep it quiet and not try to heal as many people as I can?" She looked out the car window at the snow covered street, but not really registering the scene. "Even when I was studying to become a doctor, I would take extra cases and work longer and harder... because I was there to help as many as I possibly could." She closed her eyes and shook her head, still deep in thought. "Wouldn't that be why I have this... this..."

"Superpower," Wayne said, matter-of-factly.   He smirked at her trying to lighten the mood.   "You're a super hero. Now you just need a cape."

She smiled but tried her best to look annoyed. "Right, because nothing says stealth like a superhero cape."

They both smiled and sat in a comfortable silence.

"All kidding aside, kiddo," Wayne began, "I know it doesn't seem like it... and maybe things aren't working out as perfectly and magically as you would like…   but you are helping people. You are making a difference."

"But.."

He held up his finger so he could continue his thought. "You're going to have to live… like a superhero. You can't tell people what you can do. You just had a small glimpse of what happens."

She lowered her head and her eyes followed the edge of the water stain on her foot.   "Maybe this is only a temporary thing. Maybe I have to learn some kind of lesson and then it will go away."

"I don't think that's what this is." He chose his words thoughtfully.   "You've been through a lot.   You've been derailed… a few times.   Others might not have made it through. Hell, I don't even know how you've lasted this long without cracking."

She looked away as guilt flooded her soul. She looked out the window, keeping the secret to herself how close she really came to giving it all up.

"I think it's a gift. A your-life-really-sucked-but you – have- a-giver's-heart-in spite-of-it kind of gift."

She giggled and looked back at him. "Do you think I can get a plaque with that engraved on it? I'm *so* hanging that on my wall."

He growled out a raspy smoker's laugh.

"I'd better get inside. I'm losing feeling in my nose."

He nodded.

"I have my appointment with Mosha tomorrow."

He nodded. "Hank and I will bring your car to you."

"Thanks Wayne… for listening… and… just thanks for everything."

He nodded again, not trusting his words. But his thoughts said, I*'d protect you from the world if I could, but I know you were meant for bigger things.* But his mouth said, "Get in there and get some sleep."

"That… I can do." She opened her door and looked back at him before stepping out, "Will I ever see you again?"

He shrugged, playing the nonchalant card.

Her face instantly responded in fear and sadness.

He rolled his eyes, "I said we'd bring your car back, didn't I?"

"Well, yeah, but I meant…"

"Look, I can't be your sidekick. I look terrible in tights."

She laughed and swiveled her feet to the ground, "Good, that saved me the trouble of having to ask your tight size." She slipped from the car and turned to close the door. "See ya tomorrow."

"You bet."

He waited until she was safely inside and the locks were all in place. She waved through the door window and he backed away.

Chapter Seven

"Our top story tonight comes with exclusive video footage of the young woman everyone is talking about. Who is she? Where is she from? And can the images seen on this video be believed? Good evening, I'm Vivica Caimen. Let's cut to the chase. We here at LHTV have the video footage that has spread across the social media platform and has had more views than the latest presidential debate. We've been told that there are graphic scenes in the following video. Viewer discretion is advised."

The screen behind the newscaster expanded to cover the viewing space. A loud bang was heard and the camera went from a young brown skinned woman singing at a gas pump to a blurred motion focusing in on a man falling to his knees clutching his chest. Blood poured from the hole in his chest. Another shot was fired and screams were heard outside of the viewing range. The video zoomed in on a panic-sticken, brown-skinned teenager holding a revolver. He shot off another round into the sky and turned to run. The video followed the teen for a few feet before returning back to the man who had now fallen face first to the ground.

A woman with dirty blonde hair, wearing pajama pants and a hoodie, despite the cold temperatures, ran from her car toward the victim. She pushed her way through the gathering crowd of onlookers. Several more camera phones were now pointed to the scene. The owner of the video stretched up on her toes to hold her phone over the crowd and caught the woman's head and the top half of the victim. Blood covered his shirt and was beginning to pool around his arms. He was blinking slowly, attempting to hold on to the final strands of life.

The blond woman bent down over him and lay her hand on his bloody shirt. Amidst the crowd shouting and pushing in around them, she stayed quiet and still.

Suddenly, the man gasped for air and blinked. He sat up and looked at the woman, both terrified and thankful.

Voices rose into shouts and clapping and screams as the man stood up. The camera caught a quick glimpse of the woman's profile before the man lifted his blood soaked shirt to reveal smooth, untarnished skin. The gunshot wound was gone.

The crowd swarmed toward the woman, who for just a quick second was caught on camera. A look of sheer terror showed on her face. She turned and pushed through the crowd, back to her Ford Capri. Her clothes were covered in the man's blood. She scrambled for her keys; turned over the engine and drove off, taking the gas pump with her.

"She sho dint pay for her gas…"

And the screen turned black.

Vivica Caimen's face appeared center once again as the close up face shot of the terrified woman hovered behind her.

"Do we dare believe what our eyes tell us? Did this woman in fact heal this man of his gunshot wound? Where is the woman now? Here's Larry, with more."

The scene changed to the gas station parking lot and a man wearing a red fluffy coat and a Blues Hockey stocking cap holding a microphone came into view.

"Yeah, thanks Vivica. There's still quite a bit of electric residue here at the gas station where some are saying a miracle occurred. Earlier, I spoke with fifty-two year old, Darwan James, the man who should have breathed his last breath only a mere ninety minutes ago... take a look at this..."

The scene flashed to the older man, a microphone hovering close to his face, "Yeah, I don't know what she did, but I never felt better in my life, you hear me?"

"Where were you shot? Was it a direct hit? Maybe it just grazed..."

"You see this?" Darwan poked his finger through a hole in his bloodied shirt to show that the bullet left its mark. "It hit me. Right here. I'm tellin' you it hit me. I ain't never felt so much pain in my life."

"Did you think this was the end for you?" Larry probed.

"Look, this mornin' when I lef my house, it was just another day. My bones was achin' and I was havin trouble breathing and I couldn't see without my glasses. Then I got

117

shot, and I thought, 'Well, I guess it's my time.' And now, I feel like I'm a new man. Like I got twenty years back. No lie. I'm tellin' you, I got a second chance. God bless that lady, whoever she is, and I'm not gone waste this second chance, ya hear me? Not gone waste it."

Larry came back to the center. "Pretty amazing story, I assure you. And right now, I have Teneica, the young woman who took the actual footage. Tenicia, what did you think of all that happened here?" Larry pointed the microphone toward a young woman with a head-full of long braids pulled up in a half ponytail.

"Well," she clicked her nails, "I don't even know. It could be a *beep* scam for all we know. Cause.... I mean, din't nobody actually SEE the man get shot. So, all I seen was this *beep* dude layin' on the ground and this white girl doin some *beep* praying over him, you know. Next thing I know she drivin' away with a *beep beep beep* free tank of gas!"

"You think it was all a ruse for a free tank of gas?" Larry's voice was heard off-screen.

"I think it's messed up, is what I think. I mean, who's gonna pay for the broken gas hose that girl stole? Prolly the tax payers."

"I don't think…"

"Did you show the part where I was singin? Cause baby, that was the *beep. beep* bomb!" Tenecia started in on her song, rolling her body to the beat that only she could hear, snapping her fingers over her head, "Haaaaaayyy…."

Larry turned away from the serenade, knowing that no further questions would be answered, and attempted to close out the segment with background accompaniment.

"There you have it. Here in *this* small town the jury is still out whether we've witnessed a miracle or an expertly executed gas fraud. Back to you."

"Thanks, Larry. And this just came in: another sighting of our mystery woman only yesterday. In a small truck stop just off the highway, in the same town as the gas station incident, this amazing footage was taken…"

A brief clip of the night before, also from a cell phone, showed Hannah healing a tall man right before everyone. The clip was cropped out as the crowd rushed Hannah, begging her for healing.

Vivica appeared, "We have since learned that the woman's name is Hannah Michaelson and is a resident of the neighborhood and also employed by the Route 66 Truck Stop's restaurant. We've sent our reporter, Larry, over to the truck stop to try and get some answers.

"Getting your miles in today, aren't you Larry?" Vivica smiled, to show her perfectly white teeth.

"I sure am, Vivica." Larry laughed, artificially. "The gas station and the truck stop are only twenty-two miles from each other, and I'm told that Ms. Michaelson does, in fact, live in a small mobile home park between the two businesses."

"Have you been able to speak to anyone at this second, or I guess it's actually the first location of miracles?"

"We attempted to speak with the owner, Wayne Howard, but he declined an interview, but as you can see…" the camera pulled back and panned the parking lot showing a line of people waiting for entrance into the small diner. "…there are those who are ready to believe the miracles they have seen." He walked over to a woman and poked the microphone in her face. "Excuse me, why are you here waiting in the cold?"

"I want to be healed. I've had Crohn's Disease since I was thirteen and I just want some relief."

"And you think the answer is here?"

"Well, I've tried everything else…"

"What are you willing to pay to have this disease lifted off of you?"

She thought for a second, "I would pay anything."

"So you believe in Hannah's ability?"

"I'm here, aren't I?"

Larry looked at the camera again. "The feelings of this woman are pretty much the same with everyone waiting here. They are looking for hope." Larry walked back over to the young hostess waiting for him.

"I have with me Kristy Lightner, the hostess on duty that night. Hello, Kristy, thanks for talking with me."

"Hi. You're welcome." She smiled into the camera.

"What can you tell us about Hannah Michaelson?"

"Oh, she's so nice." Kristy smiled.

"Can you tell us what it was like to work with her? Did she do this kind of healing all the time?" Larry asked.

"Oh, I only worked with her that one day, but she was really nice to me and to all the customers. Everyone came to the restaurant to see her."

"Do you really think she healed that man?"

Kristy shrugged her shoulders. "I'm not sure. I couldn't really see because everyone pushed me out of the way. Sorry."

"It's okay, it's okay. Tell me, have you seen her do this kind of thing before?"

Kristy shrugged again, "It was only my first day."

Larry looked back at the camera again, "It was only her first day. Not much to go on, back to you."

"Uh, hey! Hey! Wait a sec. I was there. I saw it all." A short, balding man ran in front of Larry's camera and talked into the mic. "I been waitin' here for her to come back," he continued.

"Is she supposed to be coming back?" Larry took the bait.

"Well, I guess so. This is where she works. Turns out she's been doin this healing stuff all week. People come in sick and they leave feeling better."

"Have you seen this for yourself?"

"I seen the finished product, let's just say." He winked at the LHTV spokesperson. "An, while I'm at it," He looked straight into the camera, "Hannah, if you're watching this, I wanna be your manager. The name's Hal. Gimme a call and I can make you millions. Ya hear me out there, sweetheart? I can make us a fortune." He pulled out his business card and held it up to the camera. "Call me. I'll set everything up."

Larry tried pulling away from the pushy little man and regaining control of his microphone. He pinched the bridge of his nose, clearly wanting to be finished with this story.

"Well, Vivica, it seems like if she is a scam artist, people are ready to buy."

Taylor Watson watched the television with her jaw hanging open. She was afraid to move away from the screen but when her phone rang, she walked to the kitchen to answer it. She looked down at the caller I.D. before answering, "Dude... what did you do?"

"I... I need your help," Hannah whispered into the phone.

Hannah pulled up in the parking lot of the Sleepytime Motel about forty miles out of town. Before she could exit the car, she heard a tap on her window. She jumped at the sound, but smiled when she saw who stood there waving.

She opened the door, "Taylor! Long time no see!"

"I know, right?" Taylor was a twenty-something respiratory technician with tightly cropped short fiery red hair with long bangs that flopped in her face when she wasn't in the mood to style them. She pushed the patience of the hospital administration on a regular basis by her nose-ring and collection of earrings that lined the cartilage of her ears. She was overly blessed with a voluptuous figure and did her best to dress it down, but even on her best days, her scrubs were tugging at the seams.

Hannah got out of the car and was embraced by her friend. "I am so happy to see you," Taylor said. "It just hasn't been the same at the hospital without you. I swear nobody else gets my sense of humor."

"Well, you are a little weird..." Hannah teased.

"See? Everyone else there is so serious! So, whatever." She hugged her again. "Okay, enough hugging. C'mon tell me. W.T.H.?"

Hannah self-consciously looked around her. "Could we not talk about it here?"

"Yeah sure, I gotcha. What do you want me to do?"

"Here," she handed Taylor a wad of money, "can you go get us a room... but... not use my name?"

A smile spread across Taylor's face, "Yeah! Course! Be right back!"

Taylor was the only person from the hospital Hannah kept in contact with. She tried to give Taylor the hint that she didn't want friends or didn't want any contact from the hospital, but Taylor would not be swayed. She text Hannah on a fairly regular basis, just to "check in" or tell Hannah who was being "lame" or which supervisor could "suck her big toe."

Hannah had no idea why Taylor attached herself, but she was there to stay.

When Taylor returned from the office she waved the card in the air. "Look what I've got!"

Hannah dropped her head and covered her face with her hand.

"Oh right," Taylor spoke in an exaggerated whisper, "My bad."

Taylor handed her the card and told her that she would meet her at the room. "I'm going to move my car around back."

"Why?" Hannah asked.

"So I can be closer."

Hannah rolled her eyes and walked toward the back of the single story motel. "Walking helps high blood pressure..." she called behind her in a sing-songy voice.

"Bite me..." Taylor sang back.

"So..." Taylor came in the room and flopped down on the corner of one of the queen size beds covered in blue and purple paisley print. "I tried to go by your house, which, by the way, I had no idea you lived there. I mean, no offense, but it's a hole. I would have let you crash at my place if you wanted."

Hannah looked at her, not wanting to discuss yesterdays.

"Yeah, so anyway... your house was surrounded by cars and vans and like news crews and stuff, so there was no way I was going to get in there. They looked like they were interviewing your neighbors and stuff. So I stopped at the store and grabbed you some toothpaste, a toothbrush, some deodorant, shampoo and conditioner, and...." she paused for effect, "A Wild Cherry Pepsi... your favorite." She offered the bottle to Hannah across her wrist as if presenting a bottle of champagne at a fancy restaurant. "Oh yeah," she reached into a second bag, "a box of Cheez-It's for you and a box of Ding Dongs for me."

"Taylor..." Hannah was visibly overcome with emotion. "Thank you so much. I just don't even know what to say." A tear slipped down Hannah's cheek and she quickly swept it away.

Taylor pretended not to notice the sentiment and shrugged her shoulder. "Eh, I needed a day off anyway."

"Yeah, aren't you supposed to be cleaning trachs or doing breathing treatments tonight?" Hannah asked.

"Called in," she smirked. "It was my peds rotation!" she laughed at her cleverness. "What's worse than dealing with snot? Dealing with snot AND kids." She did an over-exaggerated shiver.

Hannah couldn't help but laugh at her bubbly personality that had a sarcastic edge to almost everything she said. She was Hannah's kind of person. "Tell me again why you're a respiratory tech?"

"Cause it was the shortest program and the radiology tech program would have made me take out all my piercings."

Hannah nodded, acknowledging the decision. "Yeah, yes, that could be very bad…"

"Yeah, so… it's like, whatever. Beats serving ice-cream, which I did before this gig and then, before that, I worked at the Food Cart, but that was like only for four months, so whatever. I don't really even put that on a resume, you know…"

Hannah put the supplies on the sink and sat on the other bed while Taylor filled in any possible gaps that might have been silent with chatter that whether she wanted to admit it or not, helped calm and distract Hannah's fearful thoughts.

The night passed and Taylor filled her in on all she has missed at the hospital but thankfully, didn't ask how or why Hannah ended up in the situation she is in.

"Just one question," Taylor proposed.

Hannah raised her eyebrows both for giving permission to ask and doubt to it being only one…

"So… where is the hose from the gas station?"

Hannah couldn't help but laugh. She covered her face and fell to her side burying her face in the pillow. "Behind the Walmart on Lackland, near the dumpsters."

Taylor smirked and shook her head. "Nice."

Before long, Hannah drifted off to sleep. She had every intention of going to fill up the gas tank, go back home, pack the car and leave town. She didn't get that far. Now, here she was in a motel with nothing but her wallet and her hoodie… in pajama pants, hiding out like a fugitive.

"Hannah," Taylor nudged her sleeping body. "We have to go."

Just then the room's phone chimed. This woke Hannah up and she stared, terrified at Taylor.

"Should we answer it?" Taylor asked.

Hannah just shook her head and raised her shoulders.

Taylor swallowed hard and picked up the receiver, "Yeah?"

"Hi, um, I'm sorry to bother you, but the LHTV van is looking around your Capri? The silver one? I thought you should know."

Taylor looked down at Hannah and sighed heavily. "Yeah, thanks."

Hannah looked up at her, waiting.

"We have to go. They found your car out front. We'll have to take my car."

"But… I don't want you…."

"Too late, I'm already in. Let's go, before they start expanding their search."

Miracles from Ashes

Chapter Eight

Taylor pulled her car into the parking lot of the gas station/restaurant at the intersection of Lake Harmony Drive and Exchange.

Hannah pointed to a man with light brown hair who leaned against the lamppost and Taylor pulled in two spots over.

Hannah walked around the front of the car, "Wayne, thank you so, so much for meeting me here. I know it was kind of far, but I…"

He reached out and pulled her to his chest nearly crushing her. "I thought we lost ya, girl."

Hannah tensed her entire body at first and then relaxed in the embrace and lay her head on his shoulder.

Wayne pursed his lips and rested his chin on her head willing his emotions to stay hidden.

Taylor slipped from the driver's seat and spoke across the top of her car. "So, what exactly is going on here?

"No. Way." Taylor gasped. "No frickin' way." She pushed herself back away from the table inside the truck stop's restaurant. "Is that how you... Is that why we're... Dude, do I really have high blood pressure?"

Hannah couldn't help but smile at Taylor's response.. The fatigue was beginning to wear on her and now that Wayne had just bought them a heavy, warm meal, she wasn't really sure how she was staying awake. She was afraid to sleep. She really didn't know what to do next and as if on cue...

"What are we going to do now?" Taylor asked.

Hannah shook her head as she bobbed her shoulders.

Wayne took in a deep breath before he finished off his black coffee. "I think I may at least have the next step."

He turned the bill over and grimaced. "I need to raise my prices," he grumbled under his breath. "This is highway robbery."

"And," Hannah added, "not nearly as good as what Hank cooks up. But don't you dare tell him I said that."

"What are we doing? Where are we going?" Taylor asked.

No one bothered to answer her as they made their way past the souvenir magnets, key chains and trucker's hats toward the main exit.

Wayne fished into his jeans pocket and pulled out a set of keys.

Hannah and Taylor folded their arms against their chest trying to stave off the freezing air hitting them.

"Next time we make an escape, could we do it in the summer time?" Taylor whined through chattering teeth.

Wayne handed the keys to Hannah.

"What is this?"

"Keys, obviously," Taylor grumbled.

Both Hannah and Wayne looked at Taylor but kept their comments to themselves.

Wayne pointed to a 1997 Fleetwood Bounder motor home. It looked almost like a bus with it's huge front window that crossed the entire front of the rig. It stretched back for thirty feet before your eyes rested on a ladder that was attached to the back.

"What is that?" Hannah asked.

"This… is Bessie," Wayne began. "She was good to me after two of my divorces. And seeing as how I should never have to go through that again, I figure it's time to pass her on."

Hannah furrowed her brow.

They walked closer to the RV. It was light grey with darker grey and blue swooping stripes down the sides and across the back. The image of the signature kangaroo mascot still bounced over the driver's seat.

"Oh, she may not look pretty, but she's a hearty ole gal. I kept her in good shape, started the motor up every once in a while and just put those tires on for you."

"I mean…" Taylor turned her hands over and shrugged her shoulders, "It's nicer than where you live now." They both looked at her. "Just bein' honest."

"Bessie here will take good care of you. Give you a fresh start." Wayne continued.

Hannah stared blankly at him for a moment, letting his words sink in. "But... but... I..." Hannah looked at the RV and back at her friend.

"Darlin', you can't go back home. You can't ever go back to your car. You can't..." his voice cracked and he cleared his throat. "You can't ever come back here."

The reality of things weighed heavily on Hannah as she listened.

"I put all of your things inside the camper. I didn't really put anything away, seein' as how you would probably want to rearrange it your way. I filled up the cabinets and the fridge with food, so that should hold you for a bit." He cleared his throat again and dug into his coat pocket.

"Here's one of those... Go Phone things that we sell at the Route 66. You're good for a few thousand minutes. Use it... sparingly. I figure you'll need to reach me until you figure out how Bessie runs and all her quirks and idiosyncrasies." He could see Hannah's eyes well up. "Come on, let's get you inside and I'll introduce you."

"You name your camper?" Taylor asked no one in particular, knowing it would go unanswered.

Wayne showed her the basics and gave her a quick tour. In spite of the dreadful blue and grey décor, and the smell of dampness, it was pretty comfortable, and surprisingly clean for a bachelor pad. The walls and cabinets were dark, and the carpet, what was left of it, was royal blue, but the mattress was new and it was warm and safe.

Wayne leaned with his arm resting high on the wall in the door frame to the bedroom. "I filled up the gas tank, and there's a campground just aways down this road where my truck is parked. You can drive there, so I can show you how she runs. You've got two nights that you can stay there and get things set up how you like 'em."

He looked at her blank expression and paid no attention to Taylor bouncing on the couch.

"I know she's not much to look at… "

"No… no… Wayne it's not that. Not at all. I think she's wonderful and full of character. I just don't know what to say. It's… it's too much…"

"Hannah. You healed my lungs and my aches and pains are gone… do… do you know how much that would have cost me in doctor visits?"

Hannah cocked her eyebrow. "Nothing, cause you wouldn't have gone…"

He laughed. "Well, you may be right, but now I don't have to. I don't know why this is happening to you, but I know it's because someone upstairs thought you'd be up to the task and I'm for damn sure not gonna sit back and watch as some money-grubbing…." he clenched his teeth trying to choose his words gracefully, "…idiots… are going to keep you from doing what you've been given' this gift for."

Hannah nodded, her head and whispered, "Thank you."

"Now, you live in this thing for as long as she holds up and then junk it, sell it, whatever you need to do... She should hold you at least until you can get someplace new."

Hannah nodded taking in all the information.

They suddenly remembered that Taylor was still sitting on the couch between them playing with the fringe on the curtain tieback.

She felt them staring and looked back and forth between them. "What?"

Hannah sighed and looked at her lovingly, thankful for all the help and sacrifice this young woman made for her.

Taylor shook her head from side to side. "No... don't say it."

Hannah sat down on the end of the couch and turned her knees toward Taylor. "Honey... it's time."

"No... you can't ask me to go! You need me!"

Hannah bit her lip, but said nothing.

"I don't want to go back. Every superhero has a sidekick, right? I could be yours. Please don't send me away."

"Taylor... I can't thank you enough for everything that you've done for me. You have a job and a home..."

"It's just an apartment."

"But it's yours. And if you go back now, people won't know that you know me. And you can have a nice quiet life."

"See?" she curled her lip, "all the more reason I should go with you!"

Hannah looked down at her hands. "You can't."

"But…"

"I'm sorry. I have no idea what my future holds and I can't risk…"

"But *you* wouldn't be risking it… I would."

"Taylor, honey… please try to understand."

"I do. I get it. I just don't want to. I just don't want to have to say goodbye to you again." Taylor's eyes unwillingly teared up. "And this time, I know you won't be back." Her gazed lifted to Wayne and back down to the floor.

The RV was silent for a few moments as the hustle and bustle of the truck stop went on around them.

"You'll keep my number?" Taylor ventured.

Hannah nodded. "I will, but… I won't be able to use it for quite some time."

Taylor nodded and sighed. She lifted her head and looked at Hannah expectantly, "Hey, could I just stay this one night? I'm tired. I'm like SO tired and you drug me all the way out here and I've never in my entire life slept in a camper and I could help you get things set up tomorrow. You know, get this place clean and…"

Wayne cleared his throat.

Taylor raised her hand, "No offense, Wayne, but… I mean… it could use a little dusting, you know what I'm saying?"

He laughed in spite of himself and looked at Hannah with a shrug.

"Okay. One night. Then you have to get back home."

Taylor squealed and bounced on the couch again clapping her hands rapidly in front of her.

"And you can't speak of this ever again," Hannah warned her.

"I get it. I get it. I won't."

Even though Wayne had paid for two nights Hannah was anxious to get on the road to… to… somewhere else so as not to endanger her friends.

Wayne showed her all the ins and outs of the RV's secrets and they set up the beds for everyone to turn in early.

Wayne took the fold out couch. Taylor slept on the table turned bed and Hannah slept in the Queen-size bed on sheets with the perfectly squared creases still showing their newness

All three slept in after their emotionally exhausting night. The next day, Taylor and Hannah went through the four heavy-duty trash bags filled with her belongings and assigned them drawers and cabinets.

Wayne tinkered about with the engine, replaced the lock and door handle and kicked the tires a few times. By the time they were ready to set out in their three different directions, Hannah was as prepared as she could possibly be.

Hannah was almost a little excited to be off on a new adventure and the thrill of the unknown was suddenly appealing.

Taylor took the good-byes a little better, this time around and left her cell phone number on a note pad near Hannah's bed.

She hugged Hannah and pulled back getting ready to say something profound, but instead looked like a deer in headlights. "Oh! I almost forgot!" She turned away from Hannah and ran to her car.

Wayne was bringing a stack of blankets into the camper. Hannah was … content.

Taylor ran back to Hannah and grabbed her hand holding it out in front of her. "Here. Take this." Taylor deposited a wad of folded bills into her outstretched hand.

"No, Taylor, I can't do that."

"Aw, come on. I dug through every pocket of my purse and I even raided the secret stash in my car!" Her eyes lit up with excitement.

"No, honey, I can't take your money."

"I want you to. It's not as cool as a house on wheels, but…" she got serious and her voice dropped lower, "I want to help." She shrugged her one shoulder as if she hands out bundles of cash every day.

Hannah knew she had to accept the extremely generous gift. She closed her fingers around the money and said, "Thank you. You are too sweet. I will never forget you."

"Darn right you won't… I'm freaking awesome." Taylor smiled, and it went all the way up to her bright blue eyes.

"That you are…" Hannah smirked.

"And then, also, there's this." Taylor handed her a white plastic Walgreen's bag.

Hannah accepted the bag and looked inside. Hannah's eyebrows came together in confusion.

"Don't look at me like that, you might need it.

"It's red hair color."

Taylor gave her the "duh!" look. "I know what it is, I bought it."

"Why are you giving it to me? I can clearly see your roots… you need this more than I do."

Taylor rolled her eyes. "Don't I know it! But, the way I see it, you know, like in the movies, you're a fugitive, kinda, so you'll need to change your look."

Hannah sighed, "I don't think…"

"Oh my gosh! I'm kinda like a fugitive too! What if the hotel people put the pieces together and remember you and realize that we were together…" Her hands flew up in an over-excited panic and flared out on either side of her body.

"Taylor… Taylor… whoa… slow down. I'm sure that this will all blow over. The news media will try and drag it out for a while, and they'll make a big fuss about what happened but it's not like they're going to do anything about it. *That's in the movies*."

Taylor squinted her eyes not completely buying into the insignificance of the past events, but said, "Maybe I'll just change my hair for funzies, then. How would I look as a blonde? Oh, maybe I'll go goth black…Huh? Huh? Yeah?"

"I don't even know what to do with you…" Hannah laughed.

"Alright kiddo," Wayne called from the door. "If you're going to go, let's get to it. I want to do the walk through with you and see you off."

They all three did the "take-off" walk through and it was time for Hannah to say goodbye to everything she has ever known.

She walked inside to the front of the bus and sat in the driver's seat, looking out of the enormous window. It felt like she could see for miles. Wayne and Taylor stood off to the side.

Wayne nodded solemnly and Taylor waved and smiled. An entire cheering section all for her.

Hannah swallowed and looked over at the photo of her and her mother to the left of the steering wheel and then the photo of her husband and children to the right of the steering wheel... She took in a deep breath and turned the key over to bring the motor roaring to life. It startled her, but she shook it off. She sat up straight in her seat, took in another deep breath, shifted to drive and slowly eased down on the gas. Ol' Bessie inched forward and Hannah's heart skipped a beat. She released the steering wheel for just a second to wave at the last two familiar faces that she would see for a very long time. *This scene will be forever engraved in my memory,* she thought to herself. She turned the wheel and watched as her friends disappeared from sight and the new road spread out in front of her.

Miracles from Ashes

Chapter Nine

She drove in an easterly direction until she got sleepy. She was able to cross one entire state before she started looking for a place to rest for the night. As she drove she was amazed at all the beautiful scenery and all the interesting places there could have been to stop and explore. She realized that she had never been on a vacation. In her youth, she cared for her dying mother. And then it was medical school. She and Jeremy didn't even have a honeymoon. They got married between semester exams and big construction contracts.

Her eyes darted to their family picture. Four smiling faces looked back at her. They never even met Mickey Mouse. A flood of guilt rushed over her momentarily.

She looked up in time to see a small roadway sign: Pine's and Poplar's RV Park One Mile.

"Okay, Bessie, let's get some rest." She turned on the blinker and pulled off the highway.

When Hannah got to the campground, the sun was just beginning to set. The woman at the front desk, Rhoda, had showed her the site and allowed her to get set up for the night.

"I was just about to close, so why don't you get yourself all set up and then come and see me in the morning. The office opens at 8:00 and there will be fresh coffee available for you."

Hannah had a solid night's sleep and sent Wayne a text to let him know where she was. He text back a thumb's up emoji.

She walked around the park waiting for the office to open and thought that this place could really be busier, but it seemed to need so much repaired. Only one washing machine and one dryer out of three each were working. The restrooms needed a good painting and some damage repair. The pool looked like it had been closed for years. *Oh what Jeremy could do with this place. He would love it,* she thought. She pulled her coat a little tighter around her as the wind brought the smell of the pines. She took in a deep breath allowing the cool air into her lungs. Fresh air. It smelled amazing.

She turned back toward the office lodge and another amazing smell stole her attention... coffee.

"Good morning, Rhoda," Hannah called out, as she set off the clump of bells tied to the door.

"Good morning, dear! How did you sleep? You get yourself some coffee over there, alright?" She came out from behind the counter even though she pointed at the self-serve table in the corner next to a wall of maps and brochures. "Here...here... here's a cup for you. The creamer is over here and there's a few kinds of sugars. You know the regular and then the raw and the uh…" she picked up a pale blue packet, "the sugar substitutes. I prefer the real sugar myself."

"Good choice," Hannah agreed. "The substitutes aren't good for you at all."

Rhoda tapped Hannah with her elbow, "You know, I've heard that. Yes, I have heard those reports." She was nodding as she walked back behind the counter. She pulled out a four by six card and started filling out the details. "How long are you staying, dear?"

"Just for one more night," Hannah called to her, while stirring her perfect blend of coffee, cream and sugar.

"Where are you off to?" she scribbled, as she spoke.

Hannah shrugged, "Not really sure yet, just wandering."

Rhoda gasped and smiled. She rested her elbows on the counter and folded her hands, suddenly lost in memory. "Oh, I remember those days."

Hannah smiled and joined her at the counter.

"My husband and I have been to all of the fifty states except for Hawaii. We've even been a few places in Canada." She shook her head and smiled. "Oh how we loved being out on the road. We love the RV life."

"Is that how you settled here?"

"Oh yes. Ernie fell in love with these pine trees. You know he built most of these buildings himself? He was right there when they put in all the equipment for the campers. He knows every inch of this place."

"It is a beautiful place. You would think it would be packed!"

"Oh… it used to be. But, last year, Ernie had a heart attack and he's been weak ever since." She shook her head sadly. "I have never, in all of our years together, seen a man go from someone so strong to someone so… defeated. He feels like a failure." She looked away at a photo on the wall of the couple in front of the Office Lodge on opening day. "That was a long time ago."

"Where is your husband now?"

"Oh, he's in our fifth wheel. The one at the end of the row. He barely comes outside anymore. But… but… he really is a sweet, sweet man. You mustn't pay any attention to me. Just makes me sad, is all. But he is still the love of my life."

"May I meet him?"

"Oh sure… sure… he used to love to meet all the guests. Maybe this is just what he needs…"

Rhoda came out from behind the counter again and crossed the room excitedly. She grabbed her coat from the coat rack beside the door and held the door open for Hannah to walk through.

Hannah followed her down the beaten dirt road as she explained the buildings and the few residents that stayed with them all the time or seasonally.

"Honey!" Rhoda called, as she opened the door to their older model camper. "There's a guest who wants to meet you!"

The tiny home smelled a little musty and the walls were dark, but they were covered in framed photographs of all the places the couple had visited.

"Oh, well, come on in!" Ernie set the leg-extension down on his orange recliner and made every effort to stand and greet his guest.

"You don't have to get up. I just wanted to tell you how much I love your place here. I'm new to the camping world…"

"Ernie, she's a wanderer."

"Oh!" his arm went up and extended out to shake Hannah's hand. "That's what we love to hear! We were wanderers once!" Again, he attempted to stand but was stopped by a coughing spasm.

"Please, please don't trouble yourself. I… I think I can help…"

He looked cautiously at his wife, and then back at her.

Hannah stepped closer and spoke to him. "Your heart is still… blocked. Which is causing the muscle fatigue and weakness, probably your shortness of breath too. Or that could also be from your lungs. They are showing signs of lung disease which would explain your cough, and that feeling of not getting enough air?" she paused, confirming with him. He was staring at her with his mouth open in shock, but nodding along with her. "And nothing to do with your heart, the arthritis is attacking your knees making it hard for you to stand."

"How… how do you…"

Rhoda stepped back and watched the interchange with her hands folded in front of her.

Hannah leaned down keeping eye contact with Ernie, "May I?"

She lay her hand on his heart and held still.

Ernie looked down at his body and lifted his hands for inspection and then took a deep breath. His eyes locked with hers questioning what was happening to his body.

Another deep breath... "I can breathe! My hands... they don't hurt!" He looked at Hannah, afraid to ask. His face smoothed out, still showing his years, but the skin cancer spots were gone, and his eyes were clear and bright.

Hannah stepped away from him and smiled down at him. She turned to Rhoda who started and took a step back almost knocking down the shelves of collectible tourist plates.

Hannah reached out for her hands. Clasping them and looking into Rhoda's eyes, "And your arthritis... and back pain..." Hannah held her hands close to her body a moment more, "... shouldn't trouble you any more either."

A small squeak escaped her lips as she wrung her hands together. "Oh... you are an angel..." Tears appeared and slipped down her cheek.

Hannah smiled, "Not me, but I work for one."

Ernie stood from his chair and squatted. He stood back up and stretched his arms to the ceiling. "Do you see that, Rhoda?" He slammed his fists on his chest and took in a deep breath. "I... I..." his words got lost in emotion. He turned toward his wife, his eyes red rimmed and filled with tears and wrapped his arms around her, kissing her deeply and passionately. "I've been wanting to do that for so long."

Hannah looked down at the shag carpet and blushed. There was no sign of the reunited couple coming up for air so Hannah politely said, "I can show myself out. "I'll uh… meet you at the office later to finish up that paperwork whenever you're ready."

Still embraced in her husband's strong arms, Rhoda could only nod and smile.

A few hours later, Hannah could hear some banging and leaned over the back of her couch to look out the window. Just a few feet down the main dirt road, she saw Ernie on top of the laundry room's roof hammering away at the loose shingles. She couldn't suppress her smile.

Hours after that, Hannah heard a small tapping at her door. She flipped the lever and opened the door to see Rhoda standing at the base of her steps with her arms full of dishes.

"I…I hate to bother you, but I just couldn't…" she took in a deep breath and tried to calm her shaky voice. "I could never thank you enough for the gift you have given to Ernie and me. So, I thought I might bake you a little something. I love to bake, but I just couldn't the way I used to… so I… well, it just wasn't enough, so I made you a casserole, some soup… some bread to eat with it and… some cookies and muffins… for your trip. It still isn't enough, and I…"

Hannah smiled from ear to ear. "You didn't have to do that. It was intended as a gift. It makes me so happy to see Ernie back out and doing the things he loves."

Rhoda looked away and blushed as the corner of her mouth turned up. "Yes," she giggled, "*all* the things."

"Weeellll," Hannah teased, "alright then!"

She handed a casserole pan up to Hannah. "You have given us back our life." She reached over to a bag setting on a picnic table. "I could and would be happy to repay you for the rest of our days." She handed the bag of goodies up to Hannah.

Rhoda reached back over to the picnic table and grabbed the recycled ice-cream container that now held homemade beef and barley soup. "I hope you like these. I know it's too much to eat all at once, so I divided the casserole into separate servings so you can freeze some."

Hannah tried to set things down as fast as she was handing them to her. "I am so very grateful for all your kindness. I do appreciate it. It's not very much fun cooking for one."

"I was happy to do it. I... I really..."

Hannah closed the gap between them by stepping down her three retractable stairs to the outside. She hugged Rhoda. "No words... no gifts are necessary. This is my gift to you. This is my assignment."

"Assignment?" Rhoda asked.

Hannah shrugged. "That's what I am calling it. I was given this gift with instructions to heal others." She shrugged again, as if she won a free round of putt putt instead of a life-changing, miracle-causing gift from the angels.

"May I ask you a question?" Rhoda spoke, softly.

Hannah nodded, granting permission.

"Are we... immortal now?"

Hannah smiled sweetly, "I don't believe so. I have only healed your body from the ailments that you suffered from at this moment. But, for instance, if you don't eat right, you can still get diabetes. If cancer runs in your family, you may still get that. And, of course, your body will continue to age, but not as quickly."

Rhoda nodded, taking it all in as Hannah continued, "At least that's what I think is happening. I'm still new to all of this healing magic, so I honestly can't tell you the long term effects. I'm sorry. But if nothing else, you have been given more time. More time to live, to love and to do the things that made you happy."

Rhoda reached out and touched Hannah's arm and then folded her hands together. "You... are truly a miracle. I promise you that your gift will not be wasted on us."

"I didn't think that for a moment." Hannah reached out and hugged her again. "Did you want me to come over and fill out the paperwork now?"

"Oh no. No, no, no... you have no accounts due! You just go back in and enjoy your dinner!"

Hannah nodded, thankful that her tiny budget would last a little bit longer.

Early the next morning, Hannah had just taken her first sip of hot, fresh brewed coffee when a knock came at the door. She called out "just a minute" and threw on a heavy hoodie preparing to brace against the cold.

When she pushed open the door, Rhoda stood at her steps again.

Her eyes were begging for forgiveness, even as she held up another bag of homemade goodies.

"Rhoda, you didn't have to …"

She looked about her sheepishly, "But something has changed."

Hannah grew concerned, "What has happened?"

"Well, I didn't know if… what um… happened yesterday was a secret and I tried not to say too much, but, um… well, people just started asking me about this 'change' in me. And, I couldn't very well deny anything happened because they can see Ernie is back to his old self… and well…"

Hannah raised her eyebrows waiting for the other shoe to drop.

Rhoda's eyes shifted to her right and she shrugged.

Hannah opened her door completely and stepped down the stairs to see a small group of people standing just beyond her campsite.

When she looked back at Rhoda, she immediately replied with, "You said you came here to heal."

Hannah smiled. "I did say that didn't I?"

Rhoda smiled, obviously relieved. "These are a few of the wonderful people who live here for extended periods of time. They could all…"

"I see…" Hannah looked over the crowd and saw a variety of ailments mostly caused from aging, but others had some serious internal ailments.

She held her finger up to Rhoda and stepped back inside. She emerged again wearing some socks and shoes, and her heavier winter coat.

She went to the person closest to her. Rhoda introduced her to Thelma, and Hannah reached out her hands. The woman placed hers inside Hannah's and watched hopefully as her fingers embraced her frail bones.

In a few moments, her crooked fingers became straight and her rounded posture stretched her up to her full height.

Thelma's eyes glossed over with tears. "It's true. You're a miracle worker."

Hannah wasn't sure what to say.

Thelma reached into her pocket and pulled out some folded dollar bills. "It's not much but…"

"No, please, this is a gift. You aren't allowed to buy it." Hannah winked.

Thelma could not contain her tears. "There's no pain." She turned back around to face the small group that was behind her. "There's no pain!"

The group of twenty-six people pushed forward all trying to get to Hannah at once and that was when Rhoda stepped in.

"Now listen, you all. This is a blessing and if this sweet girl is able to heal anyone of you, it's a miracle. Now, you ain't gonna disrespect my friend by being rude and impatient. She's here to help. Don't be snatchin' and grabbin' like a bunch a heathens!" Rhoda stomped her foot for additional effect. "Now you can all line up here like you had some kind of training in manners."

"But what if she runs out of power?"

"Then Earl, you don't get no healin'!" a short heavy set woman called back to him.

A man looked over at Rhoda to seek permission to approach Hannah. She nodded.

He held his hand out for his wife and they walked closer. Hannah reached out her hands toward the man but he stepped back, "Her... can you please heal her first?"

"I can." Hannah leaned down just a few inches to get the wife's attention. The woman followed Hannah's eyes and returned the smile offered her. When Hannah held out her hands the woman looked at her husband questioningly. He nodded and nudged her forward. The woman placed her hands on top of Hannah's and closed her eyes.

In a few moments, tears began streaming from the corner of the woman's eyes.

Hannah whispered, "Can you hear me?"

The woman's eyes opened as tears spilled over the edges. She nodded. "I can. I can hear you. I can hear the birds... I can hear... voices." She turned to her husband, who was also crying. She wiped away the tears from his cheek. "Aren't you going to say anything?"

"You are still just as pretty as the day I met you."

They put their foreheads together and he kissed her nose.

Hannah interrupted, "Now you…"

He shook his head, "I don't need anything now." He turned back to his wife, "Want to go call the grandkids?"

A smile spread across her face.

Hannah stepped forward, "In just a moment." She turned him around and placed her hand on his lower back.

He took in a deep breath and closed his eyes. When he opened them again, he looked back over his shoulder at Hannah, confused and amazed.

"Now, you can go call those grandkids," she laughed.

Rhoda was crying and wiping her eyes with her knit-gloved hands as she directed the people forward one at a time, keeping order and respectability to the entire affair.

Finally the short heavy set woman came up to her and put her hands out for Hannah to take. "Will this make me skinny?"

"Nope, but it will take away your clogged arteries and second degree diabetes. But, you'll have to eat right and exercise if you want to lose weight and keep those things away."

"Well, my thyroid…"

Hannah cocked her eyebrow daring her to continue.

"You're fixing that too?"

Hannah held out her hands just inches from the woman's "Whenever you're ready…"

The woman, in her early fifties, took in a deep breath, "Well, here's to new changes!" She closed her eyes tight and dropped her hands onto Hannah's as if she was making a wish.

After a moment, she opened her eyes, "Oh, oh my… I can breathe. I didn't realize how hard I had to work for that. And… and my knees and my hips don't hurt… I… I don't know what to say…"

"Say you'll take care of yourself."

"I will! Oh, I will!"

Hannah went through healing each camper one by one and didn't hear her phone chirp from inside the camper.

When she healed the last one and stood alone with Rhoda, she said, "Whoo! That's a lot to do before a first cup of coffee!"

She and Rhoda laughed, and Rhoda added, "I hope you didn't mind. You have made everyone so happy today. It's not every day you get a clean bill of health. Especially at our age. And some of us were in desperate need of a miracle."

"I didn't mind. It gives me great joy to be able to see their healed bodies. I would be lying if I didn't secretly hope and pray that they don't squander it, but then again… it is a gift. And they can do with it as they will."

"That is so true, and it's a hard thing to let go."

Hannah nodded. "But, I must say, that I am a little worn out. Please don't think me rude, but I need to go and lay down for a bit."

"Of course, of course. I'll see that no one bothers you."

When Hannah woke up the sun was just beginning to set. She stretched in her bed and smiled as all the faces of the people she healed came back to her. Surely Pete is smiling today.

She stretched again and hung her legs off the side of the bed. She walked from her bedroom and saw her cold cup of coffee still sitting on the counter with the creamer separated and congealed to the sides. She picked it up and stirred it around with her finger. She sniffed at it and shrugged. She put it in the microwave for forty-five seconds. "Waste not, want not," she said, out loud.

When she grabbed her coffee and sat on the couch, she noticed that her phone had a text message on it.

She took a cautious sip and set her cup down on the coffee table. She lit up her little flip phone and saw the message was from Wayne. She rolled her eyes at her silliness. Of course it's Wayne, who else would it be...

The one sentence message was cryptic. "Read your local paper."

She furrowed her brow. "My local paper?" "Getting it" she got up and grabbed her laptop.

When the computer screen lit up and the wi-fi connected, Hannah typed in the webpage for The Herald.

She waited for the entire page to load before she slowly scrolled down, looking for whatever it was Wayne wanted her to see. She didn't have to wait long.

Just below "the fold" was a small insert photo of herself and her family standing in front of their "new to them" Victorian home.

Hannah smiled for a moment at the memory. It was the photo the realtor took when they finally closed on their home. Jeremy put so much time and effort into fixing up that antique. The smile faded as she continued reading.

"Who is Hannah Michaelson? A former doctor who lost it all…" the headline read.

Hannah gasped as her life was spelled out for all to see. Her childhood. Her father's early death; her mother's long and painful struggle and death from ALS. Her marriage, her children, her schooling… her disappearance.

"Where is she now? How many others will fall prey to her clever scams? When a person loses everything, they are capable of anything."

Hannah slammed the computer closed and tried to shake off the rollercoaster of emotions. First, anger. *Who do they think they are, accusing me of being a terrible and greedy person! Tell me! What am I getting out of all this? Where is the supposed 'pay off' for my grand schemes?* She frowned at the thought of the nonsense the media will come-up with for headlines. Then, sadness. *I am truly alone. Everyone who has ever loved me, is gone.* Then skepticism. *Gift, he says.* She chuffed as she thought about the high cost of the supposed "gift". *I don't see anyone else tripping over themselves to have the amazing gift,* she air quoted and chuffed again. *It's not like I'm charging people.* She grumbled under her breath, "maybe I should be charging…" Then, peace. The faces of those she has saved. The parents of the children. The warmth of giving a gift and expecting nothing in return. Nothing. She couldn't stop the smile from spreading across her face. *It's what I've always wanted. What I went to school for,* she thought. *I'm just giving results faster and safer. One hundred percent accuracy doesn't hurt either,* she grinned.

The good feelings weren't able to last long after her thoughts went full circle and ended up back at the article. She felt… violated. Like someone had sifted through her personal belongings and even her treasured memories. She suddenly had the feeling of being watched. She suddenly felt like she just might be in danger. She had to come to terms that the incidents in her home town might not blow over as quickly as she thought.

"I… I have to go." Hannah started packing up things in order to get back out on the road. Her heart was pounding in her chest with fear.

She paused, "Hold on…" she coached herself, "Take a deep breath, you don't know what you're doing. You don't want to skip steps." She followed her own advice and took in a deep, cleansing breath in order to slow her heart rate. She went to the driver's side pocket and pulled out the hand written list of directions to pack up and went through them one by one.

This is what she needed; distraction. And she needed mundane, uniform, repeatable tasks. She also needed to leave here as soon as possible.

The backside of the checklist was complete. Everything inside was put together and ready. She slipped on her coat and opened the door. There, at her feet... were boxes. Bags and envelopes and boxes of all sizes. They were on the picnic table, the steps and on the ground all around her door.

The light from beside her door was dim and did little to brighten up her patio area in the early darkness so she couldn't really tell what everything was.

She took a step backwards and reached inside the door and grabbed her flash light and saw gift cards for gas and restaurants and grocery chains. She saw homemade goods. She saw a crocheted hat and scarf with gloves...

Gifts. Gifts for her. Gifts for doing what she was called upon to do.

She stood there staring at the collection and couldn't stop the tears from falling. "I don't understand," she whimpered out loud, to no one. "What are you doing up there?" She flopped down on the top step and sobbed. "Why would you give me this gift and have me go out and heal people if *other* people are only gong to believe that I am a fake and want to say terrible things about me. I don't understand."

She cried. The sun had gone down but the moon was bright, showing the wind rustling the tree tops as it whisked through. A light snow had started to fall.

Don't stop now...

Hannah looked up and saw no one, the words warmed her slightly, but also sent a shiver of fear through her. She wiped her eyes and loaded up the gifts inside and went back to her tasks... all neatly numbered and in order... *just follow the list, Hannah. Don't think, right now. Just follow the list.*

Miracles from Ashes

Chapter Ten

The sun was slowly creeping up over the tall pine trees in the distance. She passed through a small city and used a gift card to fill up the gas tank. "Man, this thing sure does go through some gas," she mused. Funds were running low. She was careful to do the speed limit, even a few miles under to save on gas and to keep off the radar.

She smiled at herself when she thought about the young man she "accidentally" tripped into in front of the soda coolers. He won't have to worry about his bones crumbling away from osteoporosis any longer. She didn't even look behind her to see the expression on the man's face when he realized he could put his full weight on his left leg and stand up straight.

Hannah did a double take when she saw a woman at a rest area that resembled her mother. She struggled with her walking and Hannah raced over to "help" her step up the curb and onto the sidewalk. The woman smiled and nodded her head, but when she took her next step, she paused and looked back at Hannah.

Hannah placed her index finger over her lips. "Shhh."

The poor woman could only stand there perplexed as Hannah made her way back to Bessie.

She could hear the woman's family behind her.

"Mom! Mom! Are you okay?" It was a woman's voice. "Mom! What's wrong?"

The older woman just started laughing and hugged her daughter. "Nothing is wrong," she laughed. "Absolutely nothing!"

Hannah watched the scene from the huge window and smiled. The older woman was dancing around and hugging her children and grandchildren.

Hannah's eyes went to the photo beside her steering wheel. "I wish I could have healed you, Momma," she said out loud.

The highway was lonely and quiet. The yellow lines of the highway hypnotized her and allowed her thoughts to wander back to the days with her mother.

"This will only take a moment, Mrs. Bercerra." The nurse taped a cotton ball to the inside of Phyllis' elbow. Phyllis nodded, and looked concerned.

"Do you want a sip of water?" Hannah asked.

Phyllis strained, forcing her lips and tongue to participate, "N-n-n-n-no." She rolled her eyes and her head jerked without her permission. "S-s-s-so hard t-t-t-to talk."

"That's a first," Hannah smirked at her mother.

Phyllis' laugh filled the room and it made Hannah smile. Her mother was still inside this body. This body that was trying so hard to give up. The staff came back in and asked, if she was ready to proceed, as if she had a choice, then assisted Phyllis to lay on her side, curled into a ball. Her hands involuntary flinched which sent an unwanted response to her head and neck.

"Okay, Mrs. Bercerra, I'm going to need for you to hold as still as possible. I'm going to insert this needle into your spine, alrighty?"

Phyllis looked up at Hannah who was holding both of her mother's hands. "E-e-easy for you to s-s-s-say," Phyllis laughed along with Hannah.

Hannah was directly in front of her mother's curled, fragile body, but was steadily looking over her back to see what the doctor was doing.

"Alright, Mrs Bercerra, this is going to be uncomfortable," the doctor said bluntly, as he worked in the tiny square of bare skin along her spine.

Phyllis closed her eyes and a tear slipped from the corner of her eye and crossed the bridge of her nose. She clenched her jaw, willing her limbs to be still. Sweat beaded across her forehead and she could feel droplets run down her neck.

What in real time only took a few minutes, but for Phyllis, the time slowed to a stand still. When Phyllis' eyes flew open in a moment of pain, they locked in with her daughters, silently begging for strength.

Hannah leaned in close and stoked her mother's hair. "You've got this Mom. Just a little longer."

She ever so slightly tipped her head, hearing and trusting her only child.

Ding Ding Ding

Everyone turned to look at the machine expecting a malfunction.

Ding. Ding. Ding.

Hannah blinked and saw that the highway was still spread out in front of her. The yellow dashes marking her place.

Ding Ding Ding

She looked around for the source of the noise. A tiny light that looked like a gas pump flashed on the broad dashboard. Low on gas. Hannah recalled a note on her instruction list that if that light came on it meant that she had fifty miles (or so) left in her tank.

Welcome to Pennsylvania, the sign read.

"I guess this is as good a place as any to stop."

She drove down a busy street that doubled as the secondary highway following signs that promised a KOA Campground just a mile or two further.

Hannah filled out the form with fake information, paid in cash for a week's stay, and pulled her Bounder into the designated space.

As she went through her "set up" list, which was almost memorized by now, she took a quick inventory: three packages of microwave popcorn, three cans of green beans, one Pepsi, a box of crackers and a box of mac n cheese.

"I am literally going to die if I don't get some fresh fruits and veggies," she mumbled to herself. She opened the small drawer near her front door and pulled out her money envelope. $17.00. She took in a deep breath and let it out slowly.

"Gas, food, or lodging..." she folded the money and squeezed it in her hands. She paced back and forth down the center of her blue carpet. "Well," she spoke out loud, "I have a place to stay for six days and seven nights. I have enough food that could hold me over for a few days... so... I guess I'm going to get some gas... and then find a job."

Now ready with a plan, she stuffed the money into her jeans pocket, grabbed a ball cap and went outside to retrieve her gas can.

The closest gas station was only about six blocks from the campground.

She walked in, signaling her presence with the ringing of the bell.

"How can I help you?" the man behind the counter asked. She almost didn't see him for all of the chargers and USB displays, stickers, keychains and lighters around the pay window.

"Hi, yes... uh..." she had trouble making her words come out.

The man patiently waited for her to speak, but gave no expression of impatience or... pain.

"I um… need $15 in gas and I'll grab a bottle of water…" she paused to look at him again before turning away toward the coolers. "Are… you feeling alright?"

He bobbed his head from side to side weighing out his answer to this total stranger. "I am alright, thank you."

Hannah could see the abscess on his rear tooth and knew that he had to be in severe pain. She went back to the coolers to grab her bottle of water and came back to the front. She handed the man her money and waited for her change.

He dropped it in her hand and nodded to her, "Pump Two is ready for you."

"Thank you," she smiled. She put the coins in her pocket but just couldn't make herself leave. "Uh… my name is Hannah," she held out her hand to him.

He looked down at her hand as if he was not familiar with this American custom of shaking hands. He furrowed his brow but leaned forward on his stool and clasped her hand. "I am Nitesh, nice to meet you."

"You also." Hannah smiled, as she made eye contact.

Hannah watched him adjust his jaw back and forth. He pinched his brows together in confusion, but said nothing.

"I am staying in the area for a couple weeks and I was wondering if you knew of anyone that might need some temporary help?" she explained.

He frowned at her again, not in an angry way, but trying to calculate his thoughts. He brought his hand to his jaw and frowned again.

Hannah tried not to smile, but just waited patiently as if she was just a regular person and didn't have anything to do with his body healing and the pain just being… gone.

"You need a job?"

She scrunched her face. "Yeah, I do, but just for a little while if you know of…"

"You will work for me. I will hire you."

"Really?"

"You will come back at five a.m. and I will teach you how to make coffee."

Hannah started for only a moment… "Oh… okay! I'll be here! I'm great at making coffee! Thank you! Thank you so much!"

Hannah smiled as she walked out the door and went right past the gas pump. She realized it a few steps away as she was swinging her empty plastic gas can, and she turned around embarrassed and laughed, smiling at her new boss who was watching her from the window. She couldn't see him clearly, but there was the faintest smile as he stroked his jaw that was now pain free.

Hannah arrived at the gas station fifteen minutes early and tapped on the glass door.

Nitesh came into view and unlocked the door. He pursed his lips and said flatly, "I knew you would come."

"Where would you like me to start?"

He motioned for her to follow him, which she did. Her hair was up in a pony tail, and she even put some mascara on so she would look presentable.

"I am feeling much better today," he said, nonchalantly, once the coffee was gurgling out a fresh pot.

Hannah smiled sincerely, "I am so happy to hear that."

"In fact, I feel better than I have in a very long time."

Hannah wiped down the counter in front of the four massive coffee brewing machines. "That's really great." She looked up at him. "What would you like me to do now?"

He shrugged his shoulders. "I'm not used to having someone else here."

"You closed last night and are here again this morning?" she asked.

"Everyday," he replied.

A customer came in. He looked at her and said, "Excuse me," and he made his way behind the counter.

Hannah looked around to see what needed to be done.

For the next few hours, Nitesh had been so busy at the counter that he was unable to do anything else but take care of the customers.

Hannah restocked all of the coffee bar supplies, wiped down the walls, counters and shelves. She dusted the food shelves and pulled all of the cans of food that had long expired.

She smiled and chatted with customers, always ready with a friendly handshake or a pat on the back. She kept a broom close by so she was at the ready to go back to her sweeping.

Nitesh told her to take a break in the back room, "Get yourself some nachos and a hot dog, if you like... and a drink from the fountain soda."

Before she realized it, it was seven at night. She was exhausted.

Nitesh came out from behind the counter with a stack of bills and handed them to her. "You come back tomorrow."

"Same time?"

He nodded abruptly, and turned away.

This went on for a few days and she worked long twelve and fourteen hour days with Nitesh. He never spoke the words, but she could tell that he was deeply grateful for her help. He eventually taught her how to run the gas pumps and take care of the customers, checking the drawer counts every hour, just to keep her honest.

While she lived on gas station food the entire time, she was able to save up enough money for a full tank of gas and get some fresh food, that came from the ground, from a quick market that was on the way home from the gas station.

Hannah was prompt and worked hard, never asked for a break and never took more than he offered her in food or supplies, and never questioned or balked at the pay he gave her at the end of each day.

"Hannah, I would ask that you might do me a favor."

Hannah leaned her broom against the wall and walked over to the counter as if she were a customer. "Of course, what do you need?"

Nitesh looked down and furrowed his brow, thinking deeply before speaking. "I would ask if you would be willing to stay for an extra week and if you do," he added quickly before she could object. "I can pay you an extra one hundred dollars, on top of your day's pay."

Hannah smiled at the offer and thought about it sincerely. She had been keeping things low key. She hadn't been drawing attention to herself at all, she felt. She felt safe enough to accept his offer.

"There is one thing more," he continued. "Next week on the Friday, would you be considering running the shop for me... just on that one day."

Hannah did not try to hide her surprise. "You are actually going to take a day off?" she teased.

He graced her with a rare smile. "My son. He is graduating from his medical school training. I would very much like to see him accepting his diploma."

Hannah's heart melted. "I think you should definitely be there. I would be happy to work for you."

"I can work in the morning and then I will be back in time to open the next morning."

"Here's a thought," she counter-offered. "I know it may be a big step for you, but..." she teased. "How about you take off Friday *and* Saturday so you can actually enjoy celebrating with your son."

He stood up straight and frowned. "Oh no, no, no… that I cannot do. I can drive home after the ceremony…"

"Just think about it… I don't mind. I'll be right here when you get back. You can call me every hour and I can do a drawer count for you."

He startled her when he released a deep laugh.

"Hannah, you are…" his gaze dropped to his feet and just the corners of his mouth turned up slightly. "I will think on this offer." He opened the drawer and pulled out her pay for the day and handed it to her.

She smiled, and accepted her wages. "See you tomorrow."

"Yes. I will see you tomorrow."

The next day when Hannah got to her job, Nitesh was smiling, which caused Hannah to pause. She decided to play off it.

She looked to her left and right. "Am I in the right place? Have you seen my boss? He usually sits where you are sitting, but is always very serious," she smiled at him.

"You are making fun," he said, "I am fine with that."

"What's got you in such a good mood today?" she probed.

He smiled at her a moment more before hopping off the stool and coming around the counter. "Wait here."

"Can I wait over there so I can get the coffee started while I'm waiting."

He nodded abruptly and then disappeared into the storage room.

She pushed up the sleeves on her hoodie and went about throwing away the old, used coffee and filters from the day before and placed the clean white filters in each of the coffee pots.

She had just pulled out the decaf coffee grounds when Nitesh came around the corner balancing a dark blue ten speed bicycle beside him.

"This is for you," he said, proudly.

Hannah was obviously taken aback by the generous gift and just stared with her mouth open.

"I see that you walk every day. This belonged to my son. He stopped using it once he learned how to drive. It is several years old, but it is still good. I am hoping you will like it?"

"Oh, I do! That is… I don't know what to say…" her eyes teared up.

"It is not a big deal. My wife is ready for it to be out of the house and you are in need."

"I… I… thank you."

"Good. It is done. I will return it to the back room and you can ride it home tonight. I have filled the tires for you."

"Thank you."

"It is I who am thanking you. Istvan is my only child. And I have missed much from my work. I am so proud of him and …" Suddenly he stopped talking and just nodded his head. He turned the bike around and that was all that was going to be said about that.

Hannah smiled all the way down to her heart. The goodness of people never ceased to amaze her.

The days prior to his departure, Nitesh kept trying to get out of actually leaving. "What if there is a delivery?"

"What if there is a leak? I should stay."

"What if you run out of change?"

"I have not taught you how to read the pumps."

"Do you know where the window washer fluid is? I do not think I have told you these things."

Hannah patiently listened and then told him that he was still leaving. He would nod and still keep a worried look as he worked silently through the day.

On the actual day, Nitesh came in to get the shop open and to get Hannah settled in with the passcodes to the safe and register. He brought with him a stack of procedures and checklists and laid them next to the cash register. "These are here if you need them."

Hannah couldn't help but laugh. "One day. You're leaving for one day. I had better not need them!"

"Your saying of 'Better to be safe than sorry' applies here."

She laughed. "That it does. Thank you for getting me prepared. And, since you've done such a fine job, don't you think you should get out of here?"

He stood frozen in uncertainty.

"Go on... go... I've got this."

"Yes, you are very capable."

"Thank you, now go on..."

"Don't forget to remove your wages from..."

"That can wait until you get back..."

"But if you need it..."

She raised an eyebrow, "It's less than forty-eight hours. I'll be fine."

He stood still.

She raised her eyebrows.

He bobbed his head. "I am going now." And stood still.

She nodded at his wise decision. "This only happens one time, you know. You would hate yourself if you missed it."

"Yes. I am going."

He turned away from her and picked up a bag of candy from one of the shelving displays. "I am taking this. I have always wanted to try them and the customers always purchase this product 'for the trip'. I will try."

"You're stalling."

"Goodbye, Hannah."

"I'll see you Sunday."

"Very good." He swallowed hard and walked out the door.

Sunday morning, Hannah came into the gas station knowing that Nitesh would already be there. He's probably been there since late last night. He only called every couple hours on his drive to the graduation and the phone was actually quiet during what Hannah assumed was the actual ceremony. He was on the phone with her walking her through the entire closing procedure, even though Hannah had most of it under control.

He was standing, waiting near the coffee pots when she walked in. He beamed at her and she smiled in return.

"Hannah, I have your wages here for Friday and Saturday. And here is the additional one hundred dollars that we have agreed on, and because you have made my heart so light, I would like to add another one hundred dollars to this. I would give you more... I would give you all that you asked, because you have made me the happiest of men this day."

Hannah accepted the wages and the uncomfortable hug that came with it and no more was said about it. Work went on as usual.

Hannah came in from sweeping and picking up the random trash from the parking lot. It was late afternoon, and almost as if by clockwork, the traffic flow of customers slowed down.

"Take your break now, if you wish, Hannah." Nitesh called out, as she passed by to put the broom and dustpan back in its place.

"Okay, let me re-stock the bathrooms first and then I'll grab a couple pizza rolls today, if you don't mind."

"You can have anything you want."

She smiled at him, "Anything?"

He laughed, "Ah-ha-ha! You know me too well. But for you, I will say yes."

She laughed, knowing how much he hates having to give up packaged items over grilled items or packaged drinks over fountain. Costs and overhead, of course. Nitesh was a very frugal and wise businessman.

"Pizza rolls and Pepsi will do me just fine."

She went into the storage room to grab a new giant roll of toilet paper and the refillable liquid soap, but as she was leaving the back room, she stopped short listening to the customer that just came in.

"You are needing a receipt?" she heard Nitesh ask.

"Naw, but, you may be able to help me out in another way." The man sucked the air through his teeth as he reached into his back pocket for his wallet.

His dirty blonde hair was combed back and long enough that it almost parted down the middle. It looked wet, but didn't smell clean. He wreaked of cigarette smoke.

As he fished through his wallet, Nitesh noticed a scar above his left eye and his skin was leathery making him appear older than he probably was.

"Here's my card," he slid a thin, white business card across the counter. Black plain letters simply read, Randy Gunter, Private Investigator. "I'm looking for this girl. Young woman, actually. Late twenties, early thirties… light blonde hair or maybe even bright red hair… probably short… 'bout yay high…" He smiles at the clerk and Nitesh can see a gap in his nicotine stained teeth. "Rumor has it," he continues, "she works for you."

Nitesh picked up the card and noted that it was not a local number. He frowned at the man, "I have no employees. I cannot help you." He held the business card back out for Randy Gunter to take back.

"My client just needs to speak with her, no big deal." He produced a raspy laugh.

"Sir, this is my place of business. You have concluded your business here unless you are wanting to purchase something else."

Randy held up his hands retreating, "I hear you. I hear you. Tell you what, keep the card. If you hear of anything… I'd be willing to do more business with ya, know what I mean?"

Nitesh did not bother to reply as Randy backed away from the counter, hands still up in front as if Nitesh was holding a gun pointed at him. He turned once he reached the door and pulled it open setting off the bells. "See ya around, partner."

Nitesh watched Randy look around before slipping into his used and abused cream colored Audi.

As the car drove out into the traffic, Hannah emerged from the hallway. She and Nitesh stood quietly for a moment until Hannah looked away.

"Are you in trouble?" he asked her in a quiet, curious tone.

She shook her head "no".

"I am thinking you will be leaving soon?"

She looked up at him, feeling wounded at first, feeling like he didn't want her around any longer, but then saw by the look on his face that he was protecting her; shielding her.

She nodded. And as has become their way, that was all that was said about it. Hannah turned from him and continued on with the day's tasks.

The shop stayed pretty busy as people came in and went, grabbing a snack, quick bathroom breaks, a drink for the road and the lifeline of travel: gasoline.

As Hannah became more and more adept as a full-time traveller, increasing her awareness of traffic ebb and flow, she not only gained a higher respect for what happens on the other side of the gas station scene, but was amazed at the influx of humans and the effects their vehicles had on highways and streets at certain times of the day. Every city in every state had some sort of a "rush hour".

Today was no different. The late afternoon lull was coming to a close as the flow of people increased. Everyone was always in a hurry. No matter what. And they all complained or rolled their eyes if there was any hesitation in their progress to get their short-term goals accomplished.

People behaved as if their entire day was ruined if someone was in front of them in line waiting for the restroom; to check out or get to the pump that was on the same side as their tank. Grumbling. The fountain soda was out of ice, the melted cheese came out too slow, the slushy spilled over the edge of the cup. Grumbling. People in a hurry. People thinking that they are going to miss out on something if they don't "get there first." People pushing and shoving and frowning and feeling that they are being neglected if there isn't instant gratification. Go, go, go. Hurry, hurry, hurry. The universe can only tolerate so much…

They heard it even from the back room.

Screeching tires, the sound of metal against metal. The smell of heat and smoke and chemical. Thousands of pounds of metal, plastic and technology folding and wrinkling up with immense force…

Screams and then shouting, honking horns and the first sparks of fire…

Nitesh looked immediately at Hannah who stood by the door with a handful of other spectators pressed against the glass watching the horrors unfold.

He frowned at her and shook his head "no".

Her eyes implored him to understand.

"Hannah," he spoke from behind the counter and across the people, "don't go out there."

"I have to…" She pushed open the door almost knocking the bells completely off the arm. She nudged the person standing by the door who had started videoing the accident. "Call 911."

The man looked at her, realizing that it might be a better idea to call the police than capturing the four car pile-up on video.

Hannah ran out to the car closest to her and pushed through the gathering crowd.

A man was yelling, "Get back! Get back! Make room for the ambulance!"

Hannah ran right past him and looked in the passenger window of the closest car. No one, but a driver.

She ran around to his side. She could feel the heat from the hood of his car.

"I can't get out!" He yelled at her through his closed window. "Don't leave me here! I can't get out!" He was banging on the door's console trying to get the automatic window to roll down. Hannah pulled open the door. The man had shattered his right leg. The bone jutted through the skin, but he didn't seem aware.

"Look at me," she turned his face toward her. "I need you to get out of the car and get out of the street, okay? You don't have much time." As she held his face in her hands his leg re-fused and he nodded, turned from his seat and ran away from his car. His pant legs were torn and bloodied, but there was no wound.

Hannah made it up to the next car. People were trying to pry the doors open. This car had been crushed from the front and back. A child could be seen from the windshield, his head smashed from a direct hit. His limp body lay slumped over the dashboard with his feet dangling over the passenger seat.

Hannah saw that he only had moments to live before his brain swelled and would literally be crushed by his protective skull. She screeched out an order. "Bust the windshield!"

"I have a glass pick!" someone called.

A man took the pointed hammer and struck the center of the windshield creating a crackling effect. He brought the hammer down harder a couple more times making a hole. A handful of men were able to pull the entire front windshield from the vehicle. Hannah crawled on the hood despite it being littered with shards of shattered glass and reached in for the toddler. She pulled him close to her chest and slid off the car. As she cradled him close to her body he began to stir.

"Shhh," she coo'd holding him close. "Shh… be still. You're okay."

By the time they got to the curb, he was crying in fear. Hannah handed the child off to a bystander and went back in for the driver.

While others were trying to reach her from the driver's side door, Hannah jumped back up on the hood and dove in the opening. She stretched across the steering wheel and pushed the unconscious woman, who was slumped over, toward the back of her seat. Within moments, the woman blinked her eyes, unaware of what was happening.

"My baby! Where's my baby?" she screamed.

Hannah tipped her jaw to make eye contact with the woman. "He's okay. You're okay. I need to you to help these people get you out. There is no time to lose. Do you understand? Can you do that?"

The woman looked to her left as if this was the first time she noticed three different set of hands banging on her car door.

Hannah nodded to her again and slid back out the way she came, making her way to the next vehicle.

She heard a popping noise and then felt strong arms wrap around her shoulders and pull her to the ground. The smell of gas and blood accosted her senses but she couldn't move for the weight of the man on top of her.

Just then, it sounded like a gust of wind through a tunnel as a whoosh of flame pushed its way out from under the hood of the truck Hannah was headed for.

The man on top of her, rolled to the side to allow her to move again. "Get to the side," he yelled, over the noise of people and machines.

"There's someone hurt in that truck!" she yelled back.

"It's too late! It's going to blow!"

He lifted her up and yanked her arm pulling her away from the gnarled scene. And within moments, the hood of the truck flew up into the air and people scattered away in all directions. Flames shot up sucking the oxygen and feeding itself as it looked for directions to spread.

Within minutes, someone was at either side with fire extinguishers keeping the fire at bay.

Hannah jumped at the chance to get back into the fray.

She found the driver of the truck, an older man with barely a tuft of grey hair left on his head, lying still on the sidewalk where someone had drug his unconscious body.

Hannah knelt beside him and immediately place her hands on his heart, hoping that she was not too late. She stayed perfectly still tuning out the cacophony of voices and sirens going on around her.

The old man blinked his eyes and took in a deep breath, bringing his hand to his balding head. "What happened?

Hannah smiled down as if she had no place else to be, "You got a pretty nice bump on your head." She helped him sit up. "You okay?" she asked.

He furrowed his brow doing a mental check. "Yes. Better than…"

She patted his shoulder. "Good," she said, as she got up.

Suddenly it dawned on her that people were staring at her.

She pretended not to notice and began brushing imaginary dirt and dust off her clothes.

"Hey, who are you?" someone called out to her.

"She saved that little boy's life."

"She's a hero!"

Hannah looked around and saw that people were starting to close in around her. She saw their wounded bodies, but tried to keep her head down, making her way out of the center of the accident.

The police and firefighters were there now and asking everyone to stand back and get out of their way. She was happy to oblige. But the people followed her.

She lost track of which direction it was back to the safety of the gas station. The people came around her to talk to her, to touch her, to thank her. Her heart raced as she felt more and more like the crowd was going to suffocate her.

"I'm sorry. I'm not... I'm not a hero. Anyone would do it..." she pushed her way through the crowd begging for the edge of the crowd of people to appear.

"I got it on video!" someone called out. "This kid had like blood coming out his ears and stuff... I mean his head was cracked open and then wait... look at this ... dude. Nothing. Like it never happened, man. She's a freakin'.... I don't know, man, but she straight up fixed this kid, yo."

Hannah felt the rest of the crowd shift in her direction, once they turned from the kid with the Ipad.

As if in slow motion, Hannah pushed past people and was relieved to see Nitesh on the sidewalk holding her bicycle.

And suddenly everything went silent. She made some space and got on the bike. She could hear Nitesh's thickly accented voice say, "I knew this about you. Now go."

She looked into his eyes only briefly and saw that they had a sheen of tears over them. "Thank you," she mouthed as she pushed and pedaled through the crowd down the street as fast as she could.

Nitesh watched as she went, smiling in his success at helping her escape. He knew that people would turn their attention back to the mangled mess in front of his store in another moment or two. He scanned the accident and then locked eyes with a man who was staring back at him.

At the edge of the scene, on the other side of the street, Randy Gunter leaned against a light pole smoking. The grey smoke swirled up and around his head. He pointed at Nitesh with the finger and thumb holding the butt of the smoked cigarette. He took his eyes away only briefly as he stamped out the glowing ember on the sidewalk.

Hannah wrestled her bicycle into the RV. Her heart was beating so hard she could feel it in her ears. She leaned the bike against the passenger captain's chair and began pacing down the center of her living space.

She tried sitting on the couch to calm herself, but just got back up again, adrenaline still coursing through her.

There was so much to take in... too much was happening.

She healed all those people... they all have second chances now. She healed any number of people as they filtered through the gas station shop. She was doing what she was supposed to do.

But now... someone was searching for her? Possibly watching her? And the videos! How do you hide from modern technology and the social media craze?

Pace, pace, pace...

She shook away her thoughts and decided to concentrate on what to do next.

"Moving on," she said, out loud. "That's what's next. I have to move on." She paused for a moment and sighed. "I didn't get to say good-bye to Nitesh. I wonder if I should..." Pace, pace, pace... "No... move on." She stopped and leaned against the driver's captain chair and folded her arms sighing again, settling in to the idea, again, that running away is now her... thing.

She picked up her instructions list for packing up. "Step one..."

Chapter Eleven

Hannah Carmichael, with her new dark brown shoulder length hair reached across the folding table in the employee lounge and shook the hand of Mindy, the store manager of the Dollar General. "That sounds great," she said, smiling.

"We're happy to have you. We are definitely over worked and understaffed," Mindy smiled and straightened the stack of papers Hannah filled out.

Fake name. Fake social. P.O. Box... New location. New life. Maybe she will be able to stay for a while.

For the past three months she has traveled and stopped and traveled and stopped. She has changed her look and zigzagged across three states. Now she finds herself in Virginia, in a small town, out of money and longing for some consistency. She ached for the familiar. A place to call her own. Maybe, just maybe Huntington, VA will be just such a place.

"I don't how you settled in our little town, not much happens around here, but it's a good place to live. If you need any help finding a place, my sister is a real estate agent and we can get you settled."

"Thank you for that. I'll keep that in mind. I have to save up some money first before I can do anything."

"Preachin' to the choir, girl." Mindy stood up, signaling that her time was up. "I've been living in the same doublewide for five years. It works," she shrugged her shoulders. She walked Hannah to the double swinging doors and maneuvered around the rolling cart stacked high with boxes. "Got a new truck shipment in. See? We've got work waitin' for you."

"I... did you... I could start now, if you wanted."

"No, tomorrow is fine. It will still be here, I'm sure. Go get yourself set up and rested and it will be me and Anna Marie here with you in the morning to start your training."

"Sounds good," Hannah smiled, and shook her hand again. She left Mindy by the stacks and stacks of products that need to be inventoried and put out on the shelves and made her way down the narrow, aisles.

On her way out she smiled at the young girl at the counter with black colored hair and dark eyeliner who, did not return the smile, just went back to restocking the plastic bags on the turnstile at the register.

She walked down the sidewalk of the main street and after only a few blocks of houses and storefronts, the landscape changed. Wide fields spread out on either side of the now two lane road.

Horses followed her with their eyes as she walked along the wood-railed fence. A riding school of sorts seemed to be on the opposite side of the road as the field was dotted with jumping ramps of various levels, worn dirt circles and long barns that hinted older horses found shade and peace inside the deep stalls.

Just past that was a small convenience store that had over-priced this and that, but had scoop-able ice cream and offered old fashioned ice-cream sodas. Hannah knew that this was going to be a frequent stop on her way to or from her new job.

Then, finally, the campground. It was very small, maybe only sixty spaces. From the looks of it, most of the residents were there to stay, as they put permanent amenities on their one-time, free-roaming homes. Porches, underpinnings, storage sheds... an outdoor washing machine?

The weather was nice. Warmer than what she was used to, and she was told that the ocean was only fifteen minutes away.

The ocean. She had never seen the ocean. And now that she secured a place to live and a means to pay for it, she was bound and determined to see it.

She walked down the long entry way of the campground and stopped in at the office. The campground was owned and run by two older sisters. The story of the history of the land and being their family's plantation was always just nudge away. One only had to hint at curiosity and the tale would begin...

"Tobacco," Patty would say. "Our great-grand-daddy was a tobacco farmer."

"But he was a *good* slave owner. You know, good to his people," Clam would add. (Her real name was Jane, but since day one, she had been the tomboy, so her daddy would call her Calamity Jane, because she was always getting into things. It got shortened to Clam and that stuck.)

"Oh we had the best time growing up here."

"And when we came close to losing the property, we decided to share this beauty with others."

"And now we always have friends around us."

Hannah instantly adored the sisters. Patty was usually dressed in a long riding skirt and button down shirt. Her hair was twisted up in an elegant style on her head. While Clam always looked hot and dusty. She wore jeans cut and rolled up to her calves, and a t-shirt with a bandana tied around her neck. Her hair was pure white and cropped short around her ears. They both taught riding lessons and the land on either side of the road also belonged to them. If they had truly been close to losing the property it has long since been a memory, because they were not hurting for income these days. Turned out, they even owned the little ice-cream shop down the road.

Their shrewd business sense did not harden their hearts. They opened their home every Christmas to those residents who happened to be with them at the time and smoked an entire hog with all the "fixin's." They also offered their most gentle horses to the children far and wide with down syndrome at no charge. Busses came in from states away to introduce many of these children to the gentle giants of the range. They also have an assortment of small farm animals for these most precious of visitors: A lamb, a piglet or two, turtles, guinea pigs, an old milk cow, and so on.

They didn't slow down for much.

On this particular day as Hannah entered the small campground office she found Clam slumped over her phone, frowning. She glanced up and smiled at Hannah. "Hey, how are ya?" She pulled herself up from the lawn chair that they used as a seating area.

"I'm good. You?"

"Frustrated. I'll be darned if my granddaughter isn't gonna beat me at this Words with Friends game again!"

Hannah laughed. "I used to be so addicted to that game."

"Here," she handed the phone over to her, "help an old lady out, would ya?"

Hannah paused for a moment, ready to decline, but a small thrill skipped over her skin. "Okay, let's see what you've got." She looked over the progress of the game, the letters she had available and the points scored. "Oooo, she is good."

"I know! Little brat. I used to change her diapers!"

Hannah moved the tiles around on the scrabble-like game and came up with a solid thirty-four point word. "Here, how's that?"

"Oh yeah.. that should slow her down for a minute. Thanks." Clam sent off the word and it was her turn to wait. "Now… what can I do for you?"

"The ocean… I heard there are buses that…"

Hannah's query was interrupted as Patty came through the door with her arms laden yellow bags with black writing down each side. "Oh!" she said, as she spotted Hannah. "Were your ears ringing?" She paused and looked elsewhere frowning, "or is it your nose itching? Which one is it, Sister, when someone has been talking about you?"

"The ears ringing," Clam answered, matter-of-factly, not lifting her head from the intense game. "The nose one is when company is coming."

"Oh. I thought that was when your skin was tingling."

"That's when someone walks over your grave."

"Ah yes, yes… you're right." She walked over to the "outdoor seating lounge" that was indoors by her sister and set her bags down. "Hannah, dear, I just spoke to the ladies at the Dollar General and they are so happy that you will be joining them. I just knew you would be a perfect fit." Her light airy voice always sounded as if there was laughter just under the surface, as compared to her sister's who was deeper and more gravelly.

"I'm glad to hear it. I start tomorrow."

"So they said."

"And thank you again for the recommendation," Hannah added.

"Of course, dear. We keep pretty close tabs on what happens in our little town." Patty pulled out some Kleenex boxes, bottles of liquid soap, and some staples from the bag and brought them over to the counter. "Oh sister, I ran into

Sandy today also. That poor woman. She has been through so much."

Clam nodded in agreement. "Have you met Sandy?"

Hannah raised her eyebrows, "Uh, no… no I haven't."

"She's only been in the neighborhood for less than forty-eight hours," Patty reminded her sister.

"Poor lady," Clam continued, finally looking up. "She lost her husband about three years ago. She has three kids. The oldest daughter graduated from college about a year ago but she still hasn't found a job. Thank goodness they had her husband's life insurance to help pay the bills since neither she nor the daughter are working right now."

Patty was nodding her head in confirmation. "Yes, yes, bless her heart. She's been taking care of her husband and now her daughter… she hasn't been able to work for years now. She used to work at the furniture factory, you remember…"

Clam nodded. "You said, now the daughter?"

"How awful," Hannah offered. "Do they know what the daughter is suffering from?"

"They think some kind of stomach cancer. You know the father died of that very thing? Can you imagine?"

Hannah shook her head, understanding the pain of losing those you love.

Patty continued the story, "She also has a son who is autistic but is about to graduate high school, and another daughter…" Patty searched her memory, "who is… thirteen? Fourteen?"

"And is her favorite," Clam scoffed.

"Oh, now we don't know that," Patty waved her hand at her sister, dismissing the claim.

"You see what you see, and I see what I see," Clam defended. "But anyway... you saw her today?"

Patty laughed, "Oh yes... I did. She came into the store while I was there and she came up to me while I was shopping for some glass cleaner. And wouldn't you know it, but her boy, the middle child," she looked over at Hannah to make sure she was keeping up with the story, "woke up this morning and was throwing up blood!"

Patty covered her mouth as if she had spoken a dirty word. "And do you know, that's what she said were some of the early symptoms of the other two."

"Has she taken him to the doctor? If he's throwing up blood, that's not an early symptom... that's showing that something has been there for a while." Hannah interjected.

Patty looked at her and her eyes widened. "You know, that's exactly what I thought," she said, "but, I keep my thoughts to myself. But if you ask me, she is not doing what's best for her family. She needs to get those kids to the hospital."

"It's not like cancer is contagious," Clam frowned. "There must be some kind of flu..."

"Do... uh... they come into the store very often?"

"Oh honey," Clam scoffed, "that store is THE store. Everyone goes through that place."

"Oh yes," Patty concurred, "It's all we have. That or the Piggly Wiggly. It used to be the post office where everyone would congregate, but since the Dollar General opened up, it's where everyone learns about everything." She laughed a guilty laugh.

"It's better than a local paper," Clam nodded.

"Well, hopefully Sandy and those kids can get some help soon."

"From your mouth to God's ears," Patty added.

"Pretty much…" Hannah said under her breath.

"Lands, lands… I haven't felt this good in a long time!" Patty stretched down to reach the M slot of the mail cubby. "Usually I would dread having to reach down past the G's," she laughed.

Hannah laughed.

"No mail for you today, Sweets."

Just then, Clam walked into the office slash reception area from the side door. She was covered from head to toe in dirt and dust.

"Merciful heavens!" Patty exclaimed. "Get back outside and dust yourself off, Sister. You are a mess!"

"I'm not planning on staying in here, but, you know that crick in my back…?"

Patty nodded. "Let me get the ibuprofen for ya."

"No, that's just it. I don't need it. It's like it's… gone. No pain!"

Patty put her hands on her hips, "Well, ain't that something. I was just telling Hannah, here, that I was feeling pretty good today myself." She tipped her head to Hannah for confirmation.

Hannah nodded. "She did."

"How bout you?" Clam asked. "Any pains?"

Hannah shrugged her shoulders sheepishly. "Nope. No pain here."

Patty batted away the air. "She wouldn't have pain yet, she's still a youngster."

"It's an Angel Wind," Clam said, thoughtfully. "I'll bet that's what it is."

"You might be right, Sister," Patty agreed. "I have heard a lot of people around town have been saying that they haven't been feeling their usual aches and pains."

"What's an Angel Wind?" Hannah had to ask, keeping her smile to herself.

"It's when there's this… streak of… of… good luck or good things happening for people for a window of time. I bet that's what this is. Angels passing through our little town. Lord knows we sure could use it."

"Did you hear that Elaine quit smoking?" Patty asked. "She said that she woke up and just didn't need them any more. No more coughing fits, no more chest pains…"

"Did it fix her crabbin' and fussin'?" Clam laughed.

"I don't think anything could fix that, but at least when she insults people it's not interrupted by a coughing fit!"

The two sisters laughed and Hannah couldn't help but join in, seeing the woman-in-question's behavior first hand when she comes into the Dollar General.

An Angel Wind," Hannah said the words out loud.

"That's what I'd call it." Clam stated.

Hannah found that she enjoyed working at the Dollar General. The sister's were right, pretty much the whole town comes in from time to time for supplies and socialization. She might give off the impression that she is the clumsiest worker there, but she finds a way to bump into, trip into, twist her ankle into or just have a person stabilize her balance while she reaches a top shelf for an item.

She couldn't always heal them completely, sometimes it would take a little longer, but this actually worked out in her favor so that most of the time, people didn't realize it was happening. They knew they just felt... better.

Hannah was high on a ladder and she could hear Mindy below teasing her. "Alright, who put the accident-prone employee on the ladder." She laughed at her own joke and Hannah laughed with her, although, if it wasn't for Hannah falling into her during her first couple days, Mindy might not have been around much longer because that ulcer was burning a hole through the lining of her stomach.

"Hey, you up there," she leaned her head back at the base of the ladder. "I'm ordering food from Los Puentas, you want anything?"

Kara, the black haired teen from the register moaned. "Mexican food again?"

Mindy shook her head good heartedly, "She just doesn't get it," she said just above a whisper, for Hannah's ears only. "I haven't felt this good in ages. Do you know how long it's been since I could eat spicy food? I took a chance this morning…" she looked around her as if she was trading top secrets, "Orange juice. I had orange juice for the first time in… " she waved her hand around, "… years." She bobbed her black, permed hair. "Years." She looked back up at Hannah, "No pain."

Hannah stopped her work and smiled down at her. "Well that's good! You might not want to over-do it though."

"I know. I know… I'm just afraid that it's going to end and I'll wake up from this dream where I was able to eat anything I wanted without getting sick."

Just then, the door chime went off and a thin, pale woman came in with stringy, mousy-brown hair.

Mindy looked over her shoulder, "Oh hey, Sandy. How are ya?" she called out.

Hannah looked up to get the first glimpse of the woman whose name had been on everyone's lips.

She came in alone and waved back to the store's manager. "Hey girl," she sighed heavily, and rolled her eyes. "I don't even want to have to think about it."

Elizabeth Bourgeret

Hannah could see the cancer spots on her lungs from cigarette smoke and the results of poor nutrition on her skin and hair. Her teeth were broken and her heart was pumping harder than it should for her tiny little frame.

"Hey have you met our newest member here?" Mindi asked her. "This is Hannah, she's from Indiana, originally."

Hannah made the effort to climb down the ladder to shake hands, but Sandy waved her away and walked past the ladder's base to grab a box of cupcakes, a box of sour cream and onion crackers, a bag of tootsie rolls and a can of corn. "Don't worry about it this time. I'll see you around I'm sure."

She reached for a box of sugary cereal. "These kids, I swear, they're going to be the death of me."

"How's everyone doing?" Mindy asked.

"Oh, you know. The bills are piling up and no one is willing to get out and get a job. Linda has a degree and isn't even working."

"Is she feeling better?"

Sandy's demeanor shifted. "No… she just gets weaker and weaker by the day, and now Davy seems to be suffering too."

"Oh Sandy… I hate to hear…"

"And what about me? Who's there to take care of me? My husband is gone… I'm just so tired."

"It's going to work out," Mindy tried to console her.

"I don't know how. It's just one thing after another."

Hannah listened from her perch but said nothing. She could understand why the kids weren't in the hospital, if she barely had money to pay the bills and keep food on the table. Of course *her choice of food…* Hannah admonished herself for thinking negatively about the woman. *I'm sure she's doing the best she can,* Hannah tried to tell herself.

"How is Charity doing?" Mindy ventured.

"Oh," Sandy smiled and hugged the cereal box to her chest. "That girl is my one beacon of light. She's really all I have in the world."

"Oh, I wouldn't say that…" Mindy brushed off the statement.

"Really? You think a daughter, who's practically grown, who can't even earn an income after spending four years in college, racking up mountains in student loans is a blessing? Or a son, who only knows how to cost me money?"

"I'm sure that…"

"He's autistic. Davy is never going to be able to help pay the bills. All he can do is eat and eat and eat. I tell you, it never ends." She threw the cereal box into her little hand basket and shrugged. "What are you going to do, right? I just deal with the hand I'm dealt…" She dropped her head defeated and walked up to the front register with Mindy trailing close behind.

"Here," Mindy stood in front of Kara and swiped her manager's badge down the side of the register. "Let me help, it's not much, but a little discount might…"

"Oh, you are too kind," Sandy piled her items on the conveyer belt. "I am so blessed to have you as my friend."

She offered a meek smile and slid her debit card through the charger.

She gathered up her yellow, plastic bags, "Alright girl, I'll catch you guys later."

Mindy sighed heavily, as she came back down Hannah's aisle. "That poor woman. That poor, poor woman."

Hannah didn't like how she was feeling toward Sandy, but was anxious to be able to heal the children and her, in hopes of it easing some of the pain... both physical and emotional.

It was a complete week before Sandy came into the Dollar General again. Hannah was sitting on the floor adding the box of canned peas to the shelf. There were always so many boxes. It took them days to finally get everything on the shelves or display racks and then another truck would show up and start the entire process over again. Since Kara hated restocking, Mindy was fine with her staying at the cash register. Kara would put out the candies, the gift cards and the other items that enclosed her domain, but rarely left the front. It suited Hannah just fine. She preferred the solitude and mundane work of opening a box and methodically emptying it... over and over.

Sandy walked in and grabbed her hand-held basket. Hannah could see her pause near the door as if she was waiting for a sales clerk to greet her.

She didn't have to wait long before Anna Marie, an upbeat, bleach-blonde fifty-something part-timer came up the far left aisle. "Oh, Sandy, honey, how are you today?"

"Oh you know," Sandy replied, suddenly flustered and rushing down the aisle one over from where Hannah sat. "I'm in a hurry today. I've got to get the oldest to the doctor. Doctor bills and more doctor bills."

"Oh no, I'm so sorry," Anna Marie followed behind her, "You know my boyfriend had to go to the doctor last week. Cost him fifty dollars!" she drew her hand to her chest. "I was shocked."

"Well, now multiply that by sometimes three times a week." Sandy rolled her eyes as if no one could possibly understand what she was going through.

"Well, I've been praying for you," Anna Marie offered.

Sandy stopped and turned toward her, "You are such a good friend." She laid her hand on Anna Marie's forearm. "I am so blessed to have people like you in my life."

"Well, thank you. I believe healing is on its way, Sandy, I really do."

"I hope you're right," Sandy frowned, trying to hold back tears, "I just don't know how much more I can take. My poor husband, who was the love of my life…"

Anna Marie patted her on her shoulder and nodded sympathetically.

"And now my babies… what am I supposed to do?"

"I know. I know…" Anna Marie commiserated.

"You know what might help?" Sandy lifted her face and Anna Marie waited. "You know that icebox cake you used to make for Davy? He was just mentioning that. Maybe… if you could find it in your heart to make him one, it might help him to feel a little better."

"Oh! You think it would? I can definitely do that. It wouldn't upset his stomach?"

"Honestly, I don't know how much time he has left, just between you and me."

Anna Marie gasped, "No… I didn't realize he was so bad off!"

Sandy shook her head. "I see all the same signs as his father…"

"What did the doctor say?"

"Well, you know," she lowered her head, "they say all the things to try and make me feel better, but I know… it's just a matter of time."

"Oh Sandy, don't say that. I'll keep praying and believing that he'll be okay."

"Thank you."

"And I'll get to work baking him that cake too. I get off in a couple hours, and I can bring it by tonight, if you want."

"You are too good to us, thank you. If you're sure it wouldn't be too much trouble…"

"I wish I could do more…"

"Look, I gotta get this shopping finished, Linda is in the car and feeling sickly. I shouldn't have even brought her out, but I thought the fresh air would do her good."

"And there's the doctor appointment…" Anna Marie reminded.

"Yeah… uh yes… we got that too."

Hannah's ears perked and she wasted no time to get to the back room to her locker. Mindy was sitting at the break table going over some paperwork when Hannah came in.

"Hey, do you mind if I run to the post office really quick? I wanted to get this out before the mail runs today," Hannah asked her boss, all the while getting a pre-addressed, pre-stamped envelope out of her locker and holding it out as proof of her intentions.

"Sure. Is anyone out there?"

"Anna Marie is. She's talking with Sandy."

Mindy looked up, just as Hannah was hoping. Sandy was the serial drama that kept the gossip train running. Everyone wanted to be in on the conversation. "Well," Mindy stood and stretched, "I should probably go and say hello."

"I'm sure she'd appreciate that. I'll be right back."

Hannah tucked the bright yellow card envelope under her arm and headed toward the door calling out to Anna Marie, "I'm going to the post office. I'll be right back!"

"Alright, honey," came the answer from a voice around the automotive section.

Hannah opened the door setting off the door chime and welcomed the wave of heat that accosted her. The air conditioning was set so low that usually she had to wear a sweater while she was at work.

The store was on the main strip, so they didn't have their own parking lot. Everyone parked along the sidewalk between diagonal lines painted on spaces. She had no idea what kind of car Sandy drove or what the daughter, Linda, looked like.

She stood still for just a moment, hoping to be directed and no sooner had she prayed for direction, a car door opened. It was two spaces over from the Dollar General door.

A young woman, who moved like she was eighty, was attempting to get out of the car. Her mousy brown, thin hair was long and stringy, past her shoulders. She put her arm on the top of the tan car for support. The skin on her arm was paper thin, almost transparent, not just for Hannah's gifted eyes, but the random passerby could see her outward symptoms.

She moved closer, and when Linda stepped from behind the car door, Hannah could see the damage. Her stomach had deteriorated, but no signs of cancer. Most likely from vomiting. Her kidneys were on the verge of shutting down. There was blockage and inflammation, probably causing severe pain.

Linda stumbled as if she had been on a drinking binge and Hannah jumped into action. Just before Linda was about to topple over, Hannah wrapped herself around Linda's waist, holding her steady.

Hannah's hands slowly worked at healing the girl and gradually she stood erect.

Hannah had an odd taste, a sweet taste, in her mouth that was unfamiliar. It was heavy, but felt like a cloud against her tongue. "Are you alright?" she asked, innocently. "I thought you were about to fall," she laughed it off.

"Uh… yeah… I'm… I had to use the restroom, but… I feel…"

"Oh," Hannah interrupted, "there's a restroom in the store if you want to use that one."

Linda laughed, confused. "I… don't know what happened. I don't have to anymore. I feel…"

"Linda! What are you doing?" Sandy came out of the store.

"I was just…"

"Get back in the car!" Sandy snapped, only then noticing Hannah standing there. "You can't be out on your own without your momma's help, baby. Come on now, get back in." Sandy gently guided her oldest daughter back toward the vehicle.

"But Momma, I'm feeling better. Couldn't I…"

"Momma knows best, sweetie. I'm here. I've got you."

"But Momma, really, I feel so much better. I'm not hurting at all."

In low tones and through gritted teeth, Sandy growled, "Get in. The car."

Linda swallowed and did as her mother said.

Hannah stepped back onto the sidewalk, giving them room to back out. As she watched the car drive down the busy main street, she felt good about healing the child, but still felt a pit in her stomach. Never, in all of the people she healed did she ever feel or get any kind of residual from it. This time was different. She scanned her memory to identify the taste on her tongue as it dissipated, but came up with nothing. Sweet. A sweet, but toxic cloud.

People were walking on the sidewalks, slipping in and out of the shops along both sides, this being the busier tourist season. Hannah had to do a double take, thinking she saw Pete, walking among the crowd. She glanced over the faces once again and saw the familiar face look over toward her and make eye contact. And then he disappeared into the other faces once again.

Hannah's heart skipped a beat. *What did that mean,* she wondered. *What was he trying to tell her? I wish he would just say it,* Hannah thought to herself, *that would make things so much easier.*

Miracles from Ashes

Elizabeth Bourgeret

Chapter Twelve

The sun beat down on her pale skin as she dared to remove the worn t-shirt revealing a very simple bikini top just purchased with her employee discount. The warm winds twisted and flipped her hair away from her face as she climbed a sandy path to its summit.

The sand moved and swallowed her bare feet with every step. It felt warm and soothing. She could smell the salt in the air and her heart skipped a beat waiting for the big reveal.

As she crested the top of the dune, spread out before her was a sea of tan, sparkling sand and just beyond it… an endless body of water that danced and rolled under the sun, shining and glittering as it caressed the shore line with bold, crashing waves.

The ocean.

She finally made it. It was worth the wait.

Hannah was so much in awe that she didn't want to move from her spot. She just wanted to stand there and take it all in. She wasn't prepared, having never been, but had gathered up the necessary items from the store including sunglasses, sunscreen, waters, a small lunch bag, a huge beach towel and some flip flops. She carried it all in the signature plastic bags. As she looked along the beach, suddenly she yearned for the brightly colored umbrellas, the coolers and adorable beach bags everyone seemed to own.

The ocean. "I think I'm in love."

She spread out her new beach towel with the tag still dangling from the corner, and stretched herself out on it. She just sat, staring out into the multifaceted, mysterious waters. The waves rolled over themselves and pounded into the damp sand where it created an edge. It crashed in, throwing sand, shells and foam only to drag half of it back into its depths. Hannah couldn't turn away. She was fascinated. Amazed. She felt so very small against this watery backdrop and yet felt more safe and secure in a God that could create all of this and still know the number of hairs on her head.

Hannah heard squeals of small children and turned her head to see a young boy and girl running in the ocean after a wave and then squealing as it chased them back out. Back and forth. Back and forth until the boy decided to face his nemesis head on. The wave easily and effortlessly knocked the child off his feet. Hannah gasped for a moment trying to decide if she should run to his aid or stay put. The little warrior popped up out of the battle sputtering and coughing, but laughing. He turned and faced off again. Hannah laughed at his antics and thought… remembered…

It was November. Hannah furrowed her brow at the memory. Thanksgiving break. They were supposed to go to the beach… a vacation.

"Look Mommy!" Rosie pranced about the living room in her one-piece swimsuit with a glittery unicorn on the chest.

She wore goggles on her head and danced and pivoted in front of her exhausted mother.

"You are adorable." Hannah reached out and scooped up the child in her arms and cradled her on her lap commencing the tickling and the kissing while she screeched and giggled at the attention.

Olivia was perched on Jeremy's hip as they looked on. Olivia kicked her fat little baby legs wanting to join in on the love fest, and Jeremy obliged her. She hobbled over carefully, one step at a time, and flopped both her raised arms down on her sister's belly, releasing a high pitched baby noise.

"Oh! You got her!" Hannah encouraged. Olivia's chubby legs bounced her up and down using her mother as a brace.

Hannah set Rosie on her feet and scooped up the baby and nuzzled into her neck setting off gales of laughter.

Jeremy grabbed Rosie and tossed her up over his head and caught her only to tickle her under her arms.

Hannah brought the family together in a tight huddle and kissed each one on the nose.

She looked at Jeremy long before she could speak the words. She stroked the back of his head and neck with her free arm and begged him to understand long before she uttered one syllable.

He took in a deep breath and looked away, shaking his head. When he brought his eyes back up to hers he spoke, "We're not going are we?"

"I'm sorry. We don't have the staff to…"

He brought his forehead to hers, "Honey, they will never have the right amount of people. They had the same problem before you came along and they will have the same problem long after you leave them. It's just the way it goes…"

"But I'm almost to the finish line…" she pleaded with him to understand.

He closed his eyes and allowed her to kiss his forehead and nose. "You said that last time.

"I know. I just want to get through this and then…"

"And then what? You'll work full time, just as hard as you're working now."

"I won't. I promise," she drew his face back up to hers. "There will be other chances. There will be other vacations. Lot's more. So many more… we'll be the best vacationers ever."

Hannah blinked, her face wet with tears as the crashing waves pulled her back from her memories but mirroring her emotion.

"There were no other chances…" the wind stole her words from her and cast them out into the air.

She stood up and brushed away the sand that had stuck to her arms and stomach. She walked to the edge of the water just enough to where the ocean kissed her feet before retreating. It was cool. Refreshing.

The sand slipped away from under her feet as the wave pulled back into the single mass only to be divided again.

Hannah caught her footing and allowed herself to go in a bit deeper feeling the battle of comings and goings go on beneath her.

She knew there were people smattering the beaches directly behind her, but even this, a few feet into the water, she felt completely alone. She felt safe and secure and at peace as if she were the only one at the beach that day.

"Paschar..." she whispered. "Can you hear me? Pete?" The waves came in and out around her not inhibited in the least by her presence. "God?" She wasn't sure if she was expecting a response or not but decided to proceed. "I... wanted to thank you for the honor and the gift you have given me, allowing me to help so many people. I am grateful to be a part of that. But... I miss..." she took in a ragged breath knowing that tears were close to the surface. "I miss my children, Lord. I miss my family. I am so lonely. I am ... so, so lonely." A tear slipped down her cheek. Images of her children and her husband ran through her mind and tightened her chest.

She held her breath and fell into the water. The waves crashed over her and pulled her body to the shore. She landed on her knees and just as she was about to get her balance, another wave crashed against her knocking her down. She laughed. She laughed so hard. She got to her feet and ran back out into the water to battle another round of waves wanting to knock her down. She jumped over them and dove under them, she floated along with the rolling ones and stood firm, feet grounded as others smashed into her chest. She played, and swam and laughed and cried in the ocean that day. It was a full physical workout… and emotional release.

She walked, feeling victorious, back to the beach, making sure her swimming suit was adjusted properly. She emerged from the water feeling refreshed and renewed. The beach towel and sunshine beckoned her to stay a little longer and she obliged.

"The Angel Wind has struck again," Clam spoke, as she leaned back in the lounge chair; the local newspaper folded over in half as she read.

"What's happened?" Patty asked.

"Remember Shawn… he used to do repairs over at the Rainbow Inn Motel?"

Patty scrunched her face. "Yeah, he retired early because of a… a…"

"Tumor. Inoperable tumor," Clam filled in the missing piece for her. "Well, according to this story, not only is he claiming he is completely healed from the tumor, but feels like it's a sign to follow his dream of opening his own hardware store."

"Well, I'll be," Patty looked up from her section of the local newspaper.

"That makes him the third new business in town that credits the Angel Wind for luck."

"Kelley's Coffee and Bakery," Patty added, "She said her arthritis was what stopped her, but then suddenly, the last time she went to go buy some Arthritis pain reliever, she suddenly didn't need it any more. Who is the third one?"

"Dave's and Scott's place. Turned their garage into a mechanic's shop."

"I didn't know about that one."

"Yeah," Clam sighed out. Scott bought three lottery tickets and all three won, so he saw it as a sign from the Angel Wind."

"He's a millionaire?"Patty exclaimed, wondering how she didn't hear of it.

"Heck no. His lottery tickets only got him two dollars, six dollars and another free ticket! But you can't tell those two anything." Clam frowned and shook her head. "The Angel Wind that has blessed this town isn't something that should be mocked."

"I agree Sister. I agree."

The Dollar General was busy that Saturday afternoon when Sandy and her two girls came in. They grabbed a larger push cart this time and Charity took over. "Go ahead, baby," Sandy crooned. "You know what Momma needs. Linda, hold on to my arm so I can help you."

Linda coughed and nodded, linking arms with her mother.

"Hey Sandy," Mindy followed the three down the first aisle.

"Hey girl," Sandy called back.

Charity looked over the wall of snacks and took a few from the shelf and added them to her buggy.

"You're looking good today, Miss Linda," Mindy nudged Linda's arm.

Linda just smiled politely.

"We thought we'd get her out today. It's good for her to stretch her legs. Can't stay in bed all the time."

"I wish she would just die already…"Charity whispered under her breath. If anyone heard her, no one commented.

"We are discounting a lot of our clothing if you guys need anything," Mindy smiled and leaned in, "Look for the blue dots."

It was then that Hannah came up behind the group of shoppers and gasped loudly. She stopped so abruptly that the box of jars of popcorn kernels she was carrying fell to the floor. Several of the jars exploded sending tiny kernels rolling off in every direction.

"What on earth?" Mindy exclaimed. "Honey, are you alright?"

Hannah stared at Linda unabashedly. "I… I uh…"

With all eyes suddenly on her she quickly shook it off and looked down at her mess. "Oh… I am so clumsy. I'm sorry. I… don't… I thought I was going to run into Miss Linda here…"

"It's alright.   It's alright," Mindy came to her aid. "We'll get this cleaned up in no time." Mindy bent down and started putting the glass jars back into the box.

Hannah dared to look up at Linda. Her pale skin was paper thin again, bruised and damaged and her sunken, pink-rimmed eyes looked at Hannah willing her to hear her thoughts.   Hannah couldn't do that, but she could see that Linda was back to where she was.   Perhaps, even worse. Hannah's gaze travelled down her body and saw that her lungs were enflamed, making it hard for Linda to breath.   Her kidneys were barely functioning. She didn't understand how Linda could be walking right now, but more importantly, Hannah had healed her. She *was* healed.

Hannah locked eyes with Linda once again, her pupils were dilated and her blinking was slow. She saw the brain was swollen just behind her eyes.   Linda's gaze was hard. Imploring. "*You know. Tell me you know,*" it was saying.

"Linda!" Sandy called. "Try and keep up, Pumpkin."

Linda turned away, defeated and followed behind her mother and sister.

I don't understand, Hannah thought when she got behind the closed door of the back room. *She was healed. I didn't see anything in her body when she left last week. Is my gift only temporary? Am I starting to run out? Is it over? I shouldn't have complained.* She paced the back room trying to figure out the answers. *I need to try again.* She stood up and gathered herself before walking back out into the main room.

She saw Mindy chatting with another customer. "I'm sorry to interrupt, is Sandy still here?"

"No Sweetie, she just walked out the door."

Hannah quickly ran to the front of the store, grabbed a Snickers bar and tossed it in a bag.

"What are you doing?" Kara asked.

"I'll be right back," Hannah said breathlessly, and ran out the front door.

"Sandy!" she called. "Sandy, you forgot one of your bags." Hannah came up to the side of the car where Linda was sitting with her arm along the window frame.

Hannah rested her hand on Linda's arm and prayed that it was working. It was. Hannah could see the brain swell decreasing. She felt that odd sensation in her mouth again. That odd sweet taste that left a film on the back of her tongue. It felt that if she opened her mouth a vapor would escape.

"What bag?" Charity barked, from the back seat.

Hannah produced the plastic bag with her other hand and stuffed it in the window, not wanting to break contact with Linda. "This… was uh… laying on the counter."

"What is it?" Sandy asked.

"Not sure. I just grabbed it and came out here."

Sandy took the bag from her and looked inside. "Oh yes, silly me. I must have forgotten to grab this one."

"What is it?" Charity asked.

"It's that candy bar I grabbed. You know, I got us that Snickers to share," she looked back at Charity.

While they discussed the contents of the bag, Linda's eyes never left Hannah's face. Her pupils came back to their normal size and her eyes got their shine back. It was like her body was inflating, like a balloon, because as she was healing inside, her posture improved.

Hannah looked back and caught her intense, unbelieving stare. She smiled gently at the girl. The secret was safe between them.

"Well, thanks, we've got to be goin' now," Sandy leaned over the steering wheel to see Hannah. "Linda, tell the nice lady thank you for bringing out our missing bag."

Linda turned to Hannah and with the most sincerity she could put into two words, she whispered, "Thank you."

Sandy started to move the car back forcing Hannah from the window. "Babies, did you see I got you some Coke? Momma will fix you a nice tall glass when we get home.

She was sure she saw a tear slip down Linda's cheek, but couldn't tell if it was from happiness or sadness.

Hannah turned away from the car, pleased she could help but shivered, making a face. "Eeew, Coke."

Miracles from Ashes

Two days. Only two days later, she heard the news.
Linda Bilkins was dead.

Chapter Thirteen

Hannah was just closing out her shift when she heard the news. Mindy was saying, "I can't believe it. I just can't believe it. That poor woman. How much can one family take?" she was asking no one in particular.

Anna Marie was quick to respond, "I know. I've prayed and prayed for that family. I trust that God knows what He's doing, but oh my, the suffering they must be feeling right now."

Hannah was shaking inside and hoped that it wasn't showing to the naked eye. She closed her locker and turned to leave. "Good night, ladies," she mentioned in passing.

"Oh Hannah, did you hear about Sandy and her daughter?"

Hannah sighed out heavily, "I did... yes."

"Isn't that just awful?"

Hannah replied honestly, "It is. I... am just not sure... how to deal with it." She nodded politely and turned to leave. She heard Anna Marie say behind her, "She feels it so deeply, you can tell..."

Hannah did feel it deeply. All the way down to her core. The skies were cloudy and grey. She could feel a storm brewing both inside her and outside as well. She made a hard right once she got out of the store and started walking home.

A few droplets of rain started falling, but she was unfazed.

Near the edge of town, an old, old Ford truck pulled over beside Hannah. It was Frank. She's seen him around town and he has come into the store several times, mostly to pick up something for his wife. His gout no longer ails him. He leaned over the seats and hit the latch to open the passenger door. "Hey lady, how are ya? Do you need a lift? Storms-a-comin'."

"Thanks Frank," she leaned momentarily against the opened door, "I really need the walk. It's been a stressful day."

"I gotcha." He lifted up his dirty ball cap and scratched his forehead. He placed it back on his head and pointed at her with his wrinkled finger. "You be safe now. Gettin' a little wet is one thing, but don't get caught up in the storm. There's electricity in the air." He nodded at her with authority. "When you get my age, you can feel it."

She reached in to shake his hand. "I'll be extra careful, I promise. Say hello to Gladys for me."

He saluted her and nodded. "Will do."

Hannah backed off and closed the passenger door. It creaked against the movement but clasped into place after a couple hard bangs.

"She's a classic," he called through the open window.

Hannah laughed, "You both are!"

He rumbled out a low laugh and pulled back out into the main traffic-way.

Hannah watched him leave and couldn't help but smile, grateful to meet and get to know all these people from this town. A raindrop hit her nose and shifted her thinking.

She frowned again. "I don't... understand."

She started back on her walk back to her home. The rain really started to fall just about the time she ran out of sidewalk.

It was coming down in sheets and Hannah was instantly soaked, which did little to improve her mood. Through clenched teeth she walked and yelled out into the weather. "I. Don't. Understand!"

Her fists were clenched tight and her steps were heavy. Her clothes stuck to her skin. It was a cool rain, and had her mood been different, she would have enjoyed the rainy walk. But not today. She was hurt. Confused. Angry.

She wiped the rain from her face and turned the corner to begin the long walk to the campground. She stopped next to a small creek that went under the road. A bench was set up along side it for those who looked for a peaceful scene during their walk or a perfect place for a picnic; the creek and pastures before them. Cozy, wooded space on one side the road and horse pastures on the other.

But today, the creek waters gurgled and rushed over rocks and bounced off its enclosures to make way for more water. The rain drops soaked the bench and the ground was soggy. No picnics today.

Hannah paused taking in the scene, not knowing what to do with her thoughts and feelings. Again, with more volume, she called out. "I don't understand!"

She paced along side the bench and saw that the horses began to migrate toward her in hopes of a carrot or apple treat. She shook her head and tapped her forehead with her fingertips. "Why…. Why give me this gift if it's not going to work?" She called out to the trees and horses.

"Your gift does work," a voice came back to her. "Look at all the people you've helped in just this town. An Angel Wind, I like that." She recognized the voice. It's low tones and slight Italian accent…

"But what happened to…." She was shouting…. "Linda." She spoke her name softly. Reverently.

No answer but a thunder clapping overhead.

"Why didn't it work for her? She was suffering! I thought I healed her but then…" Hannah wiped the water dripping off her nose and chin, but it was pointless.

"I don't understand. Is it because she knew what I was doing? Did I break the rules?"

No answer.

"Please! Tell me!!"

She saw Pete emerge from the tree line. His clothes, the same ones he was wearing the last time she saw him, were completely dry. He walked closer, the rain having no impact on his presence whatsoever.

He waved his hand and brought Hannah under his protective "dry" bubble of space. She blinked the droplets from her eyelashes that were mixed with tears. She wiped away the excess from her face again. The storm raged on around them, but they were unscathed.

"Sometimes," Pete said, tucking his hands in his slacks pockets. "Sometimes there are bad people."

Hannah furrowed her brow. "I know that, but Linda…"

"It's her mother." Pete decided to get right to the point.

"Her mother is…"

"A selfish, evil human." Pete wagged his index finger at her, "Satan himself has taken great care with this one."

Hannah shook her head in confusion.

"She poisoned her husband for the life insurance money, and now that has run out…"

"What?" Hannah asked, shocked. "She killed her daughter for…"

"Insurance money. If I were a betting man, which I am not, I bet she has a life insurance policy on her kids."

Hannah shook her head in disbelief, "Poison…" Her thoughts were going in all directions. She squeezed her eyes shut and shook her head. With this new information, it became so crystal clear. "She presented with all the symptoms of anti-freeze poisoning. Oh, why did I not see that?" She recreated the scenes in her mind's eye and brought her fingers to her lips… *the taste….*

"The mother had her on a slow drip… in order to drag it out," Pete began filling in the details. "When you healed her the first time, she upped the dosage, which is why…"

"Why I saw the increased damage to her kidneys…" Hannah nodded, seeing it clearly now.

"And then the second time…"

"She must have given her more… must have thought it wasn't working…"

"Precisely."

"Oh…" Hannah covered her face. She fought the urge to pace, not knowing just how big her protective bubble actually was. But she shook her head not wanting to believe that the symptoms slipped through her fingers. "I can't believe I didn't see this!"

"No, no…" Pete drew closer to comfort her. He placed his hand on her shoulder. She could feel the warmth emanating from it through her entire body and for an instant wondered if that's what her people felt. "You are not to blame. If you were still in your hospital environment, you would have seen this in an instant, I believe. But your focus has shifted and up until now, all you've had to do was heal, not diagnose."

"But… I could have…"

"Linda…" he paused and waited for her to look up at him. "… is in a better place now. We've got her and she will never hurt again. She sends you her regards, by the way."

Hannah chuffed, tears rolling down her face. "Really? She… you… I am… so glad then…"

"Linda has completed her purpose on this earth. But her brother..." Pete continued.

"Davy," Hannah breathed out, chills ran down her spine. "He's next..."

Pete nodded in confirmation. "It's already started."

"Oh no..." Hannah frowned again. "I can't get to him. She never brings him into the store."

"Let the..." he paused for the right wording, "un-gifted doctors take care of this one. And maybe even give them a heads up?"

"An anonymous tip?" The wheels were turning in Hannah's mind. She would call the police and ask them to look into "foul play" concerning Linda's death. "But... what if they don't listen?"

Pete let out a rare laugh, "Oh ye of little faith. We have people in all the right places."

"But..."

"Sometimes, we have to allow things to happen to reap a larger result."

Hannah nodded, accepting his answer. "Thank you... for..."

She looked away for only a second but when she turned back, he was gone. She blinked away the new raindrops tapping her face and felt the cool rain drip down her scalp into her shirt.

"Go out and do what you were meant to do..." she heard his voice from far away.

Hannah breathed in deeply feeling a contentment in her lungs, "I will… but first things first…" She pulled her cell phone out of her pocket and tapped in the number for the local police department.

"Nooo," Patty gasped, leaning back in her chair. "Noooo, that's just not possible." She reached over to grab her coffee from the side table as she continued to skim the newspaper. "I just can't believe it!"

"Patty, did you read the paper… oh…" Clam came in the side door into the office and saw her sister in the reception area. She walked over to the coffee counter, pouring herself some of the fresh brew, allowing her sister to keep reading uninterrupted.

Anxious for a conversation on the matter, Clam sat in the chair directly across the pretty little white wicker coffee table that had fresh cut flowers at its center. She waited as patiently as she could, sipping the entirely too hot coffee waiting for her sister's attention.

Finally, Patty folded the paper and slapped it on her lap. "You know," she began, "I had a feeling something like this was happening."

Clam was completely taken aback. "What? No you didn't," she challenged.

Patty proclaimed her innocence. "I did. I knew it all along. I just didn't want to believe it!"

Clam squinted her eyes at her one and only sister knowing the truth. "Did you know about the life insurance policies on her husband, and only *two* of her three children? What about that?"

"Why else would she commit such a heinous crime, if it wasn't for the money?"

Clam leaned back in her chair, "Antifreeze." She shook her head again, "The youngest daughter was in on it too." She leaned back in her chair. "What makes a person do such a thing?"

"Luckily, and I say that loosely, Sister, the youngest…"

"Crystal…"

"Yes, luckily, she kept a journal. She wrote everything down. Open and shut case. Open and shut."

"She didn't even try to deny anything. I remember when that little girl was born…" Clam was lost in memories. "They seemed like such a happy family."

"Larry. It was Larry that held that family together. Sandy was all for what she could get."

"I see that now… she never could hold down a job…" Clam nodded.

"Did you read they said Davy was going to be okay?" Patty asked.

She nodded again, not knowing what to say and having the hardest time allowing the news of their small town settle into her bones.

"I guess the Angel Wind has moved on," Patty said quietly, sipping her coffee.

"Or," Clam looked over at her, "it was the Angel Wind that protected the boy." There was a pause and then she added, "I can't believe something like this could happen in our small town."

"Or that a mother could do that to her own children."

The silence was heavy in the bright, homey office until the bells that hung over the main door jingled against one another, as Hannah entered the office.

"Hello ladies," Hannah smiled at the sisters.

"Oh hello," Patty greeted. She set the paper on the small table and rose to greet Hannah. "What can we do for you today?" She asked, automatically scanning the mail bins for anything addressed to their guest.

"I think I'll be checking out in the next week or so," Hannah told her.

"Oh no," Patty replied, sadly. "You'll miss the Christmas party. We were so hoping you were going to be here."

"I am sad to miss it for sure," Hannah said sincerely, "but I think it's time to move on. It's going to be getting cold soon and I'd like to head further south. I'm looking forward to spending my first winter not being cold," she laughed.

"We can understand that," Clam called out from her seat. "When I was in Colorado training horses for a time, I was happy to get back here to Virginia. Their winters made ours look tame!"

"I wasn't fond of our Indiana winters either," Hannah acknowledged. "I sure wouldn't want to go anywhere worse!"

"That's the beauty of a house on wheels," Patty added, "You can go anywhere. But it would be okay if you stayed here, too."

Hannah laughed, "Exactly. This is my first year of my mobile housing and I want to see everything! And since I've seen the ocean…"

"Oh yes," Patty nodded, knowingly. "You see, Sister? I told you…" She turned back to Hannah, "I knew you were going to love it."

"How could you not?" Hannah beamed.

"You'll stay for the festival though, won't you?

"It's this weekend, right?"

"Yes. I'll be making jelly for the contest, and Clam will be running the pony rides. You should definitely join us."

"You can only find the best kettle corn at festivals," Hannah admitted.

"Oh yes, and there is sure to be some vendors there. It's a wonderful time. Rides for the kids, crafts and food…"

"They are trying Crystal as an adult," Clam said, her face back in the newspaper.

Patty's face sobered, "Did you hear?"

Hannah nodded. "So sad. I never got a chance to meet Davy."

"He was such a happy boy. He hugged everyone," Patty smiled at the memory. "He used to come out and visit the horses."

"He's one of the reasons we started our program for kids and horses."

"Then, one day," Patty sighed, "Davy acted out... or... was just loud, actually and I think it embarrassed Sandy so much that he was never allowed to come out into public again. He still went to school, of course, but she never took him out."

"I'm glad he's getting the care he needs," Hannah offered. "The doctors will take good care of him and then he can get treatment for his special needs."

"Amen," Patty pursed her lips and nodded along with Hannah and Clam.

She shook her head out of her reverie, "So...," she pulled out Hannah's file. "When do you think your last day will be?"

"I've already given my two weeks notice to the store, so probably right after that." Hannah twisted her body sideways to see the upside-down calendar on the counter. "Maybe the... sixteenth?"

"Very well. I'll write it in pencil, in case you change your mind." Patty winked at her.

"Fair enough. I will miss your fine little town. A lot of really great people live here."

"And a few not-so-great," Clam chimed in.

Patty looked over at her sister and pointed a finger at her, "And those people are going to be dealt with."

Both the sisters nodded while Hannah thought, *I certainly hope so.*

"Hey, what about that guy that came in the other day, Patty? No offense, Hannah. When did he want to move in?"

Patty scrunched up her face at the thought. "Oh no, Sister, I don't think we want him here. He's not our kind of people. Besides, he was asking for a cabin…"

Patty shook her head, "Dirty… greasy… smelled like smoke… I sent him to the motel on the other side of town. Maybe he'll use the showers they offer…" she curled up her lip.

Clam leaned back and laughed knowing her sister all too well. "See what I have to live with? Sending customers away like that." Clam ribbed her sister good naturedly, but knew her sister was keen on first impressions and very protective of their little community. It was probably best they sent the man somewhere else.

Mindy was truly upset. The newspaper lay out on the break room table. She sat in silence until Hannah closed her locker and looked over at her. No words were spoken at first, but Hannah's look of concern took Mindy from her reverie.

"I… just don't know what to say."

Hannah nodded.

"Her own children." Mindy was deep in her head and was obviously troubled at the news of Sandy Bilikins being arrested for the death of her husband and oldest child with the intent to murder her son. "I thought I knew her. We all tried to help her… felt sorry for her 'troubles'," she air-quoted. Her face spoke of the battling emotions within her. "How could I not see…"

Hannah walked over to the small round table and sat beside Mindy taking her hand. "You are not to blame here. You did nothing wrong. You acted with empathy and kindness to a person who took advantage of you. It's not you who are to blame. Your goodness and kindness are never wrong choices. You can't control what other people do. You can only be the best person you can be. And you are, my friend. You are."

Mindy nodded, understanding as best she could, her lip trembling. "Thank you."

Hannah squeezed her hand before patting the table like a drum, "Well, let's see if I can do some damage out there today."

Mindy attempted a feeble smile, appreciating Hannah trying to lighten the mood.

Hannah grabbed a cart from the back room, ready to roll it out front and bumped it into the door frame.

Mindy couldn't help but laugh as Hannah turned back to look sheepishly at her. "It's okay, it's just office supplies. I don't think you can break those."

Hannah shrugged, "Let's not tempt fate."

Hannah smiled, knowing that despite the Bilikins, she would miss this little town. It's the exact kind of place she could have ended up staying in, if she was ever allowed to call a place home.

Hannah moved the dolly an entire aisle up from the discounted summer decorations.

"Christmas stuff already," she sighed. "I remember complaining about this as a consumer. Now, I'm just part of the problem," she giggled.

All morning she had been clearing the Thanksgiving items off the main attraction shelves and making room for the Christmas seasonal items.

"Hey," Kara called out to Hannah after catching a glimpse of her.

Hannah looked up at her and walked toward the front counter after she gave the signal to "come closer".

Would it kill her to come out from behind that counter? Hannah thought to herself. She walked around the gift card display, batteries and make-up to reach the lazy youth.

"Some guy was looking for you today," she said nonchalantly, while leaning against the cigarette display.

"A guy?" Hannah probed further.

"Yeah, some skeezy guy. You probably don't want to have anything to do with him, if you ask me. He just put off a really negative vibe."

Hannah stared blankly at her, never feeling so old in her life. "What did he want."

She shrugged.

"What did he say," she tried another route.

"Just asked if you worked here and if you were around."

Hannah waited to see if more information was coming, but apparently not on its own.

"Anything else?"

"Asked when you would be back."

She paused again... nothing. "And you said...?"

She shrugged. "I mean, I don't know your schedule."

Hannah nodded, trying not to get upset. "There's that," she said, perhaps a bit too sarcastically. "Do you remember what he looks like?"

She scrunched up her face, "Well, yeah. I only saw him a few hours ago."

Hannah sighed... "And?"

"Like... he was dirty. His hair was slicked back, probably from yesterday's sweat..." She curled up her lip at the remembering. "He *thought* he was really cool though. You know, like he thought if he hit on me, I'd be able to give him more info. Whatever, dude. In your dreams."

Hannah recalled the same type of description from the sisters at the campground, or at least the same facial expressions.

"Did he leave a name?"

"Naw."

"Did he say if he would be back?"

She shrugged. "Just asked about you, is all."

She nodded taking in the small bits of information she pried from Kara. "Thanks."

"Oh hey," she called after her, "He had a scar on his forehead."

Hannah furrowed her brow… *it couldn't be…*

Hannah went back to her boxes and used her box cutter to open the first box of spiral notebooks. As she was stacking the notebooks fighting her organizational anxiety to color code all the stacks, she stopped short. Her mind was suddenly racing.

The guy from Ohio… the P.I. from the gas station. Could he have found me?

She tried to calm her thoughts. That was months ago. That was several states ago. She chuffed. *Why would anyone…* She wasn't just anyone. She had a gift.

There is nothing like a country festival to heal the wounds of a community.

Hannah walked among the booths admiring all of the handmade items and listening to the Bluegrass music playing in the background.

The Virginia sun took pity on them today and delivered some mild temperatures and that really brought the crowds out.

Small rides were filled with giggling, squealing children. Lines were forming at the food trucks and snack booths and everyone was smiling.

While she stood in line waiting for the coveted, authentic kettle corn, she felt eyes on her. As she scanned the crowds of people, she noticed a man leaning against a firetruck that kids were climbing on. He unabashedly stared at her.

A lump formed in Hannah's throat as she recognized the man from Ohio. Her heart raced in her chest. Neither one of them moved, but made it clear that they were both aware of the other.

She watched him as he chuffed, the corners of his mouth curled up. He reached into his pocket to retrieve a cigarette and proceeded to light it. He glanced up at her again as he inhaled enflaming the end of the cigarette. She frowned as she watched him, not really knowing what to do.

Again, he reached into his pocket and pulled out a small, flat item and proceeded to unwrap its bright red paper casing. He let the wrapping fall to the ground. He lifted his head up to her, bobbing it as if to say, "See you around". He smiled at her and turned to walk away.

That… was weird, Hannah thought to herself. She looked over the crowd to see where he went but couldn't find him. Her line scooted forward. She smiled at people who caught her glances but continued her search. At last, she saw him walking toward the barn where Clam and Patty keep the horses and ponies for festival's events.

She looked up to the kettle corn counter… she was so close. Then she looked back over toward the stables. The man, *Randy, wasn't it?* disappeared inside.

She sighed out heavily and forfeited her place in line. I don't even know what I'm doing. What am I expecting to find… or prevent? She rolled her eyes… I was so close to…

Her thoughts froze as she entered the stable. There, at the other end was Randy. He was waiting for her.

He saw her. He waited for her to come a bit closer before turning out of the other exit. Hannah's thoughts were bolting in all directions. Why is he going toward the children's area? What is he trying to tell me?

She mustered up whatever bravery she had and made her way through the crowds of people milling around cooing over the horses.

She stepped back out into the bright sunshine and immediately saw him. He stood between the pony rides and a snowcone vendor. He squared off to face her. His stance spoke of confidence and purpose as he watched her. He drew into his cigarette and released the smoke before bringing the lit end down to meet his other hand. The smallest spark began and he tossed it to the ground into the pony's walking ring.

Hannah followed it to the ground and then realized what was happening. He smiled at her before retreating into a crowd of people.

She felt like her legs were moving through molasses. She pushed people aside as she raced toward the sparks. She was too late. A series of pops and bangs; mini explosions set the crowd screaming and racing in every direction. The skittish ponies reared and threw their innocent passengers to the ground. They stomped and kicked trying to break free from wheel and the noise of the firecrackers.

Hannah flew into action. A small boy, closest to her had been thrown and lay still on the ground. Hannah scooped him up in her arms and held him close to her until he could wake up and cry out to his mother. She helped a few of the others to their feet who suffered little damage, but healed them of their wounds as she did. A young girl lay still in her mothers arms. Hannah saw that the horse had come down and shattered her back. She would be paralyzed. Hannah bent down to comfort the mother, saying, "Help is on its way," knowing while she rested her hand on the child, the bones were fusing back to where they belonged.

Luckily the damage was minimal and quickly brought back into balance. Hannah was furious. *How dare he!* What was he trying to prove?

He was no where in sight as Hannah scanned the faces in the crowd as they were trying desperately to calm themselves and get back to celebrating the day. Everyone was alright, no real damage was done. What was he doing, testing her? But Hannah then saw Clam. She was sitting against the stable, her arm folded over her stomach. To glance at her, she appeared to be sleeping. But Hannah saw beneath the surface. Her ribs were broken. She was bleeding out internally. She had been kicked by one of the frantic horses. She swallowed hard and made her way through the people.

"Clam," Hannah knelt beside her. "Clam, can you hear me?"

She attempted to raise her head to respond to the voice, but could not.

"Shh…. Shhh… it's okay. Don't move. I'm going to help you. Hannah placed her hand behind Clam's head and rested the other on her stomach. Within minutes, Clam took in a deep breath as if she were starving for air, followed by a second and a third.

She sat straight and held her head up on her own and stared at Hannah in disbelief.

"Are you alright?" Hannah asked her.

"It was you." A tear slipped down the older woman's face. "It was you all along. You're the Angel Wind."

Hannah smiled and tried to laugh it off. "Don't be silly. You're going to be okay," she nodded. She looked back over her shoulder to the line of kids standing around. "You have people waiting for you."

"Oh no," Clam shook her head, "I'm sure I'm ruined. People won't trust the horses again…"

Hannah stood up and held out her hand. "Look for yourself."

There was, indeed a gathering of children waiting for their chance to give the ponies another chance.

Clam accepted the outstretched hand and lifted herself to her feet.

"People understand the animals reacted to a prank. They know what good care you take of these precious creatures. Go on, show them that they can be trusted again."

"What about you?" Clam looked back at her. "Do they know?"

Hannah shrugged. "It'll be our secret."

"I guess you'll…"

"It was time for me to leave anyway."

Clam nodded, understanding, and went back to the kids and the animals she adored.

Hannah took in a deep breath and quietly stepped away from the scene that had barely been a blip in the events. A forgotten moment. Hannah reacted so quickly that the people barely recognized the severity of the incident.

That man, however... Randy Gunter, is no longer someone to take lightly.

Hannah walked to her trusty Bounder and saw a note tucked under the windshield. She stretched up on her toes to reach it.

"It is a pleasure watching you work," it said. "We'll meet again." It was signed, "Randy".

Hannah was not afraid. She stared off into the distance, determined. "Catch me if you can," she spoke into the summer breeze.

Chapter Fourteen

Thoughts swirled around in Hannah's head as she backed the Bounder to its new spot for... however long. "Who does he think he is?" she spoke to no one as she threw the drive shaft into park a little more roughly than necessary.

She pictured him lighting the fireworks to set off a reaction, knowing that she would respond. "What am I, your own personal wind-up dancing monkey?" She could not calm her anger. "What a coward! Skulking around in the shadows. What does he want? Just come out and say it! Do it!" She picked up a couch pillow that had fallen to the floor in the journey and threw it at the couch. "I'm not doing this anymore! I'm not going to live in fear! I have a purpose! A job to do!" She pushed the button to open the slides expanding the size of her tiny home.

When her little home was set up with water and the amenities, she ventured out into the community.

She found herself "on the other side of the tracks", so to speak. The homes here were in poor condition, the basketball hoop had no net and the fence around the court was broken and neglected. As she walked on, her heart softened. There were really no people around that she could see, which gave an eerie feeling that the neighborhood was abandoned; but knew otherwise as every once in a while, a curtain would flutter or a human would retreat to the back of a home not wanting to acknowledge the stranger in their midst.

The attitude she began her walk with was melting away. She had never lived an impoverished life and was immediately grateful for all the ways she was blessed. She admitted that she got into her own head sometimes and only focused on the things that were hurting her and the suffering that she has been through, but forgetting that others suffer too. Medically, she could see and address that, because that was her area of healing, but... this... she wished she could heal these people the ways they most needed.

As she walked, she came across a man who was slumped against a brick building next to his cardboard castle. There were clothes draped over it to create a door flap as well as a means to dry the clothes. He had a shopping cart that was filled to overflow with items, trinkets and scraps of this and that.

The closer she got to him, she saw that his body was riddled with the effects of alcohol poisoning. His liver... his kidneys, were barely functioning. His body had to be showing him signs of the condition.

Her heart went out to him and she approached.

He woke up and saw her come his direction, but said nothing. He watched, wondering what she was going to do. He frowned and sat up a little straighter.

"What? You got a problem?" he spat out, protecting his space.

She shook her head and came closer still.

"Listen lady, what's your deal? Never seen a homeless person before?"

She was not rebuffed by his tone, nor did she feel fear of any kind. "It's... your liver..."

"What's it to you?"

"I want to help." She reached him and crouched along side of his stretched out body.

"Well, you can help me by gettin me a beer."

"You could be ... so much more..." she looked into his face and saw the blood vessels expanded beyond their capacity. "You are worth..."

"Oh, I get it. You're one of those churchy people that want to save my soul, that it? Well, save your preachin' sister. I ain't buyin'"

Hannah couldn't help but snicker. "No, that's not my gift, only you can make those changes when you're ready. But..." she placed her hand on his knee, "I can help you in another way."

His eyes widened as the healing power spread through his body. His face returned to its pre-drug usage state. His teeth filled out and his lungs expanded. He took in that big deep breath. Hannah smiled but was not expecting his response.

He scrambled away from her still pressed against the wall. "What the…" His hands patted his body and fingers went in his mouth. "What did you do to me, you freak?"

She stood up, confused. She had never had this kind of reaction.

"Seriously, what the hell?" he stood up and continued to grapple with his new gift.

"I've healed you."

"What? Why? I didn't ask you…"

"I know. It's a gift. Now you can…"

"What? Now I can… what? Get back into society? Get back into the daily-frickin' grind? Forget that!"

Hannah didn't know how to respond.

"I've been there and done that, lady. I ain't goin' back. You think just because you can do this weird, freaky thing, that you're God's gift to everyone? You're not! I don't want your stupid gift!"

He was pacing and throwing his arms up.

"But you're not suffering and the pain…"

"The PAIN reminds me that I'm still STUCK here in this HELLHOLE," he shouted and turned to walk away, but thought of something else. He spun back around on her. "Let me tell you something…" he walked up close to her and leaned into her personal space only inches from her face, "… there are many kinds of suffering. And you took away the armor that I built around mine. You look at me, like I am some kind of pity project. I used to live in your world. Had the nine ta five and the two point five kids…" he swallowed hard, his voice got quiet. "Didn't work out so well for me. Not even you can fix this pain."

Hannah looked back at his pain with sympathetic eyes.

"Hey, it's cool you have this gift, but believe it or not, some people don't want it." He stepped back from her and looked at her a moment longer, his face looking at her with contempt. Finally, mercifully, he turned and walked away, cursing as he went. "I didn't ask for this!" he yelled from a half a block away. "Go back where you belong!"

Hannah squeezed her forehead and closed her eyes, fighting back tears. She stood there a moment more not knowing how to process what had just happened, and then she looked around her, feeling... guilt... shame? She was just trying to help. Why wouldn't someone want to be healthy and part of a community...

He was broken inside... just like you were...

Hannah spent the next few days holed up inside her RV. Her confidence was shaken. "To heal or not to heal... who knew that was a question," she said out loud, to her quiet, dank little home. Putting effort into the day just didn't seem like an option. Her inside voice was quiet. Pete was quiet. She didn't really know what to do.

"I've never really tried that option…" she continued on that train of thought.

And without further introspection, she hopped up from laying on her couch, grabbed a beach chair, scribbled a note on a sheet of paper and headed out the door.

This particular campsite was within walking distance to the beach. A small sandy path lead from the grounds to a small section of perfect, not heavily trafficked beach. This would be the perfect spot if she wanted more alone time to think or just appreciate the ebb and flow of the waves, but today… she was seeking people. Hurting people. Hurting people who WANTED to be healed.

She followed the path onto the beach and walked toward the boardwalk. Here, there were shops and restaurants and people. All kinds of people.

She set out her chair just prior to stepping on the main dock, and propped up her flimsy sign: I CAN HEAL YOU.

She sat in her beach chair and waited.

Hannah watched the tourists walk in and out of the shops. They would pass her chair, read her sign and walk on by, while she just smiled and inventoried their illnesses.

"You have a stomach ulcer… You have arthritis… you have a dependency on pain medications… Huh… you have migraines." She kept her voice low, but shook her head knowing she could heal all these bodies walking past her. "Ooo… sunburn, dude, you should let me take care of that for you." All kinds of people. Hardly any of them had a clean bill of health.

As she people watched, starting to get bored, thinking this was a terrible idea, someone came running up to her.

"Hey! Hey! Miss!"

Hannah looked over her shoulder at him.

"I... I need your help.... My dad... he's having a heart attack!"

Hannah jumped from her chair and followed the man to an outdoor patio. A crowd had gathered around an older man, lying on his back the color draining from his face. Someone had unbuttoned his top buttons and, someone else was attempting CPR.

Hannah pushed her way through the people with the son leading the way. "Stop," she called out to the "helpful" CPR provider. "That's not helping him." He moved out of the way so Hannah could kneel down beside him.

She placed her hands on his heart and closed her eyes. In moments, he took in a deep breath and opened his eyes to look at her.

"What... what just happened?"

"Dad! Are you okay?" The son appeared on his other side.

"You should be fine now... no more heart trouble." Hannah smiled and rose to her feet.

The crowd went silent and separated allowing her to pass. She smiled and quietly made her way back out of the restaurant.

She walked back to her chair with no one stopping her or saying a thing. She could feel eyes on her as she sat back down and watched the water, waiting for something to happen.

It wasn't long before the father and son came out. The father reached out his hand to her. "I didn't get to thank you for saving my life."

Hannah stood up to look him in the eyes. "You're welcome. I am happy to do it. Take care of yourself now," she smiled.

"Do I ... owe you anything?" the son asked.

Hannah shook her head. "Not a thing."

He smiled uncomfortably, wishing he could do more. "Then, thank you. Thank you for saving my father." He thrust out his hand which she warmly grasped. He pulled her into a hug.

"Here. Take this," the father said opening up his wallet.

"No... no, thank you. That's not..."

"Then I'll just leave it right here." He folded a few twenties and tucked them in the drink holder of her chair. "I'm not sure what the going rate is for a new heart, but I know I could never afford it. Please... take it and accept my deepest gratitude."

Hannah smiled and nodded. The two walked away from her. She noticed people watching, but she was not helping anyone if they didn't want her help.

She pouted to herself trying to justify this new attitude and flopped back down into her chair and crossed her arms. She didn't have long to wait…

It wasn't long before a few people timidly approached. And then a few more until a line began to form. Someone had set down a colorful sand pail beside her chair and now it overflowed with cash.

So many forms of cancer. Healed.

Diabetes. Healed.

Heart Disease. Healed.

Crohn's Disease. Healed.

High blood pressure and all of its symptoms… healed.

Headaches, indigestion, flu strains, kidney disease, liver disease… and everything in between… from the youngest to the oldest. If they were coming to her and asking for help, she would help them.

She was on a roll.

A crowd began to form and surrounded her, still giving her space to work, unlike the diner. They all just wanted to watch. A few would call out from the crowd, "She's a fake!" Others would call her an Angel. The people in the lines didn't care to whom they were selling their souls, only that they walked away without pain.

"Hey! That guy didn't pay!" a man yelled out from the front edges of the crowd.

Hannah wasn't paying attention, she just went on to the next person in line.

"Hey! Hey you! You didn't put anything in the pail, buddy. You think you get something for nothing?"

The man stopped. Still meek in his healed human skin. He had been sick for a very long time, and his brain hadn't caught up to the miracle. His face shown the guilt he felt.

"Hey, buddy," the first man faced-off with him and pushed his shoulder.

He took the blow and did not retaliate.

"You didn't put anything in the pail," the bully poked at his shoulder, enunciating every word.

"I… I don't have anything," the man shrugged. "I have nothing."

The bully pushed him down and pulled his wallet from his pocket. The wallet was indeed empty. It held a faded photo of what looked like a happy family at one point.

"I've been ill for … so long. I have… nothing left," he said, while still on the ground. "Insurance dropped me. Medical bills kept piling up. I lost my job… my family…"

"Get off him!" Another man pulled the bully back with a rough shove.

"Leave him alone!" a woman called toward the scuffle.

"Back off, lady, I'm just trying to keep order here!"

"Who put you in charge?" someone else yelled.

The police who were hovering around the edges, finally came forward to attend to the situation that seemed to be escalating.

The police deftly removed the cause of the distraction and slowly moved in closer to the miracle-worker.

A woman who had patiently waited in line, came forward to Hannah.

Before she could speak, Hannah smiled at her.

"I have been in pain for several weeks. I haven't been able to keep any food down and my chest hurts… here." She pointed to the base of her sternum. Acid reflux.

Hannah reached out her hand to the woman. "I'm afraid I can't heal you."

The woman swallowed hard, thinking the worst.

"Your suffering will get worse before it gets better, but I promise you, at the end of about…" she tipped her head to the side looking at the woman's mid-section, "… thirty weeks or so, it will be worth all of it." She smiled again. "You're expecting a baby."

"Really? Really?" The woman moved forward and threw her arms around Hannah. "I didn't think I could get pregnant… we've tried for so long…" Tears spilled over her eyes. "Thank you."

Hannah held her hands up, "Oh no, I had nothing to do with this," she laughed, and the people closest to them laughed along.

The woman dropped some money onto the pile and exited the line.

A police officer came up to Hannah while two others blocked the next person in line.

"I'm sorry ma'am, you're gonna have to call it a night."

Hannah looked up at him and nodded, almost gratefully. She was so tired.

"What? You can't do that!" The man who would have been next yelled out. "I've been waiting here for hours! That's not fair."

"She's leaving…"

"She's leaving?"

"The police are stopping her…"

"They're making her leave…"

"That's unconstitutional!"

"What about me?"

"The police are bullying her! Screw them!"

"I've been waiting!"

The whispers turned to panic. And Hannah stood still not knowing what to do.

The line was now closing into a crowd that began to push into each other.

"What about me!"

"But I need you!"

"That's not fair! The shouts came from everywhere.

The two officers were feeling the pressure of the pressing crowd. One spoke into her shoulder radio . It chirped back, "Sending backup. ETA seven minutes."

The crowd pushed against the resistance, feeling cheated and betrayed. People holding their cell phones, filming all of the action, while Hannah's heart rate went up reliving the emotions from the diner.

An officer scooped up her cash and stuffed it into the pail and grabbed her beach chair. He hooked his hand with her elbow. "Come with me."

Holland, his name tag said, tugged her toward the parking lot where the additional police cars had just pulled in.

The crowd wailed against the movement and nearly toppled the officers trying to get to Hannah.

The ones caught up in the motion who were weak, were pushed to the side, stepped over and stepped on.

Hannah looked back over her shoulder at the throngs of people trying to get to her. She watched as if in slow motion, the hoard pushing past her only protection, arms reaching for her, just wanting to touch her.

Officer Holland opened the back door and threw in her chair and bucket of money, but just before she was able to climb in, like a wave from the ocean, she was slammed into the side of the vehicle, closing the door. The officer holding her wrapped himself around her creating a human shield while hands reached in touching her and bodies pressed against him. He braced himself around her by locking his arms against the car. Her back pressed against his stomach, she curled herself as inward as she could.

Finally, the back-up officers created a path as they not-too-gently, tossed people to the side trying to make their way through. Upon reaching Hannah and Officer Holland, they picked the leaches off enough to allow the girl a chance to fall into the back of the squad car. Holland nodded his head to them in gratitude.

"Get her outta here," one of them yelled over the din, "We've got this."

Holland made his way to the driver's side and flipped on the blue and red lights, giving the sirens a quick "Whoop whoop" letting the crowd know that the vehicle was going to move whether they got out of the way or not.

The car inched its way through the parking lot; the last person of the crowd finally in the rearview mirror.

Holland adjusted the mirror to see Hannah. He furrowed his brow trying to analyze her expression and body language.

Was it sham? She certainly didn't look like a charlatan. But a healer? A miracle-working healer? Could there be such a thing? He's been at this job for a lot of years and have seen a lot of things, but this was new territory for him. She didn't give him any attitude... there was no defiance... other than fear, what?

When they had driven for a few minutes, and the sun had set completely, she seemed to calm down and unclench her hands from her elbows. Her arms were wrapped across her body in self-preservation.

Holland intermittently looked at her in the mirror while watching the road.

"So, what's your story?" he asked.

Her eyes were downcast and her head tipped away. She shrugged her shoulders.

"You had to know I was gonna ask."

She stole a look at him in the mirror.

"I mean, I just saved your life. You could at least tell me who I saved."

Guilt. He saw guilt flash across her face.

She straightened in her seat and clenched her leg muscles uncomfortably.

"Hannah," she barely whispered. She cleared her throat and said it again. "My name is Hannah."

"Hannah," he smiled at her. "And all that stuff out there…"

She looked away. "I'm so sorry that happened. I didn't mean… it wasn't…" She took in a deep breath and let out a heavy sigh. "I wasn't thinking."

"So… what… uh… are you for real?"

She caught his gaze in the mirror. She nodded. She could see his face cloud with confusion as to whether he could buy into such a thing or not.

She dipped her eyes down again before raising them to his. "Your body…" she began, "while you look fit from the outside, you are killing yourself on the inside." Her face told him that she knew of his steroid use.

"I don't know what you're talking about."

"Your body is trying to decide if it will send you a heart attack or a stroke first. Your kidneys are under too much stress and your liver is filled with so many cysts that you are one rupture away from death."

His face frowned. He looked back and forth from the road to the mirror in short bursts. He was agitated. "How do I know you're not lying?"

"How would I know what to lie about?"

He was quiet for a moment longer.

She drew her eyes back up to his and confronted his thoughts, "You know I'm not lying."

It was his turn to break away from her scrutinizing gaze. She could feel him warring internally.

"And you … you could… make all that disappear?"

"I can. And I will, but it's not going to help you if you continue with the same patterns. You'll end up right back to where you are now."

"I've only been using for…"

Hannah cocked an eyebrow, discouraging him from continuing forward with the lie he was about to tell.

"I will. I'll change. I promise."

"You don't have to promise to me… I am just a moment in time in your life. You're the one that has to live with yourself… and be there for those who depend on you."

"Seriously, who are you?"

She shrugged. "I'm just a woman who was given a gift, but still finding her way around how to use it."

His thoughts were going in every direction. What would *he* do if he had such a gift? His heart softened toward her. "You must get lonely."

Her eyes glistened with moisture. He touched a nerve. She blinked and a tear slipped down her cheek.

She self-consciously wiped away the tear and shook off the wave of sadness. "Where are you taking me?" she asked.

"Well, I was just driving around to make sure no one was following us and then… I figured you'd tell me where you live so I could take you there."

"Oh," she chuffed. "I thought I was in trouble."

"No, you were clearly the victim here… if you are what you say you are. But if not, I'm gonna take you down to the station and lock you up. We don't take kindly to snake oil salesmen," his voice switched to a thick southern twang.

"You're going to run me out of town?" she finally smiled.

"Tarred and feathered."

She chuffed again. The squad car was quiet with just the dashboard's glow giving them enough light to catch each other's expressions.

"I really am sorry about tonight."

He shrugged his uniformed shoulders. "We don't get much excitement here. It's good practice for my guys."

She shook her head and looked down at her hands in her lap. The floor was covered in bills. Twentys, tens, ones… If they let her keep the money, it should hold her over for a bit. She shook her head again. *What an idiot I am*, she thought.

"If I were you, I'd probably lay low for a while."

She nodded in agreement.

"You're about to 'go viral', as the kids say."

She closed her eyes and shook her head again. *Stupid. So stupid.*

"If you want, I can get some protective detail on you for a few days."

She blew out a deep breath puffing her cheeks out. "I'll be alright. I should probably move on."

He nodded. "I think it might be best."

His radio squawked interrupting their otherwise quiet ride. "10-65 at Litzinger and Maple. 10-52 en route. Be advised, gunman is armed and dangerous."

He looked back over his shoulder. "Hope you don't mind a detour."

Before she could answer, he flipped the lights on and the sirens were blaring as he took a sharp left at the next corner.

"There's an injury," he spoke over the siren's wail toward the back seat. "Maybe you could help us out?"

She nodded silently, gripping the seat cushion to brace for the unexpected turns.

When they arrived at the scene of a small corner convenience store, two other cars were there and the screeching of another, higher pitched siren let her know that an ambulance was on its way.

"Stay here." He opened the door with his hand on his holster and bolted toward the building.

Officer Holland seemed to be gone for hours when it was really only a few moments. He came out of the shop's front door and waved for Hannah to join him.

She stepped gingerly out of the car and walked toward the building. She could smell the blood from the open door. She saw the growing pool seeping beyond the edge of the counter. Without hesitation, she sprung into action. She rounded the corner and saw an Asian woman propping up an older man against her knees. She was crying, rocking back and forth speaking another language.

Hannah knelt down in front of them and saw the bullet lodged in the man's lung. She frowned, wondering how the bullet was going to come out, but she trusted her gift and lay both hands over the open, bleeding wound.

The bleeding stopped and in a few more moments the Asian man with long white hair drew in a deep breath.

Hannah gasped and pulled her hands back. She turned her fist over and opened her fingers, there, in the palm of her hand, was the bullet.

She looked just as amazed as the others witnessing the event.

"I'll be damned…" Officer Holland spoke just behind her. "Brooks," he called out. "Take this bullet as evidence."

The ambulance pulled up and the medics came rushing in with a stretcher. They lifted the man even through his protests. "I'm fine. I do not need to go."

Hannah stepped aside, quietly. Her heart missed this kind of adrenaline rush from her days of actually working at the hospital, before she could skip the guess-work and get straight to the healing.

The crime scene quieted down, all the commotion was finished and people returned to their lives… Officer Holland opened the back door of his vehicle for Hannah to slide in. "Thanks for … doin that."

"That's what I'm supposed to be doing, I think." Hannah hugged her arm, feeling guilty.

He slipped in the front seat and sat quiet for a moment. "We sure could use someone like you around here. You could do a lot of good."   He was half-heartedly looking over his shoulder.

"I'll think about it.   Having a place to call home… sounds nice."

"I can get you on the payroll… the pay is going to be crappy, but… you know, we don't do what we do to get rich."

She nodded, confirming the sentiment.

They drove in silence as he took her to the campground and delivered her to the front office.

He got out of the car, grabbed her chair and bucket of cash and walked around to the passenger side to open the door for her.

"You sure you don't want me to take you to your door? That's a lot of cash," he said, handing her the bucket.

"It's three o'clock in the morning," she looked up at him smiling. "I'm just down a short walk."

He nodded. "Thanks again for your help tonight." He pulled out a business card from his wallet. "If… if you're serious about … making a home here, reach out, 'kay?"

She nodded, promising to give it sincere thought.

"And… for all those people you helped yesterday, in case they didn't thank you, please accept my gratitude for them. Sometimes, we forget the small civilities."

"You're welcome. I wish I could have helped them all."

He chuffed, "That line would have never ended. We're all broken in some way."

She nodded and looked up to his eyes. "I know."

He held her gaze for a moment and when she looked away, she reached out her hand and placed it on his chest. Her brow furrowed as things didn't seem to be moving very quickly, but then chalked it up to his flack jacket. She set her bucket aside, dropping both hands and shook them out. She grabbed both of his hands and held them in hers, closed her eyes and concentrated.

He gave the tell-tale response of a deep cleansing breath and Hannah took a step back. He kept a hold of her hands. She looked into his eyes again.

Officer Holland looked down at her, confused. He squeezed her hands.

"I… promise… I'll get healthy. I'll never use again."

She smiled. "I'll hold you to it."

"You'd better." He stood in his space and looked at her a moment longer. He released her hands, a little embarrassed, not realizing he still held them. "Sorry. Sorry… I guess you'll be needing those," he stumbled over his words.

She laughed and blushed.

He started back toward the driver's side of his car but then stopped to look at her one more time. "There really are still miracles out there."

She nodded again, "Yes, Officer Holland. There are."

He came back over to her again and reached out his hand, "Kyle. It's Kyle. Thank you… for everything."

"You're welcome." She smiled and picked up her beach chair that was leaning against the car and tucked her bucket of money in the crook of her arm and started walking down the dark street with dim lights barely showing the way.

He watched her for a few minutes once he slid into the driver's seat and turned over the engine when she turned the corner.

Hannah reached the RV feeling mixed emotions. "A place to stay… a place to start over…" she spoke softly into the night. It warmed her. She felt guilty at her flagrant display on the beach and hoped it wouldn't come back to haunt her. She chuffed, already knowing that it would, but… how bad…

The welcoming glow of light over her door reminded her of how tired she really was. There was a business card tucked into the window of her door.

She stepped up the bottom step to read it. "You were sloppy today. So very unbecoming. R.G."

Hannah wasted no time in packing up and pulling out. She stopped for gas just on the outskirts of the quaint little beach town and as she was paying for her gas at the counter she happened to look down at the early morning paper.

She leaned over to get a better view and the boy behind the counter commented, "Just delivered. Pretty weird, huh?"

The big bold lettering at the top of the fold read "Angel or Demon. Did you get saved or sell your soul... or did you just get taken?"

When she stood back up and looked at the teenager he suddenly recognized her. "It's... it's you..."

She pursed her lips and sighed, "Yep, it sure is." Her eyes dipped down to his chest and she added. "And you need to quit smoking."

His jaw dropped and guilt covered his face. "I don't..." She glanced up at him, stopping his sentence. "I hardly... how did you know."

"Look, if you quit now, your lungs will heal themselves in a few weeks. If you don't, you're headed down a long and painful path, and I probably won't be back out this way, so... do me a favor. Quit now."

With his mouth still hanging open, he nodded vigorously. She grabbed her change from his extended hand and left the store.

She got her RV out onto the open highway headed in a south westerly direction, not really knowing where she would go next.

Without warning, the tears began streaming down her face. Pain and anguish and loneliness bubbled to the surface and were released into big crocodile tears. She could barely see the lines on the road, much less appreciate the pinks and yellows that spread across the sky from the sun bringing light to the day. Finally her vision blurred to the point that she either had to stop crying and focus or pull over and let the jag run its course. She saw a rest area and abruptly pulled in. The rows were mostly taken up with truckers and their rigs grabbing a little shut eye while en route to their deliveries, but she was able to slip into one of the long parking spaces. She threw the vehicle into park and it was only seconds later that the real purging began.

Her breath came in short bursts as the tears poured out. She covered her face and sobbed. "I didn't ask for this!" she whimpered. "I want my own life back! I want my husband! I want my children! You picked the wrong person!" Her jagged breaths trying to get air to her lungs only caused coughs and more sobs.

The crying slowed and she wiped her face with her hands. She was feeling empty; defeated. She dropped her head back against the headrest and closed her eyes. "I… am not the right person for this…"

Using the steering wheel to pull herself to her feet, she slid out of the driver's chair and out her side door.

She flung open the door of the rest stops facility, and scanned the room. The people coming and going, filling the vending machines with their money. She assessed each one... so many diseases. "They don't even know they are killing themselves." She massaged her forehead and added, "They DO know... they just don't care."

"Did you know Moses had a stutter?" She heard the familiar voice of Paschar but did not see him anywhere. She looked around the room, waiting for him to show himself, but he didn't.

"He doesn't need you to be perfect..."

"Where are you?" she whispered into the cavernous room. The people mingled around her on their way to somewhere. She stood in the center of the room full of people trying not to see their wounds. The tears began again.

"He just needs you to be willing..."

She covered her face and slipped into the women's restroom.

A mother stood by the sink soaking paper towels with cool water from the faucet. Her son, maybe six years old stood next to her wearing his pajamas and had a comforter draped around his shoulders.

He was burning up with fever.

Hannah's heart fell to her stomach. She wiped her face and chin and made her way to the boy.

"Aw," she said nonchalantly to the mother. A sentiment she'd already heard several times in the last few minutes as she tried to comfort her son.

Hannah added, "Fever, huh?"

The mother nodded. "It just doesn't want to break."

Hannah caressed the boy's head and spoke to him, "Hang in there, buddy. You'll feel better soon."

Hannah could see that the mother was next in line; that the strain had already passed on to her, so Hannah patted the woman's shoulder. "Hang in there, Momma." She disappeared into one of the stalls, so as not to be "that creepy person" when she heard they boy say, "I'm feeling much better."

Hannah smiled, realizing the change in her emotions. Because of her, that little boy was no longer in pain. *I hear you,* she thought. *Please don't answer me while I'm in the bathroom. That's just wrong.*

"It's you! Oh my gosh… it's really you!"

A woman with a small child clinging to her leg stopped in front of Hannah as she was exiting the rest stop building.

She paused, quickly scanning the woman and the child for their wounds. Nothing, really. Poor diet at the worst.

"I… I can't believe it. I've been following your page… and… and… I can't believe it."

Hannah looked at her confused. "My… page?"

"Your Facebook page," she answered.

Hannah shook her head, still not understanding.

The mother, pulled up her cell phone and opened her Facebook app. She scrolled while Hannah stood there in both panic and curiosity.

"Here… see? That's you… You are Hannah, right?"

Hannah furrowed her brow leaning in to see the lit up screen, not confirming or denying the woman's question.

There was a group page titled Finding Hannah. Below it were photos of her in various stages of her incognito. Which apparently did nothing in helping her stay hidden. She took the phone from the woman and couldn't help but stare. This whole time… she thought she was being so clever…

Photos. Videos. Comments.

"She saved my life."

"If I had only known, I could have thanked her."

"My baby is alive today because of her."

"I thank God every day for Hannah."

"My son calls her his Angel…"

"I saw her in PA where she saved seven people from a car accident…" *It was only four,* Hannah recalled, but…

"Where can I find her?   My father is dying of pancreatic cancer…"

"If you see her, tell her we miss her here in Virginia…"

"#FindingHannah"

"She's amazing. She could use her gift for gain, but chooses to use it for good. We love her so much. If you are ever in Corpus Christi, Texas, we will hide you."

"There is such a thing as miracles, and we witnessed one…"

"She saved my gramma…"

Hannah's throat tightened and she could hardly swallow the lump that formed. Her heart felt like it skipped a beat… or two.   She looked up at the woman, "I… had no idea…"

"So… it's all true?" the woman ventured.

Hannah took in a deep shaking breath not sure what was meant to happen now, but she nodded.

The woman broke down in tears. "Oh… thank God." She trembled and almost fell but Hannah caught her.

"My… my daughter…" she sobbed, "she has leukemia. The doctors have told us that we are running out of options for her. We drive three hours, twice a week for her care. And this…" her voice caught, "for some reason…" she could barely speak for crying.   "For some reason…" she pushed through, "we decided to stop here on our way home."

Hannah's heart went out to her, she was obviously in deep pain.

"And… you are here…" The woman reached out and collected Hannah's hands in her own. "Please, can you help my little girl?   I don't meant to be…. I… don't want to presume…." The woman bent over and clutched her knees trying to contain her tears.   When she stood up, more composed, she continued, "Her name is Sofie. She is a good kid. She is a good student… so smart…"

Hannah looked down at the child grasping on to the mother's pant legs and winked at her. The child smiled shyly and buried her face into the denim.

Hannah stood up tall and squared off her shoulders. She reached out and grabbed the woman's hands attempting to calm her. "I would be happy to help."

She followed the woman to her wine colored sedan and they went to the passenger side.

The younger sister pointed to the door and bravely said, "My sissy's in there."

Hannah nodded. "Can I see her?"

The little girl tried in vain to pry open the door with the car handle until Hannah helped.

The passenger seat was set as far back as it could go and a pre-teen lay still with her legs bent, just trying to find a comfortable position. She was sound asleep piled high with blankets. Hannah could tell her smooth bald head and eyebrow-less face had seen it's fair share of chemo. She covered most of her head with a turquoise colored bandana. Sofie was unaware that the door had even been opened.

Hannah grimaced at the amount of damage the deadly disease had already done to her body coupled with the poison of the chemo still glowing from the inside out.

The mother was on the other side of the open door allowing Hannah space. "You can help her, can't you? She is in so much pain… I just don't… don't know what to do for her." She wiped away the tears from under her eyes, as if there were any makeup left to salvage. "I would do anything…"

Hannah reached out and touched her shoulder "It's going to be okay." She nodded. When she knelt down, the younger sister climbed onto Hannah's knees and Hannah helped her adjust.

"Do you want your sister to feel better?" Hannah asked.

"Yeah. I got a new movie. It's *Frozen* and Mommy said she can watch it with me when she gets better."

Hannah nodded the importance of sharing such a thing. "Can you help me?"

The little girl bobbed her head, confidently.

"Put your hand on mine," Hannah instructed. The small hand along with Hannah's rested on Sofie's chest. They stayed perfectly still while the healing took place. Then suddenly Sofie took in a deep breath and her eyelids fluttered open. She jumped at the sight of her situation.

In a raspy voice, she spoke, "You're really real…"

"I helped!" the younger sister proclaimed.

Sofie's eyes opened wide and she sat up in her seat. "Oh my gosh. This feels so amazing!" She patted down her body with her hands. "Oh my gosh. Oh my gosh…" She reached out and wrapped her arms around Hannah's neck squeezing her tight getting the little one caught in the middle.

"Hey! Ow! You're squishing me!" she complained.

Hannah returned the embrace and smiled as Sofie released her. She stood to get out of the way so the mother could get to her daughter.

While mother and daughter embraced, Hannah got the younger sibling out of squishing range. "You help take care of your sister, okay?"

She nodded solemnly and Hannah set her down on her feet.

Hannah attempted to walk back to her RV when Sofie called out, "Wait!" She threw off the covers and attempted to get out of the car. Her mother cautioned her to stay put. "I'm fine, mom. Really. I don't feel any pain at all. Like… At. All."

"But you don't want to…"

Hannah looked at the mother. "She is healed. Completely. There is no disease left in her system."

The look of disbelief and gratitude mixed on the mother's face. "How can I…"

Hannah shook her head, "No need."

"Thank you… you've… I can't thank you enough. I will continue to pray for you."

Hannah swallowed hard. "Thank you. I need that."

Sofie leapt from the car and flung her arms around Hannah again almost knocking her off balance. "You are the coolest human ever." She pulled back and adjusted her bandana.

"Don't worry," Hannah offered looking up to her pale white bare scalp, "it will grow back quickly."

She shrugged, "I don't even care. I felt like my body was a prisoner and someone else had control of it. I… couldn't do anything."

"Now," Hannah paused, and smiled, "… you can do everything. Don't let this gift go to waste. Live your life to the fullest."

"Oh, I will," she beamed. "Oh hey! Mom! Take our picture!"

Hannah stiffened. "I don't know if that's such a good idea…"

"But…"

Sofie's mom intervened. "She's has to stay unnoticed as much as possible. It keeps her safe."

"But what if we just…"

"Let's be grateful for all she's already given you."

Humbled, Sofie nodded. "You're right. I'm sorry. I will never forget you." Sofie leaned in for another hug before stepping back from her. "Thank you."

Hannah nodded, her words caught in her throat. She turned to walk away and heard Sofie call out behind her. "I'm totally gonna post this though… I mean… as soon as you are far enough away."

Hannah laughed and turned back giving her a thumb's up.

Chapter Fifteen

Hannah walked along the wooded areas that surrounded her new South Carolina home. She hadn't looked for a job, or even gone into town as yet, she just needed a few days alone. The weight of her gift was heavy on her shoulders. There were so many emotions surrounding such responsibility and apparently, she wasn't allowed to just... not participate. Her own Facebook page... people she's helped... people looking for her help. What was she supposed to do with this information?

She plucked a leaf from a tree and ran it through her fingers, twisting it, smoothing it... just like her thoughts.

Lost and alone in this tropical paradise feeling calm, until she heard a faint noise. She stopped and looked around her. She saw nothing but trees. No movement. It seemed even the birds were still and silent.

She walked on, even though now she felt as if she were being watched. She cautiously took a few more steps and heard a twig snap behind her. Her heart sped up and she told herself to remain calm. Should she continue on to the beach where there would be people and openness? Or should she make her way back to the campground where there would be people, but possibly leading someone to where she lived?

She paused for a moment more. All was quiet and she chastised herself. I have become paranoid. She took in a cleansing breath and decided that she was just over-thinking things. Until…

She took a few more steps and then a few more… she definitely heard rustling behind her. She thought about running but instead turned to face whatever was stalking her. She spun around and braced herself. Nothing. No one was there.

"What is happening to me?"

Then there was movement. The tall grasses and low growing palms shifted as someone… something bent them.

Hannah's heart raced, pounding hard in her chest. She waited for whatever was to come. And soon, a pair of small black eyes peered up at her.

At first she was startled, not sure if she was the prey; but soon, the body scootched closer. A black dog, inched its way closer to Hannah's feet.

"Oh, hey, lil guy…" Hannah's heart instantly melted. "Are you okay?"

She crouched down low to allow him to come toward her at his own pace. He crawled closer and stretched his black nose up to sniff her outstretched hand. Hannah saw healed wounds on his face, head and shoulders. He was dangerously thin, but his eyes revealed his tender heart.

She reached her hand out to pet the top of his head. He flinched at first but then allowed it. His tail wagged as if he was trying to keep it a secret. She scratched the crown of his head and then behind his ears.

"Aww… you're a good boy, aren't you?" She patted his back and attempted to stand, but for this lost pit bull, he saw it as the green light to love on this new human. He pounced at her, knocking her back off her feet and licked her face and hands and arms and whatever else he could connect his tongue with.

Hannah squealed at the affection and tried to deflect the loving kisses and the painful toenails digging into her stomach. He may be starving, but he's not light!

"Okay, okay… get off me, buddy." She pushed him off and he sat obediently in front of her waiting instruction, his wagging tail betrayed his happy emotion.

She pulled herself up onto a fallen log to keep her pants from getting soaked on the damp ground. The log wasn't much better, but it was an improvement.

The pit bull sat right beside her, claiming her and allowed, or perhaps insisted the petting to continue.

"Who are you?" she coo'd, while squeezing his soft ears. She was about to stand up when he flopped on her feet and rolled over to expose his soft white belly. "Oh, I see what's happening here… Okay… fine, but then I have to go and you have to go back to where you came from, deal?"

His tail wagged happily. He would agree to anything as long as she kept scratching. Hannah scratched and patted his hollow sounding barrel chest and wondered where his family was. Maybe the campground, or maybe he ran from his people at the beach. Either way, there was no collar and he was short a few meals.

"Alright buddy, I gotta go. You go home, okay? Go on back home." Hannah stood, and the dog flipped over onto all fours and wagged his tail, ready for the next adventure.

Hannah started to walk toward the beach and the dog followed. "No, little guy… you go home." He sat in front of her and wagged his tail, smiling. He was actually smiling.

"Okay, listen… I know how this works," she crouched back down, and he immediately flopped over to his back to expose his belly, "If I feed you, you will never leave. So, don't make me get attached to you if you have a family waiting for you."

As if understanding and fully committing to this new relationship he popped back up on all fours and reached his front paws toward her shoulders. Just as she was about to melt from his sweetness, he flattened his big 'ole sloppy tongue right up Hannah's face.

"Ack! That's disgusting!" she laughed. "Okay, fine… consider yourself claimed. Now, what shall we call you?"

She stood up and began contemplating names and she almost walked right into… him.

"You know… I always considered myself one of the good guys."

Hannah stopped short seeing Randy Gunter leaning against a palm tree.

The pit bull growled at his presence but stayed beside Hannah. She didn't say anything, and didn't need to, as Randy had more to say.

"I couldn't make it through cop school. But I thought for sure that's what I was supposed to be. So I went for security. Driving around in a golf cart for hours on end, was not my idea of a good time, know what I'm sayin'?"

Hannah stood frozen, she clung to her arm and waited for her brain to tell her what to do. She absent-mindedly assessed his body for ailments. His lungs were destroyed from the cigarette abuse… from an early age, she saw. His brain also had an injury in the frontal lobe. An accident? *Some kind of blunt force trauma for sure*, she thought. There was some scarring on his face and was mostly healed, confirming her premise, but… behind it…

"Then I thought… P.I.; private investigator," he continued. "Help catch the bad guys." He sucked the air between his teeth, causing the pit bull to tip his head as if he were listening to the story. "It turned out, I was good at it. I could predict where these 'bad guys' were going to be, catch them in the act and cash in." He paused, pulling a pack of cigarettes from his back pocket and tapping one out. He lit it slowly and blew the smoke in her direction. "I figured out why I was so good." He paused again for effect, taking a long drag. "I thought like them. Hell, I could BE them, if I didn't think I'd get caught. And then came you…"

Hannah took a step back and waved the smoke from her face. The dog growled low.

"I was sent to find you by Dr. Mosha Joshi." He raised his eyebrows at her facial response. "She has a message for you."

"Then just give me the message and get out of my life," Hannah snapped, more than a little perturbed with herself for standing here and giving in to her curiosity.

He tapped the ash from his cigarette and glanced sideways at her, ignoring her request. "I didn't know anything about you. I had no idea the magic you had. And sister, let me tell you…" he took in a deep drag and moaned as he exhaled, "You are effing amazing. I can unleash all my darkest desires and you come right along behind and clean them all up… as if they never even happened. No harm, no foul right?"

Hannah couldn't help but twist her face in disgust. "That is sick!"

"Maybe," he laughed, "… but no one has been harmed, now have they?"

Hannah frowned at him. "Dr. Joshi sent you to test me?"

Randy threw his head back and laughed, "Oh no. That is for my own amusement, and let me say, you sure don't disappoint. I do like it better when we are trying to be sneaky… it's more… intimate… don't you think?" He reached out to brush her cheek with his hand but she pulled away. "It's not nearly as fun as when you put yourself on display like you did at the beach… I have to admit," he inhaled his cigarette and blew it up into the air. "I was almost jealous of all those other people. You were sharing our secret… it made it feel… almost trashy." He smirked at her, enjoying the conversation and she felt… exposed, as if he could see her without her clothes on. "If your doctor friend only knew the power you have… but then, *you* don't even know your full potential, do you?"

She frowned at his comment. She didn't know.

He winked at her, "Don't worry, we'll figure it out… together."

"Don't you have to report back? Isn't Dr. Joshi waiting for a return on her investment? Does she know where I am? What's the message?"

Randy held up his hands, "Whoa, whoa, whoa… all in good time. Your friend is very generous and understanding that a message like this takes a little… finesse. Why not see the country on her dime, eh?" he laughed, his voice raspy and thick.

She clenched her jaw. "I am not here for your entertainment…" she began.

"Oh, but you are…" he interrupted. "And don't worry… we'll meet again." He winked at her and turned away.

She watched him leave; angry that she wasn't strong enough to chase him back down and tackle him… but then what…

Exactly… then what… she has nothing in her power to stop him.

The pit bull jumped in front of Hannah and growled at the man leaving them. He snorted and kicked out his back legs signifying that he was done with the interaction.

"That's right, boy. He's gone. You're a smart one, aren't you?" Hannah tried to calm her anger. "C'mon, boy… let's go find you some food. Suddenly, I'm not in the mood for the beach."

Hannah and her new ever-present shadow walked from the tropical edges of the island and emerged onto the sandy beaches. They had been walking for miles in no particular direction until Hannah heard the sound of waves rolling gently onto sandy shores. She had grown fond of all things ocean. She took in a deep breath allowing the salty air to fill her lungs. The sights and the sounds brought a smile to her face. She looked down at Professor who sat looking up at her with the typical pit bull smile on his face.

She reached down and scratched the top of his head and massaged his ears, which he gladly accepted and laid his head in her hand to help the progress in just the right spot.

"You want to keep going? Or turn back?" Hannah asked Professor. "Whatcha want, boy? You tired?" The moment she took her hand away from his head, his tail was wagging and he bounced around her legs. "Okay, let's walk the beach on our way back, okay?" She clapped her hands and Professor took off running toward the waters edge. He bounded into the water and back out creating a figure eight with Hannah in one of the loops.

Hannah slowly walked her way closer to the water, admiring its ebb and flow, but careful not to let the water touch her tennis shoes. She'd learned that lesson. Her now long black hair blew freely in the salty air, as she tried tucking it behind her ear only for it to unfurl again in seconds.

Hannah looked up into the sky and shielded her eyes as a pair of Army helicopters flew over her head. The side doors were open and she could see a few soldiers sitting along the opening. One of the men who happened to be standing at the opening's edge waved down at her. She responded in kind while Professor barked at the intrusion on the gentle sounds of nature. A third helicopter passed and a fourth was bringing up the rear. Hannah stopped and watched as they headed out over the ocean.

She turned and looked when one of the copters made a popping sound. It sounded like a gunshot and she saw the massive winged machine dip in the sky and pull itself back up again. It was clearly attempting to stay airborne. The engine growled and whirred as it struggled to keep its cargo in the air.

Hannah gasped, as it began to spin. She saw two bodies get thrown from the wide opening on its side.

She rushed toward where she thought the uniformed soldiers could have fallen, but before she could get close, the helicopter was hovering over her head attempting an emergency landing.

She ran into the tree line as the propellers spit sand and debris in every direction. Even though she was several feet away, she could feel the sand spray sting her skin. Professor barked as threateningly as he dared, but retreated into the over brush.

The noise was deafening as the engine growled and rebelled against the malfunction.

The back wheels of the Blackhawk helicopter touched down on the sand, hopped up and then back down making tighter and tighter circles. Then finally it tipped more toward its right and could not straighten back up again, and the copter pirouetted on it's one set of wheels causing it to spin out on the ground. The propellers clipped the palm branches that got too close as the pilot desperately tried to maintain some kind of control. The metal beast touched and bobbed down again on the sand and spun several times before rolling completely over on its side. The top and rear propeller dug into the sand before screeching to a halt and spiting flames into the sky.

The smell of fuel and hot metal choked the air.

Two men crawled through the opening and stood on top of the mangled wreck. They reached down into the smoking hole and pulled up another solider from inside.

Hannah ran toward the wreckage not giving a second thought. She reached out her arm and helped the men bring the injured solider to the ground.

"Get back ma'am," one called out to her. "She's gonna blow."

"I'm a doctor. I can help" She shouted, over the screaming engine.

He nodded and slid down the metal side bringing the injured soldier with him.

The other solider called out, "Hey! Cander, Hernandez is caught!!"

Cander looked at Hannah. "I got him, go!" she called out, over the noise of bending and twisting metal.

Hannah immediately grabbed him under his arms and tugged him away from the wreck until suddenly he was able to run on his own.

Two soldiers were following close behind, carrying the wounded Hernandez. "Where's McCarty?"

"I thought she was with you. Robinson?"

One of the others shrugged his shoulders.

Only a second passed before the three men ran back toward the wreckage. Hannah held back, torn between waiting to see what was going to happen here and finding the two missing soldiers that she knew were thrown. Her answer was made for her when the helicopter burst into flames followed by a second explosion. The three soldiers were blasted backward but they were unharmed.

Hannah took off running into the tropical wooded area to search for the two that were missing.

She heard someone trying his best to keep his screams quiet as he wrestled with the pain. His helmet had cracked and blood soaked his short blonde hair. His sunglasses still covered his face and his jaw was clenched tight. He growled through clenched teeth and waves of pain.

When Hannah came up close to him, she said nothing but immediately saw the damages. Both legs were broken, his spine and neck had compressed. His lungs were pierced and his organs were rearranged.

Hannah approached him cautiously not wanting him to move.

"Please be still. I'm a doctor. I'm here to…"

"Tell my wife…" he gasped for air, "…and… and my mom…"

Hannah knelt down beside him. "Shhh… you tell them…" She placed her hands, one on top of the other, on his blood soaked chest and closed her eyes. She felt his erratic heartbeat become regular. She felt his spine stretch back out to it's regular length. His vertebrae decompressed and the swelling in his brain subsided. He drew in a deep breath as his lungs sealed back up and were once again protected by his spine and not pierced by it.

He lay still feeling as if he had been dreaming and watched her kneel silently over his mangled body and felt it rearrange itself under her hands. His lungs took in another deep breath and he reached out to grab her hand on his chest. She tipped her head to the side, almost listening for something before opening her eyes.

He stared at her in amazement and she smiled down at him. Her face was smooth and full of peace.

"Am I dead?" He furrowed his brow and couldn't take his eyes off of her.

She smiled again, "No. You are very much alive." She suddenly perked her head up and scanned the landscape. She leaned down closet to him, "Go to your people. They need your help." She pushed off his chest and stood.

"Wait! Who are you? How did you…"

"I have to go, I'm sorry."

Hannah took off running in search of the tiniest whimpers from the other fallen solider.

Hannah could hear the healed man running but wasn't sure if it was toward her or away from her, but she had no time to waste.

She found the other soldier splayed out across a fallen tree trunk. The legs were in an unnatural position and her spine was clearly broken in half.

She could hear the whimpers but the body was otherwise still. Her chest rose and fell in short, shallow bursts in an effort to breath.

"It's okay. It's okay. I've got you."

"It hurts." The voice was tiny and weak. Her pulse was faint and her skin was pale. She didn't have much time left. "My son…"

"Just a moment more, hang in there with me." Hannah knelt down beside her broken rib cage and placed her hands on her chest. Before she closed her eyes, she noticed the name badge. McCarty. "They are looking for you, don't let go. Stay with me," Hannah smiled, and closed her eyes.

McCarty's body began coming back together and as the bones reconfigured themselves, Hannah did not hear the approach of the other man she had just healed.

The woman's body slid off the log as it realigned.

Hannah heard the expletives coming from her witness and she opened one eye and looked at him. "Shh," she whispered.

"Sorry, ma'am."

McCarty opened her eyes after taking in a deep breath. She stared at Hannah in disbelief. "What the f… What did you do to me?"

Hannah stood up and held out her hand to the soldier. She accepted it and pulled herself to her feet.

She looked down at her healed body and open and closed her hands. She closed her eyes and took in a deep breath. "I… I don't understand… who…. I thought I was…"

McCarty took in another deep breath and forced it out. Only then did she notice her comrade, "Holy hell, Robinson, what happened to you?"

He looked down at his bloody uniform and frowned. "I don't even know. But she does."

"Please, you can't tell anyone what happened here."

"Seriously? How are we going to explain this?"

Hannah shrugged, "I… I don't know, but I can't…"

Robinson looked her over, and nodded. "I understand."

"Where's everyone else?"

"Hell if I know," Robinson said, looking guiltily at Hannah, "Sorry, ma'am. All I know is I'm walking and not even ten minutes ago, I was six inches shorter and barely breathing."

"Thank you. I don't even know what…. It's true… that whole life-flashing-before-your-eyes shit…" McCarty's eyes filled but she swallowed down the emotion, shaking her head.

"You need to go see if the others are okay. Your helicopter exploded."

Both shouted out expletives and took off running toward the wreckage. Hannah followed but stayed behind just in case she wasn't needed, she could easily sneak away.

Two of the soldiers were sitting on the sand with their heads down. The heat from the blast could still be felt. A third was pacing and shouting into their oversized radio. Hannah could see that they had burns but none of them were life threatening. But there was another person. Lying on his back. She couldn't see very well, but did see some head trauma. She crept up closer to the trees edge. The two that were sitting jumped up at the arrival of the two that were thrown from the copter.

There were hugs and more cursing, before they questioned the blood on Robinson and McCarty.

"Just lucky, I guess. Nothin' but a scratch," Robinson lied to his co-hearts. They looked skeptically at the pair.

McCarty shrugged, and decided to stay silent.

"You mean to tell me you busted your helmet and you come out without a scratch?"

"I'm wearing my lucky sunglasses, what can I say?" Robinson laughed.

Out of the corner of his eye, he could see Hannah emerge from the thick underbrush, "Where the… uh… heck are we?" he asked distracting the team to face out toward the ocean.

"Only about forty miles from base. I'm sure they'll be sending…"

And as if on command, the loud clacking of propeller blades rattled in the distance. "Your chariot, Sergeant."

Robinson nodded and looked back over at Hernandez who was sitting up and rubbing his head after receiving the "gift". He looked around him on both sides and jumped to his feet looking into the foliage.

"Hey, Hernandez, you gonna siesta all day?"

Hernandez said nothing but stared at his commander completely dumbfounded.

"What the hell? Hernandez! How are you even standing?"

"There was this girl…"

"Man, he really bumped his head…" Robinson glanced over at McCarty who attempted a fake laugh.

"No sir, you don't understand. We pulled him from the cock pit and his knees were shattered…"

"And there *was* this girl…" Another soldier rubbed the back of his neck suddenly uncomfortable with his next words. "At least I think there was…"

"You're right, there was… she said she was a doctor," Cander added.

"All I know is my lungs were on fire and my neck was barely keepin' my head connected and when she helped me off the side of the helicopter, it was like I was fricken' brand new. I mean, my OLD aches and pains aren't even bothering me."

Robinson stood there and listened to his story with his hands on his hips. He nodded, acknowledging that *THEY* believed it, but was letting them think that he didn't completely buy it.

McCarty nudged her Sergeant and pointed to the landing helicopter with her head.

Medics jumped from the helicopters while it was still a few feet from landing. They tossed out first aid bags and stretchers.

The team of five just stood by and let them come to the rescue even though the only rescuing they needed was a change of clothes and to get back to their mission.

Sergeant JR Robinson separated from the hustle and bustle and walked to the edge of the beach and scanned the thickly shrouded South Carolina jungles for any sign of the mystery healer. "Thank you," he whispered out into the flora, and saluted before turning back to their ride off this island.

Hannah leaned against a fallen pine tree to catch her breath. Her heart was pounding in her chest. Professor sat at her feet, his tongue flapping along with his heavy breathing.

She smiled, knowing that her gift saved at least four lives in that fateful moment. She had stopped wondering how she just happened to be at the right place at the right time to heal people. The true meaning of divine intervention. *Either He plans these incidents for wherever I'm at or He plans my steps to make sure I'm in the right place at the right time… or maybe both,* she thought to herself.

Hannah tried to keep a low profile but still help as many people as she could. Still, money was tight again, and she was going to have to settle down for a little while to build up her stockpile. Would this be a good place? Her camp fees were paid for two weeks, she could go out and look for a part time job tomorrow.

After having been introduced to the ocean, she could understand why people uproot their lives to own a piece of it, or become snowbirds to take the edge off the winter's chill.

Hannah scanned the path that she had just come from to make sure no one was following her. Her heart was struggling to get back to its regular pace. "You ready to go, buddy?" Hannah reached down and scratched Professor's head. He looked up at her and responded with his smile still panting. "Okay, fine. If you insist, we can wait a couple minutes more."

About a week later, Hannah and Professor were walking through the tropical woods near the campground and the pit bull took off running out in front of her. This didn't alarm her because she was used to his taking off to chase one thing or another. *Besides,* she thought to herself, *technically he's not my dog anyway. He found me and he could just as easily find someone else.* Although, instantly after thinking those thoughts, she hoped that he wouldn't. Never having been a "dog person" in the past, she was quickly seeing the appeal in having one around to keep the loneliness at bay.

She walked on, enjoying the day. She could hear Professor sniffing and snarking around at something that probably dove underground for safety.

"And then, she appeared…"

Hannah jumped at the sound of the male voice and scanned the area for its source.

"I was just about to give up ever finding you again."

Her eyes came across Sergeant Robinson whom she had saved from the helicopter crash. He was leaning against a shattered tree stump with his hands folded in front of him. He wore his sunglasses, was in civilian clothing, and his blond tightly cropped hair was neatly brushed to the side, minus the caked on dried blood from their first interaction.

Hannah's fight or flight reflex warred within her but she couldn't move. Her legs instinctively braced for the slightest instruction to run.

He held out his hands passively, "I am not here to hurt you or exploit you in any way."

He stood up and took a potential step toward her and he could see every muscle in her tighten.

"Please. Please don't run." He stretched his hands out palms facing her. "It took me a while to find you."

Her brows furrowed and he proceeded to answer the question she was thinking. "Young woman, dyed hair, obviously trying to stay under the radar, but has an amazing gift that shines a neon light over her head...Hannah, isn't it? A couple different last names to choose from and a few social security numbers too?" He raised his eyebrows, "It's all good. Your secrets are safe with me. As for the rest, it was pretty easy. I assumed you didn't have a vehicle, so I followed your trail from the crash site to the campground a few hundred yards that way," he nodded with his head, " and decided to wait."

A flash of panic crossed her face.

"Relax, it's what I do. Not many people have as much access... and time on their hands... and a penchant for finding the person who saved his entire team..." He paused, waiting to see if she would respond... or take off. When she didn't he continued, "I didn't want to *really* freak you out by knocking on your door, so I decided to wait out here in the woods, like a perfectly normal human would do." He laughed at his own humor.

She looked down and away, identifying with his description and the peculiarity of the present situation.

"You're doing a pretty good job… keeping low profile." He shrugged, "But you've also done some pretty amazing things."

"What… what now…?"

"No… you misunderstand. I need your help. Not… me personally." He paused and released the air in his lungs and rolled his eyes. "I'm sorry. This isn't coming out right. I'm sure you get asked to do something for everyone else, all the time. But this… it's not for me. You have given me more than I deserve and have, without a doubt, shown me that I am on my correct mission. Not professionally… well," he stumbled, "I mean, yes, professionally, but also personally."

Hannah held her ground, not wanting to give up the space between them. *Where is that stupid dog? So much for protection.*

As if on cue, Professor bounded over the plants and fallen bits of trees to sit at Hannah's feet. Immediately he sensed the presence of someone else and turned his entire body to face off with the stranger. A low growl escaped uttering a warning for the human to keep his distance.

Hannah relaxed her stance a bit and cocked an eyebrow in a show of confidence.

Sergeant Robinson bent at the knees and held out his hand toward the terrifying pitbull that squared off before him.

"Hey boy… how are ya? What'cha say? Huh?"

Professor broke his stance and lopped over to the man, tail wagging and smiling away.

Hannah couldn't help but roll her eyes.

As the man and beast were becoming fast friends, Robinson asked, "What's his name?"

Hannah shrugged at first. "I call him Professor."

Robinson looked up at her, "You found him?"

"He found me, actually." Hannah couldn't help but smile at the memory.

JR got back down to business, "Uh... my wife and I would like to invite you over for dinner... You and Professor, here..." He made baby noises in the dog's face who wagged his tail even harder, that it almost made him fall over.

"Your wife... she is sick?" Hannah asked, tentatively.

"No. Not at all. Probably one of the healthiest people you'd ever meet," he laughed, and settled back on his ankles. "In fact, after..." he nodded up to her, "my uh... new lease on life, I went home and threw out all my junk food and beer..." he nodded again, affirming his decision and keeping his emotions under control. "I... have ... a second chance at life. I don't know why I was chosen, but I don't intend to squander it." He looked away from her and squeezed Professor's face and flopped his ears about.

"What is it you need from me?"

"Oh yeah, so... at dinner I was going to give you all the details, but the BLUF, sorry, bottom line up front is... I'm running a mission to Brazil and I'd really like for you to come along. It will be an exclusive mission, so, for your safety, only the personnel that.. uh... you have already been in contact with, so to speak, will be there. You won't have to worry about anyone else finding out about… uh… that thing you do."

"Brazil?" Hannah questioned, warming up to the idea, "I have never been out of the country! Wouldn't I need like, a passport or something?"

JR stood and put his hands on his hips. "No ma'am. You will not have to worry about any of that. I will be flying this mission and…"

"Hang on," there was a sense of teasing in her voice, "I've seen what you do to a helicopter… no thank you."

He laughed, lifted his glasses, and wiped the sweat from his brow with the back of his wrist. "Uh, THAT won't happen again, and technically I wasn't flying the craft, and plus, we have *you* in case anything goes wrong."

"Sure sounds great for you, but what if something happens to me?"

He furrowed his brow. "You mean, you can't… on yourself?"

She shrugged. "Don't know… Haven't needed to yet."

He put his hand over his chest. "I promise I will protect you with my life. This mission means a lot to me and I know it will to you, if you just give me a chance to explain it."

Hannah nodded her head yes before she could talk herself out of it. They made arrangements for his wife to pick her up at a nearby gas station and then bring her back again.

You direct my steps…

It was literally only two days following the wonderful home-cooked meal, that she was staring at the huge military helicopter that was going to carry her to Brazil.

Sergeant Robinson walked up to Hannah and gave her a jumpsuit to slip on over her clothes.

"You may want to bind your hair back. We leave in fifteen minutes."

She nodded.

"Yes, I checked and double checked. We are a go for a boring, uneventful flight to Brazil," he smiled.

"My first helicopter ride? Boring? I hardly doubt that!"

He laughed at her and flagged Sergeant McCarty with his fingers in the air, who came up and hugged Hannah. "It's so good to see you again. I'm super stoked that you're coming with us."

She held out her hand, leading the way toward the helicopter.

"Oh, wait… I have to…" Hannah held out the coveralls she had just been given.

McCarty nodded, not wanting to compete with the deafening motor. She helped Hannah balance while she stepped into the jumpsuit and then zipped up the front folding the zipper under the flap.

McCarty asked her with a thumb's up and Hannah responded in kind.

Her first helicopter ride.

Luxurious was not a word to be used to describe her first helicopter ride.

Hannah stayed buckled in her seat gripping tightly to the handles on either side of the seat. Even with the headphones they had her wear, the noise was deafening. The wind whipped around inside and caused her ponytail to whip her cheeks whenever it freed itself from the headrest. She tried to listen closely whenever instruction was given to her but could only nod her head in reply. Words just wouldn't come.

They invited her to unstrap and look out the gaping doors on either side, but she had no intention of doing so. Instead, she made an effort to stay calm and enjoy the view from her strapped down seat of the blues of the skies, passing through clouds, and the expansive mass of water underneath them.

They landed on a rectangular shaped clearing that was marked with a big red "X". The six person team jumped into action even before the engine stopped whirring and the propellers stopped spinning. They unloaded boxes and backpacks and Hannah waited patiently until she was literally unloaded as well.

The variety of green tropical trees and plants made her feel small. The twisting branches and vines stretched up to the skies and were bustling with activity.

They stood in a small clearing. Next to the helicopter were a few tents and trucks. Stacks of black boxes lined the inside and outsides of the heavy canvas tents. Tables and wooden folding chairs were haphazardly set about. Hannah could only see about three or four other people, all wearing camouflage and busy doing... things.

While everyone bustled around her Hannah looked on with awe. Sergeant Robinson came up behind her and grabbed her arm moving her closer to one of the tables. He tossed a backpack on the table.

"See if you can carry this. It has water and food and a few other supplies that we may need."

Hannah obediently threw it over her back and tucked her arms in the straps. She nodded her head, her words were obviously still not functioning.

"Alright then," Sergeant Robinson raised his voice with military authority. "Let's move out."

He came back over to Hannah and again tugged on her arm to lead her down a well worn path.

"Stop manhandling her, Robinson!" McCarty scolded as she came up behind him, "She's our guest... our guest of honor, I might add."

JR pulled back and looked shocked. "Ma'am. I am so sorry. The job just took over. There's a military side and a human side. I get the lines blurred every now and again. I'm sorry. Please," he held his hand out for her to follow two soldiers ahead of them, "after you."

The openness of the airfield and Army base was quickly replaced with the looming tangled darkness of the overgrown jungle.

The path was relatively short, but it felt longer to Hannah having never carried a backpack before, and the humidity and heat was sweltering. Her hair was soaked and she could feel drips of sweat trickle down her back. She adjusted the backpack to find a new spot where it didn't ache, but that was short-lived as well.

"Almost there," Hannah heard McCarty call out behind her.

True to her word, the stifling jungle opened back up to reveal a very lived in village.

The dirt under her feet was soft and there was not a single speck of green within the outline of this small village.

Small huts were scattered about in no particular order, some were in disarray with pieces of the roof missing, gaping holes in walls or shells of what could offer some kind of protection from the elements. People were everywhere. They were standing and sitting, leaning against the American trucks or sitting in circles talking.

The soldiers set to work right away setting up tables with supplies. Hannah stopped dead in her tracks. Her eyes saw so much and it was troubling to her brain. She had trouble taking it all in. So much disease, malnutrition, weak organs, and joints... she didn't know where to begin, but she saw her purpose immediately.

Her vision of grey and weak organs was interrupted with a pink, healthy, beating heart. She looked up to see the face of Sergeant Robinson.

"You can see it, can't you?"

She nodded.

"They are hurting and we can only do so much. Can you help them? Any of them?"

A broad smile spread across Hannah's face. "I can. Yes, I can."

Chapter Sixteen

"Momma, you would have been proud of me."

Phyllis, with an ethereal glow, walked toward her daughter and grabbed her face. Her smile was gentle and pure. "I am always proud of you, Baby Girl. There's nothing you could possibly do…"

Hannah felt the warmth of a tear slip from her sleeping eyes. "I couldn't save you."

"Oh… oh, now… don't be sad. You weren't meant to save me. I told you, you were meant to do great things." She laughed and shrugged, "I was just in your way."

Hannah shook her head protesting.

"I know. I know. You know I'm just teasing. What happened to your sense of humor? You used to always laugh and smile…"

Hannah paused, reveling in the sight of her mother in front of her, but then reflected on the question. "I know… I just… I think… I miss you… and Jeremy and my babies… so much."

"But you are doing amazing things."

Hannah nodded, the tears flowing freely. "I know. And I am so happy I get to help so many people, but… and I know I should be thankful but…"

"You're lonely."

Hannah nodded and allowed the dreamy image of her mother to kiss her forehead. "Hold on tight, Baby Girl… things are about to get messy."

Hannah flinched in her sleep as the image of her mother was replaced by Randy Gunter.

"That's not very nice of you to keep ditching me like that."

Hannah scoped out her dream's setting. She was standing in the burned out remains of her home she shared with Jeremy and the girls. The walls were charred with just a hint of the original color peeking through. The roof and second level were completely gone but a blinding stream of sunlight was shining through the tall, window which was still intact. "We aren't finished yet." He laughed and laughed and laughed until Hannah sat up straight in her bed, heart pounding in her chest. Her cheeks were moist from fresh tears but she was in her own space. Her bedroom. Her pajamas. And a snoring pit bull at the foot of her bed.

She took in a deep cleansing breath and flopped back down on her pillow. She was restless now, but didn't want to move for fear of waking her furry friend. A stream of sunshine was forcing its way through the closed blinds.

She looked over at her clock, amazed at the late hour. How long had she been asleep?

It's true that when they returned her from the Brazil Mission, she was beyond tired. Drained, even. It was the middle of the night and she had no problem falling right to sleep.

She smiled. All those beautiful faces. So much transformation. So many children that now have a fighting chance. Their sweet, little, sad, brown eyes that were filled with so much pain and despair brightened up immediately. Their brown, patchy skin, evened out to a smooth glowing coffee color.

Her gift could not replace the lack of food, but at least they had a new opportunity. Sergeant Robinson was working on the food-side of things, but they just couldn't get the medicines they needed. "Now, thanks to you," Sergeant Robinson told her, "we can offer them a better chance. You have done more in these two days than we've been able to accomplish in the two years we've been here."

Hannah smiled again, feeling... purposeful. "Yes, purposeful," she said, out loud.

As Hannah and Professor were returning from their walk, Professor's tongue lagging out of the side of his mouth, smiling and wagging at everyone in the park, the office clerk came out to greet her.

"Hey, Miss Morganson, a man came by earlier to see you, but he didn't have a pass so he wasn't allowed in the park. I'm sorry if this was an inconvenience for you, but it's more of a safety precaution for our guests. If you are expecting visitors, could you let us know ahead of time?"

"Oh, of course. I wasn't expecting anyone, so…"

"He left you this note." She handed a sealed envelope to Hannah and smiled. "You have a great day." She patted Professor on the head and made her way back inside.

"Thank you," Hannah called after her. She and Professor proceeded around the circle as she pried the envelope open.

A scribbled note read: *Meet me at La Triviata on Bay Street at 7:30. I'll deliver the message as promised. R. G.*

She sighed heavily and crumpled the note, stuffing it into her pocket.

She walked around the final corner onto Bay St. and saw him leaning against the wall of an older brick storefront building under a sign written in script, La Triviata- Fine Italian Dining. On one side of the building a small parking lot catered to the patrons. On the other side, the brick structure continued into another store front. A shoe store, which seemed to be closed.

It was a touristy part of town and there were people walking up and down both sides of the street window shopping.

He saw her coming, and cocked one foot against the wall striking a confident pose. He leans down to cover his cigarette as he lights it, blowing out the smoke as she approaches. She was wearing jeans and light colored loose top and sandals. "I wasn't sure if you were coming," he blew out a dirty cloud of smoke as he spoke. "You look nice. Anyone might think this was a date."

She rolled her eyes in disgust and kept things on topic. "You said you'd give me her message."

"She must be pretty important to you."

"Friends are hard to come by with this gypsy life-style."

He nods, not really caring. "I picked a nice place, huh? You ever eat there?" He nodded to the restaurant he leaned against.

"No, I haven't." She closed her eyes and drew in a breath, struggling for what little patience she had left.

"I have. Once. Pretty good, if you like Italian." He tugged at a bandage that was wrapped around his hand between his thumb and index finger. He grimaced at the twinge of pain. She could see a fairly deep cut surrounded by some minor burns. She furrowed as she looked at it, thinking it was an odd combination.

"Don't worry about this little scratch," he smirked at her. "I can tell you're dying to heal it."

"Hardly," she snorted, putting her hand on her hip. "The message."

"Right. Right. So, your doctor friend apparently needs you. Only you."

Hannah dropped her hand from her hip and gave him her full attention.

"She sent me all over the place trying to find you, because you're the only one who can save her. And now I understand why." He inhaled and exhaled the toxic fumes, making her wait. "She has an inoperable brain tumor. She's kinda hoping you'll come back and take care of that for her."

Hannah's expression told him that she interested in the new information but he couldn't read what she would do with it. "Is that it?" she asked.

He shrugged. "That's it."

She looks at him warily but he doesn't offer any other information. "Thanks," she says, and turns to walk back across the street.

"It's been a pleasure getting to know you Hannah Michaelson. I'd be lying if I said I wouldn't miss our little tete a tete."

She paused for a moment and was about to say something, but decided better, and continued walking away, but his next words held her in place.

"Let's play one more round, shall we?" He called out across the street. Then laughed low and guttural.

Hannah turned and frowned. "You've done your job. You've seen what you needed to see. Let's call it a day."

"But… you are so amazing to watch," he purred. His words felt like the smoke he breathed out wrapping and wafting around her. "Besides, aren't you curious to know just how powerful this 'gift' is?" He cocked his eyebrow knowing that he had touched a nerve. "The uh… 'tests' up till now, have all been child's play."

She walked back in his direction a few steps and pointed a finger at him. "These stupid games you're playing are getting in the way of my helping people who need me."

"Awww, that's so sweet. But humor me, won't you?"

"No, Randy… no. I'm finished being your entertainment. You've done your job. It's over."

He startled her when he threw his cigarette down and leaned toward her yelling, "Not until I say it's over!"

They stared at each other for a moment that felt like hours daring the other one to blink. It was Randy.

He looked down at his wrist, lifting the bandage to see his watch. "You have … twelve minutes." He jerked his head toward the building behind him. The two huge scenic windows on either side of the entrance showed a room full of unsuspecting, happy patrons. "It's gonna blow. You might want to take cover."

Hannah shook her head… "No."

"Suit yourself." He shrugged his shoulders. "It's happening with or without you." He twisted his foot on the cigarette butt he threw on the sidewalk, grounding out the glowing ember and walked past her. "Ten minutes."

Hannah's heart raced and pounded inside her chest. She didn't waste a moment more, as she ran to the entrance door.

"Everyone get out!!" she yelled. "There's a bomb! It's going to explode! Get out!"

Some people jumped from their seats and others just stared at her like she had three heads. Some even had the nerve to go back to eating their food. Hannah went from person to person. "Please! Get out! We don't have much time!"

And before it could have been anywhere near ten minutes, they heard screams from the kitchen. Billows of flames whooshed through the waiter's swinging door followed by another, louder explosion.

Then the panic hit the dining room as the remaining patrons screamed and ran over each other trying to reach the exit in search of safety. Hannah ran into the crowd trying to quickly heal the ones who had fallen. A few were able to get to their feet and run.

A third explosion boomed directly behind Hannah. She felt the heat behind her and the pressure knocked her off her feet. Black clouds coiled up through the missing roof pieces and darkened the sky. Hannah lay face down on the tile as flames and smoke engulfed everything around her.

In an extended moment, Hannah's body took in a deep breath of air and she lifted herself to her feet. She stood unscathed by the destruction around her. A light, almost like flames themselves, seemed to be emanating from her body.

She looked around her for people she needed to help. There were so many. She went to the woman closest to her. Covered in burns, lungs black with smoke. Hannah stretched her hand out toward the woman and saw that a glow reached out from her fingertips, and spread to all the bodies that lay still in the charred dining area.

Flames still licked the walls and furniture starving for more oxygen as it made its way up to the roof. But the carnage ceased within the glowing reach of Hannah's healing power. The people scrambled to their feet not knowing who they owed their lives to, as instinct kicked in and forced them to make their way to the door. To freedom. To safety.

The fire trucks rolled in and immediately set up a perimeter, sending waves of water onto the building fragments. Hannah collapsed, so close to the door, reaching her hand just outside it; her hair sprawled around her; her heart barely beating.

The scene was pure chaos. The fire trucks and police cars had blocked the streets and directed traffic to go blocks around the disaster. The back and the parking lot side of the building had fallen at least three quarters of the way from the roof, destroying several cars in the parking lot. The windows from the shoe store had exploded and the hair salon down from that had their windows broken, as well.

Smoke still wafted its way into the early evening sky. Ashes that were being blown around by the sea breeze dimmed the setting sun and added an eerie feel to the otherwise gorgeous pinks and golds.

Easily, three inches of water filled the cavernous restaurant that was now black and charred and soaked. Three German Shepherd dogs led their partners around the premises sniffing for specific scents. AFT labeled jackets were seen milling around among the white head to toe suits of inspectors.

The site inspector walked over to the officers who were first on the scene. "What are all these ambulances doing here? Why are we not getting these people to the hospital?"

The two men shrugged as one spoke, "No one's injured, sir."

He looked at them, puzzled. "You mean to tell me, an explosion of this size and no one is injured? No deaths? Were they not in the building?"

"Everyone we spoke to were either dining or working at the restaurant. They all say there were three blasts but by the time they got out into the street, they were not burned or wounded in any way."

"I don't understand."

The two men shook their head, just as confused. "I don't know what to tell you, sir. That's just what we've discovered so far."

"You've detained everyone?"

"Everyone."

Guests of the restaurant, now victims, were being interviewed while standing around in the street, while others were sitting along the curb waiting for their turn to be questioned or cared for.

Hannah lay on a stretcher with an oxygen mask covering her mouth and nose. Her eyes were closed and she was unresponsive.

"Doctor, I can't find a pulse," an EMT shouted across to another ambulance.

"She's dead?"

He frowned. "I don't think so. She's breathing."

The doctor rolled his eyes before speaking, "Then she has a pulse."

"You don't understand… uh… she has no heartbeat."

Exasperated to have to leave what he was doing, the medical examiner made his way over to the gurney. He picked up her wrist and placed his two fingers on her vein. He frowned, confused. And just as he was leaning in to place his head on her chest, Hannah gasped. She inhaled a deep breath and sat up, startling everyone around her.

"Miss… are you okay?"

Hannah had to think for a moment. She felt like she had just run a marathon was out of breath, and every muscle was sore. "I'm… I'm fine," she answered, looking around her, remembering what had happened. She swung her legs over the side of the stretcher.

She slid off the side and landed on her feet.

"Ma'am… we really need to check…"

"I'm fine." She looked up at the medical examiner. "Really."

"Yes, ma'am." The doctor waved his two fingers signaling for someone to take the freed gurney.

What an odd sensation, she mused. She felt a prickling on her skin, followed by warmth. And then she felt fine. No pain. She looked around and saw that everyone was trying to be patient as the ATF crew sorted things out. Then she saw him.

Randy Gunter stood less than a few feet away admiring his work. Admiring *her* work. Was he smiling? They made eye contact but before she could do or say anything, she heard a young police officer call out to him. "Sir. Sir? Are you okay? Have you been seen by a medic?"

The officer took a few steps toward him. Randy was able to snatch a quick glance at Hannah before he turned away from the officer and ran.

"Stop!" he called out. "We have a runner! I need backup!" The young officer called back to his people.

In a matter of seconds, four more uniformed officers joined the chase.

Randy pulled a gun from his boot and fired a random shot back toward the men who were chasing him. A return fire commenced and one officer hit Randy's thigh causing him to stumble. It wasn't long before they were able to apprehend Randy and wrestle him to the ground.

They brought him back to the scene limping and losing blood from the wound in his leg. They rolled him onto a gurney and cuffed his wrists to the side grates.

A member of the CSI unit came up to Randy and misted his bandaged hand and the front of his button-down plaid shirt with a solution. The technician nodded his head to the police officer. "Positive for explosives." He then grabbed a swab and ran it under Randy's fingernails, tucking the swab into a protective tube.

"That's the man!" someone yelled. "He came barging into the kitchens yesterday saying he was the health inspector, but he had no credentials."

The police checked his wallet. "Randy Gunter, Fort Wayne, Indiana," the senior officer looked down at him. "Well, you're a long way from home, Mr. Gunter. What brings you this way?"

Randy looked briefly at Hannah then looked down choosing to shrug his shoulders.

"That's a pretty bad wound you got there."

"You shot me!" he yelled.

"I bet it would feel better if you got some medical attention, huh? Why don't you tell me what happened here?"

Randy just snarled and watched the blood soak through his jeans.

"Suit yourself. We'll talk more when we get to the station." The police officer started clearing the area, sending the ambulance vehicles on their way, since they really weren't needed. The street cleaning crew were coming in to follow up and try to put things back together to get the busy little tourist street back in business. The utility trucks were on stand-by waiting to move in.

Hannah took this opportunity to walk over to Randy.

He blinked slowly in disgust at her hovering over him. He would not look at her.

She could see the bullet had severed his tendon which would make if difficult for him to walk again. The cancer that blackened his lungs was spreading to his stomach and pancreas.

She spoke no words and turned to walk away.

He coughed, feeling light-headed, "You're no angel… you're just a freak."

She paused and turned back to him. She slams her fist down on his chest as if she could be stabbing him with a knife. He grunted under the blow and curled his lip in disgust. "That's for all the harm you have caused. And now," She then spread her hand out to heal him. "I want to make sure you are plenty healthy to serve out your long, long, miserable prison sentence." She opened her eyes after she felt his deep breath. "But I can't heal what's really broken."

He said nothing, but swallowed hard.

She turned and walked away from him, never to see or hear from him again.

Chapter Seventeen

Hannah pulled over into the registration parking and stepped out of the RV. She extended her arm over her head and twisted her body to stretch out the kinks. She looked back over her shoulder and could see Professor watching her from his favorite spot; back paws on the passenger seat, front paws on the dash.

She shook her head and laughed at his antics, thankful that he'd found her to help dodge the loneliness.

She tucked her newly cropped short haircut behind her ears as she made her way to the office to register.

It was wonderfully warm for being late in the year and she didn't mind it a bit. At home, she knew she would be shoveling snow by now. She stopped short before going inside. A year, she realized. It's been a year since this whole thing began. She looked down at her feet. How much longer…

She walked up the ramp into a refurbished Airstream motorhome decked out in its original 1950's glory, complete with the starburst clock on the wall and pink counter tops in the kitchenette.

"Hey, how are ya?" An older stocky woman sat in a recliner in front of a fifty-five inch screen TV. It took up most of the wall and covered what used to be one of the windows. She rocked herself forward a couple times until her own weight propelled her to her feet. She pushed her glasses back up onto the bridge of her nose and made her way over to Hannah, still standing by the postcard rack and the service counter.

Hannah smiled at her greeting. "Hi, I'm uh, Hannah Connors, I called about an extended stay lot?"

"Oh yeah, sure, sure."

Hannah could see the reason for her limp was from a hip surgery that healed incorrectly, doubled with arthritis. Her lower spine had a slight curve too for how she catered to her weaker side.

The woman flipped through an index card file and pulled one out. "Alright, sweetie, if you could fill this out for me... the only one we have left is a back-in site, but it's close to the laundry room and the lake. Gorgeous view of the lake." Her thick New York accent told Hannah that she was probably hiding out from the cold too.

"Is there someone who could help me back in to the site," Hannah asked. "I'm not too good at that." She scrunched her face at her shortcomings.

"Sure. Sure." She limped over to a charging station and lifted one of the heavy walkie-talkies from it's charging stand. She clicked the button and the black box screeched in return. "Hello, uh Manasseh... this is Susan, do you copy? Over."

"I hear you, what can I do you for?" the box crackled back.

"Can you guide someone in to site seventy-four, please?"

"On my way."

"Oh… okay… uh… over and out." Susan shouted into the speaker. "How many in your party?" she asked, returning to her notes.

"Just me and one dog."

"Oh… we love dogs here. But there is a gator sometimes in the lake, so be sure he stays on a leash."

"Yes ma'am. I can do that."

"Okay, uh, Hannah," she scanned the form. "Here is your parking pass, be sure this stays on your mirror and this is your rent amount due on this date every month." She pointed to a number written into one of the blocks next to the date. Hannah pulled out the cash from her pocket and counted out the correct amount.

Susan adjusted her sweater and added, "It's pretty chilly here right now, which is rare, but it should warm up by next week. Something about a cold front blowing through. We were all in shorts on New Year's Day," she laughed.

"Now we're talking!" Hannah noticed it gradually getting warmer the further south along the coast she went. "Oh," Hannah remembered, "Where is the closest beach?"

Susan pulled a slip of green paper from below the counter. It had a map in the corner and step by step directional instructions written on it along with a few local dining favorites.

"We have a really nice beach here. You'll love it. But, like I said, this early in the year we have little cold spells so just keep an eye on the weather."

Hannah acknowledged her advice and looked over her "Welcome Sheet". "Within walking distance?" Hannah briefly scanned the page.

Susan weighed the question in her mind. "I guess you could, if you wanted…" she paused, "I know I wouldn't want to. Manny takes his Gator there, but…" she threw her hands up in indecision. "Up to you."

"I'm sure I can figure it out," Hannah laughed.

The door of the office opened and a man walked in. His hair was just starting to grey around the edges and his skin was tanned and weather worn. Hannah could see his inner turmoil immediately and was wondering how he was still walking upright.

He crossed the small room and nodded at Hannah. "Site Seventy-four?" he asked.

She nodded, "Yes, but you can call me Hannah."

He laughed. His eyes wrinkled at their corners and he had a nice smile, Hannah thought.

"Sorry. Habit."

"Alrighty. You're all set." Susan handed her a receipt. "Manasseh will get you settled in and oh, we'll be having a bonfire the first Saturday of every month if you'd like to join us. Everyone comes and brings something to share, and whatever you want to drink. It's a nice way to get to meet everyone."

Hannah didn't shrink away from the thought, which she had done every other place before. She just thought it was better to keep to herself. This time... this place seemed... different.

Manasseh drove the Gator and had Hannah follow him to her site. He helped back her in and get her lined up with her utilities. He walked up to the driver's side window, "Okay, looks like you're good to go. You need anything else?"

She called down to him. "Nope, I don't think so. Thank you."

"If you do, go ahead and call the office or I'm usually around someplace."

"Will do, and thank you again."

Professor ran back and forth, the length of the RV. He was anxious to get out and stretch his legs.

"Hang on, hang on," Hannah tried to calm him as she made her way to the door. "You wait here. I'll be right back."

Hannah slipped out the door and closed it behind her and she could hear Professor galloping from one end to the other. He'd jump onto the front dash and look out the massive window trying to keep and eye on her, then he would run all the way to the back, jump on the bed and nudge his nose through the curtains. Rinse and repeat.

Hannah went around and pulled out the long heavy cord that she plugged into the electric outlet and also

Professor's lead so she could let him out, before he wore a trench in the carpet.

She went back inside and pushed the buttons to extend the sides of the RV getting Professor wound up again with new space to conquer. Now instead of a straight path, he included bouncing off the couch as well.

Hannah rolled her eyes and went about her set-up list.

With the inside put together to her satisfaction, she and Professor moved to do the same to the outside. Professor waited patiently to be attached to his lead and then promptly chased a squirrel up a tree, where he continued to harass the pit bull from his safe vantage point.

Awning extended. Check.

Lawn chairs, check.

Sewage line, check.

Water hose… water hose…

Hannah was getting frustrated. She was unable to get the water hose connected to the RV properly. "C'mon, you stupid thing!" she grumbled at it. She tightened it again and turned the main water on, only to see sprays of water shooting up and out in all directions. She sighed and turned the water off so she could try again.

"Need some help?" Manasseh pulled up along side her.

She frowned and sighed, exasperated. "I can't get this thing to hook up right."

"Let me take a look at it for you." He slipped out of the driver's seat and stopped at the back of the Gator to grab a wrench. "I've got tools." He smiled at her.

She couldn't help but laugh at his easy demeanor. As he worked with the hose and the nozzle she assessed the damage in his body. There was so much… A spinal injury that went all the way up to his neck. He had to be in pain. Fluid around his knees and hips… and heart. Dark spots… is that metal? There's no way he doesn't know how sick he is, she mused. "So… uh… have you worked here long?" she attempted the lost art of making small talk.

He answered, "Bout three years."

"From the area?"

"Not at all," he grunted, turning the wrench against the stubborn nozzle. "Wisconsin, originally, but when I retired from the Army, I settled here."

"You like it here?"

He stopped and looked at her putting thought into his answer. "I do, actually. I was… lost for a while… travelled around, but," he shrugged his shoulders, "It's a good place here. Plus, they let me work off my rent," he laughed, and went back to his work. "Could you see if that water is off?"

"Oh, yes, of course." Hannah moved over to the water spigot and turned the knob… the wrong way. A fountain of water shot from the hose and drenched Manny. "Omigosh!" Hannah apologized, frantically trying to turn off the water, only making it worse before she switched directions. "I am so sorry! Oh… I…" she stuttered. "Let me… get you… oh…" she left him and went inside to grab a kitchen towel that was closest to the door. Professor bounded and barked at the excitement.

She handed him the towel seeing that he was so wet that it wasn't going to do him a bit of good. "I… am so… sorry."

He looked up at her, blinking away the water on his lashes and wiping away the dripping from his hair. He accepted the towel and wiped his face and then his arms. "No harm done."

Hannah could only gape in embarrassment. "I am so… so sorry."

"It's fine. It's fine," he laughed. "The good news is, I know where the problem is now. You need another piece to replace the one coming from your rig."

"Oh… oh… okay… I can get that…"

"No, no… not necessary. I have one at my shop."

"Your shop?"

"Okay, it's a barn that they let me keep stuff in. I just like to call it my shop."

She held out her hands in defense, "Not judging…" she was laughing and it felt… good.

"Let me run and get that… maybe change my clothes," he shot her a look, followed with a smile, "… and we'll get you all set up here."

"You still want to help? You must be bored to death."

He paused for a moment looking at her, his entire shirt soaked clean through, "Guess I can't abandon a damsel in distress."

Hannah looked away, her cheeks feeling warm.

"I'll uh… I'll be right back."

Hannah stretched out on the beach feeling the warmth of the sun on her skin. She pulled her hair back into two tiny pig tails and wore her swimsuit and coverup. Professor came along and lay beside her panting but refusing to drink from the dish of water that was next to his head. She shook her head at her dramatic dog and pulled her sunglasses over her eyes and rested.

She could hear the crashing of the waves and the squeals of children; the barking of dogs and general noisiness of a crowded beach, but her thoughts went back to the explosion. It had been a few weeks or so but it still haunted her. She was able to save every one that was there, but Randy's words bothered her. "You don't know just how powerful you are…" He tested her gift. And even she was amazed at what she was able to do. If she had to put hands on each of those people, she might not have been able to save them all.

Her breathing grew deeper and her eyes grew heavier as she drifted deeper into her thoughts.

The thrust of that third blast knocked her to the floor. She could feel the heat all around her. The screams… the screams were so real… so close…

"My baby!! Someone help me!"

Hannah's eyelids fluttered open. She saw the ocean waves roll onto the shore, but there was tension.

"Somebody! Please! My babies!"

Hannah sat up and looked down the beach. A woman was kneeling over two small bodies, screaming. A crowd was beginning to circle her.

"Call an ambulance!" a man yelled out.

"Please! Please!"

Hannah jumped to her feet and ran over to the scene. Professor was right beside her, but he wasn't barking or bouncing around as if he knew it wasn't the time or place. Hannah bent down beside the mother and pulled the oldest child close to her body and cradled him. His wet hair was plastered to his head and sand was stuck to his skin. Hannah closed her eyes and in a few moments, the boy coughed and spit up water. He gasped and choked and choked but sat up and was crying.

Hannah crawled over to the mother who clung to the smaller of the children. A girl. Her little pink and green swimsuit had ruffles along the edges.

"May I see her?"

"No!" the woman cried. "The ambulance is coming!"

"Please," Hannah pleaded, "let me try and help."

The mother looked up at Hannah and silently pleaded with her. The little girl was limp, her blonde ringlets were pulled straight from the weight of the water.

The waves flowed up and wrapped themselves around the two women and the bystanders.

"Can you save her?" the brother asked crying. "I didn't mean…" he went to his mother's open arms and crawled onto her lap.

Hannah held the child close to her and closed her eyes. She felt nothing. "Please… please… please…" she whispered and clung to the girl.

Tears streamed down Hannah's face. "No… don't let it be too late… please… let me heal her."

The girl remained still. Hannah laid the child back down on the sand and resorted to chest compressions and mouth to mouth.

Even the waves responded to the heavy emotion by rolling gently onto the wet sand. It would come up and sweep under the child's body drawing her hair back out to sea; the only movement she would give. She was gone.

The ambulance pulled onto the beach and the paramedics came running to relieve Hannah of her compressions.

Hannah relayed to the two men that there was no pulse and she had been working over the body for approximately five or so minutes.

"We'll take it from here," one said and picked up the lifeless child from the sand. He cradled her to his body and ran toward the ambulance with the mother and brother close behind.

Hannah fell back to the sand on her knees and sobbed. "I couldn't save her. Why couldn't I save her…"

She was already gone. It was too late. Some people are not meant to be saved.

"She was a child!" Hannah screamed out into the vast, empty ocean.

Chapter Nineteen

A couple days after the hose debacle, Manasseh stopped in front of site seventy-four as Hannah sat outside reading.

"Hey you," he called out to her.

"Hey yourself," she called back, not upset by the distraction. She had spent the day prior inside her home, not wanting to get out of bed. Her heart was still wounded from the day before.

"Do you drink wine?" he asked from his seat.

She furrowed her brow at the strange question but answered, "I've been known to imbibe every once in a while."

He nodded, taking in the information. "What wine goes with chocolate?"

She chuffed, "I'm not sure that I know that answer." She thought a moment more. "But my guess would be... maybe... a nice pinot? Can't go wrong with a nice pinot noir."

He paused a moment more, just bobbing his head as if he were pondering her answer as being the meaning of life. She sat quietly and didn't interrupt his pondering.

"I... was wondering..." he began, as she waited, "... would you go to the bonfire with me? I'm in charge of bringing the chocolate… for the uh… s'mores…   and… I thought…" he breathed out heavily; nervously. "Would you like to go?"

A dark shadow flashed over her face and she looked away briefly, her mind racing. He was waiting… waiting for an answer. She swallowed the pain that left the lump in her throat. You can't change the past. You can't bring her back. He's staring… Would it be so wrong to change my future? Let everything else go? Begin again…

Answer him!

A smile spread across her face and a flutter danced in her stomach. "I would like that, yes."

Since the evening of the bonfire, the two found reasons to share the same space. She would have issues with a clogged sink and he would be passing by to bring Professor a treat…

Manny would get down and rough house with the pit bull, which Hannah wouldn't do and they would play until both were worn out.

"He sure does like you," Hannah would observe.

"I used to have a pit when I was in Basic in the Army. Great dogs. He was a merle."

"What happened?"

"The uh… ex won him in the divorce." He shook his head and ruffled Professor's ears. "I was getting ready to be deployed to Germany for three years. It seemed like the right thing to do."

They would do their laundry at the same time… Folding and chatting about life, and love and dreams.

"I didn't think I would enjoy living this lifestyle as much as I do," Hannah mused. "I wish I could take more time…"

"Why can't you?"

"I… just…" she shrugged nervously, "I… get spooked, I guess and feel the need to run."

He stopped folding and looked at her. "You're safe here. I would protect you."

Her heart skipped a beat and she wanted to believe him. If only he knew…

"Did you know you fold your towels wrong?" she laughed, changing the subject.

Manasseh stopped in mid-fold and glanced over at her, challenging, "Funny, I was thinking the same thing about you…"

He would invite her to watch the sun set over the lake which became a regular, standing date and they would talk long after the moon rose high in the sky.

"You're a doctor?" he asked, raising his eyebrows.

She shrugged. "Technically? I never finished. Didn't take my boards." She looked down and away.

"Is that still something you want to do?" he asked sincerely, not judging her.

"I… just lost the passion for it after my family… I walked away and never looked back."

He nodded, understanding. "Shame. I sure could use a doctor," he laughed trying to lighten the mood.

"So I see," Hannah said.

"That bad, huh?" he chuckled.

"Oh… uh… I just mean… I can see the tell-tale signs that you're in pain." She looked away nervously. "Once a doctor always a doctor… you know."

"Yeah, we have Afghanistan to thank for that." He lifted up his shirt to show her the scars. "I was literally blown out of our jeep. Landed on my head. Only me and one other of my team survived."

"I'm so sorry." *The dark spots… metal shards,* she recalled seeing so much more than scars.

It was his turn to shrug it off, "Yeah, well, they stitched me back together and sent me home. Medical termination. I was three years away from retiring." He shook his head. A wound for him that Hannah knew she could not heal. But she could heal all the others… She shook away the thought not wanting to confront those emotions.

They sat in silence enjoying the beauty of the moon's reflection on the water.

He looked over at her profile, taking in the sight of her before speaking. "Thanks for hanging out with me. It's been a long time since… I've… taken time for... the moon is so much prettier with company."

She nodded, looking at him. "Same."

He held her stare for a moment more. *He wants to kiss me,* she thought and her heart skipped a beat in anticipation, but before acceptance, panic took over. "I… I have to go." She looked away and stood up.

"Oh, right… yeah. Right. Me too. Sorry, I kept you out so late."

Her face softened, "Don't be." She dipped her eyes then returned them to meet his, "I am just… tired." *Read: scared*, she thought.

"Let me walk you home." His hands were in his jeans pocket, so he thrust out his elbow so she could link hers, which she did… and they walked.

The Gator pulled up and stopped in front of site seventy-four. Professor was already anticipating his best friend.

Manasseh hopped out of the driver's seat and came around the front of the vehicle just in time to catch the leaping pit bull in his arms. Hannah could see in all the ways that this one action caused him physical pain, but you would never know it by the look on his face.

He accepted the love that came in the form of slobber and returned the affection in the form of scratching Professor's head and back.

Professor jumped from Manny's arms as if to announce his arrival to Hannah.

"Yes, yes, I see," she laughed. She scooped the dog's face in her hands, "You know he comes to see you…" She coyly looked out of the corner of her eye to see if she garnered a reaction.

He smiled and continued to talk through the dog who came back over again, "She knows I use you as an excuse to see her, doesn't she, boy? Doesn't she? Yeah, she does… she just doesn't want to admit it."

Hannah gasped, "Admit what?"

Manasseh grinned, "That you love it when I stop by."

Hannah looked away feigning disinterest, "I mean, I don't mind… I guess."

"Mmm-hmm," he challenged. "Maybe… if you could stand my company, you'll have dinner with me tonight?"

She turned to look at him and unconsciously bit her lip, "I would like that, actually."

"Great. I'll pick you up at six." He pulled a dog treat out of his pocket and told Professor to "sit pretty". The dog sat up on his hind feet and Manny placed the treat on his nose. "Hold it… hold it…" Professor trembled as he tried to maintain perfect stillness, not wanting to drop the treat. "And… go!"

Professor popped his head up, tossing the treat into the air and catching it.

"Good boy… good job." He scratched his head. "See you tonight."

He picked her up right on time. It was already dark out and it looked like it could be nine o'clock already. While Manasseh preferred the long days of summer, this night was perfect for his evening plans.

Professor bolted out of the door and into Manasseh's arms and then bounced off his chest back to the door only to spin out in the sand and head back to the Gator jumping into the back, not to be left behind.

Hannah came out and closed the door behind her. She wore a long white skirt and a lime green tank top with a white coverup over it.

Manasseh's face said more than his words, because all that came out of his mouth was, "Wow. You look amazing."

Hannah blushed and looked away and tried to shrug off the comment. "Stop. You see me every day."

"Yeah, but this time you dressed up just for me."

Hannah swallowed the nervousness and smiled.

"Your chariot…" he escorted her to the passenger side of the Gator.

Manasseh had made a picnic basket of wine, cheese and grapes, and then heated up the pulled pork he slow cooked all day, along with some potato salad and coleslaw, compliments of the grocery store deli.

They sat on a huge blanket while Professor sniffed close by or slept on one of the edges. They talked and star gazed or watched the bonfire's flames reach up and disappear into the night sky.

Manny did most of the talking, which Hannah was grateful for because she was extremely confused with her thoughts and feelings at the moment.

He laid his head on her lap and talk about his days in the military, the things that he'd learned, the friendships and bonds he made and if he could go back... he would, but his body just turned against him.

"They say it's only going to get worse, these injuries of mine, but, I'll cross that bridge when I get to it. It's tough admitting you can't do all the things you used to do. I just don't feel as old as my body says I am."

Hannah responded when prompted, but he seemed content to carry most of the conversation. Hannah leaned back on one hand and watched the fire, or the water or the stars while the other hand stroked his hair.

At some point he grew quiet and Hannah leaned over to see that he had fallen asleep. She looked at his sleeping face and wondered if she could be happy here, forever, with this man... but then she remembered who she was. How long could she keep her gift to herself? Was it really so wrong to be selfish for just a little while?

Even if her selfishness was keeping this man... this kind, and gentle man in pain?

Guilt flashed across her mind... "If I heal you... I'd have to leave..." she whispered into the wind, verbalizing her tormenting thoughts. "If I stay, I'll fall in love with you… and…" She swallowed hard, not wanting to think of what people like Randy Gunter would do with fuel like that.

Hannah sat on the bench along the edge of the lake in the campground. She hugged her one leg to her chest and rested her head on her knee. The sun warmed her skin and she stared out at the calm waters. She has been unable to go back to the beach during the day, despite several offers from Manasseh to take her there. She just couldn't go. She couldn't shake the image of the little girl in her arms.

Professor lay in the grass beside her, his tongue flopping out, laying in the dirt, which he didn't seem to mind.

Suddenly, Hannah was not alone. She looked to her left and saw Pete sitting at the opposite end of the bench.

She turned her head to the side and rested her cheek on her knee and looked in his direction. She felt… relief in seeing him. Her eyes burned with tears threatening to spill over.

"I know," he said, comfortingly. "I know."

She said nothing, but turned back to the water again.

They sat there in silence as Hannah watched the sun glisten off the peaks of water being moved by the gentle breeze.

She could feel him looking at her.

"You haven't been using your gift," he finally said. He looked at her from the corner of his eye. "It's been a few months now."

Hannah tucked her face down resting her forehead on her knee now. "I know."

He nodded silently, accepting her answer.

She looked back at him, a tear making its way down her cheek. "What if…" she began, recalling the children at the beach, but paused. She took in a deep breath and tried again, "If I had gotten there sooner, could I have saved her? If… if I had taken her first…"

"No."

Her breath caught in her throat giving way to new tears.

"It was her time," Pete explained, as gently as he could.

"But she was just a child," she whimpered.

Pete drew in a deep breath and released it. "Sometimes, that's all the time they need to serve their purpose."

Hannah furrowed her brow, not even thinking of that.

"You have to let that go, Hannah. The boy… is going to grow up and do great things."

"And the mother?"

Pete looked down at his hands as he folded them on his lap but remained silent. "You can't heal everyone. You're not supposed to," he spoke, staring out over the lake. "But… there are people put in your path for a reason."

"But how do I…"

Pete rubbed his balding head with his stubby fingers. He squinted as if composing the perfect answer. "People…"

he looked around before looking over at Hannah. "People… were given a vessel." He put his hands out in front of him to help him explain. "Just one. No refunds, no exchanges."

The corner of Hannah's mouth lifted slightly as his Italian accent soothed her.

Pete smiled, encouraged. "They are in charge of taking care of it. Some do. Some don't. Everyone is given discernment…" he waved his hand around searching for the word, " and… and discipline to turn away from things… that can cause them harm." He bobbed his head liking the way his words were coming together. "Each one of them… has a purpose. And sometimes, we need to assist them to stay on track to complete their purpose."

"Is this my purpose?"

He nodded his head, "Yes."

"How will I know when I have completed my purpose? Do I live forever, or something?"

"On earth? No."

"So… how…"

"You don't need to see the whole path, you just need enough light to see the next steps."

"But…"

"Have faith, Hannah". Pete frowned and looked out across the water. "But know this, you can't move forward if you are not using your gift."

Hannah blinked sending two tears down her cheeks following the rivulets of those that fell before. "Pete… what if I don't…want… "

Pete spoke softly and asked, "Are you sure that it is something you want… or are you hiding from your calling?"

She knew it was a rhetorical question, but just once, she wanted him to give her full details. All of them. The good and the bad so THEN she could decide. But she already knew that when she turned to look to the other side of the bench… she would be alone once more.

Manasseh met Hannah as she was walking back from the lake. Professor tugged on his leash and she released him. The dog ran straight for Manasseh and jumped into his arms. Manasseh grimaced but was laughing while Professor covered his face in puppy kisses.

"Oh, who's a good boy? Who's a good boy!" he growled baby talk and Professor loved every second. Manasseh looked up at Hannah as they walked back to site seventy-four and asked, "You okay?"

She half-smiled. "I am. Just have a lot on my mind."

He nodded, deciding not to pry. "I… uh… I have something for you."

Her eyes lit up and she rewarded him with a smile. "For me?"

"It's not much, but I thought… Hang on. Wait here." He nudged Professor to jump down and he bounded along behind him while he walked over to his Gator.

"I'm pretty sure you've stolen my dog," she called after him.

"What can I say? Dog whisperer, right here." He looked over his shoulder at her and smiled.

She swallowed the lump in her throat, and fought back the tears that threatened to spill.

He came back with a backpack slung over his shoulder. She scrunched her face, wondering what he was up to. He was all smiles.

She didn't have to wait long because he gently unzipped the bag and started to remove the items hidden inside, one by one. First, he displayed a college-ruled spiral notebook and set it in her hands. She pinched her eyebrows together but let him continue. He then, dramatically pulled out a twelve pack of black ink pens and rested those on top of the notebook which she held out like a shelf on flat hands. "And if you're worried about mistakes..." He produced a box of wooden lead pencils.

"What..."

"Shhh... there's more..." He silenced her and pulled out a child's pencil box that had a picture of a black and white pit bull wearing sunglasses.

"Awww... it's Professor!" She coo'd. "But what..."

"Just wait a second more...". He hooked the strap of the back pack on her thumb and reached around to his back pocket and pulled out a brochure.

Hannah glanced down at it briefly and then back up to his eyes, still not understanding.

He raised his eyebrows, "It's a brochure."

"Yes, I see that... but for..."

He opened up the full color booklet to show the beautiful green landscaping of the local college campus and the list of important professor's and instructors.

"It's for you... If you wanted... you could get your doctorate... from right here." He pointed to a specific building on the center layout of the map of the campus.

She covered her face with her hand, "I... I... don't know what to say."

"I don't mean to assume, but it would be a great place to learn... and to... finish your schooling and... stay..." he looked deeply into her eyes begging for her to understand his feelings.

She looked down at the items in her hands and could feel the tears coming, "Thank you. I love it. You're so thoughtful... and I'm...". She looked away from him not able to complete her sentence.

He came closer turning her face back towards his with his finger and tucked a strand of her pitch black hair behind her ears. "I wish I could heal what is broken inside you."

And with that the tears poured from her eyes. Here she has had the power to heal his pain for months, but kept it to herself so she could keep her secret ... and him a little longer.

"Oh, Hannah... don't cry. Please don't cry. What can I do?"

Her voice shook as she spoke. "I have to go."

His face registered confusion, "You mean like... go inside and sign up for classes or..."

"I have to... leave."

"Oh, I see." Manasseh dropped his hands to his side and took a step back.

"I'm sorry... I..." She set the backpack and the stack of school supplies down on the picnic table. "It's complicated... I... " She closed the gap between them and paused for just a brief moment before reaching her lips up to his.

He breathed her in and entwined his fingers in her hair. He kissed her deeply and backed her up against the side of the RV. The salty tears Hannah wept for this moment and all the moments she would be leaving behind tainted their kiss.

He reluctantly pulled back to look into her face, trying to read her inner thoughts. He furrowed his brow and stared deeply into her eyes, using his thumb to brush away a new tear. He brushed the tip of his nose against hers before closing his eyes and claiming another kiss.

She responded in kind and this time placed her open hand on his heart. He thought she wanted him to pull away, but she held him in place with her kisses.

He gasped and his lungs filled with air. He stumbled backwards and looked at her. He looked down at his body, expecting to see some outward change.

"Did you... feel that?"

She nodded.

"Did you... did you... do that?"

She nodded again.

"What did you do to me?"

In a low, emotional voice she said, "I healed you." *And the cost of that, is my having to leave you,* she told herself.

"Hello? This is Dr. Joshi." Silence. "Hello?"

"Mosha?   This... this is Hannah.   Hannah Michaelson."

Chapter Twenty

Hannah cried for the entire drive to Pensacola, Florida, where she decided to stop for the night. She opted to get a room at a hotel instead of a campground so she could just wake up early, enjoy a hot shower before making her way up north to Indiana.

Her tearful good-bye was more than she thought she could bear. She handed Professor's leash over to Manasseh and he sat beside him, smiling at her; tail wagging. When she turned to leave, he tipped his head and whimpered but Manasseh told him they would be okay. He looked up at him and then back at Hannah and accepted this new chapter in his story.

Hannah healed as many of the residents as she could, as discretely as she could before leaving in the early evening hours. She knew she couldn't stay one more day for fear she would change her resolve.

Her life was not her own. Her gift was not meant to be kept to herself.

The temperatures were slightly colder here but it still didn't feel like Spring. She ate dinner alone at a hotel restaurant with all the other travelers. A room full of happy people off on family adventures or even some on business trips to the beautiful city by the beach... and yet, she had never felt so alone in her life.

She leaned against the headboard of the queen size bed as the television provided background noise. She was staring at her flip phone. She hadn't opened it in months. Her thumb caressed the cover as she tried to decide what to do. It had been charging the whole time she was at dinner and so it now read one hundred percent charged.

She tucked her thumb between the two main pieces and popped the top up, lighting up the screen.

Forty-eight messages. Twenty-nine were from Taylor, two were from Wayne, and seventeen were claiming to help her pay off her student loans.

Wayne's first one: Things are quieting down here. Hope you're safe.

The second one, more than a month later, "Kiddo, I don't know how this place stayed open before you came along. No news is good news, I'm hopin'. Miss ya, Girl."

Taylor's were her usual chatter and gossip. There was one about Dr. Joshi: "O.M.G. Something must be happening with the boss lady, you know, Dr. J. She asked me if I knew where you were or if I'd heard from you. How creepy weird is that? Whatevs, I told her I didn't know. Oh also... my hair is pink. You heard me. Pink. I am so cute. So yeah, later."

The latest one from Taylor was only a few days ago. "So... get this. Dr. J comes up to me out of the blue and says she has a special job for me. One that I'll like. How does she even know what I'd like? She has been like mega absent lately and between you me and the fly on the wall, she looks like crap. Like she hasn't eaten a real meal in months. Now she has to single me out? Seriously? Doesn't she have like four million employees or something? Yeah, weird. P.S. It's totally flippin' freezing here, dude. My life sucks."

"A brain tumor will do that to a person," Hannah said out loud, thinking of her former mentor. "I hope I am doing the right thing." She drew in a deep ragged breath and released all the heavy emotions she had been dealing with. She turned out the light, grabbed the corner of the comforter and wrapped it around her, still dressed; she flopped over to lay on the other pillow. The television chatted in the background as she drifted off to sleep.

The door opened to room 226 and Taylor's jaw dropped. "Oh. Ehm. Gee," she stuttered. "You're my 'special job'? Shut the friggin' front door."

Hannah couldn't hide her smile as she swung the hotel room door closed in Taylor's face.

Taylor banged on the door and Hannah could hear her inside, "Omigosh, I can't believe you just did that!" She was laughing.

Hannah opened the door again, "Well, you said…"

Taylor cocked her head to the side and stuck out the tip of her tongue. "Very funny."

"It's nice to see you again, too."

"How long have you been here? Where's Bessie? I can't believe you didn't flippin' call me!"

Hannah stepped aside and opened the door wide so Taylor could come inside the room. "Why don't you come in here so everyone else doesn't have to hear your potty mouth."

"Seriously? I'm totally curbing it 'cause it's you."

"Well thank you for that. You've been hanging around with sailors?" Hannah laughed.

"No, but I was hangin out with that guy that sold the Dippin' Dots in the lobby? Remember him?"

"Taylor... I don't want to hear about..."

"Yes you do. You've been gone forever! I haven't talked to you... I love your hair. I need mine cut like, so bad. Maybe I should go black again."

Hannah closed the door to the hotel room and braced for the update on the missing pieces of her hometown life.

Taylor leaned against the headboard with her legs crossed in front of her, Indian style and was just about spent of the built up gossip. "Oh, and last thing... I promise. Nicole... remember her?"

Hannah nodded, but it was not required for Taylor to continue.

"She had a baby. A boy. A boy? Yeah, I think a boy... but get this. The rumor is that one of the Attendings is the father!" She squealed at the juicy gossip. "Can you believe that? The one who turned her nose up to everyone? Classic," Taylor shook her head laughing. "Just classic." She shook her head at the amount of stories she's been keeping inside. "Oh yeah, that and you totally missed my birthday." She held up her hands in front of her, feigning insult, "… but I guess that's okay since you were out saving the world."

A moment of silence and Taylor bounced her shoulders, already bored. "So, what about you?"

"It's not important," Hannah was exhausted with listening.

Even if she did have a story to add, the window was closed as Taylor thought of new things to fill up the silence. "So… now this all makes sense." She nodded thinking to herself. "Dr. J gave me her credit card and told me to pay for your bill here and if you needed anything, we were supposed to go get it." She pulled out the shiny platinum card from her back jeans pocket and waved it at Hannah. "Shopping spree? I've already paid the bill here for a week."

"I do need a heavier coat."

"Yeah, it's freezing here. It's supposed to be Spring. Where have you been that you didn't need a coat?"

"At the beach."

Taylor rolled her eyes. "Ugh. Bite me." She looked over at Hannah again, "Are you still… you know…?"

"When I can," Hannah admitted.

"Is that why you're here?"

Hannah nodded.

Taylor started putting the pieces together. "Dr. J? Is she sick?"

Hannah nodded again, not giving away too much.

"I knew it. I knew it. She just looks meaner." She scowled. "So then what, heal her and you're gone again?"

"I think so. I've learned that it's not safe for me to stay in one place for long."

Taylor was bobbing her head in understanding. She hopped up from the bed and went to the window to peer down to the parking lot. "Where's Bessie?"

"I've… parked her some place else, just in case I need to make a fast get-away."

"So if you leave early can I use up your other hotel days?" Taylor looked over her shoulder at Hannah and bounced her eyebrows.

"Be my guest."

Dr. Mosha Joshi opened the door to her apartment on the eleventh floor. Hannah's face reacted immediately at what she saw.

Dr. Joshi folded her arms across her chest and without changing her expression, commented, "That bad?"

"You must be in a lot of pain."

Mosha's eyes dipped down and then returned to hers without answering. "Where is Miss Watson?"

Hannah nodded backwards, "She's waiting in the car."

Mosha, satisfied with the answer, stepped back to allow Hannah passage into her home.

Hannah took in the room. It was very elegant; plain, simple lines. White furniture accented with red pillows and rugs. It transitioned into the kitchen which looked like it could have been used in a photo shoot for a magazine. It certainly didn't look… lived in.

Mosha walked toward her couch, arms still folded. "I hadn't heard from my investigator for some time. He hadn't sent me any new invoices, so I assumed he had found you and delivered my message. He wouldn't return my calls."

Probably won't be doing that for some time… Hannah thought to herself.

"It's my fault," Hannah offered. "I'm sorry it took so long to get back to you."

She sat on the edge of the sectional white couch and invited Hannah to do the same. "You must know how grateful I am to you for… coming here." Mosha looked away, almost guilty. "At first, I was willing to accept that it was, perhaps my time. But..." she shifted nervously, as if her sweater was strangling her, "the… hospital is all that I have. They were trying to remove me from my position. I could not let that happen. I have worked too hard… gave up…" She didn't finish.

Hannah said nothing and allowed her to continue.

"I have to do… what I must."

Hannah tried to smile to alleviate the uncomfortable static that was just below the surface. Hannah did not feel their friendship like she once did, but then again, she left without saying a word and made no attempt to keep in contact. Her reasons for doing so were valid, but at the moment, they seemed … lacking.

"Will this take long?" Mosha asked, shifting in her seat.

She wore a grey colored turtleneck sweater that hugged her slender form and black slacks, her socks matched the color of the sweater and her black shoes, that looked brand new, would never touch the snow or salted ground. Hannah tried to recall the last time she saw this woman without her pure white, starched lab coat… maybe only a handful of times.

"Uh, no," Hannah snapped back to the present. "When ever you're ready."

Mosha frowned and pushed herself to the back of the couch taking up the full seat, probably for the first time ever.

She set her hands beside her body and then nervously back across her chest, only to rest them in her lap. "I am ready."

Hannah stood and removed the long wool coat setting it at the edge of the armless couch. "Thanks for the coat, by the way. I really needed one. It's so cold here… I'd forgotten…"

"Yes. Yes. You are most welcome," she interrupted. "If we could…"

Hannah nodded. "Of course. She walked over to stand beside her former boss. "I'm going to touch your chest, okay?"

Mosha nodded nervously and leaned back further and turned her chin up in case Hannah needed more space.

"You're fine. Just relax. Your pain will be gone in just a few…" Hannah sat rigidly beside her and pressed her hand against her soft sweater. She closed her eyes and felt the warmth under her hand. She waited a moment more until she heard Mosha draw in a deep breath, hold it, and then release it.

Hannah looked up at the shocked face. "Better?"

Mosha blinked unable to find the words. Her eyes darted back and forth mentally checking her body for the symptoms she's lived with for months. She furrowed her brow, confused, disbelieving. "There is no pain." She sat still, searching, confirming, not wanting to react. "I feel no pain. Is it gone?"

Hannah nodded.

"Forever?"

Hannah shrugged, "Let's hope so."

"What I mean is, it is completely gone? It will not go into remission?"

"My gift has healed your body completely," Hannah began, "The only way for you to suffer from this again is for it to start the tumor process completely over. But as of today, right now, all of your brain cells… and body cells are healthy." Hannah noticed a large round mirror against the wall going down a hallway. "Go look."

Mosha looked at her skeptically. Her face betrayed a smile, but she quickly caught herself. She stood up and walked to the mirror. quietly gasped at the reflection staring back at her. She looked over at Hannah and then back to the mirror. Her hands traced the outlines of her face and pulled and pinched at her skin. She ran her fingers through her shiny black hair and was astonished that none came out in her hands. "I am… amazed."

Hannah stood up and went to grab her coat and slip it back on. "I don't mean to heal and run, but…"

"No, wait…" Mosha walked over to her. "Please don't leave. I mean… I have to go into the hospital today but…"

"It's okay. I should probably get going anyway."

"No… uh… please. Come to the hospital, won't you? I…" she seemed to be struggling to find her words. "I have never gone over those results with you of… all the tests we took. I still have them."

Hannah laughed. "You do? Did you find anything interesting?"

Mosha swallowed hard. "There are things that might surprise you. You come to the hospital today, yes?"

Hannah shrugged. "I guess I can."

Mosha offered a weak smile. "Very good. Thank you."

"You're welcome." Hannah fastened the buttons on her coat and reached in the pocket for the matching hat.

"I have money," she added, as almost a passing thought. Mosha tentatively reached out to touch Hannah's sleeve. "You will allow me to pay you?"

"You don't need to, Mosha. You are my friend. I would have come sooner but…"

Mosha shook her head, "No… please. Let me pay you. You need money to live. I have money. More money than I need. I have worked so hard and now have no use for it. Let me do this for you."

Her beautiful healthy brown-skinned face looked panicked; almost worried that Hannah might decline her offer.

"Okay, okay… if it would make you feel better, I accept."

Mosha breathed out a sigh of relief. "Yes. Yes it would. I can give you a check?"

"If you'd like."

Mosha walked quickly to the small table near the front door where her pocketbook was laying. She pulled out a leather checkbook case and scribbled away. Tearing out her work, she folded it in half and handed it to Hannah. "This, this… will help to make amends."

"Make amends? Mosha, you don't owe me anything."

Mosha swallowed hard. "You'll come to the hospital at one, yes? I will see you then."

Hannah nodded and felt the pressure to leave. "I'll see you later?"

Her eyebrows pinched, creasing her otherwise smooth forehead. "Yes. Yes, I will be there."

Miracles from Ashes

Chapter Twenty- One

Dr. Joshi met Hannah and Taylor in the hallway outside of one of the rooms that was once used for classes.

"What are we doing way down here?" Hannah asked.

"That's what I said! I dunno," Taylor offered. "This is where Dr. Joshi told me to bring you."

Dr. Joshi looked down at her shoes as they approached as if she was mentally preparing for the interaction.

As they got closer she raised her head and smiled. It looked forced if Hannah had to guess.

"Hello again, Hannah."

"Hi? Is everything okay? How are you feeling?"

She closed her eyes as she nodded for emphasis. "Yes, I am well."

"Why are we down here?"

Mosha looked down at her folded hands in front of her before raising her eyes back up to Hannah's. "I wanted to bring in some specialists. I have a neurosurgeon …"

Taylor stuck out her neck and her jaw dropped. "There's something wrong with Hannah's brain?"

Mosha closed her eyes again at the interruption and took in a deep breath.

Her pause made Hannah uncomfortable. "*Is* there… a problem with my brain?"

Mosha shook her head "no". She leaned back and opened the door closest to her, calling into the room, "She's here, whenever you are ready to proceed." Mosha turned back to Hannah, who was once her friend, but now was being treated very formally. "In fact, there is nothing wrong with you at all. You are the most healthy body any of us have ever seen."

Taylor curled her lip and scowled. "I'm so confused."

"Miss Watson, could you please go work on your charting? I'll page when you are needed."

Taylor's shoulders sunk; dejected. "I was just…"

Mosha raised an eyebrow.

"… fine…. Whatever. That is so unfair." She leaned in and gave Hannah a quick side hug. "Catch ya later, I guess."

"Of course," Hannah smiled, "I'll see you before I go, I promise."

Taylor half smiled and walked further into the hospital down the dark hallway muttering under her breath, "Until I'm needed…"

Hannah stifled her giggle and looked back at the serious face of her friend.

"Are you okay?" Hannah scanned her physical body and seeing nothing that would distress her friend. "Is there something else…" Hannah leaned in and whispered.

Mosha took in a ragged breath. "I am well. I… have not felt so…" she cleared her throat, snapping back to her emotionless persona. "I need to do what is best for the hospital. My position… I hope you understand."

"Of course, but, what does that…"

"Ms. Michaelson?" The side door opened and three men and one woman emerged from the room.

"Yes. Hannah, please."

"Of course, Hannah. Thank you. I am Dr. Romero. This is Dr. Brazier, and Dr. Hallifax and Mr. Schisler. We'd like to run a few tests on you."

Hannah nodded. "May I see the results of the tests that were already run?"

Dr. Romero gave Dr. Joshi a sideways glance, not sure how to answer the question.

"Dr. Michaelson," Dr. Joshi corrected him, "was a third year medical resident. Top of her class, a brilliant doctor."

"Ah," Dr. Romero smiled, as a used car salesperson would at a mechanic coming in to buy a car.

Hannah smiled at her praising. "That feels like a lifetime ago. Please, Hannah is fine."

Dr. Romero's eyes darted about as he thought of his next plan of action. "So, let's get, uh, Hannah's brain scans and MRI's pulled up," He looked back over his shoulder at Dr. Hallifax.

She nodded and left the gathering to go back into the room.

"So, Hannah," Dr. Romero, rubbed his hands together. "We are privy to your... gift, shall we call it? And... we... have a few patients set up. Uh... I'd like to hard wire you so we can see how your body responds when you... uh... do what you do." He didn't wait for a response, but turned to the other doctor, "Do you want to go ahead and get that set up for us?"

"The last time I was here," Hannah interjected, "Dr. Joshi asked me to assess some patients by looking at them, I was curious to know what the results were on that."

Mosha looked to the ground and said nothing, allowing the third man to step forward.

"You were one hundred percent accurate." Mr. Schisler spoke. He was a shorter, heavy-set man that forced himself into a suit that was one size too small and his extra weight squished out over his collar and his belt.

He furrowed his brow when he noticed Hannah slightly tipped her head to the side and looked like she was looking through him.

"Dr. Michaelson?"

Hannah blinked and looked back at his face, "I'm sorry, you were saying?"

"You were correct in all of the cases that you were asked to assess. To the point where... the doctor's sometimes had made an erroneous diagnosis, but did find a basis for all of your guesses."

Hannah smiled coyly, "They were not guesses."

"Dr. Michaelson, you could not possibly have known…"

This was going to take all day at this rate, Hannah thought. She creased her eyes slightly. "Mr. Schisler," she began. "You already know that you have high blood pressure and it had gotten so bad at one point that you had to have the fluid drained from your lungs." Her eyes bobbed up to his to make sure she was hitting her mark. He fidgeted and tugged on the collar of his button down shirt. "However, you have taken no precautions to correct the situation and are dangerously close to having a heart attack. Your left ventricle is thick and stiff causing your heart to have to work three times as hard to pump your blood, but you already know this because you've been having … chest pains?"

He unconsciously nodded.

"… and shortness of breath."

He cleared his throat and was about to speak when she asked, "Do I need to continue? Because we can discuss your kidneys because they are gonna go next."

Mr. Schisler twisted uncomfortably fighting the urge to cover himself with his hands.

Dr. Romero was fascinated. He narrowed his eyes. "That's amazing. How… how are you doing that?"

She stopped frowning at the man that she verbally stripped and assessed and turned her attentions to the other man.

"I just see it."

"I mean... can you see everything? Do you see it like an x-ray? An MRI? What do you see?"

Hannah took in a deep breath and glanced at Mosha before beginning. Mosha was shaking her head "no", subtly but enough where Dr. Romero caught it. "I think we can take it from here, Dr. Joshi. Thank you. You've been most helpful." He put his arm around Hannah's shoulders just enough to guide her into the side room.

Hannah looked back over her shoulder and saw Mosha massage her eyebrow, not making eye contact and she turned to walk away.

The room in front of her had a hospital bed on one side with all the hook-ups and machines that would keep a scientist busy for days, and on the other side was a table and chairs, a light board hung on the wall and was covered in the various scans of Hannah's insides. Her charts were also hung on the wall, along with several photos of herself, her husband and children, the car she drove, the house she grew up in and her parents.

She said nothing as they led her into the room and pulled out a chair for her.

She sat, but couldn't stop staring at her life, inside and out, displayed on the wall. A photo of her mother and father's wedding was off to the side and closer in, one of her mother, in a hospital bed. Hannah swallowed hard with emotion seeing her mother like that again.

"You were close to your mother," Dr. Romero asked.

Hannah nodded, not wanting to look, but not wanting to look away.

"How did she die?"

She looked back at the doctor insulted by the question, knowing that the answers were right there next to her photo.

Dr. Romero raised his hands in submission. "I'll rephrase... how was your relationship with your mother through her illness?"

"I was her main caregiver." Hannah spoke softly, her voice heavy with emotion.

"You were awfully young, weren't you?"

Again, Hannah knew the information was there on the wall for all to see, but she felt compelled to answer as she followed them down the rabbit hole.

"I was seventeen... no, sixteen when she had to stay home..."

Hannah's mind took her back to that time. She opened the front door of her house; a heavy oak door with stained glass and the original glass door knobs. The floor creaked six steps in. The thick velvet-textured wallpaper was beginning to peel away around the top edges and along the seams. In some areas, her mother used scotch tape to try and save the seams from lifting, even though it didn't work and it was blatantly obvious, she refused to part with the unique paper. Hannah allowed her hand to run over one such section of wall. She continued to walk in her dreamlike state to a large opening on the left. The doorway, which at one time housed two pocket doors that would slide into the wall to allow a breeze or easy access to the parlor. The doors were long gone and the wide framing boards were layered with years and years of paint.

A couch was almost in the middle of the main room. Other furniture lined the walls, but mother always liked the couches to be the center of the room. A long couch faced a smaller loveseat and an individual arm chair. A narrow coffee table separated them and an end table sat at the side of the love seat. *It makes for a nice place to have company*, her mother would say. *Nobody wants to have to shout across a room.* Even though her voice was naturally loud and did a fine job carrying across any room... or grocery store... or playground...

This was her home, growing up. It made her love older houses. Their character, their charm, their uniqueness.

"Zat you, Hannah?" her mother called from the kitchen.

"Yes," Hannah tried out her dream voice, "It's me."

"Come in and eat. I know you're hungry. Come on... come and tell me all about your day. Any cute boys talk to you today?"

She walked into the kitchen and saw her mother's back. Her hands were working wildly on something. Her hair was pulled up in a loose bun, it was a dark brown color and had natural waves, which Hannah got none of. It hung down to the middle of her back when she allowed it to hang freely.

Phyllis Becerra turned around and smiled at her only daughter. "Aw, there's my princess." Her smiled reached her eyes that were magnified by glasses. "I made you some cookies. Peanut butter. Your favorite." She reached behind her on the counter and picked up a plate of neatly placed cookies in a swirl design. She held out her one arm to embrace her daughter as they walked toward one another to meet in the middle at the kitchen table. On the way, Phyllis tripped and fell forward catching herself with her one hand. The cookies spilled across the floor. Phyllis immediately started laughing. "Oh, what a mess I've made! I bet that was a sight to see!"

"Mom, are you okay?" Hannah rushed to help her mother to her feet.

"Of course I am. Blame it on these weak ankles. Got 'em from my mother, your gramma. See what you have to look forward to?" She bent over and struggled to close her fingers around the cookies.

"Ma, I got it. Let me get those, you sit here."

"It's no big deal, I can get 'em."

"Let me."

"Okay, fine." Her answer to everything that didn't go her way. She sat in one of the metal legged chairs with plastic seat covers to protect the original plastic cushion. She smoothed her hair and checked that her bun was still intact while Hannah picked up the remainder of the cookies.

"I'll make you some more tomorrow." She flapped her hand at her daughter.

"You don't have to." Hannah came and sat down next to her mother and took her hand into her own. "Ma... maybe you should go to the doctor. That's the third time you've fallen this week... that I've seen anyway."

Phyllis cupped Hannah under her chin. "Oh, you worry too much, daughter of mine. It's just a few muscle cramps, that's all. I told you, your gramma had those same weak ankles. I'll be fine..."

A tear slipped down her cheek when she blinked. Dr. Romero's voice was right behind her. "It was ALS, wasn't it?"

Hannah nodded, speaking mechanically, "Amyotrophic Lateral Sclerosis." Hannah looked at her mother's picture again. "We didn't know until..."

"Hannah," Dr. Romero did his best to sound calming... reassuring..."You know that there's no known cure for that, don't you?"

Hannah cleared her throat and wiped away her tears and turned away from the wall of her history. "Yes... I do know that... now. But as an eighteen year old, trying to save her mother..."

Dr. Romero dropped his head knowing that there are no words to make her internal wounds heal.

"So, Doctor, why is my life spread out on a wall?" Hannah asked, suddenly impatient.

"Well, Hannah... your... um... circumstances are very... unique. We have a lot to learn from you."

Hannah nodded, conceding his point.

"You will help us, won't you?"

"I'll do what I can."

"So… if you don't mind," he leaned forward and folded his hands in front of him on the table, "could you go back to telling us what it is you see?" He bobbed his head at a quiet woman in the room who responded to his silent order to turn on a recording device.

"I see the affliction."

"So, when you were looking at Joel here, Mr. Schisler, do you see everything? Bones? Veins? Organs?"

She thought about how to answer that, which caused her to look at the man once again, scrutinizing even more. "I see only the areas that need healing. I don't see anything on his arm, for example. I can't even see skin. My vision goes directly to the disturbed area, nothing blocks it. No bones or other organs that I know should be in the way. I see past those… or through those… "

"Fascinating."

"Without going into detail," he probed further, "does anyone in this room have a clean bill of health?"

Within seconds, she answered, "No."

The room responded with looks passing from one to the other.

"Really, that fast."

"It's kinda the first thing I see. Where you may notice someone because they have red hair or blonde hair, I see oh, they have arthritis, or they have failing kidneys, or they have a nasty rug burn… it can be very distracting."

"How do you cope with it?"

She thought about it for a moment. "I either keep my head down, or try to make eye contact only, hoping that they have a healthy brain."

He chuckled at that.

"And when... did all this start?"

Hannah looked away, "It's been about a year now."

He nodded, letting the information sink in. "And... how did it come about?"

She looked away at the floor thinking of her answer. She decided to keep her near death and guardian angel to herself. "I just woke up with it. It started as a ... " she searched for the right word. "... a sensitivity... and then, the small ailments began appearing. It was quite by accident that I found I could heal them."

Dr. Brazier leaned in with a question, "Do you have to do anything special? A chant? Or... or... summoning or something like that?"

Dr. Romero looked over his shoulder at his colleague, "Did you need to grab your crucifix, Brian?"

Hannah's heart sped up a little, hoping that it would continue to be dismissed as the higher power that it was. "No, I just lay my hands on the person."

"What do you feel?"

She looked away, thinking, "Warmth. A tingle in my fingertips." She smiled at the skip of her heartbeat. She didn't add the feeling of oxytocin rushing through her body as she could no longer see the wound, whatever it may have been. The person was healed. Some knew, some didn't.

"And how do you feel? Do you feel any different?"

"I'm more tired."

"Is that it?"

"Yes."

"Well, as Dr. Joshi told you, you have a clean bill of health. So, if you were wondering about inheriting your families ALS, it seems to have… skipped a generation."

His implication hit Hannah hard, "My… children?"

"One, we believe, yes. If the blood work is accurate."

Hannah looked behind her at a picture of her children at a local fair. They were getting their faces painted. She didn't ask which one… she didn't need to know.

"And now, if you'd be willing to indulge us, we'd like to run some tests of our own. See what is happening with your body while you are…"

"Healing."

"Healing, yes." He tapped his fingers a moment. "I wonder if your cells breakdown and you are only able to heal so many people… in your lifetime, or… do your cells regenerate… have you the answer for the fountain of youth?" He inadvertently looked over at Joel Schisler, and bobbed his eyebrows.

"Dr. Joshi took some of my blood. What did the tests say?"

Dr. Romero turned his hands over and let them fall again on the table, "That your blood is perfectly healthy but just the same as anyone else's. Nothing spectacular about your blood." He spoke quickly and dismissed the topic as he rose from his chair.

Hannah had to admit that she was finding this information very interesting. Even being a spiritual person, she has always been interested in the science of things. She has always been eager to know how and why things worked and not afraid to research new ways to help people to heal. If her blood could help others, then she could reach and heal more people than she could ever do on her own.

"Let's get started, shall we?"

Hannah was dressed in scrubs, which she usually found very comfortable, but she only had thick socks on her feet with little rubber pads and she was hooked up to every kind of electrode they could plug into a machine. The room was cold and she was not given any kind of sweater.

They took another round of her blood, enough to use for testing and storing.

They put her next to patient after patient. All were completely sedated so they couldn't speak of what had happened to them in the small room of the hospital basement. But she healed them. One right after the other. They gave her simple ones, like a broken bone to more difficult like kidney disease and three different types of cancer.

They had her heal "Jack Smith", a patient who had an inoperable tumor. If a surgeon had gone into his intestines with a scalpel, he would have died, but Hannah was able to remove the tumor or rather, make it disappear.

The doctors were in awe. They couldn't write their notes fast enough.

"That is absolutely amazing," Dr. Romero said, sincerely. "I am completely amazed." He watched as the nurses wheeled out her last patient. "I can't figure it out." He shrugged his shoulders noncommittally, "I... I am stumped." He looked around the room for confirmation from the other "experts" and they all admitted to being at a loss. "If this is some kind of magic trick, it is the best I've ever seen. I mean... your vitals stay even, your heart rate doesn't even go up. If I wasn't standing here, watching you, your vitals would tell us that you are resting." He made a face, "Resting!" he laughed. "What am I supposed to do with that?" He seemed to be getting himself worked up the more he spoke. "We have watched you supposedly heal these different types..." he sighed and pinched the bridge of his nose. "How do you do it? How are you doing this?"

"Does it last?" Dr. Brazier asked.

"Do you feel anything?"

Hannah padded her way over to the rolling stool next to the long white table.

"I'm feeling tired and hungry right at this moment," she said, with a little more edge to her voice than she intended.

Dr. Romero pulled back abruptly and looked at her strangely.

"Everything about my body is normal. You keep saying that. I'm not an alien, I need to eat and I need to rest."

"But we still have so much to do."

"I understand that, and I'm perfectly willing, I just need a break."

Dr. Romero looked around the room at his colleagues. "Let's uh... let's order some food and we can have it delivered. What would you like?"

Hannah tipped her head to the side, "Here's what I was thinking." She rested her hands on her thighs. "Let's just call it a day. Let me get back to my room, get some food and a good night's sleep."

"Oh... uh, no... No," Dr. Romero hesitated.

"But I am tired."

"And... I can see that. Yes, I can see that. The latest reading, your body is at the level as if you had participated in a marathon at a high altitude."

"Then wouldn't me getting some sleep sound like a good thing?" Hannah raised her eyebrows, as if to say, isn't it obvious?

"I can't let that happen, Dr. Michaelson." He closed the chart and leaned back on the table. "We are... tracking everything, right now. And... we need to gather readings on your body, even under these conditions while you are healing." He looked down at his hands and back up to her, his demeanor changing like that of a stern parent. "So... I need you to stay here. I've got a bed all set up for you and you can sleep for three hours, if you'd like, when we are finished here today. And… like I mentioned before, as for food, we would be happy to have something brought in to you." He raised his head, silently saying that the discussion was over. "So, Dr. Michaelson," he rubbed his hands together, "What would you like?"

Hannah bit her tongue and let his words sink in. She was a prisoner. If she fought back, they would restrict her even more.

"Chicken?" she offered.

A roomful of doctors responded as if chicken was the best thing they'd ever heard of.

"Chicken it is," Dr. Romero smiled, as if he had won the chess championship where it's poor sportsmanship to gloat, but the crowd knows you've won.

Hannah's mind began racing… *Dr. Joshi… what have you done?*

Miracles from Ashes

Chapter Twenty- Two

An elderly woman lay on a hospital bed in front of Hannah. Her brilliant white hair was splayed out on the grey striped pillow under her head. Her face was reposed as she rested in her sedated state.

Hannah lay her hands on the woman's shoulder and furrowed her brow. She pulled her hands away and looked at the woman. She wrung her hands and then shook them, releasing the tension from them. She stepped back away from the bed and took a deep breath before returning to the woman's side.

Hannah lay her hands once again on the woman's shoulder. She furrowed her brow deep in concentration. She was visibly holding her breath.

The doctors in the room glanced at one another as writing utensils scribbled madly on the paperwork in front of them.

Hannah blew out her breath and frowned. She glanced up at the doctors suddenly self-conscious of their scrutiny.

"I... I... I'm sorry... I don't understand... "

"As in... you can't?" Dr. Brazier asked, his pen hovering over his clipboard.

Dr. Romero held up his hand, "Okay, okay… let's take a break, shall we?"

Dr. Halifax stood by one of the machines. "It looks like she's running a slight fever."

The other two doctors nodded. More scribbling.

Mr. Schisler had fallen asleep hours ago and was still bundled up in a standard white knit hospital-issued blanket, snoring softly.

"Maybe… using her powers wears her down?" Dr. Brazier offered.

Dr. Romero rolled his eyes. "She's not a superhero, Brian. You've been reading one too many comic books, I think."

He shrugged, "So, you have a scientific explanation for what she's been accomplishing all night?"

Dr. Romano gave him a sideways glance. "I'm not even completely convinced that what we've seen here is real." He looked back at Hannah waiting for a reaction. "Quite an elaborate ruse, and it does look pretty convincing, but I'm not quite ready to sell the farm, as yet."

"But…" Brian complained.

"Ms. Michaelson…"

"Doctor…" Brian corrected.

He glanced back over his shoulder at Dr. Brazier, "Exactly." *Check-mate.* "She knows about medicine and how the body works." He turned away from his counterpart and cocked an eyebrow at Hannah. "For the sake of argument, on behalf of my colleague here, have you ever been bitten by a radio-active spider?"

"Trent, really?" Dr. Brazier complained.

Dr. Romero held up his hands, "No, no… let's be thorough. Dr. Michaelson?"

She drew in a deep annoyed breath. "No."

"Fallen into a vat of chemicals? Been to another planet? Have a secret cave somewhere? Been injected with any kind of serum?"

"Dr. Romero. I am tired. I am drained. Maybe it doesn't work after two a.m." she looked up at the clock on the wall. "Maybe I'm only allotted so many patients in a day. Maybe you have used up all of my gift with these experiments."

She had lost her sense of humor, and if it wasn't for the fact that she was indeed healing all the patients she was the dog and pony show for, she would have stormed out hours ago. That… and she couldn't help but be curious as to their findings.

"Don't *you* have any answers, yet? You've run every single test. Why am I still hooked up?"

"Well, isn't it obvious?" Dr. Romero cocked an eyebrow with a look of arrogance, "Now we need to find out why you *can't* heal anymore."

Hannah dropped her head and shook it, disappointed. She scooped up the various wires to make it easier to walk. She lifted them up and over the bed with the sleeping elderly woman and she sat on the empty hospital bed on the other side of her.

"I am going to bed. I am tired. I can't keep my eyes open any longer."

The other doctors all looked at each other at her defiance, but no one knew how to respond.

Dr. Brazier spoke first. "Maybe she's right," he spoke softly, preparing for a rebuttal.

"I do agree. I know that I am exhausted," Dr. Halifax added.

Hannah was paying no attention to their quiet conversation and pulled back the covers and climbed in. She neatly placed the wires above her head over the headboard and the monitors responded immediately at her calmed demeanor.

Dr. Romero threw his hands up and let them drop at his sides. "I thought I chose the best doctors for this team. How can we leave now with so much left to do?"

"It won't help us if she can't perform when…"

Dr. Romero shot Dr. Halifax a look silencing her, and looked back at Hannah, who lay perfectly still with her eyes closed.

"Fine," Dr. Romero sighed, "Fine."

"She's hooked up to the monitors, we'll know if she's doing anything crazy."

"Those don't tell us if she's escaping!" Dr. Romero hissed, in a harsh whisper.

"But they'll tell us if her heart rate goes up, any kind of activity, any kind of movement. "

"And Joel is still here. Let's just leave him in the chair."

"Trent. We'll be right next door. I'm beat. I haven't called my wife all day."

"I'll stay." A small voice came from the side of the room.

"Nurse… uh… Nurse…"

"Beckett," she offered.

"Ah yes, Beckett." Dr. Brazier raised up to his full stature again, gaining authority. "I think that's a fine idea. Does that ease your anxiety, Trent?"

"I have no anxiety. She doesn't need to stay. You are dismissed, Nurse Beckett. We can take it from here."

She nodded obediently and went to pick up her clear, see-through bag.

"Oh, and Nurse Beckett, please be reminded of the non-disclosure agreements that you signed. You are not to discuss the events in this room with anyone else. Not even your husband. Not even God, Himself."

Her eyes widened at the sternness of his voice but she nodded again and waited for him to jerk his head toward the door before she left.

Dr. Romero waited for the door to close behind her and then spoke. "Tomorrow we're hooking this place up with cameras. I can't take any chances. Joel is only the tip of the iceberg. If he was willing to offer us that kind of money for just a vial of her blood, just imagine what other offers are waiting…"

"But... she won't..." Dr. Halifax spoke low looking beyond Dr. Brazier at the sleeping Hannah, "She won't be harmed... right? I'm not in this for the money, Trent. I am in it for the healing potential"

Trent bobbed his shoulders. "Call it what you want, but you know how much people are willing to pay to be instantly healthy again. *Instantly.*" He stressed the word. "They can go on about their lives and eat what they want, smoke what they want. Dabble in whatever drugs they fancy. Jump off buildings. They can basically do what they want, and we can heal them and all of their stupid decisions. And they will pay. They will be lined up to pay. So, call it what you want, but there's a payday at the end of it, and it's going in your pocket. So, you can try and get all judge-y and preachy, but you're in it for the same reasons as everyone else."

Dr. Brian Brazier raised his hand, like a child afraid to speak. "Do you really think she can live forever? In all plausibility, she should be able to heal herself. So, if we inject her blood in our veins, would we get those powers? That's what I want to know."

"I didn't realize you were a Fountain-of-Youth chaser, Brian."

He looked almost hurt by their judgment. "Aren't we all? Aren't we all looking to live just a little longer, stay younger-looking? Younger feeling?"

They both nodded, admitting that the thoughts had already crossed their mind.

"I think that's how we should start the day tomorrow. A blood infusion." Dr. Brazier introduced the idea.

"And I suppose you're wanting to be the guinea pig?" Dr. Halifax snarled at him.

"Yes, I mean, yeah, I would."

"Of course you would," she glared at his shallowness.

"Let's not bicker between us." Dr. Romero interrupted. "We all have the same goals in mind. Let's get some sleep, since ten minutes ago you were all so in favor of that and we can get serious tomorrow. Now that we are eighty-five percent sure that she is the real deal, we can get experimental and really see what kind of 'gift' was dropped in our lap." He looked up and put praying hands together, "Thank you, Dr. Mosha Joshi."

And with that, they flipped the switch to the room, plunging it into darkness and exited. The only sounds were the steady beeping of the monitors, and the gentle snoring of the business man in the corner.

Hannah forced her eyes to stay open in the dark room. She took in slow, deep breaths and moved at a sloth's pace. She looked to her right to see that Joel Schisler was still sleeping in the corner of the room. He was stretched out with the blanket up to his chin and his business shoes peeking out from underneath at the bottom end.

To her left, the elderly woman was sleeping. She wasn't sure how the patients were chosen for her "test" but this woman, at the very least, deserved healing. It took Hannah all the power she could muster *not* to heal her earlier.

She wasn't sure if it would work. They were watching her every move.

When she lay her hands on the woman's shoulder, she could feel the warmth moving through her, transferring to the patient's brain, where Alzheimers had made its home. Hannah prayed and fought back against the warmth. "Please, God, please, let me have some control... please do not let her heal right now. I'll fix it later, but please, my life depends on it. Please hear me... please..."

Her head was aching and she felt dizzy, but she was able to maintain control of the gift. She had never tried to withhold the gift. Never thought that there would be a need. She *was* tired, so, she didn't have to pretend on that account. Her body was physically drained and she needed sleep, just like everyone else. She was not such a superhero that she could simply ignore common sense and proper health care.

But now, as the room was quiet and dark, she slipped from the bed, literally sliding down over the edge until her socked feet touched the cold linoleum floor. She paused before standing up, by testing the monitors with a deep breath.

No peaks. No changes.

She moved so slowly that she could feel each muscle respond to her silent commands.

No peaks. No changes.

She made her way to the head of the elderly woman's bed. Her wires still hooked up to the machines followed along dragging the floor.

She stood there for a moment looking down at the sleeping patient. She took in a deep breath... and then another. Hannah looked back over to Joel Schisler, still unmoved.

She raised her hands to her temples, and in one quick smooth movement, she pulled off the electrodes and stuck them on the elderly woman's temples.

She paused, waiting for backlash. A slight beep on the monitors, but that was all. So she went on to the next... and the next... and the next. And with only a couple interruptions to the steady beeps of the machines, Hannah's electrodes were all successfully attached and reading the woman's vital signs.

The heart-rate began to slow and the blood pressure was suddenly showing a different reading. Hannah, now free from her wires, moved to her side and laid her hand on the woman's chest.

She whispered softly as she felt the warmth move through her body. "I'm sorry that I had to take so long in this healing and I'm sorry that I had to borrow your vitals. But I give you this gift of a healthy mind and I hope that it helps you to reconnect to your family. Thank you." The vitals began to change to that of a healthy woman and no alarms were set off.

Hannah tiptoed to the board where her entire life was on display. She took the pictures of her parents and her children and her husband. She grabbed her coat and snuck over to the door.

She slipped on her coat as she opened the door silently, but on the other side someone was trying to come in.

Hannah squeaked and the photos flew into the air and scattered about them.

"Oh… I'm sorry…." A woman whispered.

Hannah froze, staring at her, wondering what was going to happen next.

"Shh… shhh… it's okay." She looked past Hannah to check the status of the room. "How did…." She shook her head realizing that an answer wasn't important so she bent down and scooped up the photos and then pulled Hannah from the room and locked the door from the outside.

Hannah was terrified and wasn't sure if she should take off running or stand and fight. She didn't know how to fight. Her heart was racing as she attempted to slink down the wall away from her.

"Wait… Don't… I'm not here to hurt you…." She turned the light on from her cell phone.

"Nurse Beckett?"

She nodded. "I… I've come to help you." She swallowed, looking nothing like the hero she so wanted to be.

She begged Hannah to follow her with her eyes. Beckett turned and quickly walked down the hallway. She turned to the right and then to the left. She looked through the window of the doors in front of them and looked down at her watch. She tugged Hannah's arm and pulled her into a side patient room.

They were still in the part of the hospital that wasn't used regularly, but the rooms were set up to house two patients per room in case the need arose or if there was a tornado.

"We have to wait here for a couple minutes."

"Thank you," Hannah reached out for her hands.

The nurse pulled them away. "Before you thank me. I am doing this for selfish reasons. I've seen what you can do. And… and I need you… to…"

"You want me to heal you?"

She shook her head "no". She didn't even ask what Hannah saw in her. "My child. My child… was in a car accident. We were hit by a drunk driver and my daughter will be in a wheelchair and fed by a tube for the rest of her life." Nurse Beckett's voice cracked as she attempted to swallow the lump caught in her throat. "She's just a baby… a seven year old that will never know what it means to run and play," the tears poured down her cheeks, "or taste cake…"

Hannah's heart went out to her.

"Please, can you heal her?"

"I can," Hannah nodded. "I'd be happy to."

"She's outside… in my van."

"Can you take me to her?"

She nodded. "I'm parked on the other side of the baseball field. My husband is waiting there for us. We can at least give you a ride somewhere."

"I'm afraid this may cost you your job."

"You can save our daughter," Nurse Beckett looked into Hannah's eyes. She grabbed both of her shoulders in her shaking hands. Her eyes brimming with fresh tears, willing her to understand. "That is worth any cost. But I can only imagine the cost for you. I wish…"

"You're doing what you can. And I thank you."

"I don't deserve your thanks, like I said, I'm being completely selfish."

"I would have done… anything… to have saved my children. I do not blame you."

Beckett's fingers squeezed the small stack of photos that she forgot she held. She took this opportunity to give them back to their rightful owner.

Hannah smiled as she took them. She tucked them into the pocket of her coat. "What now?"

Beckett's eyes went wide and she looked as if she were called on by the teacher with a question she wasn't prepared for.

"No plan?" Hannah asked.

The nurse slowly shrugged her shoulders and bit her lip. "I… I don't really know what I'm doing. I've never stolen a superhero before."

Hannah couldn't help but snicker.

"There were people standing out by the doors."

"Guards?"

"I… uh… I don't think so. They didn't think you were real, so they didn't put the precautions in place. But, this place is about to be on lockdown. I heard Dr. Romero talking to someone on the phone about security. So... we really don't have any time to lose. I knew that if you didn't get out in the next hour, it would be too late... and..."

Hannah was listening but then something else caught her attention. "Wait... wait a moment... shh..."

The nurse immediately fell silent. She was visibly shaking with fear.

Hannah stepped closer to the door to listen.

"Yeah, so there's this Pokemon... one is ekans, which is snake spelled backwards. And then theres arboc, which is cobra spelled backwards, and then there's Grimer... which, I don't really know what he does..."

"Taylor?"

Taylor stopped and looked around her, before spotting Hannah peeking from the doorway.

"Hey, what's up, woman? Are you just now..."

"Taylor, I need you in here, quick."

She straightened with importance and dismissed her friend, "Dude, I gotta go. Catch ya later." She darted for the room and shut the door behind her leaning against it. Her eyes widened and she smiled, "What are we doing? Whatever it is, I'm in. Why are we in here and why are we sneaking, and who is that?"

"Taylor. I'm in trouble. Can you help me?"

"I'm totally in. I just said that."

Hannah nodded, "You did, ... but..."

"Do you have a brain tumor?? Oh my gosh... is it that? What's happening?"

"You have a brain tumor?" The nurse asked. "Is that what gives you your power?"

"Power?" Taylor scrunched her face. "What the sugar cookie? She knows?"

"I need you to..."

"What? What do you need me to do? I can do it."

"It involves your car..." Hannah flinched knowing how Taylor would respond.

"What the hell? How am I everyone's chauffeur all of a sudden?"

"I know. I'm sorry... but..."

"It's cool. You're lucky I like you." She smiled. "When are we leaving. My shift technically ends at..."

"I have something to do first but, they don't want me to leave the hospital... so I have to..."

"Like, 'we have a hostage situation'?" she dropped her voice to sound official.

Hannah released the air she didn't realize she was holding in. "Yea... something like that, actually..."

"Seriously? That's so cool!"

"No... no honey, it's not. This is very real."

She closed her eyes to slits and put her hands in front of her, "I got this." She nodded her head conspiratorially.

"Okay, can you pick me up at the gas station just beyond the baseball field in about twenty minutes?"

"Twenty minutes." She nodded, as she repeated. "Twenty minutes, got it."

"And please, don't tell anyone…"

At that moment the door opened and a short brown-skinned man stepped into the room, "Hey Ta…"

Without thinking, Taylor turned and crammed her thumb and fingers into the guy's throat and pulled his head down to meet her knee knocking him unconscious.

"Holy crap! Did you see that? That was me! I just did that!"

"Taylor! What did you do?"

"Oh, snap… that was Dre…" She checked his pulse. She stood up and faced the other women. "He'll be alright. Defense training." And then a smile spread across her face again. "Omigosh… did you see that?"

Hannah shook her head, "We did, and now we really have to get outta here."

"Oh!! Oh! I know, we can dress you like a patient and wheel you out the front door." Taylor was beaming.

"Honey, this isn't the movies… "

Visibly dejected, "It could work."

"*You* just meet me at the gas station and if anyone finds out, don't come, okay?" Hannah cupped the young woman's cheek, "Thank you."

She shrugged off the affection, "No biggie. This is the most I've done the last three days."

The three women stepped over Dre's still unconscious body and back out into the hallway.

"Want me to cause a distraction?" Taylor whispered out of the side of her mouth.

"No... definitely no. If we could just quietly sneak out, that would be great."

"Well, you have on scrubs. So... technically, you look like everyone else that works here," Taylor stated the obvious. "And you've got that crazy black hair that I mean, no one would recognize you..."

Hannah laughed out loud. She looked over at her co-conspirator, "We've been trying too hard." Hannah palmed her forehead. "Taylor, you're a genius." She beamed under the praise. "Let's just chat as we calmly walk out the main door," Hannah suggested.

Beckett hugged herself, uncomfortable in this new "fearless rescuer" persona, "You just want to walk through the main lobby?"

"It's three o'clock in the morning. There shouldn't be too much happening," Hannah said.

Beckett nodded, accepting the logic, but was still terrified of being seen. They all three took in a deep breath and proceeded through the double doors.

The hospital's main entrance opened to a huge main lobby, complete with a coffee bar, benches, and chairs and the main Information Station.

From the central lobby, hallways wagon-wheeled out in four different directions with a formal staircase in the middle leading up to a second floor.

A two-story water fountain nestled between the elevator doors leaving a pool for people to toss coins into as they wait for their elevator escort.

The three woman walked calmly down the hallway. The fountain was to their right, another hallway and the staircase was to their left.

They walked nervously chattering, when they reached the opening to the lobby. Nurse Beckett froze and had to be nudged forward by Hannah. Taylor calmly and confidently took a left .

"Almost there," Hannah encouraged by tucking her arm into that of Nurse Beckett's. "Just keep walking... tell me about your daughter. What is her name?"

Beckett stared at the Information Station. The two older women were both looking down at their cell phones. An older gentleman with a bit of a belly and greying around the temples of his brown curly hair acted as security guard. He had his thumbs tucked into his utility belt and leaned against the wall. He scanned the room and nodded to those who acknowledged him.

"Her... her name is Mickayla." She stared at the Information Station as they walked closer and closer toward it.

"Just relax. They are not looking for us. We are just nurses... "

"Just nurses..." she repeated, giving herself strength.

"We're doing this for Mickayla. Let's think about her."

They walked past the fountain and were making their way past the seating area when their ears perked at a conversation happening on the other side of the room.

"Hey T," someone called out to Taylor.

She inadvertently glanced back at Hannah, but recovered quickly. "S'up?"

"You know that doctor you used to hang out with?"

Taylor looked at the young man like he had three heads. "Uh, hello, I'm a respiratory tech, I hang out with doctors all day…" she cocked her head to the side to add to her annoyance.

He shook his head, "No, I mean that one… she had long blonde hair. She was a third-year, I think?"

"Dude, she's been gone for like-ever."

"I know, but they are looking for her."

"Who is?"

"The police or something. There's these dudes running around downstairs like crazy. They say she's here."

"Here like… in town… in the state…."

"Like here… in the hospital."

Taylor bobbed her head trying to think of what to say next, but he spoke first. "They're offering a reward."

"Why? What'd she do?"

"I think she killed somebody."

"What? That's just stupid." Her eyes accidentally looked past him and willed Hannah and Beckett to walk faster.

"You seen her?"

She chuffed, "No."

"It is kinda weird how she like, just stopped coming to work, don't you think?"

"Dude, show some respect, her family had just died. And that was like a year ago."

He winked and tisked, while pointing at her, "Exactly."

"You're an idiot, Glen."

"What if she was the one that…"

"Excuse me? Ma'am?" The security guard stood up and nodded his head in Hannah's direction.

"Oh my gosh, Dude, back up!" Taylor's voice filled the entire lobby and all eyes turned to her direction.

"What the…" Glen frowned at her as she flailed her arms and pushed him away.

The security guard came from around the desk and looked at Hannah and Beckett and then over at the noisy respiratory tech. He started walking toward Hannah..

"Seriously? I'm SO not into you like that!" Taylor pushed off Glen and pretended to fall into a metal cart that an orderly was pushing toward the hallway Taylor was standing next to.

The security guard, nodded to the nurses, "'Scuse me, ladies, I was just gonna remind you that it's mighty cold out there. Y'all need to give up smokin', or at least put ya coats on. An I mean one fo each of ya."

Hannah nodded, "Oh… Oh yes, of course. My car's right outside."

He nodded again, "Excuse me," He turned his attention to the commotion, "Hey... Hey, what's all this goin' on over here?"

Taylor was on the floor "accidentally" kicking metal trays in every direction making as much noise as possible.

Hannah and Beckett kept their heads down and braced for the cold temperatures. "I guess a distraction *was* a good idea." Once outside, they took off running across the parking lot, through the vast sea of cars to the local baseball field and a special needs van with precious cargo waiting for them on the other side.

Hannah could see the fear in Mickayla's eyes when her mother started taking the tubes off. Her eyes darted back and forth from Hannah to her mother. Her father looked on skeptically and his breathing was rapid as his wife began to release their child from all her restraints. Mickayla tried arching her neck and drool spilled from her lips. Her father was close by with a washcloth to wipe his child's face.

When Hannah lay her hands on her tiny little heart, she locked eyes with her. The sweet little girl gasped for air only once but then, her eyes were wet with tears. Her arms that were locked tight against her chest, relaxed. Her mouth opened and closed as if she'd acquired a new skill. Mother and father stood off to the side to give Hannah some space. It was only a few moments more and Mickayla turned her head. For the first time since the accident, she was able to look at her mother and father on her own. She next tested her arms, stretching them out in front of her, then wiggled her fingers. "Ahh! Momma!" she called out perfectly clear. "My Daddy…" Unable to control her tears, she held her arms open for her parents to fill. Tears of joy united that family once again. And while they embraced their daughter, not having to manipulate her limbs or head again, Hannah placed her hand on the base of Nurse Beckett's back and healed her damaged spine that was also caused by the accident. And before they could come up for air and thank Hannah, she had disappeared.

Miracles from Ashes

Chapter Twenty- Three

Hannah smiled to herself as she watched the sun begin to come up in the rear-view mirror out of the passenger window. She and Taylor traveled in silence for the first twenty minutes of the trip.

"What are you smiling about?" Taylor asked, as she looked over to her passenger.

"Family…"

Taylor nodded, not wanting to get into all that mushy stuff.

Hannah looked back over and studied Taylor's profile briefly, trying not to look elsewhere. "Hey," she said finally.

Taylor glanced over at her.

"Thanks…" she swallowed, "You saved me again."

Taylor chuffed. "I know."

Hannah looked away and back out to the window. It was Taylor's turn to look at her passenger. "You must have really pissed some people off."

"Not on purpose."

"You're taking off again?"

Hannah opened her mouth to speak, but no words came out. She apologized with her eyes but could offer no other consolation.

Taylor shrugged her shoulder, "Whatever, you know? I kinda figured. You're suddenly all secretive and stuff. Got the cops after you, probably."

"Can't get anything by you, huh?" Hannah teased.

"I got mad detective skills," Taylor laughed.

They both fell silent for a few moments before Hannah burst out laughing. Taylor couldn't help but smile listening to her laugh and finally she had to ask, "What? What, woman?"

Hannah yelled in the small Volkswagen Bug, "Dude! I'm SO not into you like that!"

Taylor's whole face lit up and she joined in the laughter, "That was messed up. I can't believe I did that. I totally saved you."

"That you did. Oh, that was so funny. I was so scared at the moment, but being able to look back at it now, that was so, so funny." Hannah had to wipe away the moisture beneath her eyes from laughing.

"I'm probably going to have to go through drug testing when I get back."

"And poor Glen."

Taylor laughed again, "He'll get over it."

"Speaking of testing, you'd better get that high blood pressure under control before it does some serious damage."

"What high blood pressure? I'm flippin' twenty-three years old."

Hannah looked at her skeptically. "Now you have been in the medical field long enough to know that you don't have to be a certain age to be affected by high blood pressure, and in your case, too much salt."

"What? Salt is my friend."

"Uh, no… it's not. And you'd better back off of it before…"

"Yeah, yeah, okay, mom. Jeez, so I like salt."

"It doesn't like you."

"So fix it, you got all these superhero skills and shhhhh…. uh stuff."

"I did. Fix it, that is, but it's not going to do you a bit of good if you keep eating the same way."

Taylor squinted her eyes, grinning slightly she replied with, "I'll think about it."

They pulled into the hotel parking lot and saw three black SUVs parked haphazardly, blocking one side of the parking lot.

Taylor quickly turned back out of the drive looking in her mirror. "Dude…"she whispered in her own car, "they aren't playing around. Think they are here for you?"

Hannah frowned. "I don't know, but let's not chance it." She slumped down in the passenger seat a little lower.

"You were right by parking ole Bessie somewhere else."

Hannah pulled up the collar on her winter coat and stuffed her hands in her pockets. She felt the paper copies of the photos in one pocket, in the other, there was a single piece of paper. She pulled it from her pocket to look at it. The check.

Hannah unfolded it and gasped at the amount. In the memo section she had scribbled, "I'm sorry."

"What?" Taylor looked over at her.

Hannah tipped the check so she could see it.

"Holy… sugar cookies!" Taylor's mouth was hanging open. "She sold you out! She straight up sold you out."

"It appears that way." The sadness on Hannah's heart weighed heavy. Suddenly it was all so crystal clear.

"So… where am I going?" Taylor asked.

Hannah read from the corner of the check. "The First Bank of Trust on Manchester."

"Yeah… I like what you're thinking!"

Hannah was able to cash out a good part of the check as long as she agreed to open an account with the bank and they would deposit the rest. She gave them her old address from her old driver's license and they seemed to be fine with that.

She came from the bank with a thick envelope of bills and climbed into Taylor's car. She tucked a stack of bills in the center console.

"What's that for?"

Hannah smiled. "It's just paying you back when you helped me out… and maybe a little interest," she laughed.

Taylor dropped Hannah off at her camper, which was parked in a Walmart parking lot. "So, how long are you going to stay?"

"Probably not long," Hannah shrugged "…with all this stuff going on… Hopefully, they'll just chalk it up to a loss and it'll be over but, it's probably better not to beat the beehive."

"Good call." She nodded toward the superstore,"You picked a good place to get stocked up."

"That was the plan."

"Text you tomorrow? I work early, so I get off at one. I mean, technically I work early every day this week because Janet is trying to kill me, but whatever, you want to do lunch before you head out?"

Hannah nodded. "Sure. Where would you like to go?"

"Anywhere. Wait, anywhere but Chinese. I really hate Chinese food."

"Fair enough. Let me think about it and we can meet somewhere on the way out of town."

Taylor pursed her lips and nodded.

They both sat in silence for really only seconds before Hannah leaned across the console and hugged her. Taylor accepted the love and blinked her eyes as they watered up. "Stupid mascara," she said, brushing her lashes with her index finger. "Got in my eyes."

Hannah nodded, understanding. "Stupid mascara…"

"Hey," Taylor said, causing Hannah to pause, "I'm going to miss you. Answer your freaking texts every once in awhile will ya?"

Hannah laughed. "I promise. Quit crying, I'll see you tomorrow."

Taylor pouted, "I'm not crying... you're crying..."

Hannah decided to stay in the Walmart parking lot for the night. She splurged on a steak dinner at the Texas Roadhouse that just happened to be in the parking lot. She sat close to the televisions to see if there was any "breaking news" about a missing superhero that was being held hostage at the local hospital... but all seemed to be quiet.

She was expecting some kind of smear campaign or bogus missing person's tripe, but so far, it was just the usual news stories. Still, she shouldn't wait around too long for them to change their minds.

She wasn't so naïve as to think there wouldn't be any backlash of her sneaking away and ruining all of their plans of torture. And yes, she had to admit that she was curious about their theories in reference to using her blood, not enough to become a prisoner, but curious, nonetheless. They had plenty of vials of her blood that should keep them busy for a while. *And if it made them billions, whatever; knock yourself out,* she thought as she finished off her drink and tossed her napkin onto her plate.

The next morning, she text Taylor to see what time she wanted to meet for lunch and where. She waited and waited, but no response came. "How's she gonna yell at me about returning texts," Hannah mocked, as she put away her groceries.

She tried a couple more times but Taylor didn't answer. Hannah didn't really think much of it because... well, it was Taylor.

But right before she was about to doze off, her phone lit up. It was a text from Taylor.

"Hey, sorry about today, I had to work late. How about tomorrow?"

Hannah tapped the tiny keys with her thumbs in response. "Sure, what time?"

"How about ten a.m."

"Don't you have to work?"

"No. I'm off."

Hannah looked suddenly wary at the blinking curser on her phone's screen. Hannah shook her head, feeling silly and typed back. "Sure. Where?"

There was a pause... "Where are you now?"

Hannah furrowed her brow, now suddenly a little concerned. "Same place."

The curser blinked and blinked and blinked for what felt like hours waiting for a reply.

"K," came the responding text. "You can pick where we eat."

Hannah swallowed hard before typing her response. "How about the Chinese place on Shackleford?" her thumb hovered over the send button for a moment more… *Please come back with a smart-aleck answer. Please. Please…*

"What time?"

Hannah's heart sunk to her stomach and her skin prickled down her arms. "Omigosh… Omigosh… that's not Taylor. What do I do? Who is on the other end of this conversation?"

She began to type a response and then deleted it… you don't know, Hannah…. Stay calm… She typed, "How about one? I know you don't like your Chinese food too early."

"Yes. You're right."

Hannah felt sick. This is not Taylor. This is not Taylor. Hannah's eyes burned with tears. The phone slipped from her hand onto the couch as she rubbed her eyes. She was trying to stay focused, but just knew that something bad had happened. She wrapped her arms around her stomach and rocked back and forth on her couch.

The phone lit up again and Hannah didn't want to touch it… but she had to. She turned it over to see the bright screen?

"So, I'll see you tomorrow?" it asked.

Hannah grimaced and wiped away her tears before responding. "I'll be there. See you soon."

Hannah did not sleep all night and jumped at every little noise. How she wished she still had Professor with her to protect her. She went through bouts of crying as her mind raced wondering what might have happened to Taylor. And then she would battle those thoughts, trying to talk some sense into herself. "I'm sure they just took her phone. She probably doesn't even know it's missing. They are probably asking her questions, trying to figure out where I am."

She sat up in her bed. "What if she tells them? I know she wouldn't do it on purpose, but…"

She threw her legs over the side of the bed and crawled over the furniture to reach the front of the RV. Everything was still closed up, as is the Walmart rule, so it was pretty cramped on the inside. She peeked her face through the curtains in the front half expecting her camper to be surrounded by police or black sedans. It looked pretty quiet and thanks to all the parking lot lighting, she was able to see the entire parking lot. The only movement was the customers who took up the first few spaces near the door.

"I'd better move… just in case." She pulled up the legs and slowly pulled out of the parking lot. She didn't go too far, but headed out of town, close enough in case the real Taylor reached out to her, but far enough away that Taylor couldn't accidentally tell anyone where she was.

She felt so helpless. She had no way to get in touch with her: No way to go and check on her.

She had decided to go and visit Wayne tomorrow, regardless, but now she would ask him to go and check on Taylor for her. She breathed in deep, letting the solution settle in. "That's the best I can do, for now," she told herself. She climbed and crawled all the way to the back of the camper and got back into bed. *Sleep, Hannah,* she told herself. *There's nothing else you can do right now.*

Hannah tucked her hair behind her ears and pulled her ball cap down low over her eyes. She parked her rig at the far corner of the gas station parking lot. She stuffed her hands in her coat pockets and walked cautiously across the slick parking lot.

She walked into the once familiar diner and saw that quite a few changes had been made. The walls were cleaner and everything was... brighter. Painted? She couldn't help but smile. There were flower vases on each of the tables. She looked around, not seeing any familiar faces. There was a new face behind the counter cooking on the grill, and new waitresses bustled around in jeans and colorful t-shirts advertising the diner... t-shirts which were also available for purchase, she could see.

She smiled at the changes but a moment of panic flashed through her as she wondered if Wayne was still even here. But then she heard:

"Who in the hell left this crap in the middle of the walkway? You girls tryin' to break this old man's neck? Melissa, get this box where it belongs."

Hannah couldn't hide her smile as she saw his grumpy face emerge from around the corner. He looked at her and nodded informally.

She took off her hat and ruffled her hair and smiled at him again.

"Well, I'll be damned. Look what the cat dragged in." He walked around the long counter and took her by the shoulders. He paused to look at her face and then pulled her into a deep embrace. "You're a sight for sore eyes, Girl," he whispered.

He pushed her body away from his once again to get a good look at her and embraced her once more, tighter. "It is good to see you."

Hannah's eyes had filled with tears and words would not come to her, but they were really not necessary.

"Hey, you want me to feed ya? Come on over here and sit down." He led her to "his" table and pushed his papers and catalogs to the side to make room for them both to sit.

"Hey, uh… Skylar," he waved one of his girls over. "What do you want to drink?"

Hannah looked up at the young waitress, "Uh… Pepsi, please?"

"She wants a cherry Pepsi," Wayne corrected. "And can you grab my coffee from the office?"

"Thank you," Hannah added.

She smiled and nodded and was on her way.

"Man," he reached across the table and grabbed her hands. "It's good to see you. How the hell have you been? Where have you been? Can you... do you..."

She laughed and nodded, "Yes. I can see you've quit smoking and for the most part, you're pretty healthy." She looked around at the diner again. "I love what you've done with the place. It looks nice."

He scrunched his face. "That's all Julia's doing."

Hannah cocked her eyebrow, "Oh? And who is Julia?"

Wayne, clearly embarrassed, smirked. "Now, let's not make a big deal out of things, she's this gal I've been seeing."

"Must be pretty serious to make you part with your money."

"I've got to admit, it's been good. I mean, the business and, you know... the other too. I increased my prices and cleaned the place up and now I make enough that I don't even need to be here if I don't want to ."

"That makes me so glad," Hannah smiled, genuinely happy for her friend. "So, why are you here then?"

"What the hell else am I gonna do?' he laughed. "Wanna quick tour? Wait till you see the other side!"

Skylar brought their drinks back and set them on the table. "We'll be right back," he told her and placed his hand on Hannah's back to lead her to the gas station side of things.

New neon signs announced what delectables were hidden in the coolers. Wayne waved an arm, proud of the new Shoppette.

Hannah responded appropriately. "Oh, I love it! It's so clean and bright!"

"Well, *that's* thanks to Paula here." Wayne indicated the older woman behind the counter. "Come on out here and meet this special lady."

Paula's step was small and pained, but she kept a smile on her face. "I'd know you even if he didn't introduce you," she smiled. "This one is pretty proud of you," Paula hitched her head toward her boss.

Hannah saw immediately the cause of her pain. Spinal Stenosis. Hannah could see that herniated disks were fractured causing the space between the vertebrae to be limited, and therefore pressing on the nerves, making walking or standing for long periods of time very painful.

"Wayne," Hannah scolded, "Why are you making her stand so much? Don't you need office help?"

"Ah, my medical student," Wayne grinned proudly. "Hell, I can't make her sit down. I put a stool back there for her and everything."

"He does spoil me. Don't be too hard on him."

"Well Paula, it is really nice to meet you." Hannah reached out for her hand and held it in both of hers. "He's so lucky to have you."

Confusion crossed Paula's face, but she smiled politely through the odd sensation.

Wayne looked over the counter pretending not to notice a thing.

Hannah dropped her hand and watched the woman stand up tall, testing her spine for the piercing pain that was sure to come.

"Well, let's get back and get some grub, shall we?"

"Nice to meet you," Hannah called out again, and turned to walk back to the diner side. She looked up at Wayne, "You did that on purpose."

He shrugged. "I might have."

After placing their order with Skylar, he folded the menu and set it to the side. "And that gets me all caught up. Tell me... how's my girl?"

"I'm fine," she blushed.

"No, no... not you," he winked at her, "How's my Bessie."

Hannah laughed out loud. "She is a trooper. Put a lot of miles on those wheels. Want to go see her?"

He nodded. "Later. First, I want to hear about your adventures."

They talked for hours and he fed her anything and everything she could possibly eat. While she poked at the slice of key lime pie, attempting to make room for it, she brought him up to date. "I got a text about fifteen minutes before I got here that asked if we were still on for today..." she crumbled the chunk of pie crust on her plate with one prong of her fork. "I text back, 'Sure, is Glen coming?'...

Glen was the guy she embarrassed at the hospital but in *no way* has any relationship with her. She would have sent me back some... something... her sassy little self could come up with..." Hannah swallowed the lump in her throat and pinched her forehead.

"What did they say?"

"They said, and I mean after a really long pause, 'Not sure, he's busy, I think.'"

Wayne shook his head in disbelief.

"I know," she said, reading his thoughts. "I took the battery out of the phone and threw it away before I got here in case they could trace it or something."

"Good thinking." He folded his hands and tapped them on his lips. "So what now?"

She shrugged, "I was hoping that you could maybe go check on her or something today? Or call... or..."

"Yeah, yeah sure... we can make that happen."

"Thank you. I'm so worried about her."

"I'm worried about you. As much as I'd love for you to stay, you need to get out of here."

She flopped her head down on her arms. "I am so tired of running, Wayne. I just want some kind of... normal."

"I hear ya, Kiddo. But that's not something you can have." He talked to the top of her head knowing that there were tears on the other side. "I don't know why you were chosen to be given this gift, but... it's not something that you can just ... stop doing."

"Oh... I know," came the muffled reply.

"Well, okay then… we need to get you out of here."

Her head shot up and she looked across the table at him with red-rimmed eyes and fresh tears welling up. "Where? Where, Wayne? What's to say these guys won't follow me where ever I go? Or… THEY hire someone to follow me? To what end?"

He shook his head and grabbed a napkin from the holder at the edge of the table. He leaned forward to wipe away her tears, "I wish I knew, Girl. I don't have the answers…"

"What?" Hannah gasped. "Can we turn that up?" Hannah was looking behind Wayne at the television mounted in the corner. She slid out from the booth to get a closer look.

Wayne was behind her with the remote, turning up the volume.

"Dr. Mosha Joshi, the CEO of Saints Memorial Hospital has been arrested today for allegedly embezzling funds from the charitable donations made annually. Reports indicate that this behavior may have been going on for years." The film footage behind the reporter showed Dr. Joshi being led out of the administrative building in handcuffs. She was given no coat, but only wore a cream colored turtleneck, and brown slacks; the picture of elegance. Her head was bowed down, not responding to the reporters sticking their microphones in her face or the cameras trying to get another view. As the camera panned back claiming a wider view, showing Dr. Joshi being put into the back seat of a police car, Hannah gasped. There, standing on the steps was Dr. Romero.

He was taking reporters questions, and shaking his head solemnly.

"That's one of the doctors!" Hannah turned back and looked at Wayne! "He… he was there! He was the one who was leading the testing!"

"Hannah…" Wayne paused, looking up at the TV and lowering the sound again.   She looked up at him with fear. "She didn't do what they are accusing her of. She's innocent."

"Hannah," Wayne said again, placing his hand on her shoulder. "…this is bigger than a hired, slick P. I. This is… serious."

Hannah swallowed the lump in her throat. Her mouth was dry. She stared at the television but nothing was registering. Finally, she meekly asked, "What should I do?"

"Get the hell outta Dodge." He grabbed her arm and led her back to the table and leaned in conspiratorially. "You know what to do… you've done it before. You've got to go underground. These guys aren't playing and they have boatloads of money they can spend."

Hannah nodded, understanding.

"I'm sorry. I don't want you to go. Hell, I just got ya back… but you…"

"What about Taylor? Do you think she's in danger?"

He shrugged. "Maybe she's not important enough for them to mess with. But, I'll go into town later and see what I can find out."

She wrapped her hands around Wayne's. "Thank you. I would be so lost without you." Tears poured freely down her cheeks.

"Don't…" Wayne looked away, not comfortable with her tears, "Don't give up on me now." It was his turn to squeeze her hands, "You gotta stay strong, you hear me? There is obviously a reason that you're still here. You need to get out and find out what it is. You need to go heal people." He waved his hand in the air, nonchalantly, "Somewhere else, obviously, but… this gift is your purpose. Go and do it."

She nodded, knowing he was right. She had to get herself together and figure out where Pete needed her to go next.

"Go get freshened up. Can't have you lookin' a mess. We'll get you settled and on your way." He looked out the window and down at his watch. "It's only five-thirty, but it looks like it's nine o'clock. You go to the break room and get cleaned up and I'll go see if the evening newspaper is out yet. Let's get the whole story."

She swallowed hard but followed directions and walked past her waitress, Skylar, toward the back room.

When she came back out to the dining floor, she saw Wayne standing by their table rubbing his face with his hand. He was stressed too, she knew.

He saw her coming and stopped her from sitting down by grabbing her shoulders. He forced a smile and said, "You sure wore some life out of those tires, Girl. Did you not think about maintenance?"

She looked up at him guiltily. She pouted and shook her head "no."

"I sent Bessie over to the boys in the mechanic's shop. They're gonna replace your tires, and give 'er a once over." He paused and made sure she was looking at him. "But you have to learn to do these things for yourself. I may not... always be around..."

"Don't say that. Don't even talk like that."

He released her to rub his face again and run his fingers through his hair. "Okay, listen, there's no other way around this." He turned around behind him and flipped the folded newspaper over so she could see the main story.

Hannah's eyes scanned the page and then her jaw dropped. She didn't realize she was holding her breath until it was forced from her lungs along with wailing sobs. There, on the top of the fold was the headline: "DUI Takes the Life of Yet Another Underage Drinker". A photo smiled up at her. Taylor Watson's bright blond hair and sparkly nose ring... she had her hands pressed together against her cheek... and ethereal glow softened the edges.... It was an older photo, but it was Taylor.

Hannah's blood drained from her face and cold chills ran over her body.

Hannah shook her head. No..." She skimmed over the teaser paragraph not believing what she was seeing.

"This can't be right! Taylor doesn't drink!" Hannah said. "This can't be..." She stopped short, gasping for air. "She's twenty-three! What have they done to you?"

She gathered herself long enough to unfold the paper and follow its prompts to the appropriate page to read in full detail...

Had been missing... didn't report to work... was disruptive employee of late... car found in head on collision with a tree on the side of winding road... popular place for parties...

No...no...no...no..... Hannah couldn't read anymore. She dropped the paper from her hands. It fell to the floor and fanned out over the floor. *This isn't right... this can't be right...*

Skylar silently came over and picked up the newspaper and folded it neatly and laid back on the table. Wayne picked it up and continued reading the article. Skylar asked with her expression if she should clear the table of dishes, not wanting to interrupt and Wayne nodded with a gruff, "Thanks."

Hannah froze; the implications sinking in.

It wasn't an accident.

It wasn't an accident.

It... wasn't... an ... accident...

"Did I do this?" Hannah's brain went crazy? Is this because of me? Did I get Taylor killed?

Hannah squeezed her forehead trying to keep her thoughts straight. She paced back and forth in front of the small area. Skylar was weaving in and out trying not to make a sound.

Hannah's eyes burned with tears. "What have I done? What have I done?"

In this moment in time, Hannah was caught in fear for her own life and in mourning for that sweet girl who only wanted to help. Hannah didn't have time to cry; couldn't reach out to Taylor's parents...

"Hang on, it's about to get worse," Wayne said, as he scrolled down the paper. At the very bottom of the article it said, "Last seen with Hannah Michaelson" and an older photo of her was posted beside it with a hotline number. "If you see this person or have any information of her whereabouts, please call the number."

Hannah dropped her head into her hands. She looked up at the last person on earth she could trust.

"Get the hell out of this town and don't look back."

"Hi, uh... is this the hotline?" Skylar turned her back to the dining room and tucked a loose strand of hair behind her ear. "That girl you are looking for. I've seen her... she's here."

Miracles from Ashes

Chapter Twenty-Four

It was about one in the morning when the RV was ready to get back out on the road. Wayne loaded her up with supplies and a full tank of gas and was giving things one last look. Hannah watched from the window inside the diner and sipped on her hot white chocolate latte waiting for the signal to come out.

Skylar came out of the back room and buttoned her coat. She slipped on her knitted hat and looped her scarf. She watched Hannah for a moment before throwing her purse over her shoulder and walked toward her.

"Um... hey..." Skylar approached.

Hannah turned toward her and smiled warmly. "Hey Skylar, thank you so much for taking such good care of me today. I'm sorry I was such a mess. I hope we didn't steal too much time from your other tables."

Skylar looked down at her shoes and back up to Hannah. "No, you don't have to worry about that, Mr. Wayne takes care of us. He tipped me more today that I would have earned in a week."

Hannah nodded, knowing Wayne's generous nature. "He's a good guy."

Skylar agreed. "He really thinks a lot of you." She turned away, shyly before continuing, "I'm uh… getting off for the night and… I… "

Hannah turned to face her, listening.

"I… just wanted…" The girl's face became emotional and she swallowed hard between her sentence fragments."

"Are you okay?" Hannah touched her shoulder.

She nodded, causing the little yarn ball on top of her hat to bounce back and forth. Hannah didn't know how she could help. She was obviously struggling with something. It was nothing Hannah could heal.

"I've heard things… about you..." she gulped. "I didn't know if they were true…"

Hannah didn't interrupt, waiting to see which of a million directions that last statement would go.

"I called the hotline." She finally spit the words out.

Hannah took a step back, her mouth opened but no words came out. She tried to speak "Why?" but her voice box wasn't cooperating. Hannah's face showed sheer panic. She closed her eyes and tried not to let the information take over her emotions.

"It's okay though…" she barely touched Hannah's forearm causing her to open her eyes again. "I didn't tell them that you were here, necessarily…" her eyebrow pushed up her usually smooth forehead in worry. "Please don't be mad."

"Skylar," Hannah began calmly. "What did you tell them?"

"I told them that you were at my old job. It's a truck stop, like this one only on the other side of town, heading in the opposite direction. I was hoping..." she swallowed hard, "That it would give you some time to... you know... get away..."

Hannah tried to smile, understanding her sentiment. "Thank you. I hope they take the bait." She reached out and held Skylar's hands, "I guess I know which direction I won't be going," she attempted a laugh.

Skylar pushed out a half-hearted laugh. "There's something else..."

Hannah swallowed hard, bracing for the worst.

"Paula," Skylar's eyes subconsciously looked past Hannah toward the gas station side, "she's... she's my mom. And... I think you... uh... you saved her or ... healed her... or whatever you call it..." Skylar felt suddenly self-conscious and looked away at her boots. "Don't worry. I won't tell," she added quickly. "I... just wanted to thank you... and try to ... help."

Hannah drew the young woman into an embrace and held her for a moment. "Thank you," she whispered into Skylar's thick scarf.

Skylar looked around as she smiled sheepishly, "Good luck," she finally said, and left the diner to go pick up her mother so they could end their shift.

Hannah drove through Illinois in the dark and reached Missouri just as the sun was coming up framing the St. Louis Arch. She wondered if she should stop, but the gas tank said she should be able to go a few more miles.

She glanced at herself in her visor mirror while stopped at a red light and saw the stress and emotions all over her face. Not only were her eyes swollen from crying but the dark circles showed that she was severely lacking in sleep. She actually wondered how she was still going. She glanced down at her cup holder and acknowledged the empty coffee cups may have something to do with her progress. Her eyes inadvertently dipped over to the passenger seat where a brand new "go-phone" package rested.

Wayne had tossed it there, just before he let her go. She was terrified to use it, but terrified also of never being able to speak to him again. This brought tears back to her eyes even though she tried to fight against it. The light changed and crying through downtown St. Louis made things extremely difficult. She dried her tears to be able to focus on the complex interstate system.

"I will never forget you Wayne. I hope that we can meet again someday."

She leaned over and pushed the package to the floorboard, so she would no longer be distracted with the option.

Hannah sat in the chair at the beauty salon getting her hair colored back to its original brownish-blonde color. She sat patiently flipping through an entertainment magazine shaking her head because she didn't know a single celebrity that covered the pages, but at the same time, felt their pain of wanting a "normal" life.

She couldn't help but smile as she heard her stylist talking to a co-worker in the back room.

"I don't know what it is, I just… feel so much better."

"What happened?"

"You know, you're going to think I'm crazy, but I just felt this … like… warmth go through my body and it's like my hands and my back… they just stopped hurting."

"You have time for a quick smoke break?" the other woman asked not really wanting to participate in the conversation.

She laughed, "I… I don't really want to. I can't explain it… but … I … it's like the craving is gone."

"Suit yourself."

Then, a woman with long straight, thick brown hair sat in the chair next to her and Hannah couldn't help but overhear their conversation.

"So the full twelve inches, huh?" the stylist asked.

The customer nodded, "More if you can. I want to donate it for a wig."

The stylist nodded understanding and began sectioning off the hair.

"I was just at the grocery store," the woman continued, "and this little girl came up to me and tugged on my finger. I looked down at her and she said, 'You have pretty hair. I hope I have hair just like yours when I feel better.' I tell you, that broke my heart." The woman placed her hand on her chest, reliving the moment. "I decided that I would donate the hair, specifically to her. She's getting ready to be hospitalized. That poor, sweet little girl."

Hannah's heart went out to the child that she didn't even know. In her travels she has seen and was thankful that she was able to help so many children along the way. She wished she could save them all.

She was so tired of living in the shadows and keeping her gift a secret. But for her safety…

She paid her stylist for the service and was ready to go out and… hide again… waiting for the next person she could help.

As she walked out the door, she saw a shiny black SUV, the only vehicle in the parking lot that didn't have salt and snow residue on it. There were two men. One sitting in the driver's seat and one standing outside the truck, smoking.

Hannah knew they were there for her. She stood and looked directly at them, surprisingly not feeling any fear. They saw her and froze, neither side really knew what the next move was supposed to be. The driver, instantly picked up his cell phone.

Suddenly, something inside Hannah… shifted. She turned around and went back into the beauty salon. She leaned over the counter and directed her question to the other customer halfway through with her service. "I'm sorry, what was the name of that hospital you mentioned?"

The woman looked over at her, "The Children's Cancer Institute."

"Thanks."

Hannah walked back out the door and stared at the men both watching her. She walked across the plaza's parking lot and slid into the vehicle she rented and drove off, practically daring the men to follow her. Frankly, she didn't care anymore if they did or if they didn't.

Hannah walked into the sliding doors of the Children's Cancer Institute. There was happy music filtering through the speakers and a wall of bubbles that needed to be passed through before you came into the cavernous lobby. It was brightly colored and there was a permanent hot air balloon "floating" overhead. Several other hot air balloons were painted on the walls and some were "half real and half painted".

A genuine smile crossed her face as she thought, "I'm about to put this place out of business."

She followed the signs to the first wing of "extended stay" patients.

There were two rows of beds filled with children of all ages in various stages of the deadly cancer disease.

Hannah felt light headed as she made her way into the room. She saw so much damage... tissues, organs... she wasted no time and went to the first bed.

She spent a few hours talking, hugging, shaking hands with the children, of course healing them as she went. No alarms went off, no alerts to raise suspicions… just laughing, loving and healing.

She went from wing to wing, floor to floor healing as many as she could.

It wasn't until she reached the top floor, the intensive care unit that she knew her time was up. She saw them at the opposite end of the hallway. The two men in black. They were escorted by someone wearing a suit, a man in scrubs and a nurse. She wondered what story the men told the staff to make them believe she was the one who could be dangerous.

There were still so many children on this floor to heal, and they were the worst off. No one on either side moved and Hannah stood firm.

She heard a nurse come from one of the rooms and it startled her. She was about ready to run but decided to try one more thing before they catch her.

She crouched down low to the floor and closed her eyes. She reached her hand out as far as she could stretch and willed her body to repeat the mass healing like she did at the bombing scene.

She took in a deep breath and released it. Nothing. Come on… she pleaded with her gift. She stretched out again, spreading her fingers wide…

She opened her eyes and saw the band of people from the other end of the hallway move toward her.

She pulled her arms close to her sides and shook out her hands. She balanced her body on one bent knee and one foot, in case she had to take off running. She breathed in and exhaled. She twisted her neck and rolled her shoulders. On the next exhale, she reached out her hand again.

She felt the warmth filling her body... it tingled her skin as it radiated from her center outward. She stretched her hand and fingers and felt the heat follow. She could see a light, like a mist or a vapor-with-a-mission emanating from all around her. It hovered just above the ground until it lifted and moved down the hallway.

The others must have been able to see it as well, for they stopped dead in their tracks to witness the strange occurrence.

She concentrated, but watched as the golden light took on a life of its own, almost and tucked in and out of each room. Hannah's gift healed the entire floor.

Her body gave way and she lost her balance falling to her side. She was breathless and dizzy. The light was gone and only the two men were coming toward her.

She barely had enough time to smile triumphantly at her suitors before she forced herself to get to her feet and run down the stairwell behind her.

Hannah was able to make it to her car without getting caught and did happen to see the men come out a side door as she was speeding out of the parking lot.

She screamed in her closed up vehicle and slammed her fist against the steering wheel in triumph. "This was the best day ever!!"

From that moment on, she decided that she was going to do as much good as she possibly could before she got caught.

She turned in her rental, fired up the RV and headed into her new life.

Chapter Twenty- Five

Hannah's picture was in every newspaper and her videos went viral. She was everywhere. She would blow into town, and go to the first hospital or clinic she could see, heal as many people as she could in one day and blast out again.

She would have to disappear for a few days at a time to recuperate and to change direction so as not to become too predictable.

In some towns, she saw her shadows and in others, there was no sign of them.

She was afraid of what would happen when they finally caught up to her, and she was certain that it would indeed, happen, but since her gift was so public now, they would have no other option than to lock her away, and proceed with their originally intended testing... Hannah was not looking forward to those dark times as her imagination took her down every scenario of what they would want to do with her, and she knew none of them would be noble or selfless.

She, herself, also didn't know the answers to the questions they would be wanting. Was she able to heal herself? Would she live forever? Does she age? Does her blood or tissues or other pieces and parts create some level of healing? Or cell regeneration? Or any number of other magical things?

In some cities she had just barely escaped her trackers. She wondered if Pete was keeping her safe. Is this what he was wanting her to do all along? Or is it all too impersonal and showy for his liking. He hasn't made his displeasure known so...

Hannah had to admit that she missed the interaction with each person she healed, but was so caught up in the adrenaline rush that she couldn't very well stop now.

Hannah rushed across the massive parking lot of the largest hospital in Austin, TX. She looked up toward the sky not yet tackling something so immense. This would be her biggest "save" to date.

She whisked past the rows and rows of cars not paying attention to the people or anything else that was around her.

She walked right past Pete who was standing among the cars watching her make her way with purpose toward the front door. He wasn't the only one watching.

She barely looked both ways before crossing the busy thoroughfare; her eyes on the main entrance. Just prior to the huge automatic sliding doors opening, she saw Pete standing at the corner of the building and stopped cold.

She tried to read his face, knowing that he was there to tell her something.

She stood for a moment looking at the Main entrance to the hospital wondering if she should go in. Hannah glanced back over and saw Pete shake his head "no".

She frowned, unhappy about being delayed. She didn't see anything out of the ordinary. This would be her finest achievement. There were thousands of people in there. The largest hospital, she argued with herself standing just outside the doors.

She looked back over toward Pete and saw that he was gone. She frowned again. "What?" She spoke under her breath and looked around her for any suspicious activity. "I've got this." She took a step toward the building and the magical doors opened for her, inviting her in.

She heard Pete's voice, *"Pride goeth before the fall..."*

She gasped as two men came from the other side of the welcoming doors, and without laying a hand on Hannah, maneuvered her back out toward the curb where a black SUV was waiting. They shoved her in the back seat with one smooth move, shut the door behind her, and the vehicle screeched off.

The SUV pulled up alongside a warehouse and Hannah was escorted into a side door. They kept a tight hold of her arm as three men lead her down a hallway and into a large open space.

A make-shift hospital room was created with plastic sheeting for walls, lights on stands, a hospital gurney and machines hooked up to long extension cords disappearing under the plastic walls. Hannah could hear the hum and growl of a generator that must be powering this portable facility.

Hannah could see movement on the other side of the plastic but when she was escorted into the center of the room, it all felt very familiar.

"Ms. Michaelson," the voice said. "You have been very troublesome." Dr. Trent Romero set down his clipboard and turned to face her.

She said nothing but her expression showed contempt and honestly, she felt no fear.

"I hope you don't mind," he continued, as he pinched the bridge of his nose, "if we skip the formalities this time. You have cost me… " he laughed out… "quite a bit of money, with your… activities."

She struggled against the grip on her arm and Dr. Romero nodded to a chair. One of the men brought her to the chair and forced her to sit.

"What now?" Hannah sighed.

Dr. Romero laughed. "We pick up where we left off, of course."

Two nurses came into the room pushing a tray filled with shiny objects, empty vials and other tools designed to intimidate her.

"Where are your co-harts?" Hannah ventured.

"Funny you should ask…" he smirked. "They were so valiant in the early days. They decided that they, themselves wanted to be the guinea pigs for our initial testing of your blood. The results…" he looked at her to see if she knew the answer before he spoke it, "… were quite surprising."

She furrowed her brow in confusion.

"You don't know, do you?"

She shook her head, honestly.

"Well, here's the short version. Our friend Mr. Schisler accepted a direct injection of your pure blood." He made the symbol of the cross on his forehead, waist, shoulder to shoulder.

"What? What happened to him?"

"His heart rate sped up, and a fever broke out. Basically, his heart exploded and his brain … cooked."

Hannah gasped, her jaw dropped.

"Right," Dr. Romero nodded, and pointed at her. "Not unlike the expression I had." He paced in front of her shaking his head. "Never seen anything like it, and it happened so fast," he threw out his hands, "… there was nothing we could do to save him."

He slid a stool out and moved it in front of her before sitting on it. He leaned forward and nodded to the nurse who was standing beside Hannah.

Hannah startled when the nurse reached for her arm but then Dr. Romero explained, "She's just getting your vitals. Believe me, no harm will come to you as long as you cooperate. But, I will let you in on a secret. While I'd much rather have you alive, I have no qualms about severing our little partnership, if you understand my meaning." He leaned back almost disappointed that her face did not yield the results of terror he was hoping for.

"Which brings me to Dr. Halifax," he continued. "She decided that your blood should be diluted and dispensed in smaller intervals. However, when I suggested we wait for a patient, *she,* despite standing very much the same distance you are from me now, from Mr. Schisler when he literally cooked in front of us, decided to perform the test on herself."

He wheeled the stool back to a side table with drawers and claimed his clipboard before scootching his way back in front of Hannah.

He flipped through the first few pages, scanning the documents, before speaking. "She..." he continued to look over the flipped pages, "Ah yes... she claimed 'levels of euphoria, feeling warm sensations, and no pain. A light, floating feeling...'" He looked up at her to see if anything resonated with his prisoner.

Hannah listened, not giving him any facial feedback, but when he didn't continue she asked, "And then?"

He took in a deep breath and pulled the pages back to their original position and breathed out. He slapped the clip board against his thigh and pursed his lips. "The damnedest thing." He looked sideways at her. "Before we could administer her next dosage, she..." he shook his head looking for words, "She... I don't know how else to say it, but... she turned to mush. Her body lost all fluids, which poured out of every opening," he rolled his eyes in disgust, "and her bones lost all consistency. She was flesh J-ello."

Hannah was horrified at his non-emotional description. "How awful!"

"You have no idea." He rolled his eyes. Dr. Romero looked at her a moment more trying to read her.

He shook the clipboard at her, "And *you...* obviously have no idea just how... powerful you are."

I was working on finding out, till you interrupted me, she thought, but said nothing.

"You have definitely increased in your skills since last we met though, I'll give you that." He cocked his eyebrow challenging her to deny it. "Multiple healings at a time. Impressive. Very impressive."

She scowled at him, not the least bit interested in his praise.

"Oh yes, where was I..." he searched his thoughts. "Ah. Dr. Brazier. The third partner... our friend who was determined you were from a comic book."

Hannah nodded, seeing the face of Dr. Brazier in her mind.

"Now he..." he paused. "He got wise. Our good friend, Dr. Brazier suddenly decided that it was too dangerous to run the tests on his own person, as much as he wanted to be the next Spiderman, he refused." Dr. Romero was shaking his head being dramatic, enjoying the storyteller's spotlight. "However, he was foolish enough to think he could just walk away. But... we both know what happens to those in our inner circle who... know too much, don't we."

Hannah's heart skipped a beat and a lump formed in her throat as she thought of Taylor and Mosha. "What... what happened to him?"

He brushed away her question with the wave of his hand, "It's not important, really. He wasn't much of a team player, anyway."

Hannah swallowed the lump finally and dared to ask, trying to keep the quivering from her voice... "There... there was a nurse that night, is she here?"

Dr. Romero looked down at Hannah, a slow smile spreading across his face, "Nurse Beckett." He wheeled his stool closer to her. "Funny, she never showed for work the next day... in fact, she just..." he blew into his hands, "disappeared..."

Hannah looked down at her hands, relieved.

"Don't worry. We'll find her. We found you, didn't we?"

Hannah rolled her eyes at his cockiness. "It's not like I made it too difficult for you. All you had to do was read the paper."

He frowned as his gentlemanly façade faded before her eyes.

"You think this is a game? You think I have invested all of this time and money on a game of tag?" His voice boomed in the open room. "Or perhaps you think you have been a challenge? The Midwest has been your chess board?

You are sadly mistaken." He clenched his teeth attempting to control his temper. "Your days of running are over. Now your next move has been narrowed down to two choices: if you are going to play nice, or not. Check mate."

Despite her best efforts, Hannah couldn't resist closing her eyes. She knew she hadn't been drugged, because Dr. Romero was particular about not wanting to taint her blood in any way, but he was getting irritated with her onset of narcolepsy.

"Dr. Michaelson… Dr. Michaelson," he repeated. "I'm going to need you to stay with me. You're giving off false readings."

She forced her eyes open and stared blankly at her captor. "You just took fourteen vials of my blood, have not given me any water or food and put me on your stupid tread mill for an hour, what do you expect?"

He looked at her and then down at the scribbled notes. Conceding, he said, "Yes, I can see that your blood sugar is low. I'll have some food brought in for you right away." He nodded at two of the men standing at either side of Hannah and they immediately left the room through the overlapping plastic edges and disappeared into the darkness.

The lights flickered and the machines beeped at the electrical surge. Dr. Romano looked at Hannah. "Are you doing that?"

Hannah, as tired as she was, laughed. "No, of course not. Not my superpower."

He looked to his third hired hand, "Didn't you put gas in the generator?"

"Yeah boss, but it's been going all day."

Dr. Romero pursed his lips and spoke through his teeth. "Then, fix it."

The man simply nodded and he too, left the plastic research room.

All that was left was the good doctor, a nurses and a hostage. A sleepy hostage. And Hannah couldn't help herself, she fell into a hard sleep.

When she woke up, she had no idea if it was day or night. She had a painful crick in her neck from sleeping in the chair. She saw a Styrofoam container on the table beside her. When she lifted the lid, it revealed a sandwich and some chips, an apple and a bottle of water tucked inside. She devoured the food as fast as she could chew and swallow.

She looked around her and she seemed to be alone. The steady beeping of the machines were familiar... almost comforting to her, but there were no people... no sounds of people, it was like everyone had disappeared.

She took a moment to scan the room and saw the mini fridge in a back corner. She stood up and stretched her tense muscles and walked toward the fridge. When she opened the door, she saw the vials of her blood, all dated and lined up on the top shelf.

She pulled them out and was getting ready to smash them on the concrete floor when Dr. Romero pulled back the plastic sheeting to enter the room.

"Well, well... look who's awake and hellbent on making my life difficult."

Hannah faced off with him and threw the four vials that were in her hand on the floor. The thin glass shattered and the thick liquid oozed into a puddle around it.

Dr. Romero fluttered his eyes, exasperated. "Marco," he called out. "Could you please come in here and... detain our ... guest." He seethed, clenching his jaw as the giant man came into the room and grabbed Hannah by the arm and escorted her, with her feet barely touching the floor, back to her chair. Hannah didn't fight but kept her fist closed tight around a hidden vial.

"I see you've mauled your food."

Hannah didn't reply. But reached for the pickle sliver that was left in the tray.

"Yes, yes... eat, please, because today, since you are rested and fed... we are going in to retrieve some marrow from the center of your bones." He looked over at the dark colored puddle on the floor. "And apparently, draw some more blood."

"So… what… You're going to become this snake oil salesman and sell bits and pieces of me from a cute little corner voodoo shop?" Hannah defiantly munched on chips while the doctor talked about his plans.

A smile spread across his face. "Oh no… your little bits and pieces… are being sold to the highest bidder. Just one of these vials of blood is worth more than you could even imagine." He spread his hands out and whisked them up and down Hannah's body as if showcasing her on a game show as the prize. "And here, I have an unlimited supply…"

She squinted her eyes and jutted her neck forward. "Seriously?"

He was a little taken aback by her comment. He frowned, not understanding.

"This," she spread her arms out including the room, "this is what your future holds? Keeping me alive so that you can make more money than any human alive only to spend it on keeping me hostage? Why bother? What's the point of having all of that money… if you don't get to enjoy it?"

A nurse came in wearing gloves and a breathing mask carrying a fresh new tray. She looked at Dr. Romero for unspoken permission, when he nodded at her she walked over to set the tray beside Hannah.

The nurse made eye contact with her patient and proceeded to tie a stretchy plastic band around Hannah's upper arm, and tapped the vein at Hannah's inner elbow with her fingers waiting for it to respond.

Dr. Romero curled up his lip, "For the prestige," he snarled at Hannah. "I will be the most honored physician in the world when we discover the secret to everlasting youth."

"But will you though?" Hannah taunted.

"Of course I will!" Dr. Romero roared at her slamming his hand down on the gurney.

"But how is that possible when you can't really tell anyone how you came up with this formula. You can't divulge your sources... you can't even release the ingredients to mass market this magic ... whatever you're proposing." She waved her hand in the air.

"There is a black market for everything."

Undaunted, Hannah smarted back, "The whole purpose of the black market is to keep everything a secret... where is your prestige now?"

"Why don't you let me worry about those things?" Dr. Romero replied, clearly annoyed.

And as if on command, the lights flickered causing all the machines to shut down and start back up.

Hannah spoke under her breath. "You can't even keep the lights on." The nurse withdrew the needle from her arm, pursed her lips together and looked away, pretending not to listen.

"What? What did you say?"

Hannah allowed the nurse to place a cotton ball held on by a bandaid on her arm. "How do you expect anyone to respect you when you are doing business out of a portable hospital?"

"If you hadn't been running…"

"Oh?   Now you're going to blame me for your situation? How selfish of me to want to have a life… and do GOOD for people, instead of…"

She didn't get to finish her sentence as Dr. Romero charged at her and lifted her from her seat. He expected to shout at her, show her who's boss and put her in her place; but he did not know she took the vial of blood that she had hidden in her hands and could not have expected her to smash it against his cheekbone.   The vial cracked and sent blood splashing across Dr. Romero's face. The fine shards of glass cut his cheek and blood seeped into the thin cuts and into his mouth. He screamed, releasing her, and tried to wipe his face and spit out the blood that lined his lips, but with every wipe, he dug the glass… and the blood deeper into his skin.

In a quick movement while Dr. Romero was trying to save his own life, Marco attempted to intervene.   Hannah grabbed the syringe from the table and jabbed into the large man's shoulder and depressed the plunger.

The nurse pushed herself away from the commotion and held her hands up in front of her, telling Hannah she wanted nothing to do with any of it.

Hannah lost no time in exiting the plastic room under the cover of chaos. She heard the screams of Marco and the crashing of equipment, but she didn't look back.

She side-stepped into the shadows of the huge empty room as two men came in the door, running toward the commotion.

Hannah waited until they were past her before escaping out the same door.

"Go after her!" she could hear Dr. Romero screaming. And she couldn't help but surmise that death did not come with a small dose of her blood administered by mouth. So... she ran.

Miracles from Ashes

Chapter Twenty- Six

Her heart pounded and her lungs burned, but she ran. She didn't know how long it would take for them to begin their pursuit, so she was determined to put as much space as possible between them.

She ran through the industrial neighborhood. The sun was high in the sky; it was early in the day. People were at work. Should she go for help? She decided that it would be too risky, as she wouldn't be able to explain any of this and she may run into someone just as bad, if not worse.

She came to a parking lot full of cars. As she wound her way through them, she tugged on handles to see if any happened to be unlocked. I'm sorry," she said breathlessly, "I just need to borrow one…"

All of her efforts proved to be fruitless. Out of the corner of her eye, she caught a glimpse of a man running. He was running in her direction, she didn't know if he saw her yet, or if it was even one of Romero's men, but she abandoned her planned car thievery and took off on foot once again.

She ducked toward the right, and the warehouses turned into low income homes. As she hid behind a tree, she caught the gaze of someone watching her. An older man sat on his front porch that was barely wider than the old lawn chair he sat on.

Her chest heaved but they just looked at each other. Hannah thought she was ready to run again, hoping that this man wouldn't betray her, but as she was ready to round the edge of the tree, she saw the familiar black SUV slowly roll down the street. She stepped back behind the tree again and held her breath.

Don't cry... she told herself. *Stay focused.*

She looked over at the man again and he nodded his head at her. He waved at her to go, but pointed for her to go down his street.

She swallowed hard, and nodded, thanking him with her eyes. And she ran.

The lower class neighborhood, upgraded slightly the farther she got from the warehouses. The houses were larger, there were lawns and driveways, and small playgrounds. She slowed to a walk, no need to call extra attention to herself...

She walked at a quick pace, looking through every yard and down every street for evidence that they were still after her. *Of course they are,* she told herself. Dr. Romero is convinced she is the answer to all his problems. He will never let her live in peace. She paused for only a moment to mourn the life she complained about because it was ... hard. She actually laughed at her present circumstance.

Her pause was not to last for long as she saw the SUV in front of her. It pulled over to the sidewalk and Hannah thought it was over. She thought she'd been spotted. She slid into the closest driveway and crouched down low watching the SUV through the parked car's window.

She saw the man that was chasing her walk up to the window of the black vehicle. The window rolled down. She couldn't see the driver, but they were talking. An arm came out of the window and pointed back where Hannah had just come from. The man nodded and took off in that direction while the SUV took a right turn at the corner.

Hannah took off toward the left.

The residential street she walked down opened up to make room for a parking lot and it's own crosswalk. She looked to her right and saw an elementary school. The parking lot was half full of cars and the busses were parked and unmanned since classes were underway.

Hannah thought she heard fire crackers and paused at the middle of the length of the parking lot. She assumed it was something else, because she couldn't detect anything wrong so she continued forward.

When she looked ahead of her she stopped, frozen in her tracts.

Pete stood, blocking the sidewalk. He said nothing, but she could see tears rolling down his face.

She looked quizzically at him, expecting him to speak. "Pete, what's wrong? He said nothing, but looked toward the school.

Hannah's eyebrows came together, confused. "You want me to go in there?" she asked.

Pete said nothing, but looked into the building again.

"They are chasing me. What am I supposed to do? If I stop, they'll find me!"

Just then, she heard gun shots. They were definitely gunshots. She turned and looked back at Pete. She nodded to him, telling him that she understood and was going in.

Hannah crept along the busses and made her way to the front door of the school. As she entered the building, the smell of iron accosted her senses. All was still. Maybe she had been mistaken?

She walked into the first room, which was the office. It was empty of faculty.

Hannah frowned. It was too quiet. Eerily quiet. "Where is everyone?" she whispered into the stillness.

The silence was broken by a smattering of rat-a-tat-tat sounds of an automatic rifle being fired.

She rounded the corner and saw the bodies of small children scattered about the hallway. Hannah gasped at the horror. Her stomach rolled as she swallowed the bile that was forcing its way up.

"No… no… no…." she dropped down to all fours and felt the pulse of the first child. None. She crawled to the next. No pulse. She crawled and checked all seven children, smearing a path of blood as she made her way from one still body to the next. She couldn't help them. Tears filled her eyes.

Shouting interrupted her grieving. She forced herself to move toward the noise. Her hands, tank top and cargo pants were now covered in blood.

She gingerly stepped over the dozens more lifeless bodies and made her way down the hall. A classroom door was open only to reveal a bloody massacre inside. The children never even left their seats.

"God," Hannah pleaded, "…please…"

She walked further down the hallway not daring to look in any more of the rooms. Tears blurred her vision. She rounded a corner toward the back of the building and heard the screams and cries of a group of people.

Hannah pressed herself against the wall and caught a glance at little eyes looking back at her. Her eyes adjusted to the dim light and she could see three maybe four children hiding in the janitor's closet. Hannah held her hand up flat, telling them to be still and placing a finger on her lips, reminded them to stay very quiet. The little boy in front bobbed his head causing the tears to slip from the edge of his eye. Hannah looked to her left, toward the sound of the commotion. She couldn't see anything, but there were two separate voices, shouting.

Hannah took in a deep breath summoning all of her courage and opened the door a bit wider allowing the children to follow her. "You must be very quiet," she whispered. "Follow me… don't look around… just stay focused on me, okay?"

She grabbed the tiny hand of the little boy who was closest to the door and drew him out, praying that they didn't distract the gunmen. "Come on… here we go… good job, hold hands…. Quickly and quietly now…"

She led them back down the hallway. A little girl started crying at the site and Hannah rushed them through. "Just a little more, sweetie… come on…"

They reached the front door and Hannah opened it as quietly as she could. She looked down at the five children. "You all hold hands and go the neighbor's houses. You bang on any of the doors until someone answers. Tell them to call the police, okay?" They all bobbed their little heads. "Good job… go now… run! Run, babies…"

Hannah watched until they reached the edge of the parking lot all linked together with clasped hands. They took the sidewalk to get to the first house. Hannah nodded, satisfied that they would be safe and be able to send help. But for now…

Hannah looked back to the elementary school and had to force herself to go back inside. If she could save any others, she had to try.

Two gunmen had gathered everyone into the cafeteria at the end of the hall.

Hannah flattened herself as close to the wall as possible to try and see inside. She saw two people with automatic weapons. They wore black ski masks, one had on shorts, hi-top sneakers and the other wore jeans and they both wore black shirts.

There was crying and screaming. A few adults had wrapped their arms around as many children that they could reach, attempting to be strong for them.

"Shhh…. Shhh, babies… stay by me…."

They had all seen too much and knew full well that they were not going to make it out alive. The crying and the ear piercing screams of the little ones pushed the gunmen over the edge.

"SHUT UP!" One shouted, screaming expletives at the crowd of frightened children.

Suddenly, the two gunmen just opened fire. The screaming and scrambling and gunfire created a cacophony of chaos.

Hannah ran into the cafeteria and tried to yell over the gunfire. "NO! STOP!" They did stop and turned to face her.

"Look, we missed one."

"I can fix that." The one in jeans fired two short bursts in Hannah's direction.

Hannah gulped in air as she clutched her stomach, blood seeping through her fingertips. She doubled over in pain, but struggled to keep upright. "Why?" she demanded. Hannah fell to her knees fighting against the stinging pain of the bullet wound to her abdomen. "They were innocent children…"

"We did them a favor," one said, his words muffled by the black knit ski mask. "Kids don't matter… you people tell your kids to come to you if something's wrong… that's a lie. You don't care. You just want to get on with your life."

"She doesn't care, Brett, why waste your time?" He pulled off his mask to better survey their work.

They were just teenagers. *I can't heal them*, her heart broke. *I can't heal what is destroying them.* She fought against the pain. *"Say something!"* She admonished herself. *"God! Let me save them! Please!"*

She thought briefly about letting the bullets do its work, the burning pain was so intense, but her body had other plans. She couldn't give up. It couldn't end this way. Her body was rejecting the metal intruders and Hannah could feel it slowly making its way back out the way it came.

Hannah fought against the pain stood up and took in a deep breath. She had a metallic taste on her tongue and the smell of death filled her senses. She felt the warm sensation building up inside her. She rolled her shoulders back gaining strength and balance. The blood slowed and finally stopped. She closed her eyes and produced the two bullets in her hand.

The screaming had died down as only a handful of survivors shivered, crying in the corner. Their voices were merely whimpers. The one who removed his mask looked at Hannah standing, bullets in hand, after being shot; he was unfazed. He turned back to the survivors and raised his gun finishing the job.

"Please, please, nooo!" Hannah managed.

"Too late," he growled.

Hannah could see that he spoke the truth. The last person standing in the corner, fell onto the heap of bodies.

The room was suddenly quiet and the air was heavy. Even the assailants stood quietly, almost in reverence to the carnage.

Hannah could barely breath. "NO! No....no...no..." she fell to her knees again, helpless... defeated.

"You be sure to tell everyone that we are heroes," the other said, removing his mask.

She didn't have the chance to do anything. They faced each other, as if it was part of their rehearsed choreography and pointed their guns toward the other. "This is it," one laughed. They paused for a moment. The other's last words were, "We're going to be famous, dude."

Simultaneously, they opened fire, finger tight on the trigger until they fell lifeless to the floor adding to the carnage.

It was over. She hadn't been able to save one child... not one. Hannah was overwhelmed with guilt. She looked around her and saw the damage that had been done by these two misguided boys.

"God..." Hannah whimpered, "Where are you...". She dropped her head and sobbed.

Miracles from Ashes

Chapter Twenty-Seven

Call upon me in the day of trouble; I will deliver you and you shall glorify me.
Psalm 50:15

Hannah could not contain her sorrow.   Deep sobs rocked her body as she ached for the lost and even more for those left behind.   There is no sadness or healing the pain of the loss of a child.   Hannah lifted her hands in front of her. They were covered in blood from her own body and so many of the tiny victims that lay all around her.   She shuddered and she cried and cried and cried.   Her wailing echoed off the walls in the heavy silence of a building filled with death.

"Hey… hey now… no more tears…"

Hannah's breath caught as she lifted her head.

Phyllis leaned down and stoked her daughter's face and lifted her chin.

"Mom?" Hannah looked at her mother's healthy face smiling down at her.

"No more tears, now."   Phyllis crouched down in front of Hannah and wiped away her tears with her thumbs.

"Mom… what do I do?   All of these…"   Hannah attempted to look around at the room but Phyllis held her jaw and kept her still.

"You have to fix it."

"But I… I can't… " Hannah started to cry again.

"Oh now," Phyllis brushed away the comment with a wave of her hand. "My Hannah… my strong… brave… beautiful girl…" she smiled, so tenderly at her daughter, "… she doesn't know the word 'can't'."

Suddenly, an explosion came from the kitchen and blew out the wall separating the kitchen from the serving area.

The blow back launched Hannah a few feet backwards into the far wall.

She heard police sirens in the distance and hoped they would be here in time to save the school.

She stood up and faced the fire that was now licking up the walls toward the ceiling engulfing everything in its path.

Phyllis was gone and Hannah felt so alone and powerless. She blinked her eyes to make sure she was seeing correctly. In the thick of the fire she saw an image…It was a human form… tall… the head reached the ceiling. The image split into two and the smaller of the cloudy forms moved forward.

The form came through a wall of smoke and emerged as Pashar.

"Pete! Pete!" Hannah rushed to him. "Pete… please tell me I can fix this. Please… let me fix this."

Pete reached out his hands to her, "… your time here is through."

Hannah paused, "What? It can't be. Please, don't let it end like this."

"Momma?"

Hannah looked beyond Pete locating the source of the familiar voice "Rosie?" Hannah sobbed.   Her daughter emerged from the flames. "Don't... don't come out here, baby... stay there."

She looked beyond her daughter and saw Olivia and Jeremy standing just behind Rosie.

Her heart pounded as it dawned on her what was happening. She looked at Pete and back at her family. "You.. you are making me choose?"

He shrugged. "You don't have to choose. Your time can be over. It's what you wanted, isn't it?"

"Pashar, please. Please don't make me choose."

Pete stood quiet with his hands folded, resting on his belly.

"If... if I stay... we can fix this? We can... turn back time?"

"We cannot turn back time."

"I could heal them? If I stay, could I heal them?"

He nodded.

She looked beyond him at her family standing in the fire from the explosion but not being affected by the flames. She didn't have to look around her to remind her of the damage; the amount of lives lost that she had recently witnessed.

Tears slipped from her eyes. "I'm sorry."

"Mommy..."

She wiped away the tears from her cheek. "I'm sorry. I have to save them. Wait for me… say you'll wait for me…" She reached her hand out and her husband reached toward her. They were inches away from touching when the wall of flames hid them from her once again. Hannah's head dropped and she felt the pain of losing them all over again. "I'm sorry. I'm sorry." She was inconsolable.

Jeremy smiled at his wife. "Go honey. Save them. We wouldn't expect anything less. We're here… waiting."

Hannah nodded, encouraged. She watched until Jeremy's face disappeared into the flames.

"We don't have much time."

She took in a ragged breath and attempted to calm her sobbing. She nodded more for herself than for the Angel. "I'm… I'm ready."

He looked into her eyes and nodded his head. He closed his eyes and in a bright flash of light and blast of air, huge tan wings appeared behind Pete's body.

He turned her around positioned Hannah to stand in front of him as he rested his hand on her shoulder. She could feel heat flood her body emanating from Pete's hand, giving her additional strength.

The fire roared behind them, but Hannah concentrated on the carnage in front of her.

She wasn't sure what to do so she reached her hand out in front of her and waited. Nothing was happening. She was out of breath and sweating as if she were holding onto a heavy weight.

She crouched down to the ground, closed her eyes and extended her hands out inches above the floor. Pete hovered behind her and extended his arms out to the sides.

Ba-bum, ba-bum…she heard a heart beat… and then another… and then another.

Tears streamed down her face and she took in another deep breath and held her hand out. Her body tingled and heat poured out across the floor. Hannah opened her eyes and saw a golden glow coming from her finger tips and reaching out to the scattered bodies across the floor.

Ba-bum… ba-bum… ba-bum…

She turned her hand over so that her palm was facing toward the ceiling and tried to extend the glow upwards.

It expanded it's girth as she raised her arm higher.

She slowly stood up to her full height and extended her other hand. The warm golden glow was now emanating from her entire body as she was encompassed in the wave of a glowing life force. It spilled out from her person onto the entire room. It twisted and wound its way through each body causing them to suddenly take air into their lungs.

Tears flowed from Hannah's eyes as she saw the life returning to the children.

The glow drifted through the open doors and Hannah grew dizzy until Pete touched her shoulder again. The entire cafeteria was blindingly bright and she could hear the laughter of children.

The police, guns drawn and expecting the worst, made their way to the entrance of the cafeteria. What they saw, they would never be able to explain to another living soul. They saw children running and laughing when only a few feet away the entire wall seemed to be engulfed in flames. The children showed no fear. But then, between the two, a woman... an angel hovered above the floor.

The officer's jaws dropped as they looked up at the celestial creature before them.

She was surrounded by a swirling golden glow that seemed to take on a life itself. Her brilliant white wings stretched out and were barely contained by the room.

Her eyes were closed. Her face was at peace and had a gentle smile. Her arms were outstretched controlling the glow as it moved about from child to child.

The police holstered their weapons and just stared in awe. There was so much warmth in the room.

Hannah's head was filled with the deep bass of heartbeats and the high tingling sound of laughter. Her own heart swelled as the sound of the heartbeats grew faint and then silent.

That's all of them... she mused. They are alive.... The room showed no sign of a massacre, the children having no memory of what had transpired in this very room or others. The teachers wrangled the children to move them away from the heat of the fire.

She opened her eyes and made a connection to one of the officers. She told him in a voice only they could hear, "These boys..." Hannah nodded to the two teenagers. Her voice not sounding like her own, "See that they get the help they need."

The man nodded his head in understanding.

Hannah smiled at the children and looked into the eyes of the teenage boys. Her voice was only heard by them, "You have been given a second chance. Find the ways that this world is good, and if you can't... become the good. Be the person you needed when you were younger."

They looked at each other and back to Hannah, nodding their head vigorously.

The police took the two teens into custody and began escorting the children and teachers from the room so the firefighters could come in and contain the blaze.

They looked back over their shoulder and saw the angel wings fold in neatly and disappear behind the woman's body as her feet came back to the floor. Her brilliant white robes were replaced with olive green cargo pants and white tank top.

She smiled and winked at them as they reluctantly escorted the last of the children from the room.

Hannah looked over the room once again and knew that her work here, was finished.

She calmly and quietly turned away from the now empty room, to the Angel that no one else could see. Pete stood off to the side in his usual clothes, hands in his pockets as if he had no place else to be. He smiled at her.

She furrowed her brow, emotions warring inside her. She felt so full, so blessed for being chosen to be able to give these innocents another chance to complete their lives, but for just a moment in time, she was so close to being with her family again. And now… and now…

"Thank you… for allowing them to all be saved. And now…" she lowered her head, willing to honor her promise, the tears beginning again. "Where will you have me go?"

Pete looked into her eyes and smiled. "Well done good and faithful servant." He stepped to the side to reveal her mother.

"Baby Girl." Phyllis walked forward and tucked Hannah's hair behind her ear and stroked her jaw. "I am so proud of you. Come on… let's go. I've been getting to know those beautiful grandbabies of mine…". She linked her arm with Hannah's and started walking toward the kitchen.

Firefighters raced into the room, assuming that it was clear for them to start the hoses. Hannah heard voices call out behind her, "No! Ma'am! Don't!"

Hannah turned and looked into the faces of the firefighters, calming them. "It's okay. It's going to be okay, now."

When she turned back around, she saw in front of her was her family. Her heart was so full. Her husband smiled at her and held out his arms. She walked into them allowing them to wrap around her. Her children attached themselves to her legs embracing her.

The firemen watched helplessly, as the flames engulfed the woman.

The hoses flooded the wall with water. The flames were doused and when the water was turned off, steam and a soft golden glow rose from the ashes.

Inspectors came in with trained dogs and found the source of the explosions. It was a pipe bomb with a timer that was placed under the gas valve of the oven.

The kitchen and outer wall can be rebuilt and the school will be no worse for wear.

On the interior of the cafeteria the fire singed a pattern on the walls . Some say it looks like the outline of angel wings.

There was no sign of a body.

The black SUV sat in the back corner of the school's parking lot.

The tinted window of the back seat rolled up hiding the occupants that rode inside.

Dr. Romero tapped his face with a tissue to wipe away new droplets of blood from the scratches on his cheek. He took in a deep breath and audibly released it.

"Where to now, boss?" the driver asked.

"Back to the lab. The real lab. Gather up the supplies from the warehouse and meet me at the Square One labs. We have more work to do."

He frowned and looked down at his hands. He folded them into fists and felt a tiny buzz of electricity in his fingertips. He unclenched and did it again, with the same result. The tingle spread down to his wrist. The corner of his mouth tipped up ever so slightly.

"What about the girl?"

"I believe…" he looked at his reflection in the window and where there were once scratches from the broken glass vial, his skin was soft and smooth. He rolled his tongue along his teeth, "… I have all we need."

The End

Elizabeth Bourgeret

Miracles from Ashes

Elizabeth Bourgeret

Acknowledgements

They say that writing a book is a solo sport and while that may be true for the hundreds of hours that is spent in the creation, the telling and then the finessing of the story, but it is also inadvertently creates a team of sorts. Some may not even realize they are even on the "team", but they are. In my mind at least, and I am grateful for their input.

Many will not be named, as they were perhaps, the profile of a character, a participant of a conversation, a piece of an "overheard" nugget of information, or even those who ask me, "Can I be a character in your book?"
Yes. Yes, you can.

The people named below, are so very valuable to me and to the completion of this specific story. Without them, it just wouldn't have been the same.

Always first, is my family. My mother is my biggest fan and my hardest critic.
My husband is learning his way around living with a "creative" and tries to be patient with my manic and sometimes isolated ways. And unfortunately, he is usually the recipient of my million and one questions or the audience (willing or un) of any number of scenarios that my characters have to go through.

My children encourage me to always keep creating. My youngest offspring, and fellow author is my springboard. Some of my happiest memories during story creation is our brainstorming chats. She is brilliant in her own right and I will be so sad when she finally becomes too successful to rattle story ideas out with her momma.

My medical advisory team was indispensable!! Samantha Dennison, Terri Goolsby and Robyn Smith- thank you for enduring the many questions and helping to come up with new scenarios.

My research assistant- Robyn Smith. She was more help than she even realizes. I would send her off with a random thought from my head (as in... "see if this or that theory would be possible." "What are the side effects for...") and without batting an eye would come back to me with everything and more than I could possibly need! A creative in her own right- a brilliant artist. She is the talent behind all of the amazing logos for my business. She is a treasure, to be sure.

My editors, Barb Bourgeret, Pat Lambert and Nancy Marling. Thank you for shielding the people to my poor writing skills.

And finally, thank you to Henry, the inspiration for Professor. He is our rescued pit and has that sweet telltale smile of the pit bull breed and a heart as big as they come.

Find me on social media:

www.facebook.com/EBourgeret

Instagram and Twitter- @ebourgeret

Website: www.elizabethbourgeret

Elizabeth Bourgeret

Elizabeth Bourgeret

Elizabeth Bourgeret

Made in the USA
Columbia, SC
26 January 2022

54803053R00283